ADVENTURE TIME™

with

Fionna & Cake
CARD WARS

kaboom!™
WWW.KABOOM-STUDIOS.COM

CARTOON NETWORK.
FREDERATOR

ADVENTURE TIME™ WITH FIONNA AND CAKE: CARD WARS, May 2016. Published by KaBOOM!, a division of Boom Entertainment, Inc.

A catalog record of this book is available from OCLC and from the KaBOOM! website, www.kaboom-studios.com, on the Librarians Page.

BOOM! Studios, 5670 Wilshire Boulevard, Suite 450, Los Angeles, CA 90036-5679. Printed in China. First Printing.

ISBN: 978-1-60886-799-8, eISBN: 978-1-61398-470-3

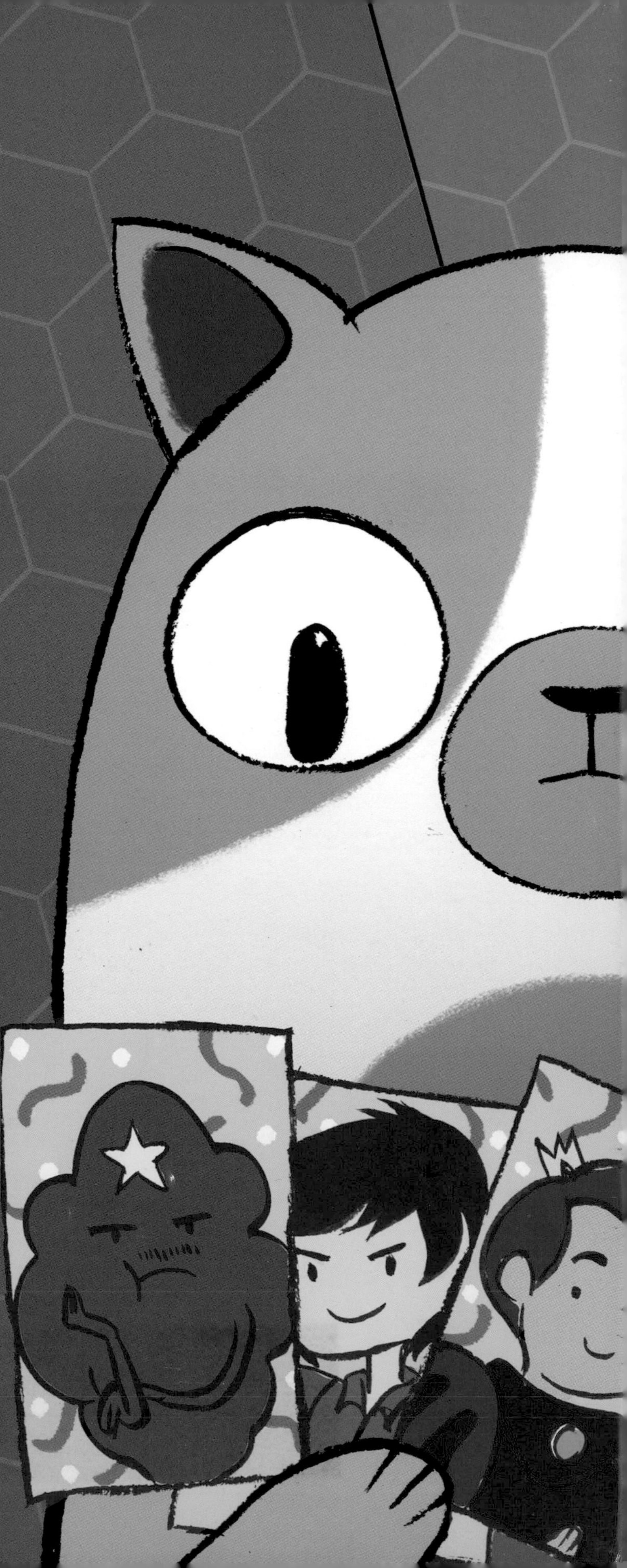

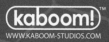

ADVENTURE TIME™ *created by*
PENDLETON WARD

written by JEN WANG

CHAPTER ONE
illustrated by BRITT WILSON

CHAPTERS TWO-SIX
pencils and letters by BRITT WILSON
inks and colors by RIAN SYGH

cover by JEN WANG

designer JILLIAN CRAB
associate editor WHITNEY LEOPARD
editor SHANNON WATTERS

with special thanks to
MARISA MARIONAKIS, RICK BLANCO,
CURTIS LELASH, CONRAD MONTGOMERY,
NICOLE RIVERA, MEGHAN BRADLEY,
KELLY CREWS, SCOTT MALCHUS,
ADAM MUTO AND THE WONDERFUL
FOLKS AT CARTNOON NETWORK

chapter one

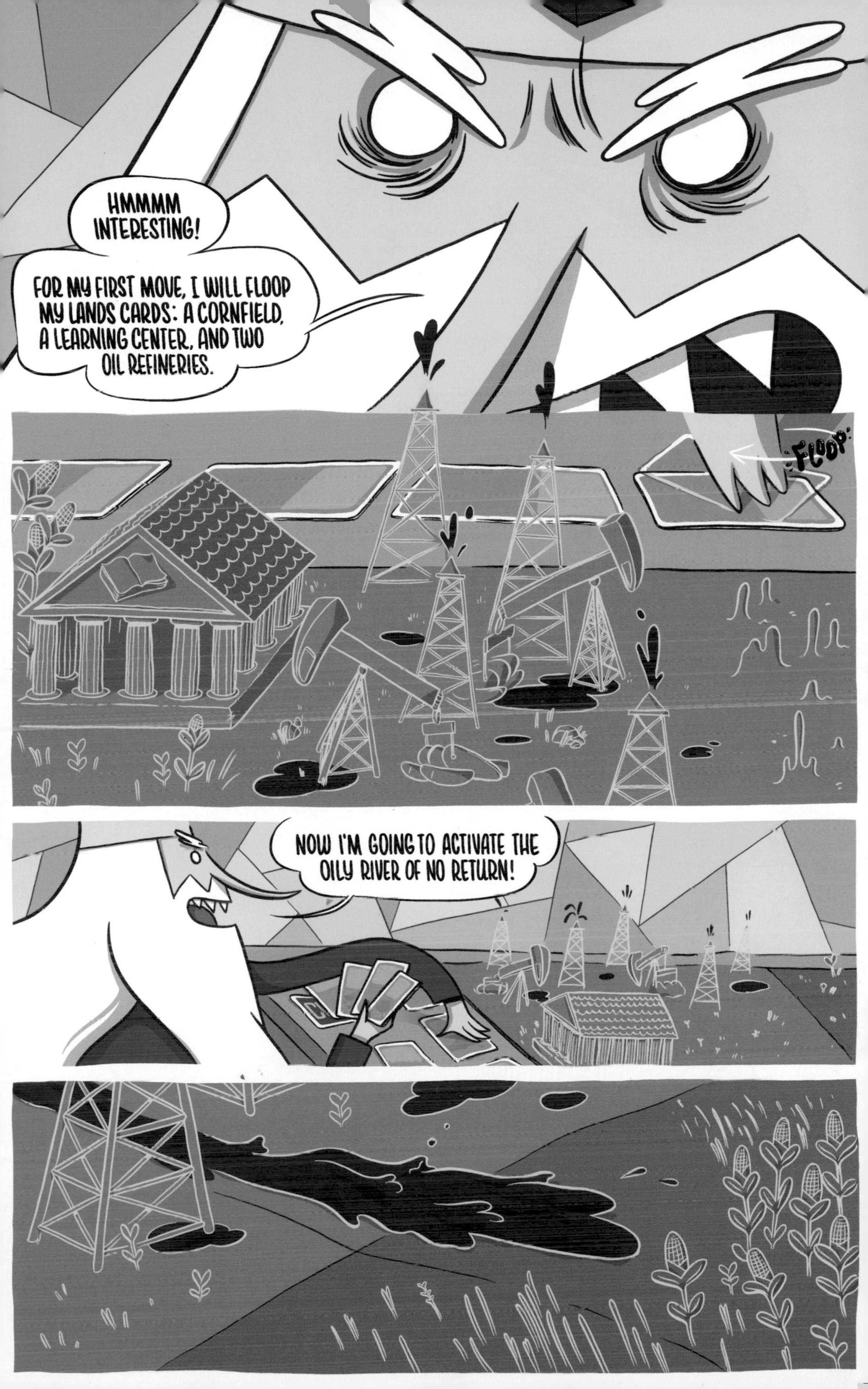
HMMMM INTERESTING!
FOR MY FIRST MOVE, I WILL FLOOP MY LANDS CARDS: A CORNFIELD, A LEARNING CENTER, AND TWO OIL REFINERIES.
FLOOP
NOW I'M GOING TO ACTIVATE THE OILY RIVER OF NO RETURN!

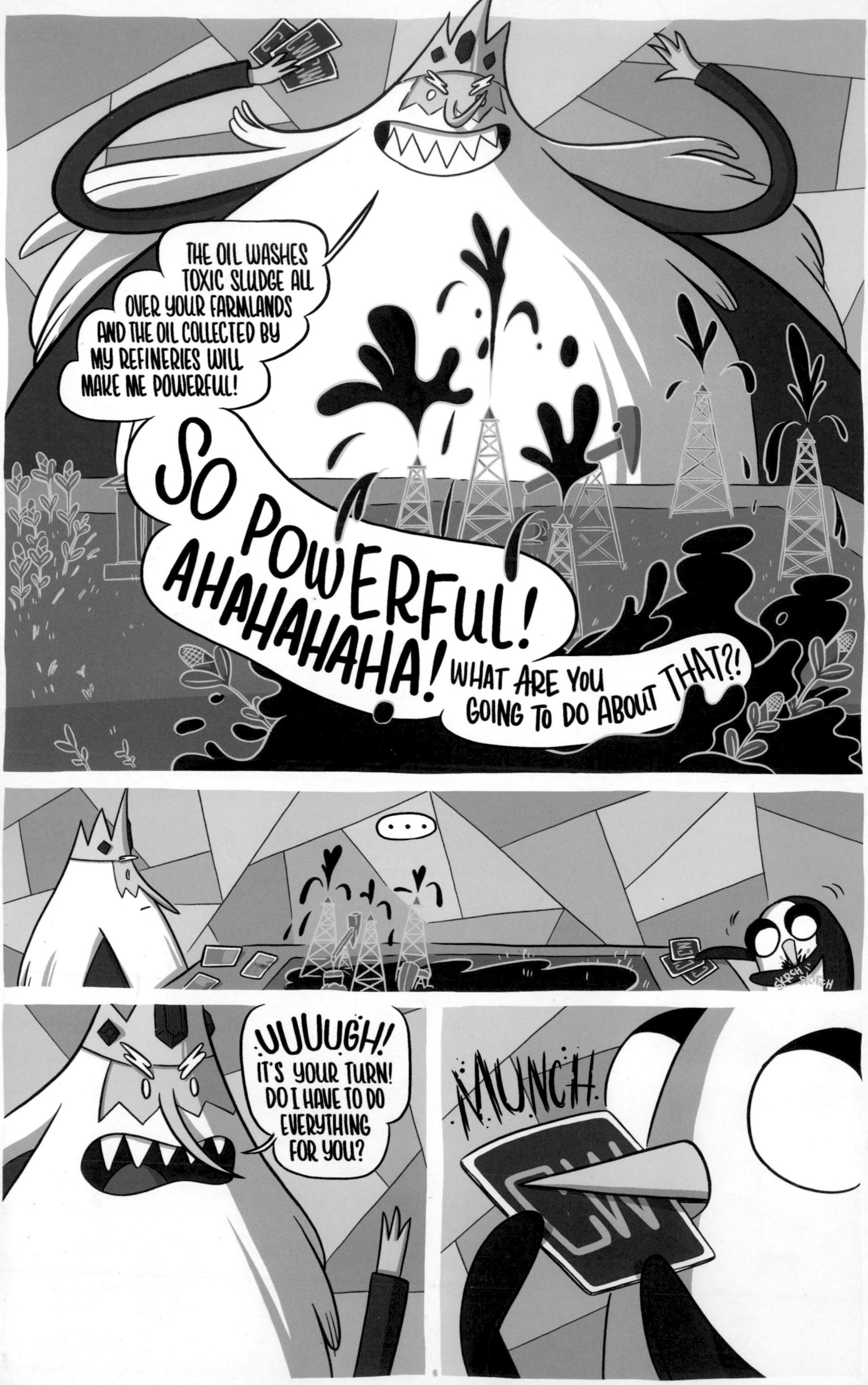
THE OIL WASHES TOXIC SLUDGE ALL OVER YOUR FARMLANDS AND THE OIL COLLECTED BY MY REFINERIES WILL MAKE ME POWERFUL!
SO POWERFUL! AHAHAHAHA!
WHAT ARE YOU GOING TO DO ABOUT THAT?!
...
SKRSH SKRTCH
UUUUGH!
IT'S YOUR TURN! DO I HAVE TO DO EVERYTHING FOR YOU?
MUNCH

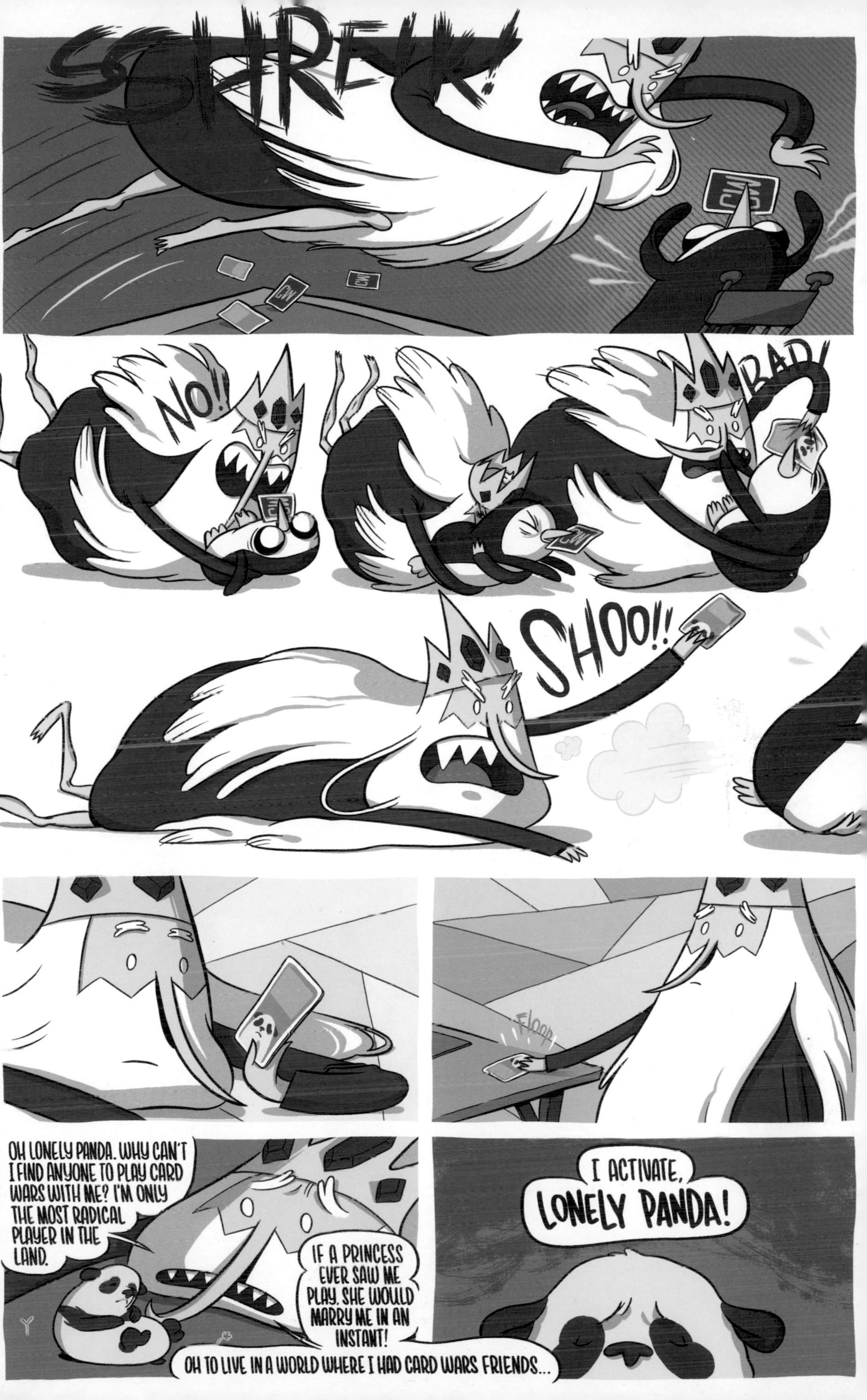
NO!!
SHOO!!
OH LONELY PANDA. WHY CAN'T I FIND ANYONE TO PLAY CARD WARS WITH ME? I'M ONLY THE MOST RADICAL PLAYER IN THE LAND.
IF A PRINCESS EVER SAW ME PLAY, SHE WOULD MARRY ME IN AN INSTANT!
OH TO LIVE IN A WORLD WHERE I HAD CARD WARS FRIENDS...
I ACTIVATE,
LONELY PANDA!

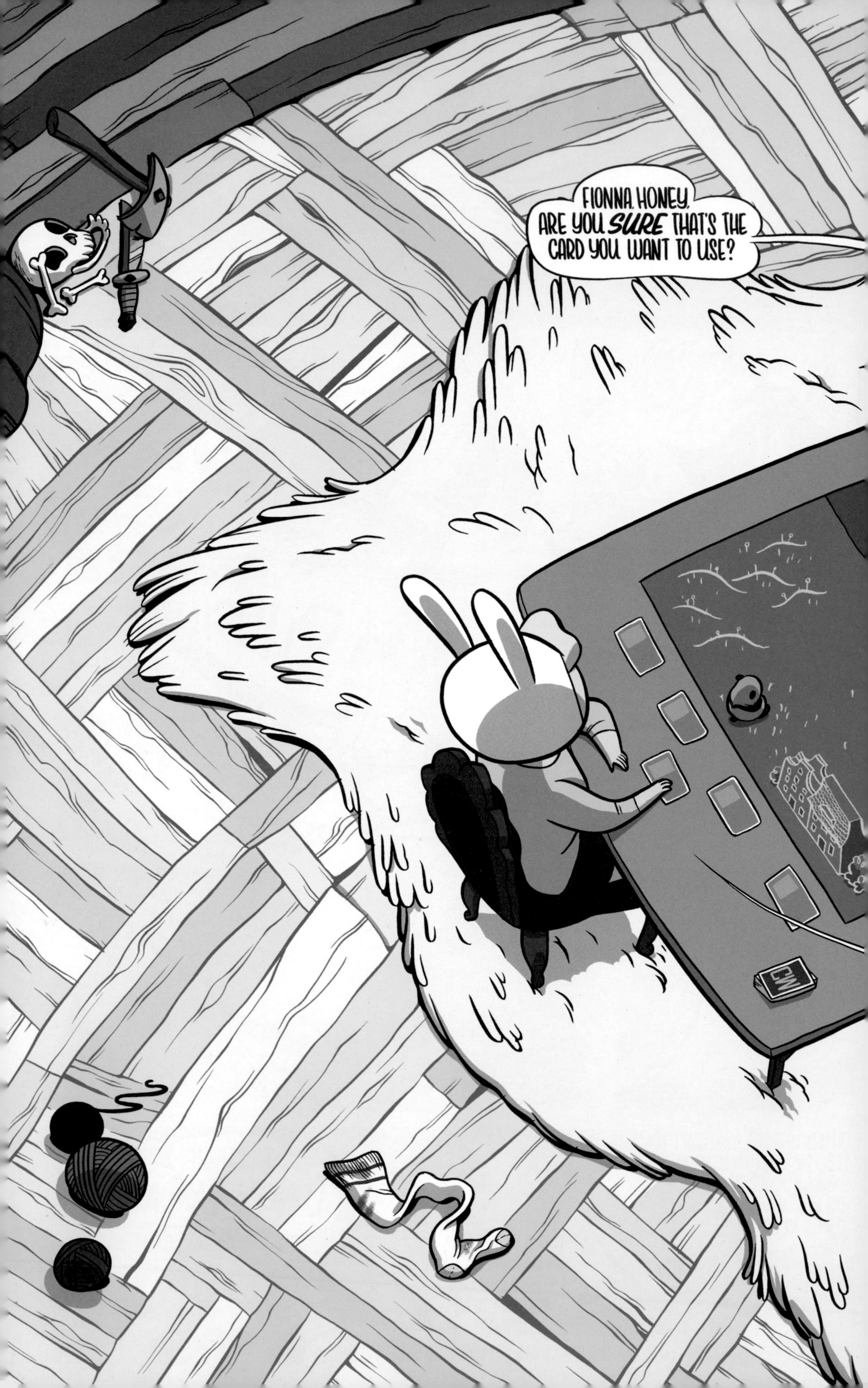
FIONNA, HONEY, ARE YOU SURE THAT'S THE CARD YOU WANT TO USE?
CW

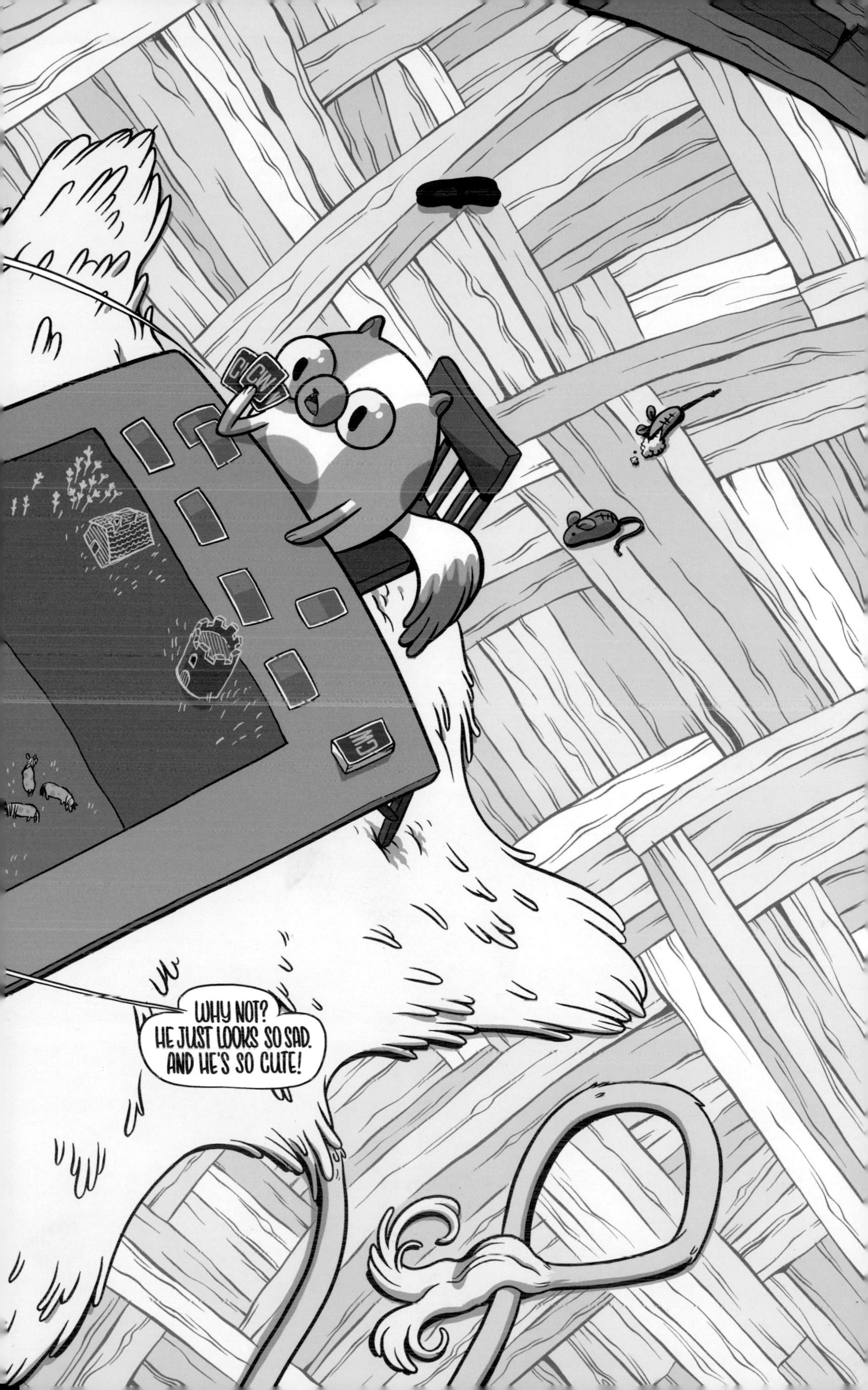
WHY NOT? HE JUST LOOKS SO SAD. AND HE'S SO CUTE!

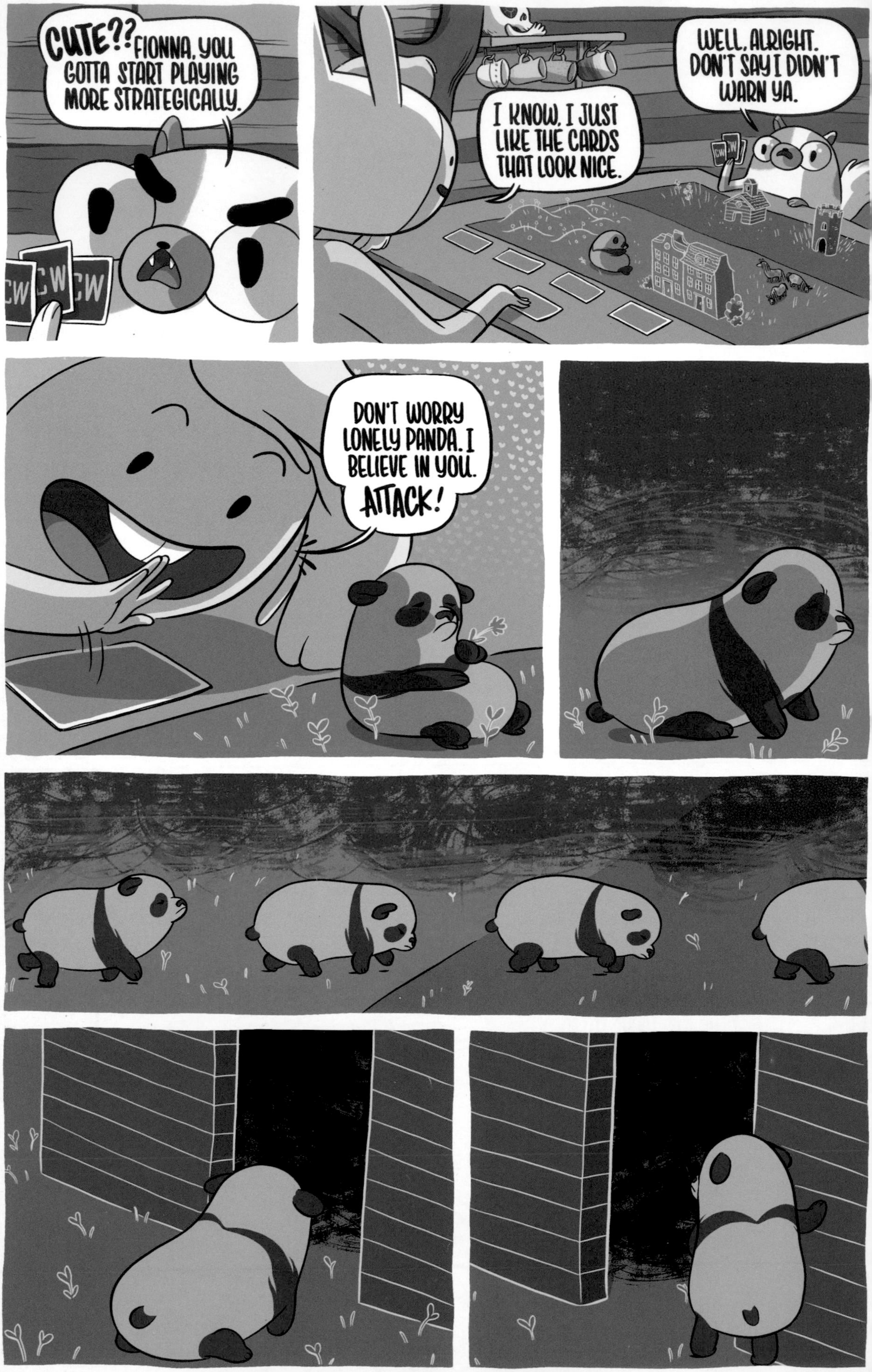
CUTE?? FIONNA, YOU GOTTA START PLAYING MORE STRATEGICALLY.
I KNOW, I JUST LIKE THE CARDS THAT LOOK NICE.
WELL, ALRIGHT. DON'T SAY I DIDN'T WARN YA.
DON'T WORRY LONELY PANDA. I BELIEVE IN YOU. ATTACK!

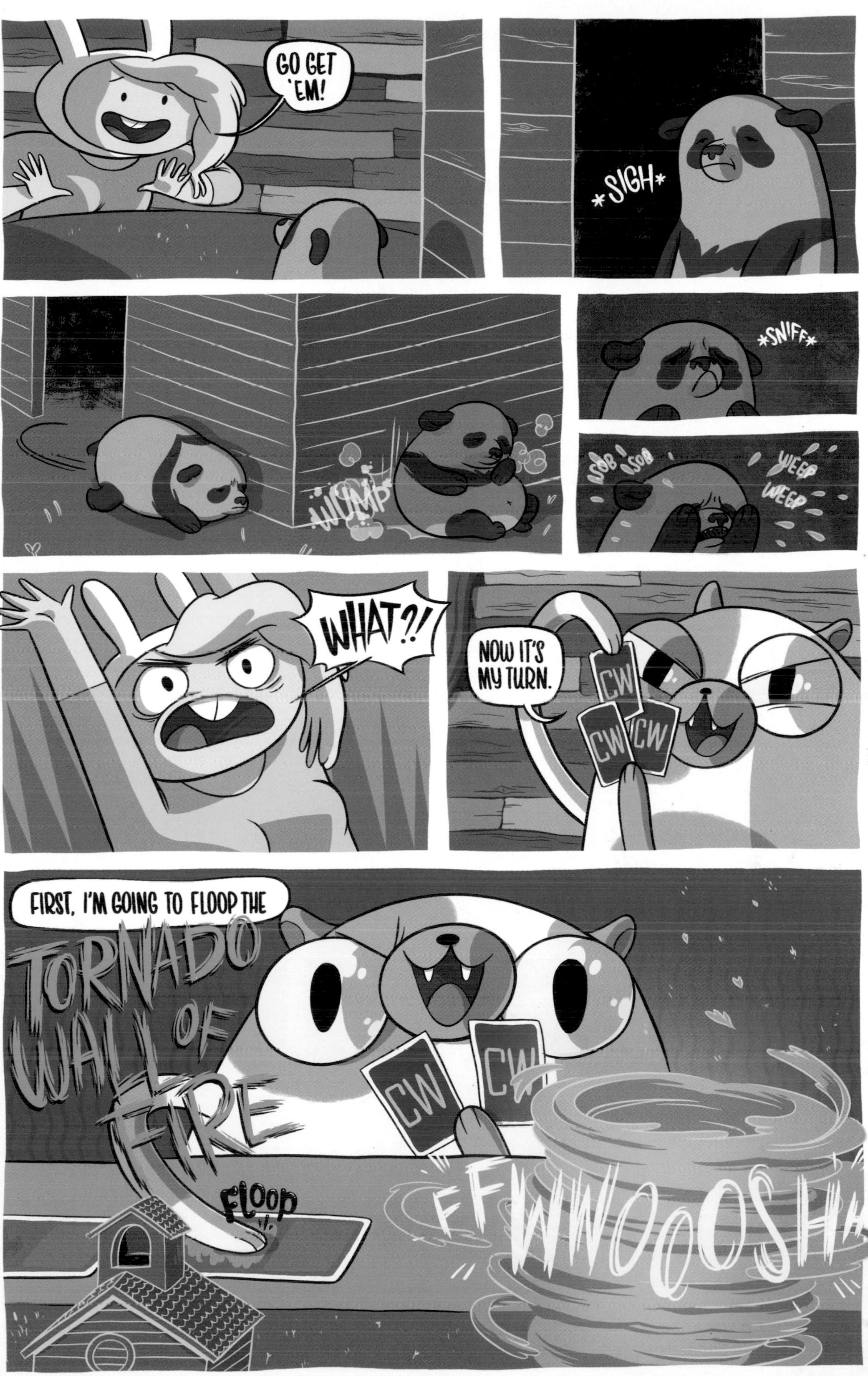
GO GET 'EM!
SIGH
WOMP
SNIFF
SOB SOB
WEEP WEEP
WHAT?!
NOW IT'S MY TURN.
FIRST, I'M GOING TO FLOOP THE
TORNADO WALL OF FIRE
FLOOP
FFWWOOOSH

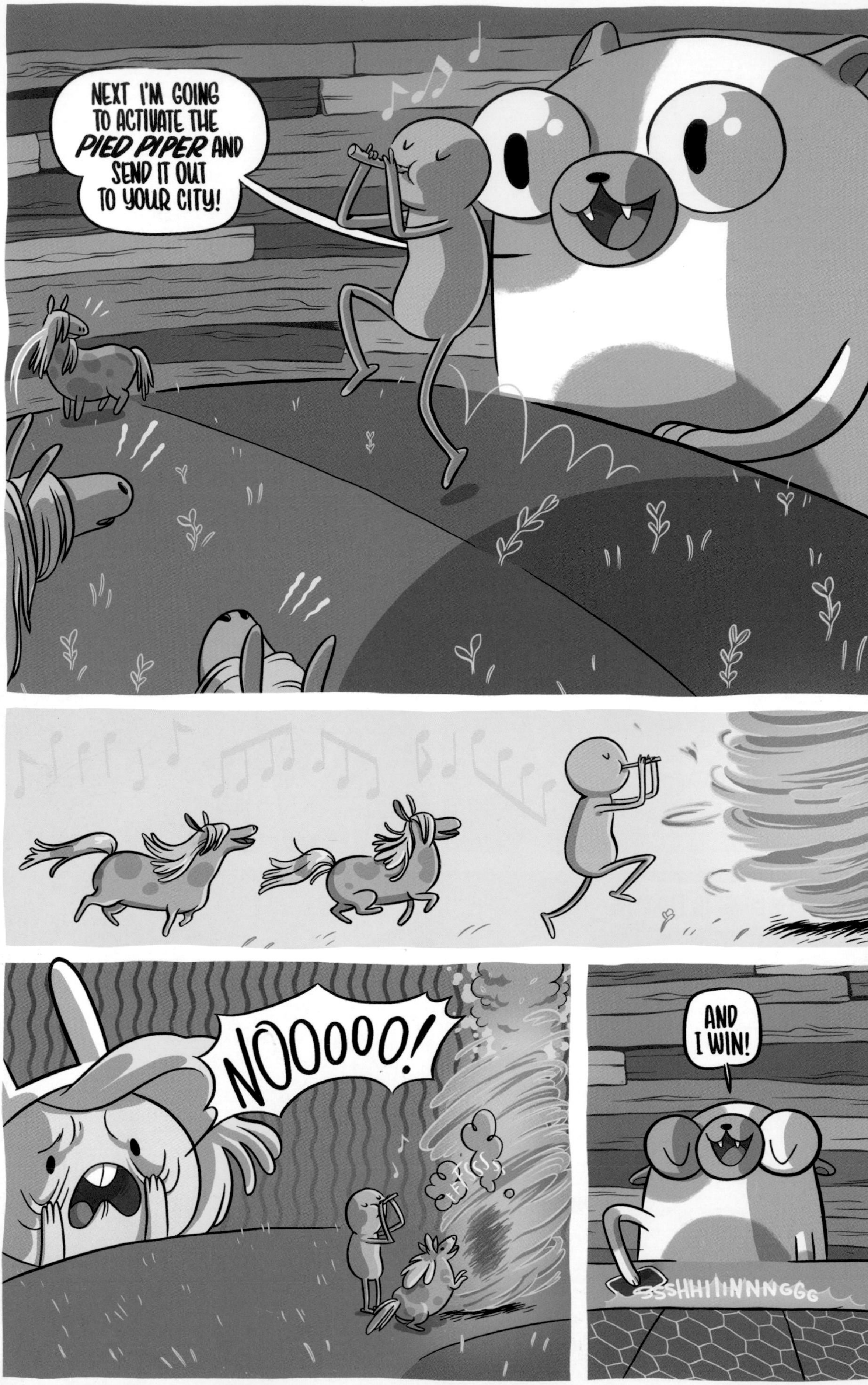
NEXT I'M GOING TO ACTIVATE THE PIED PIPER AND SEND IT OUT TO YOUR CITY!
NOOOOO!
AND I WIN!
SSSHHIIINNNGGG

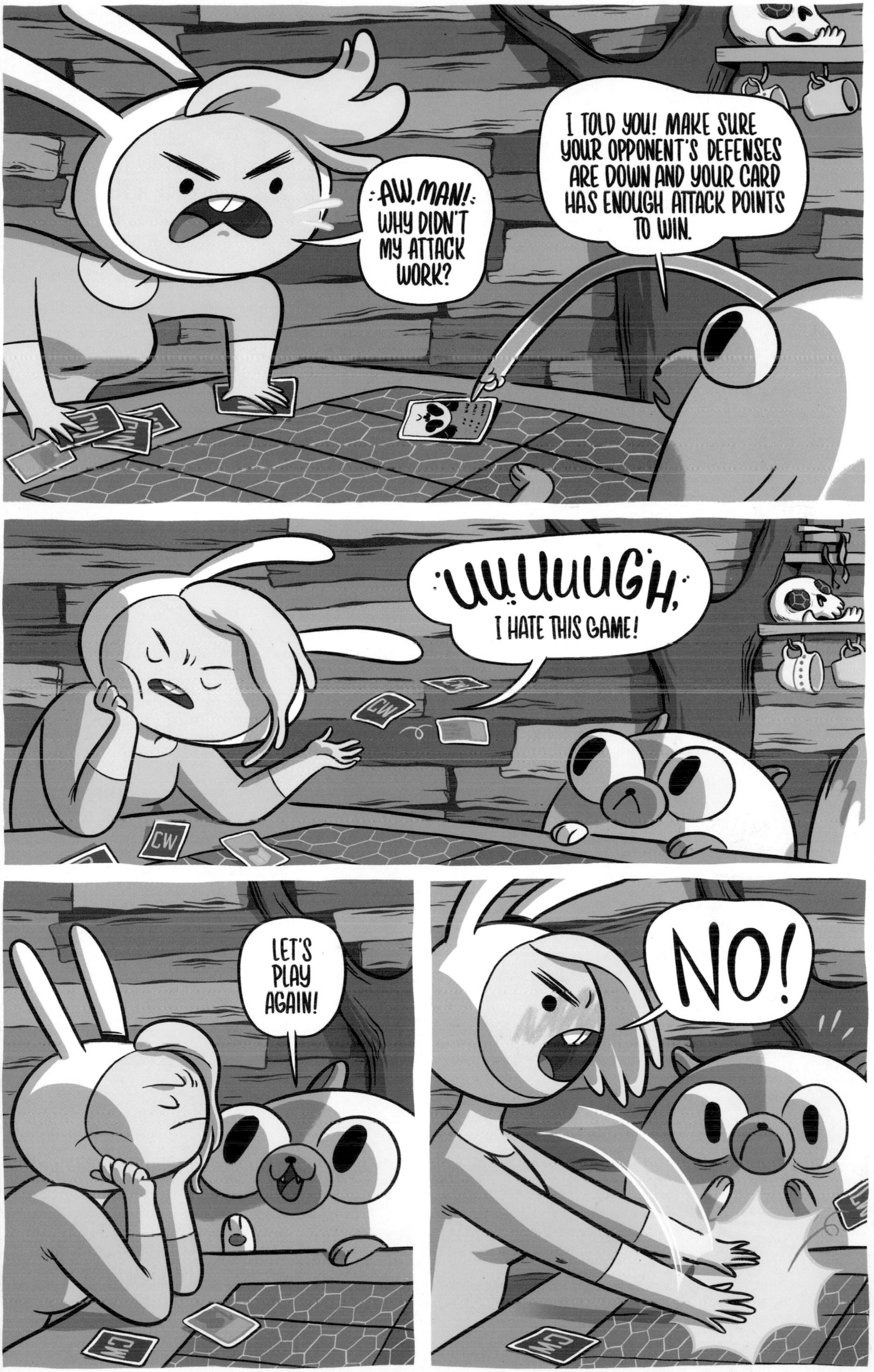
AW, MAN! WHY DIDN'T MY ATTACK WORK?
I TOLD YOU! MAKE SURE YOUR OPPONENT'S DEFENSES ARE DOWN AND YOUR CARD HAS ENOUGH ATTACK POINTS TO WIN.
UUUUUGH, I HATE THIS GAME!
LET'S PLAY AGAIN!
NO!

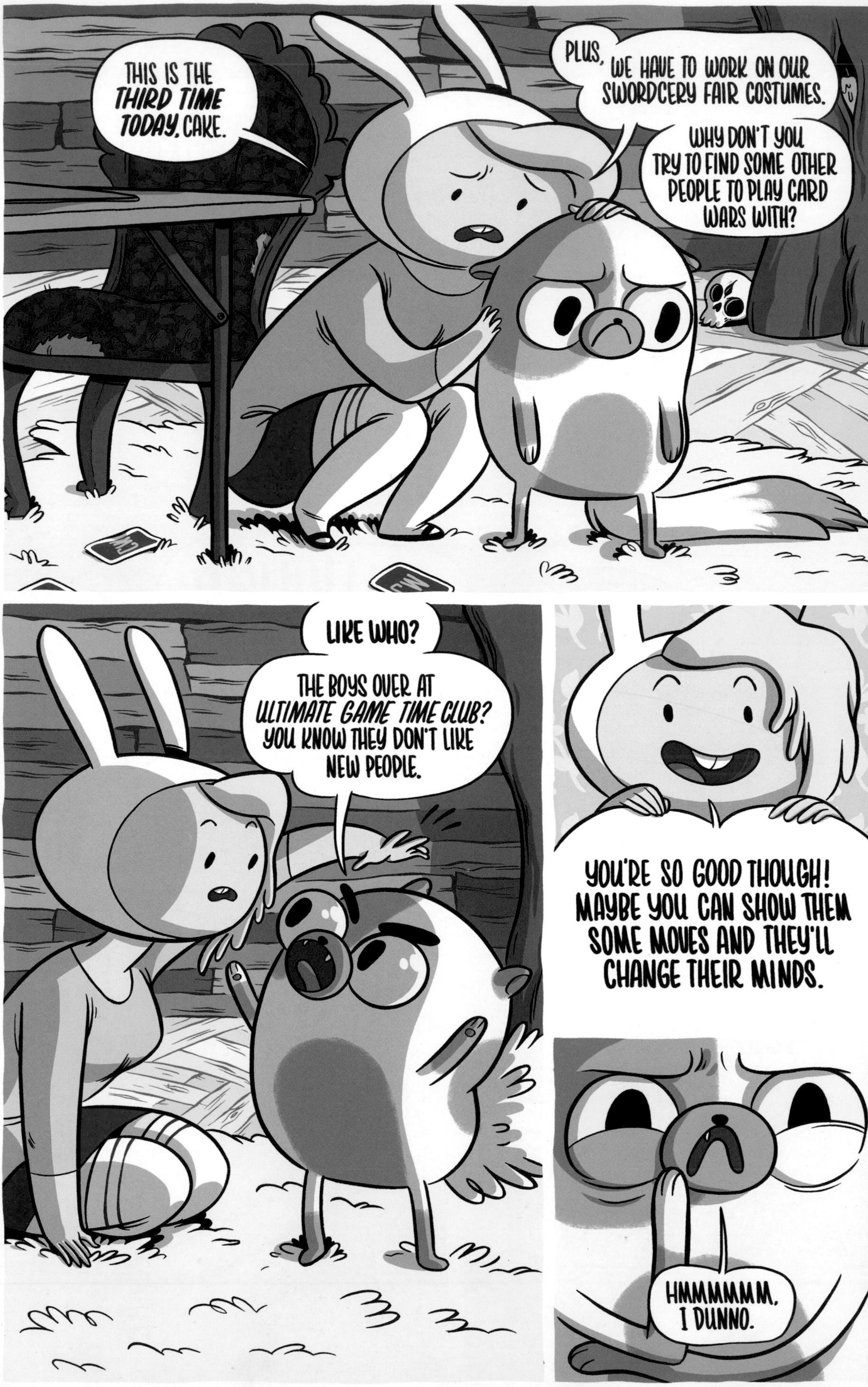

THIS IS THE *THIRD TIME TODAY*, CAKE.
PLUS, WE HAVE TO WORK ON OUR SWORDCERY FAIR COSTUMES.
WHY DON'T YOU TRY TO FIND SOME OTHER PEOPLE TO PLAY CARD WARS WITH?
LIKE WHO?
THE BOYS OVER AT *ULTIMATE GAME TIME CLUB*? YOU KNOW THEY DON'T LIKE NEW PEOPLE.
YOU'RE SO GOOD THOUGH! MAYBE YOU CAN SHOW THEM SOME MOVES AND THEY'LL CHANGE THEIR MINDS.
HMMMMMM, I DUNNO.

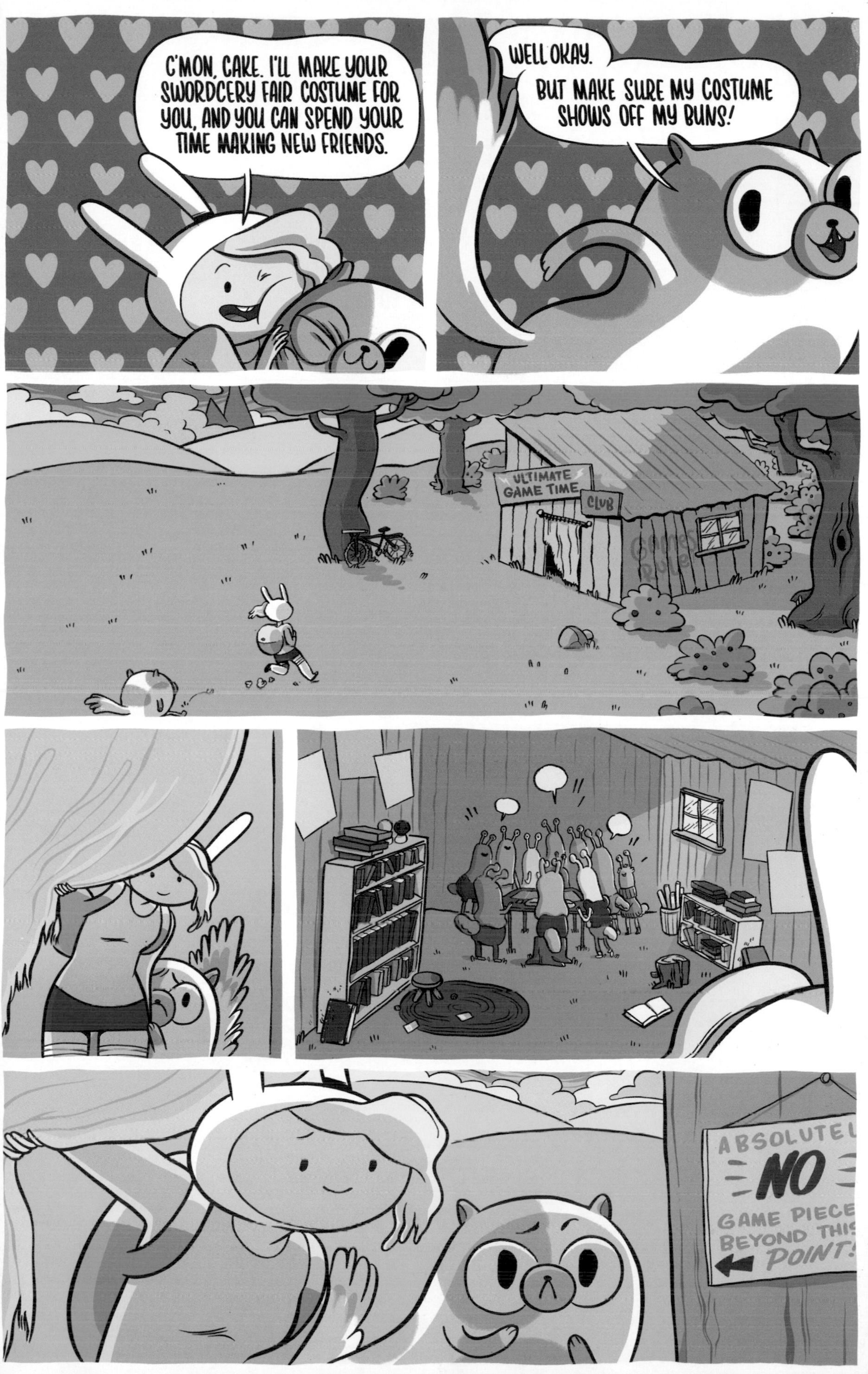
C'MON, CAKE. I'LL MAKE YOUR SWORDCERY FAIR COSTUME FOR YOU, AND YOU CAN SPEND YOUR TIME MAKING NEW FRIENDS.
WELL OKAY.
BUT MAKE SURE MY COSTUME SHOWS OFF MY BUNS!
ULTIMATE GAME TIME
CLUB
Games Rule
ABSOLUTELY
NO
GAME PIECES BEYOND THIS POINT!

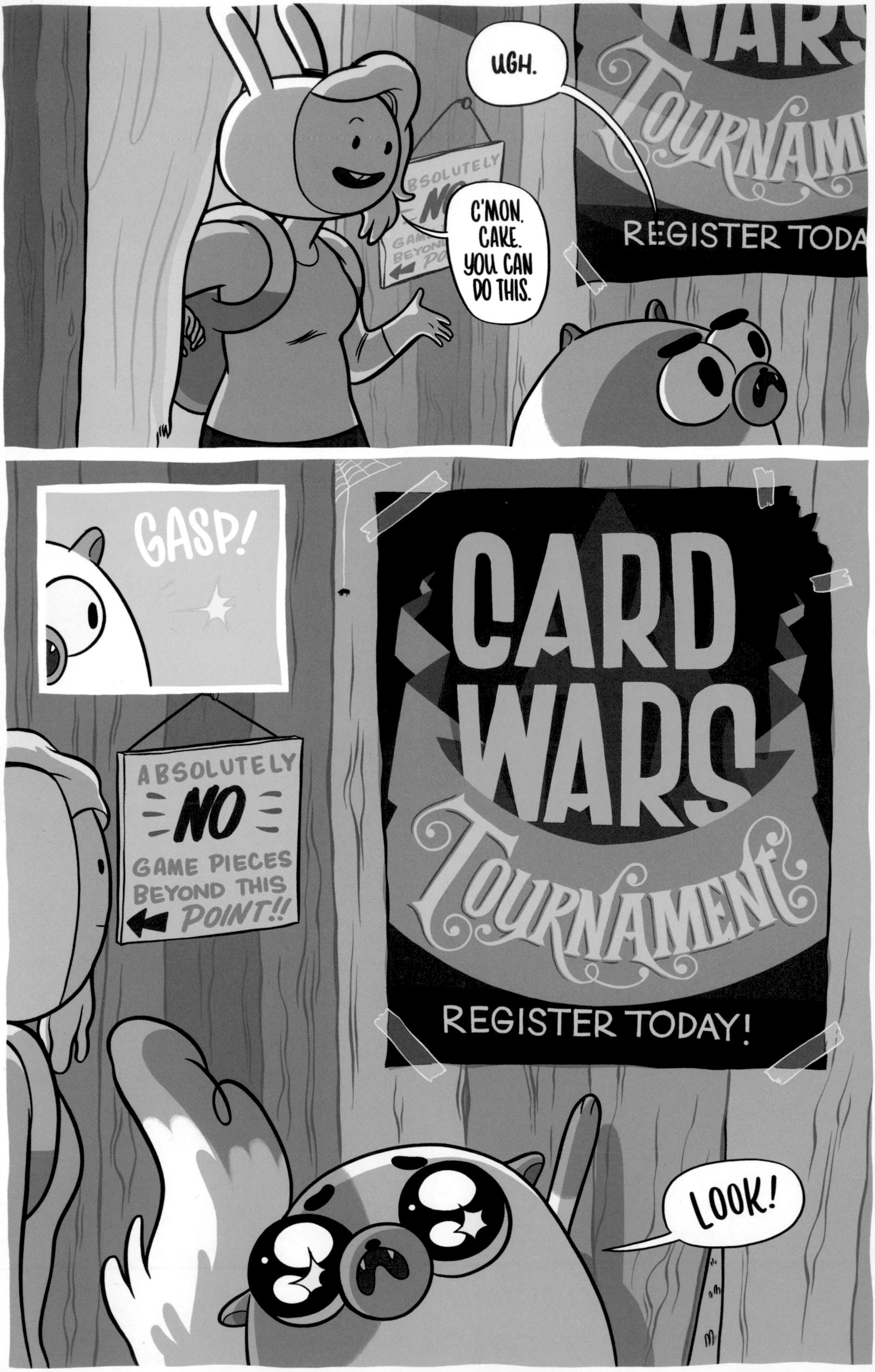
UGH.
C'MON, CAKE. YOU CAN DO THIS.
GASP!
ABSOLUTELY NO GAME PIECES BEYOND THIS POINT!!
CARD WARS TOURNAMENT
REGISTER TODAY!
LOOK!

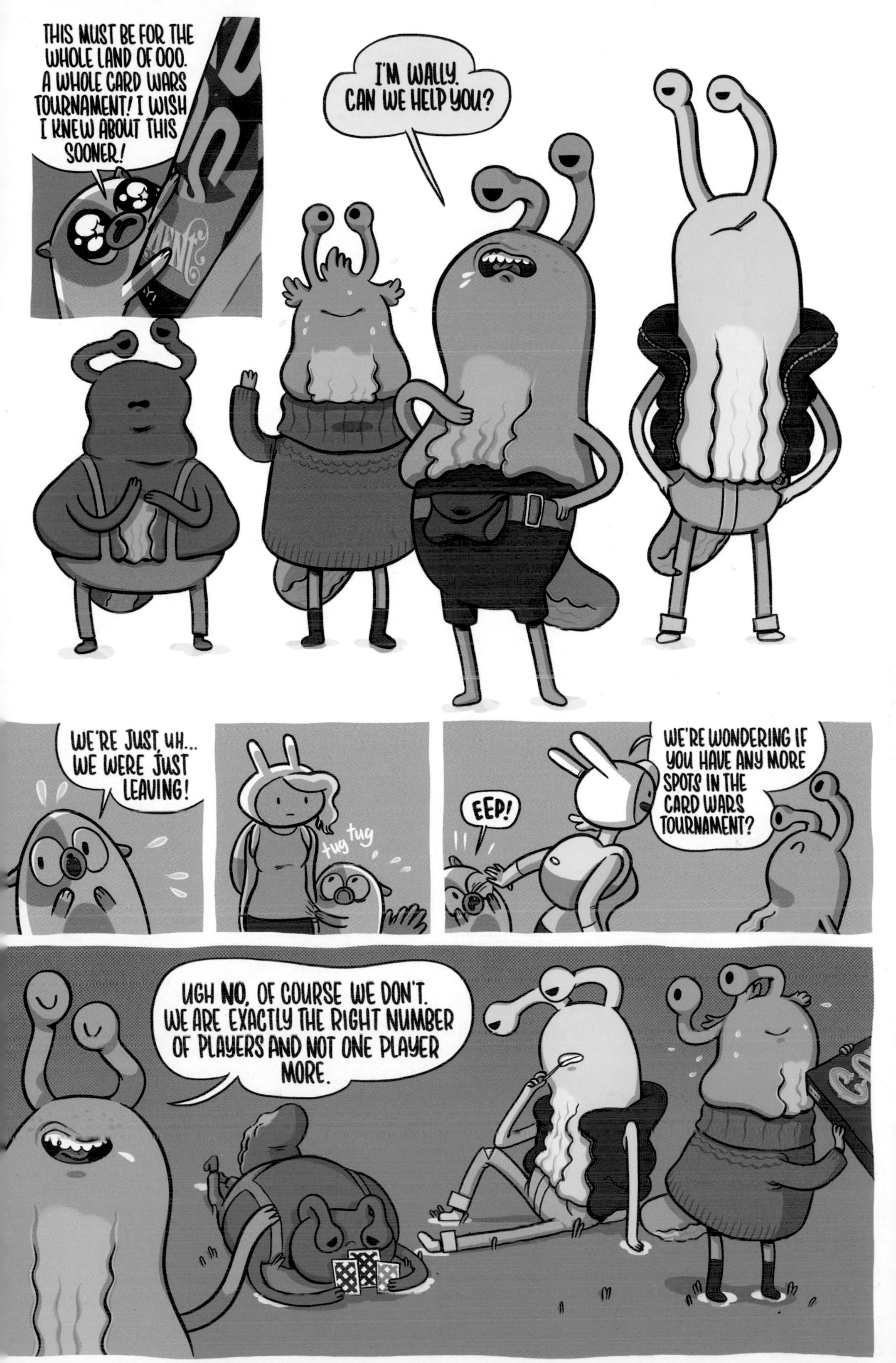
THIS MUST BE FOR THE WHOLE LAND OF OOO. A WHOLE CARD WARS TOURNAMENT! I WISH I KNEW ABOUT THIS SOONER!
I'M WALLY. CAN WE HELP YOU?
WE'RE JUST, UH... WE WERE JUST LEAVING!
tug tug
EEP!
WE'RE WONDERING IF YOU HAVE ANY MORE SPOTS IN THE CARD WARS TOURNAMENT?
UGH NO, OF COURSE WE DON'T. WE ARE EXACTLY THE RIGHT NUMBER OF PLAYERS AND NOT ONE PLAYER MORE.

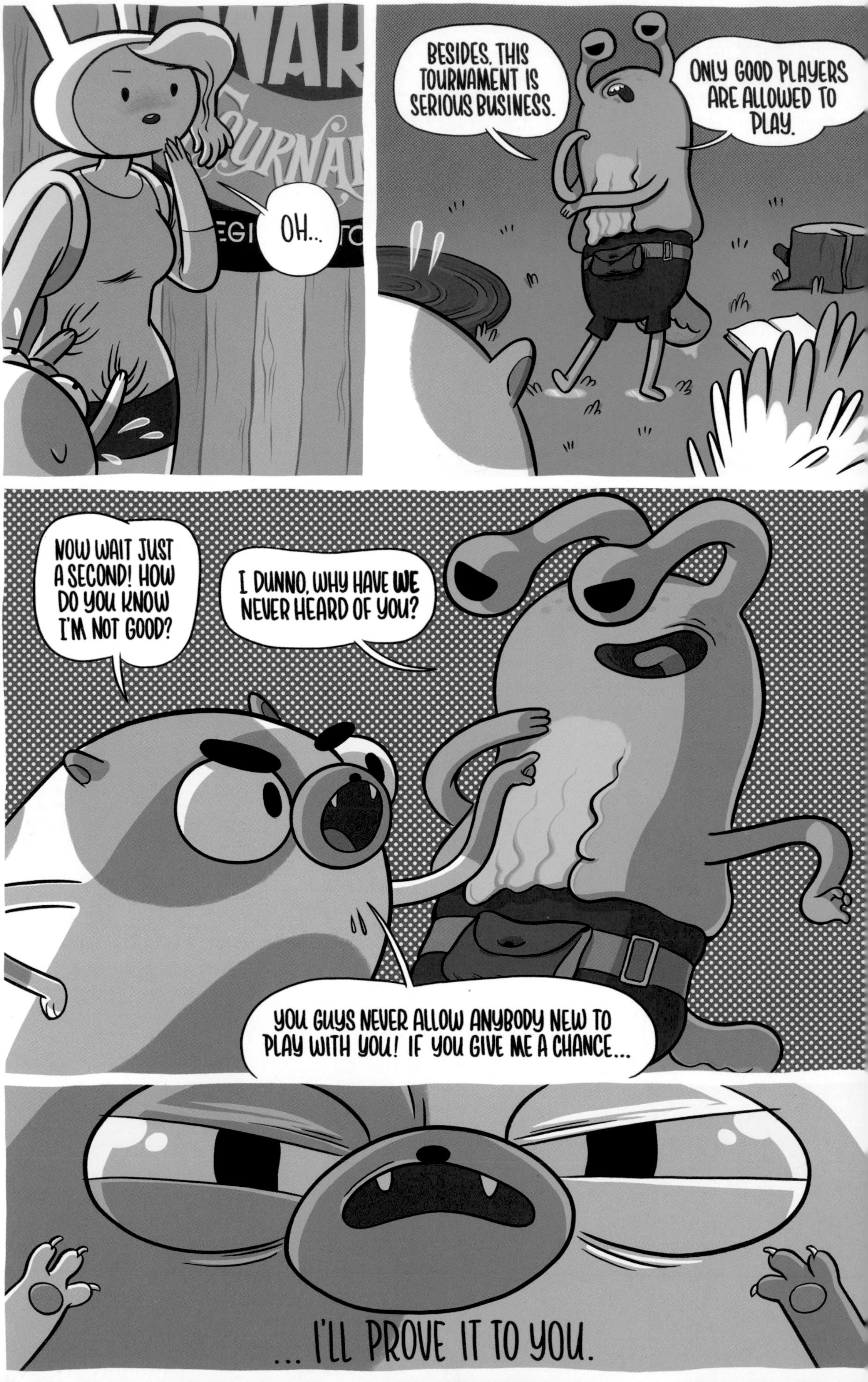
OH...
BESIDES, THIS TOURNAMENT IS SERIOUS BUSINESS.
ONLY GOOD PLAYERS ARE ALLOWED TO PLAY.
NOW WAIT JUST A SECOND! HOW DO YOU KNOW I'M NOT GOOD?
I DUNNO, WHY HAVE WE NEVER HEARD OF YOU?
YOU GUYS NEVER ALLOW ANYBODY NEW TO PLAY WITH YOU! IF YOU GIVE ME A CHANCE...
... I'LL PROVE IT TO YOU.

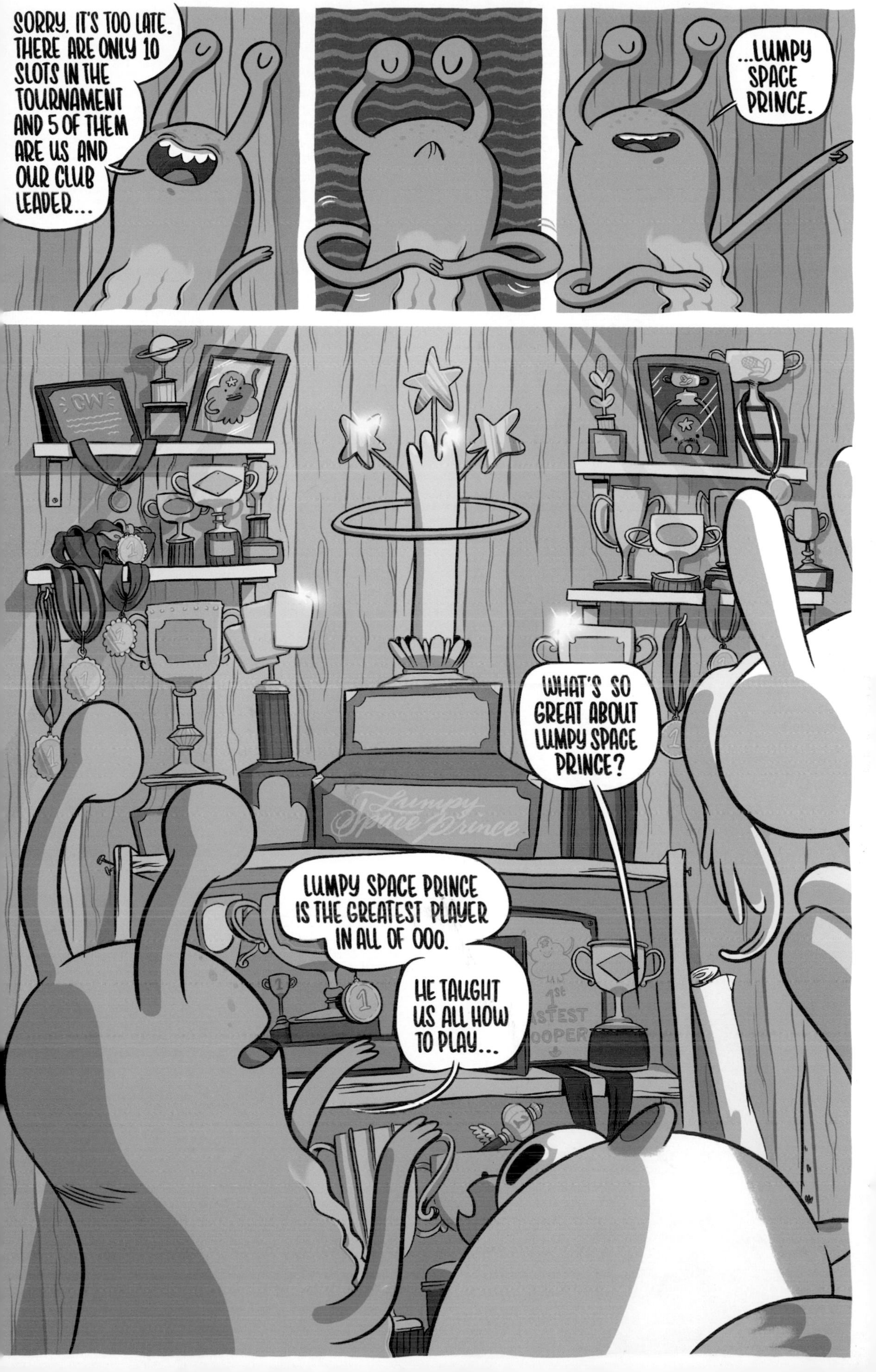
SORRY. IT'S TOO LATE. THERE ARE ONLY 10 SLOTS IN THE TOURNAMENT AND 5 OF THEM ARE US AND OUR CLUB LEADER...
...LUMPY SPACE PRINCE.
Lumpy Space Prince
WHAT'S SO GREAT ABOUT LUMPY SPACE PRINCE?
LUMPY SPACE PRINCE IS THE GREATEST PLAYER IN ALL OF OOO.
HE TAUGHT US ALL HOW TO PLAY...

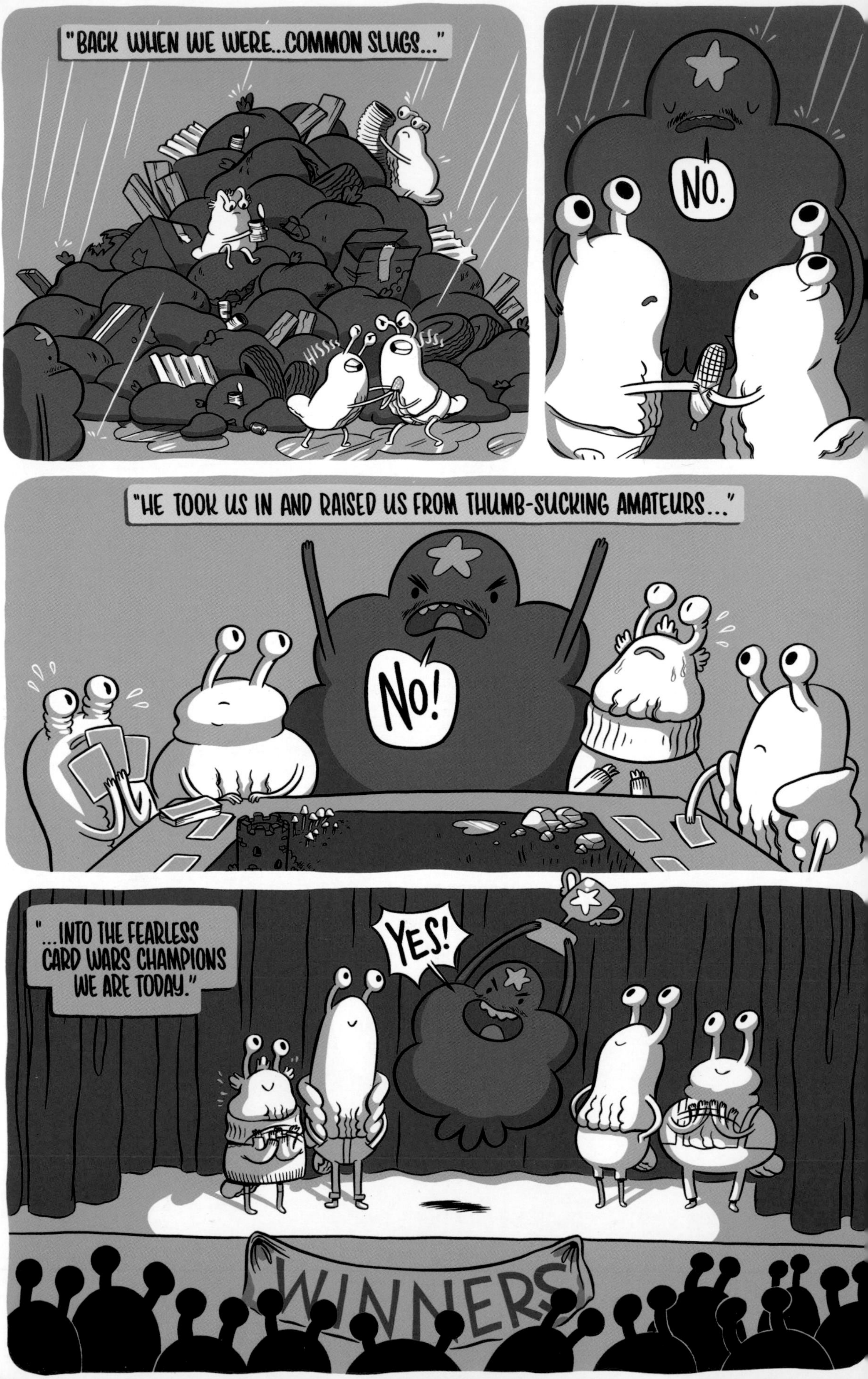
"BACK WHEN WE WERE...COMMON SLUGS..."
NO.
"HE TOOK US IN AND RAISED US FROM THUMB-SUCKING AMATEURS..."
NO!
"...INTO THE FEARLESS CARD WARS CHAMPIONS WE ARE TODAY."
YES!
WINNERS

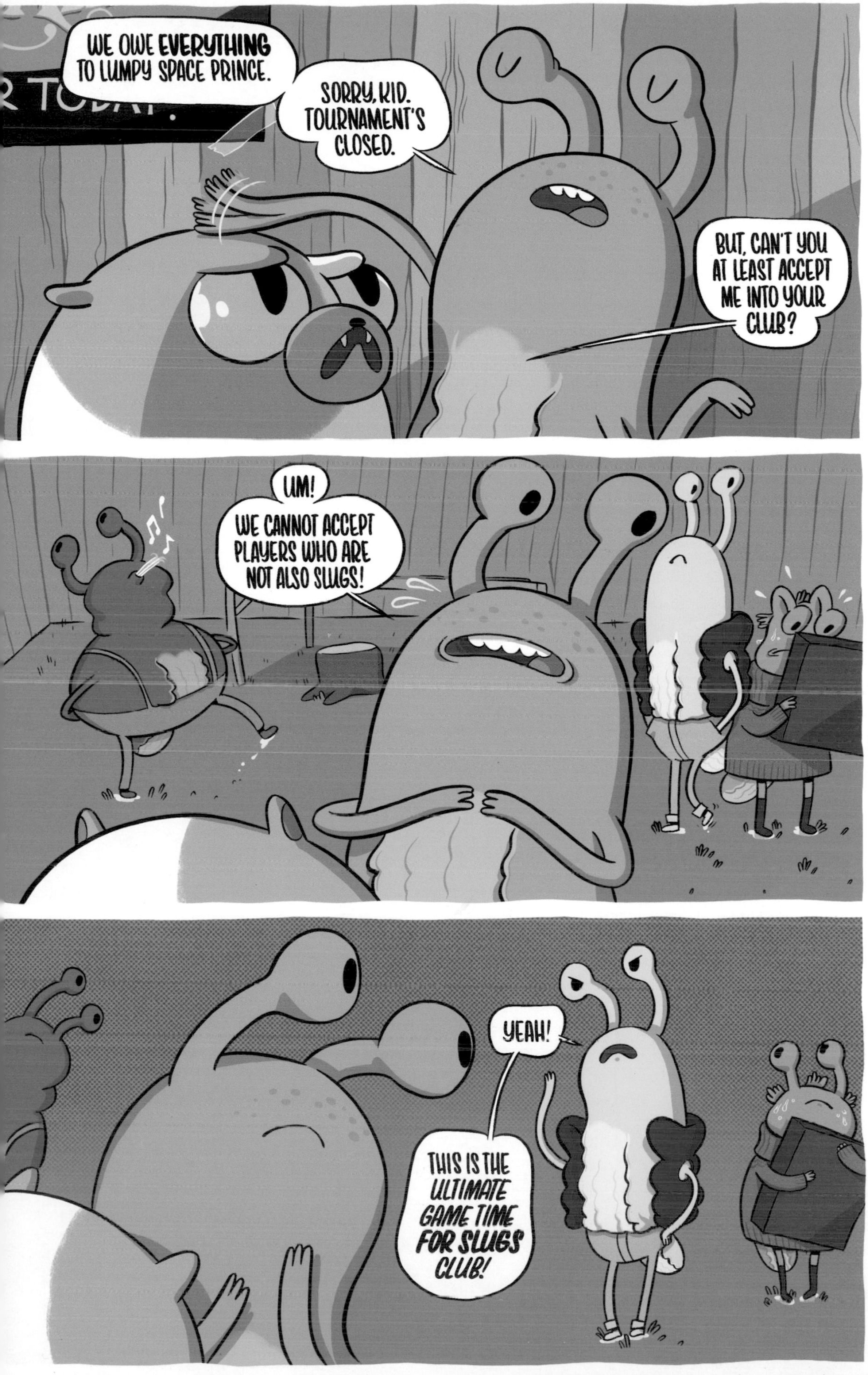
WE OWE EVERYTHING TO LUMPY SPACE PRINCE.
SORRY, KID. TOURNAMENT'S CLOSED.
BUT, CAN'T YOU AT LEAST ACCEPT ME INTO YOUR CLUB?
UM!
WE CANNOT ACCEPT PLAYERS WHO ARE NOT ALSO SLUGS!
YEAH!
THIS IS THE ULTIMATE GAME TIME FOR SLUGS CLUB!

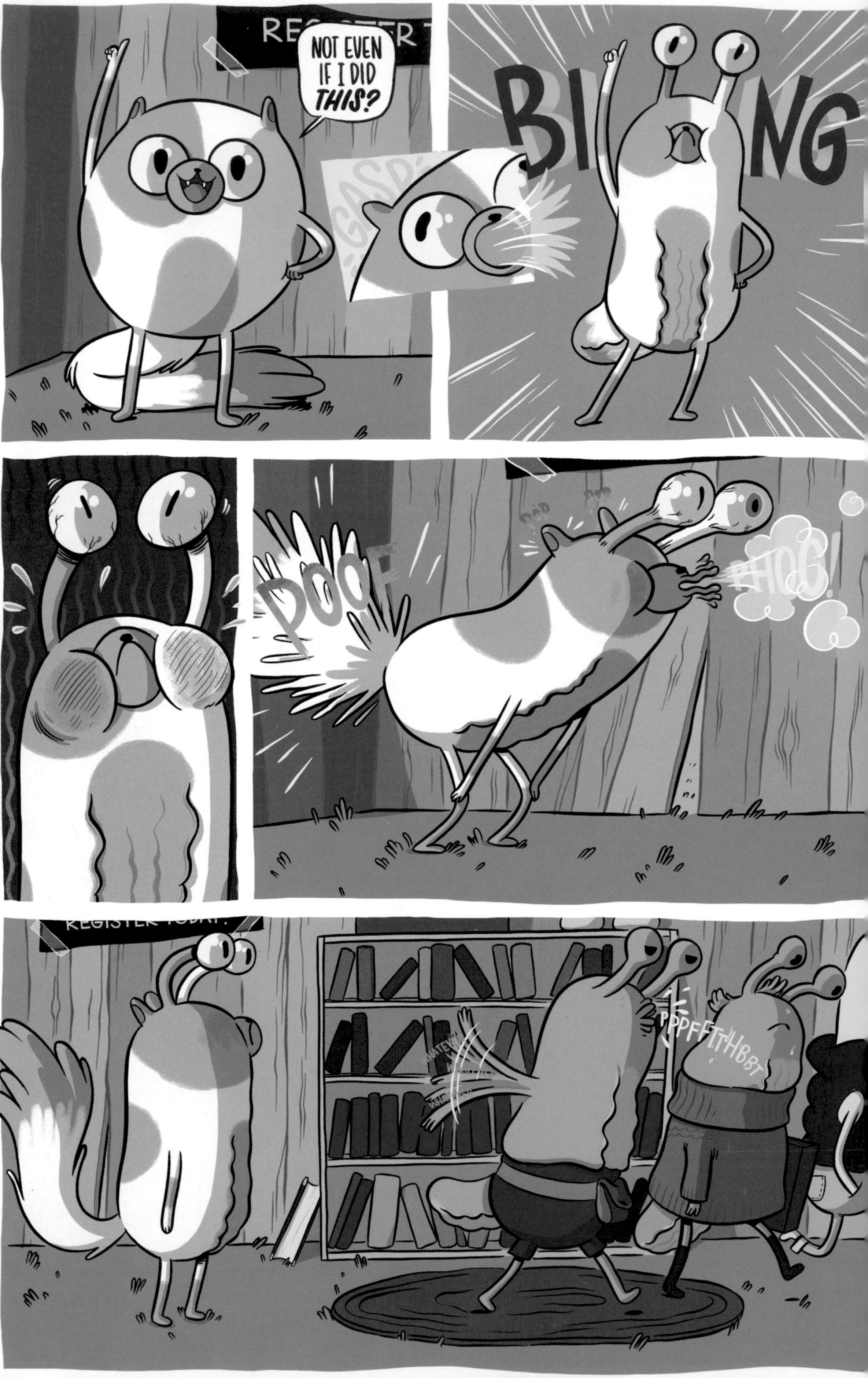

NOT EVEN IF I DID *THIS?*
GASP!
POOF
PPPFFTTHBBT

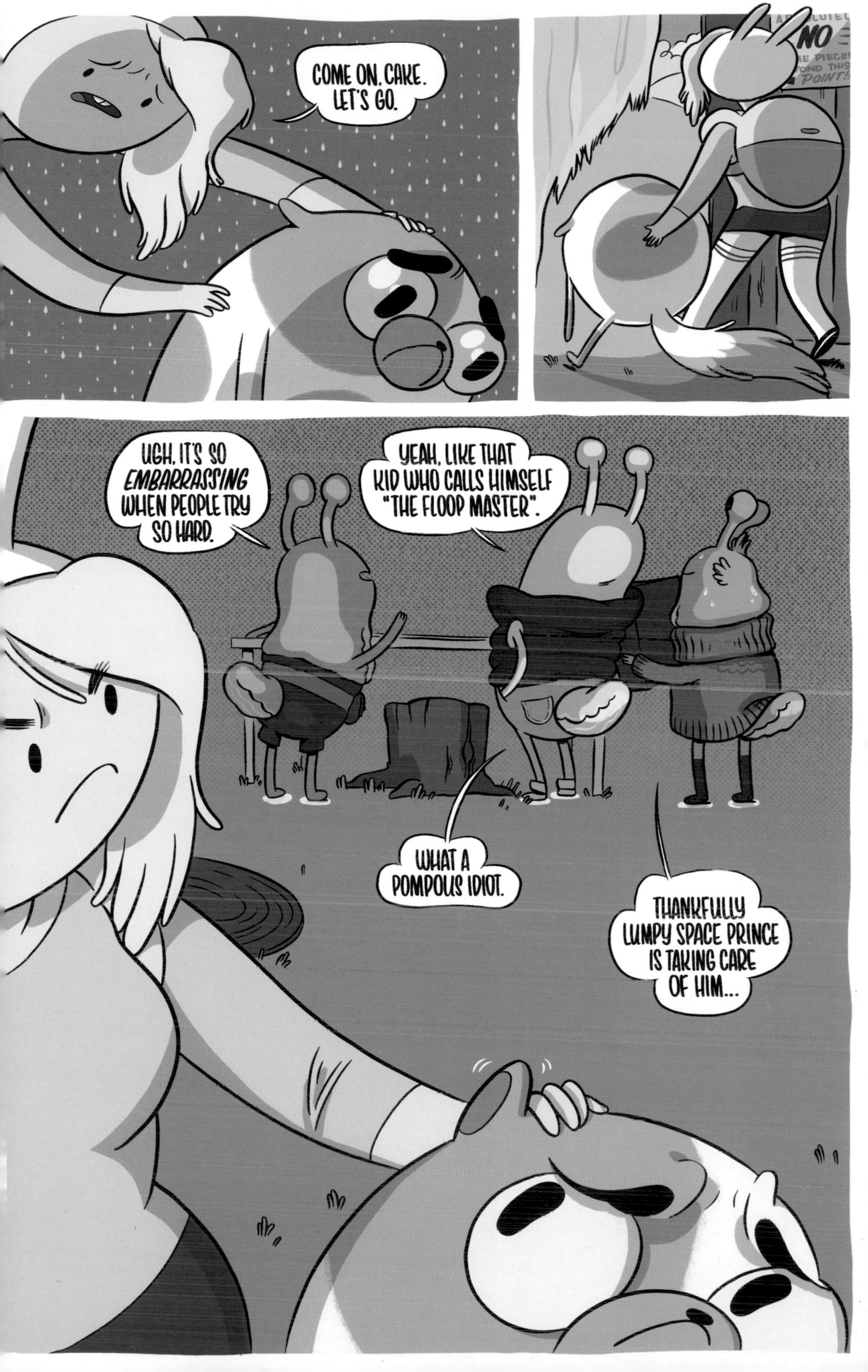
COME ON, CAKE. LET'S GO.
NO
POINT!!
UGH, IT'S SO *EMBARRASSING* WHEN PEOPLE TRY SO HARD.
YEAH, LIKE THAT KID WHO CALLS HIMSELF "THE FLOOP MASTER".
WHAT A POMPOUS IDIOT.
THANKFULLY LUMPY SPACE PRINCE IS TAKING CARE OF HIM...

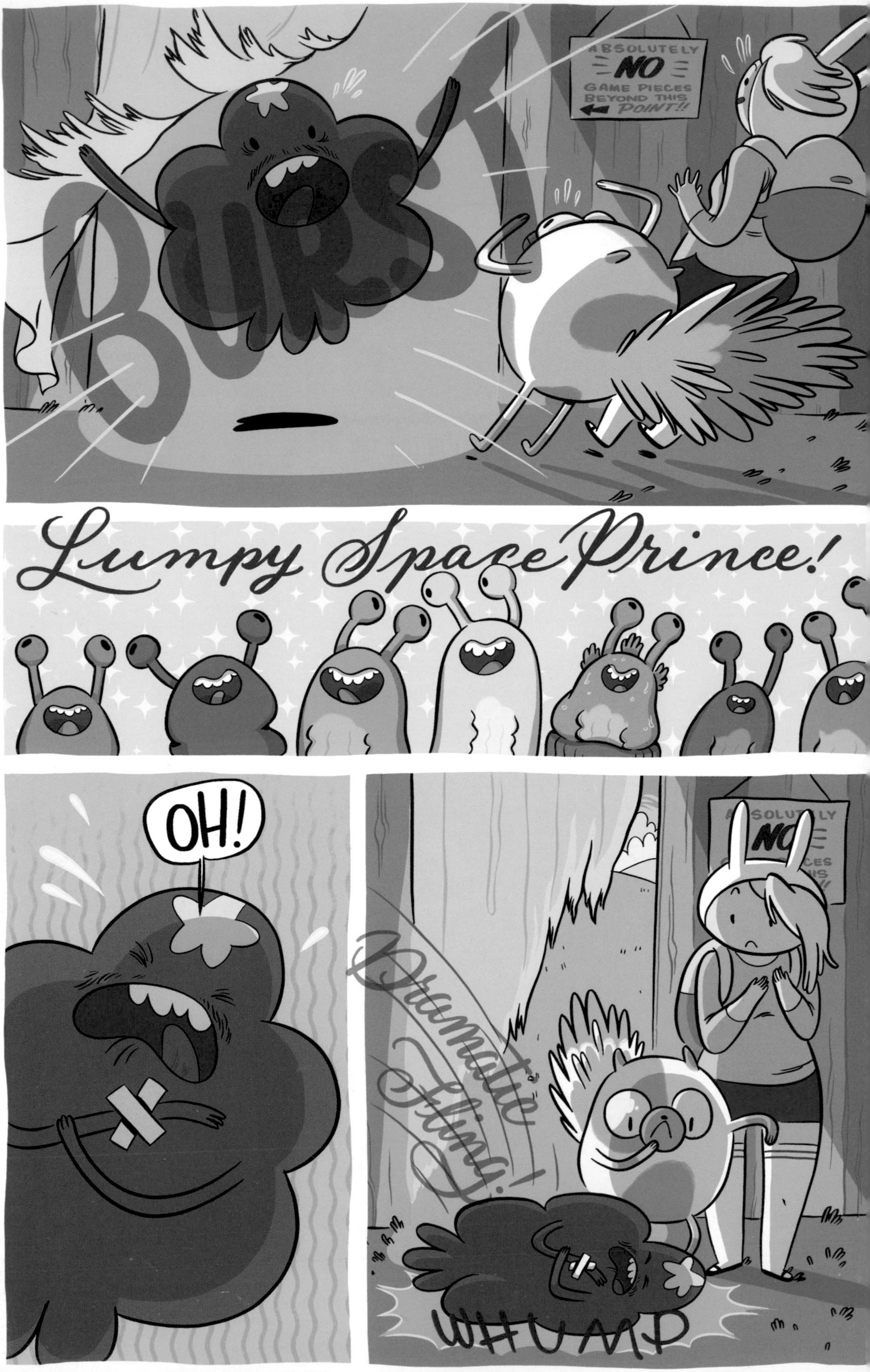
ABSOLUTELY NO GAME PIECES BEYOND THIS POINT!!
BURST
Lumpy Space Prince!
OH!
Dramatic Fling!
WHUMP

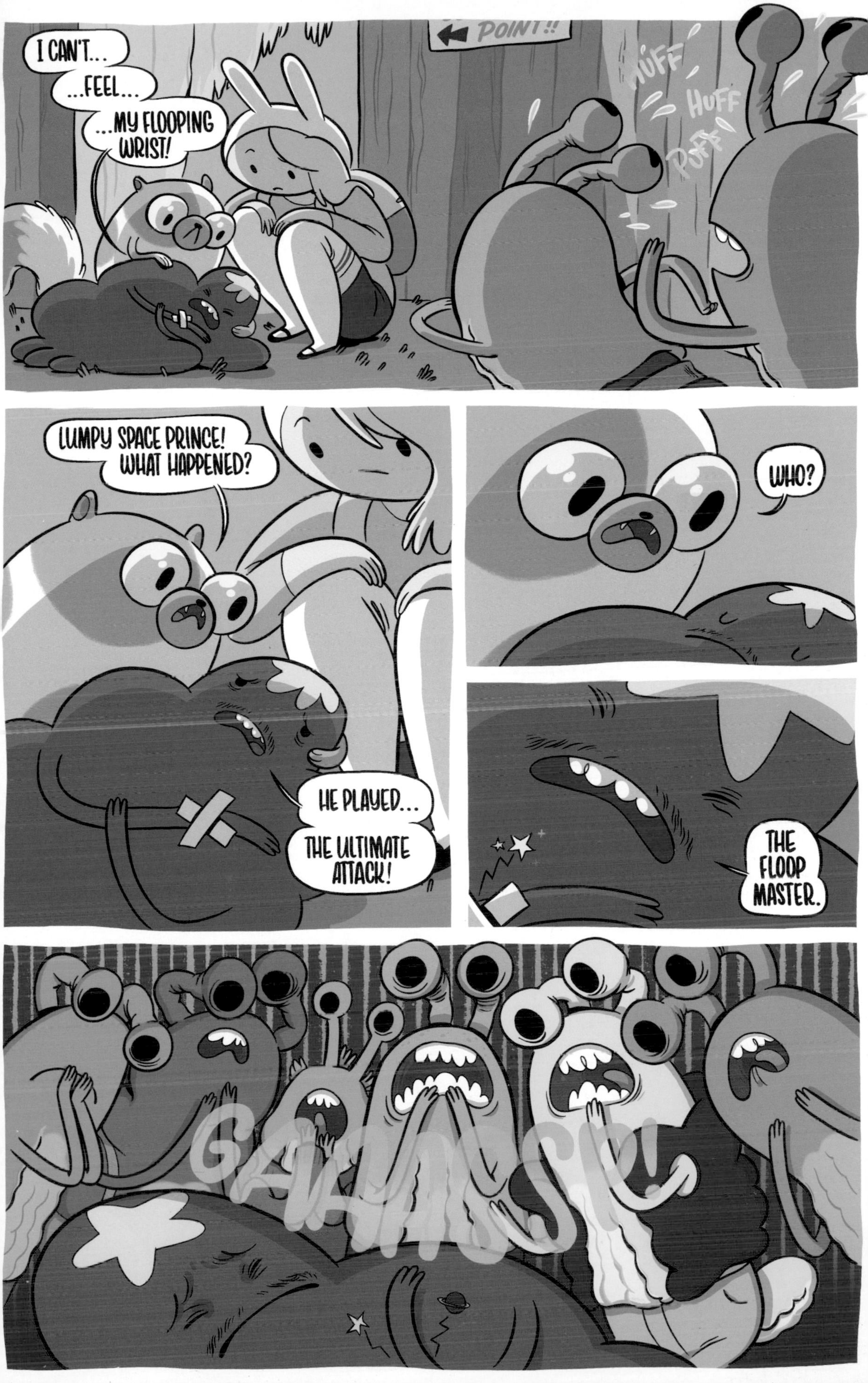
POINT!!
I CAN'T...
...FEEL...
...MY FLOOPING WRIST!
HUFF
HUFF
PUFF
LUMPY SPACE PRINCE! WHAT HAPPENED?
HE PLAYED...
THE ULTIMATE ATTACK!
WHO?
THE FLOOP MASTER.
GAAASP!

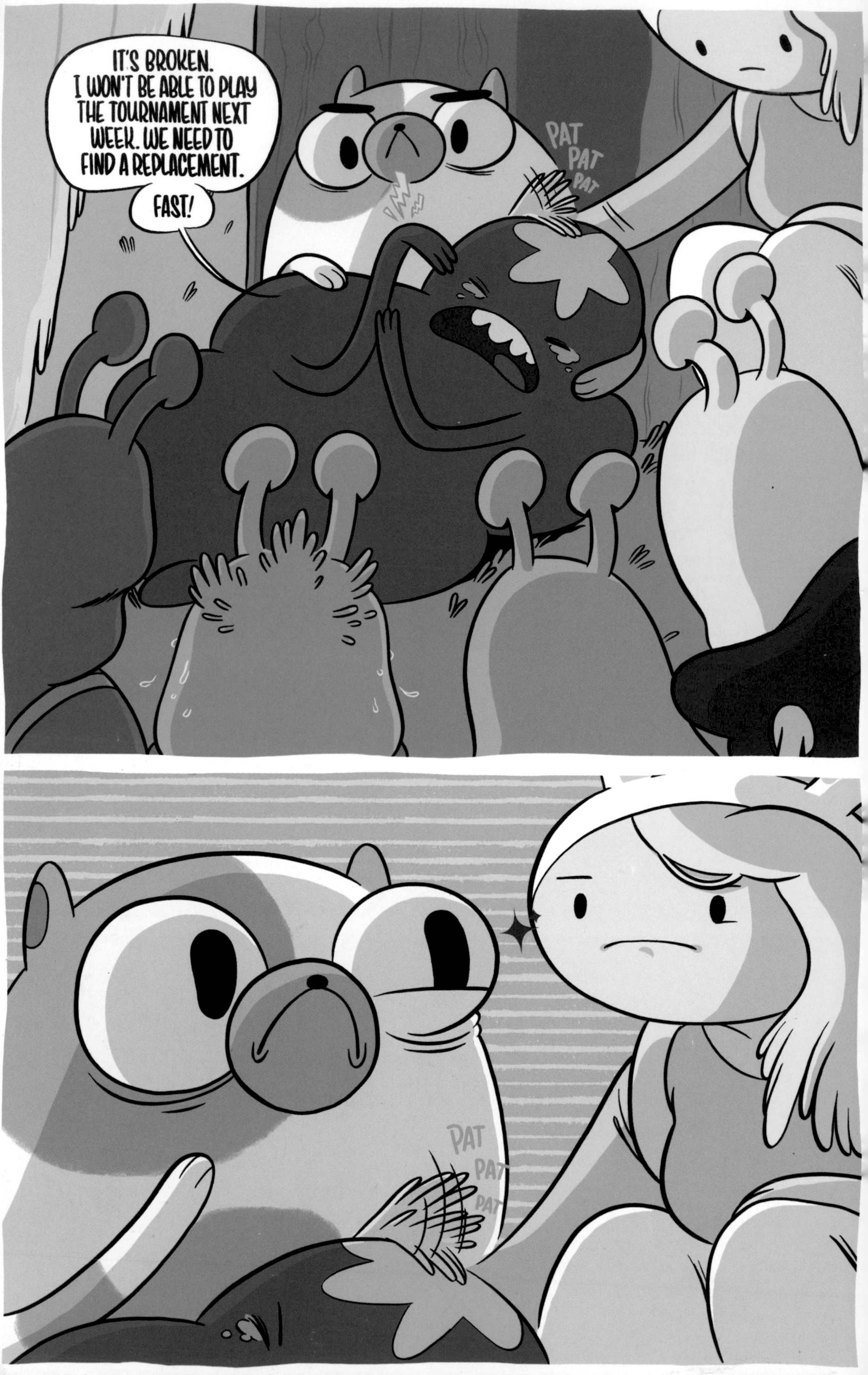
IT'S BROKEN. I WON'T BE ABLE TO PLAY THE TOURNAMENT NEXT WEEK. WE NEED TO FIND A REPLACEMENT.
FAST!
PAT PAT PAT
PAT PAT PAT

chapter two

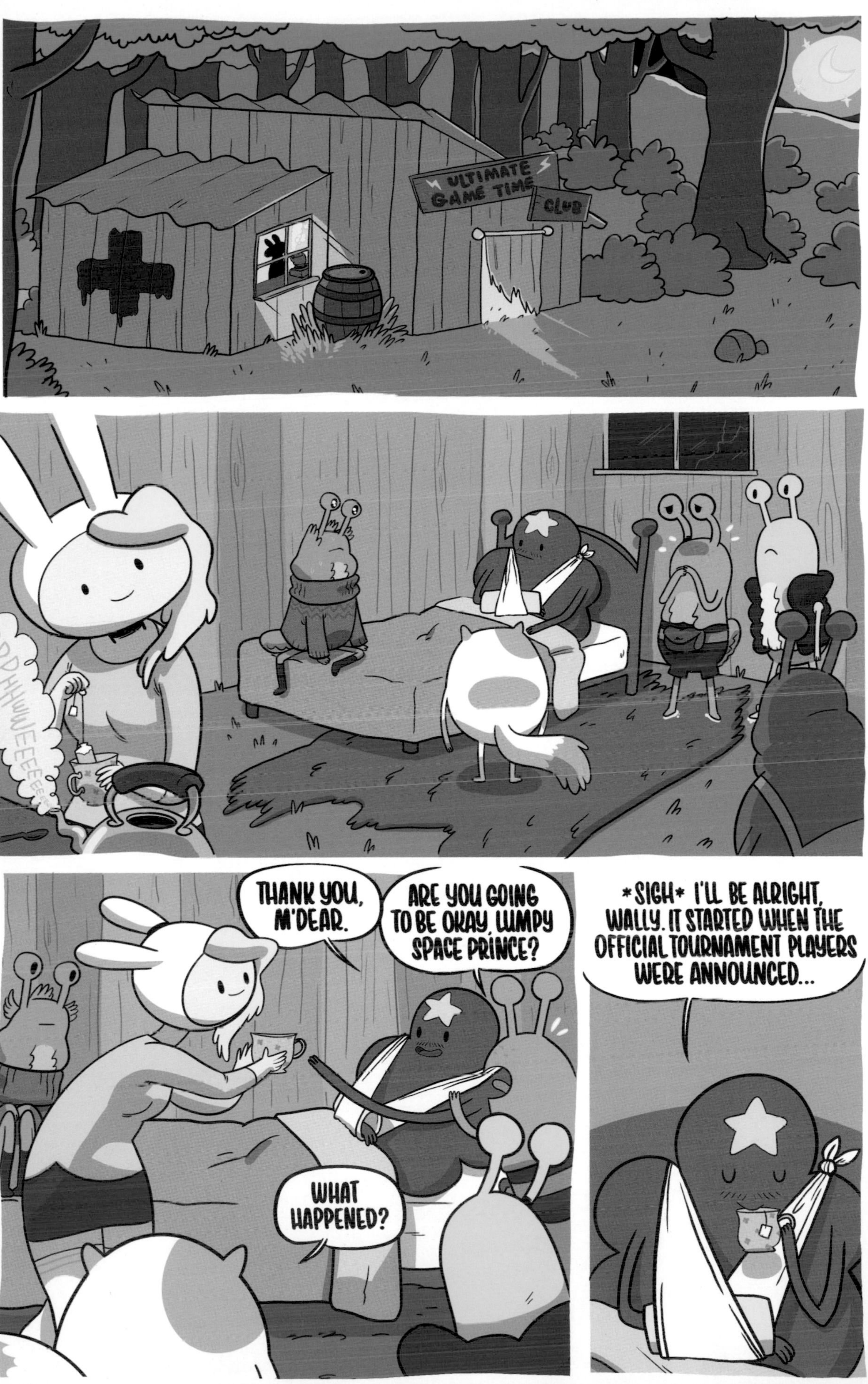
ULTIMATE GAME TIME CLUB
THANK YOU, M'DEAR.
ARE YOU GOING TO BE OKAY, LUMPY SPACE PRINCE?
WHAT HAPPENED?
SIGH I'LL BE ALRIGHT, WALLY. IT STARTED WHEN THE OFFICIAL TOURNAMENT PLAYERS WERE ANNOUNCED...

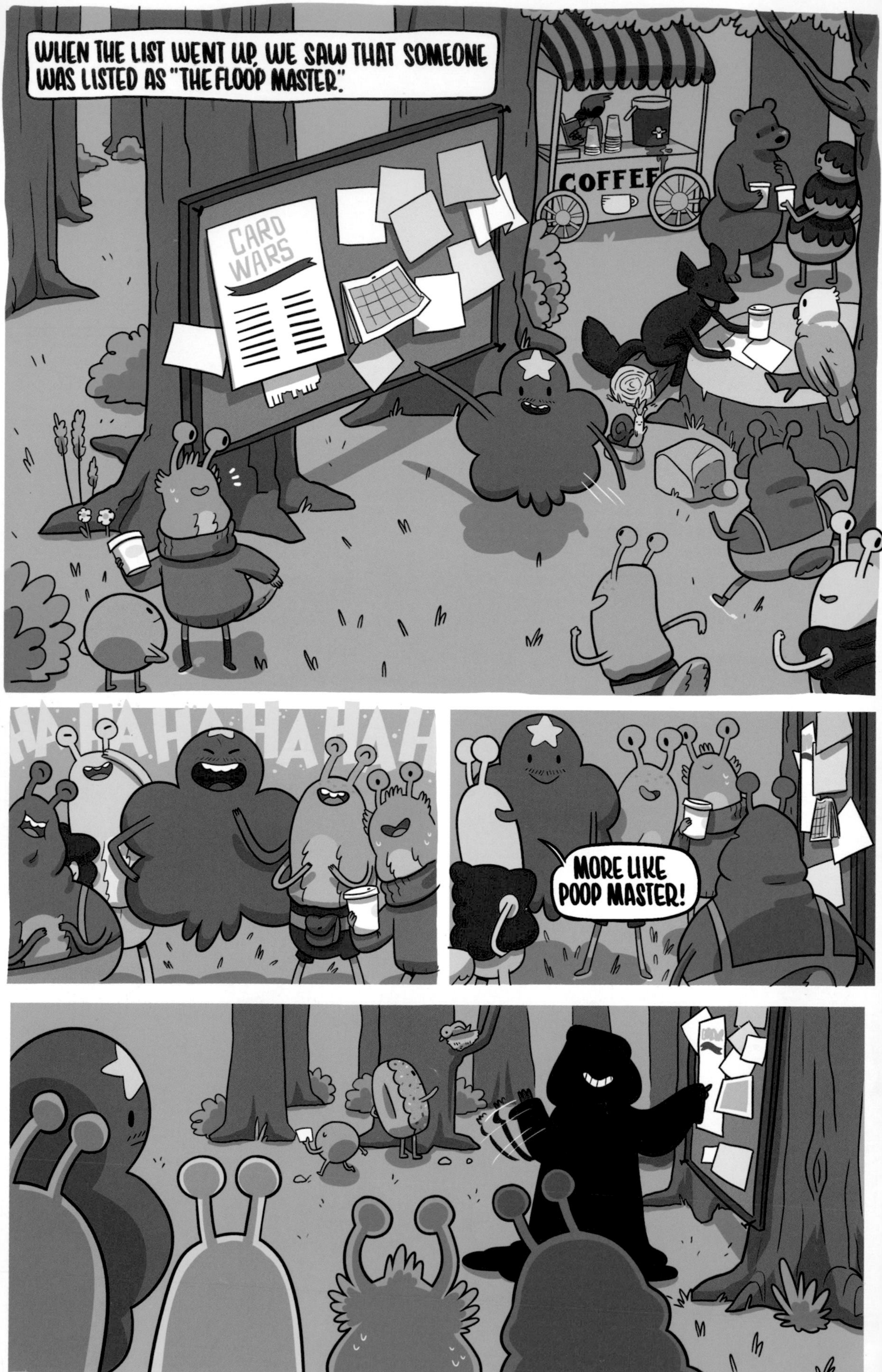
WHEN THE LIST WENT UP, WE SAW THAT SOMEONE WAS LISTED AS "THE FLOOP MASTER."
CARD WARS
COFFEE
HAHAHAHAHAHAH
MORE LIKE POOP MASTER!

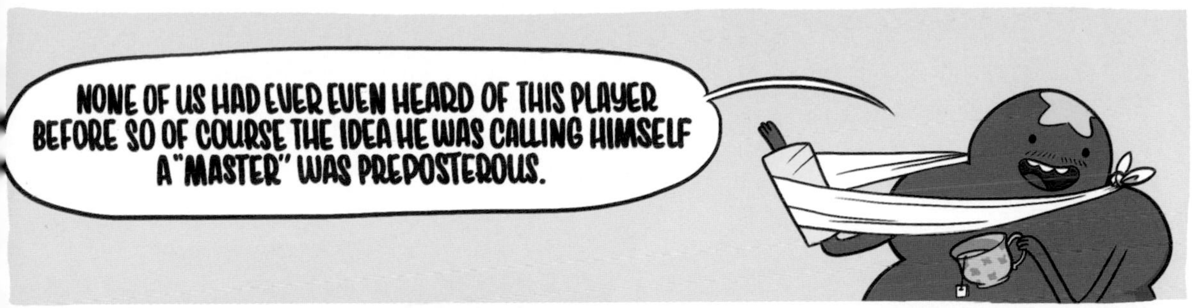
NONE OF US HAD EVER EVEN HEARD OF THIS PLAYER BEFORE SO OF COURSE THE IDEA HE WAS CALLING HIMSELF A "MASTER" WAS PREPOSTEROUS.

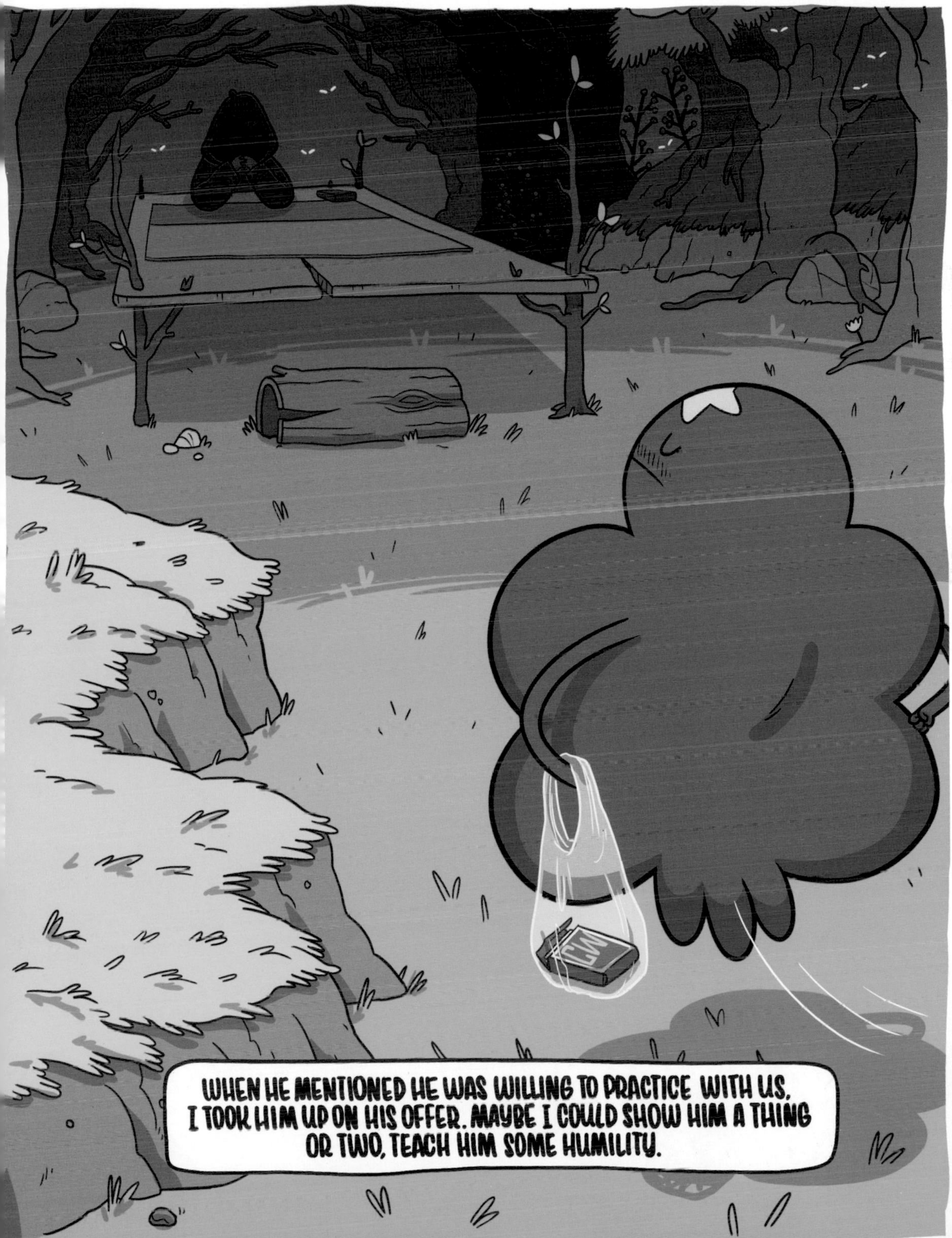
WHEN HE MENTIONED HE WAS WILLING TO PRACTICE WITH US, I TOOK HIM UP ON HIS OFFER. MAYBE I COULD SHOW HIM A THING OR TWO, TEACH HIM SOME HUMILITY.

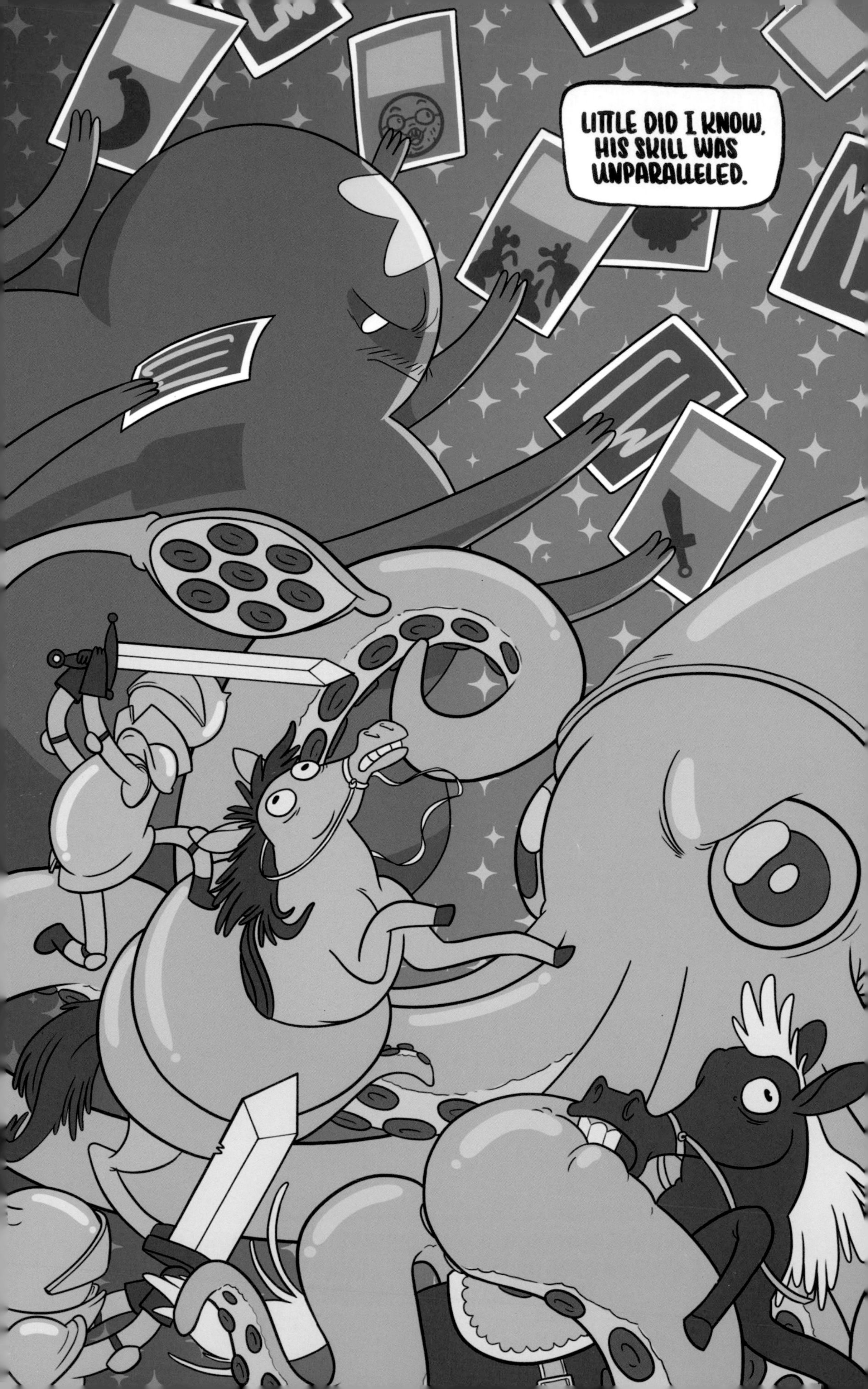
LITTLE DID I KNOW, HIS SKILL WAS UNPARALLELED.

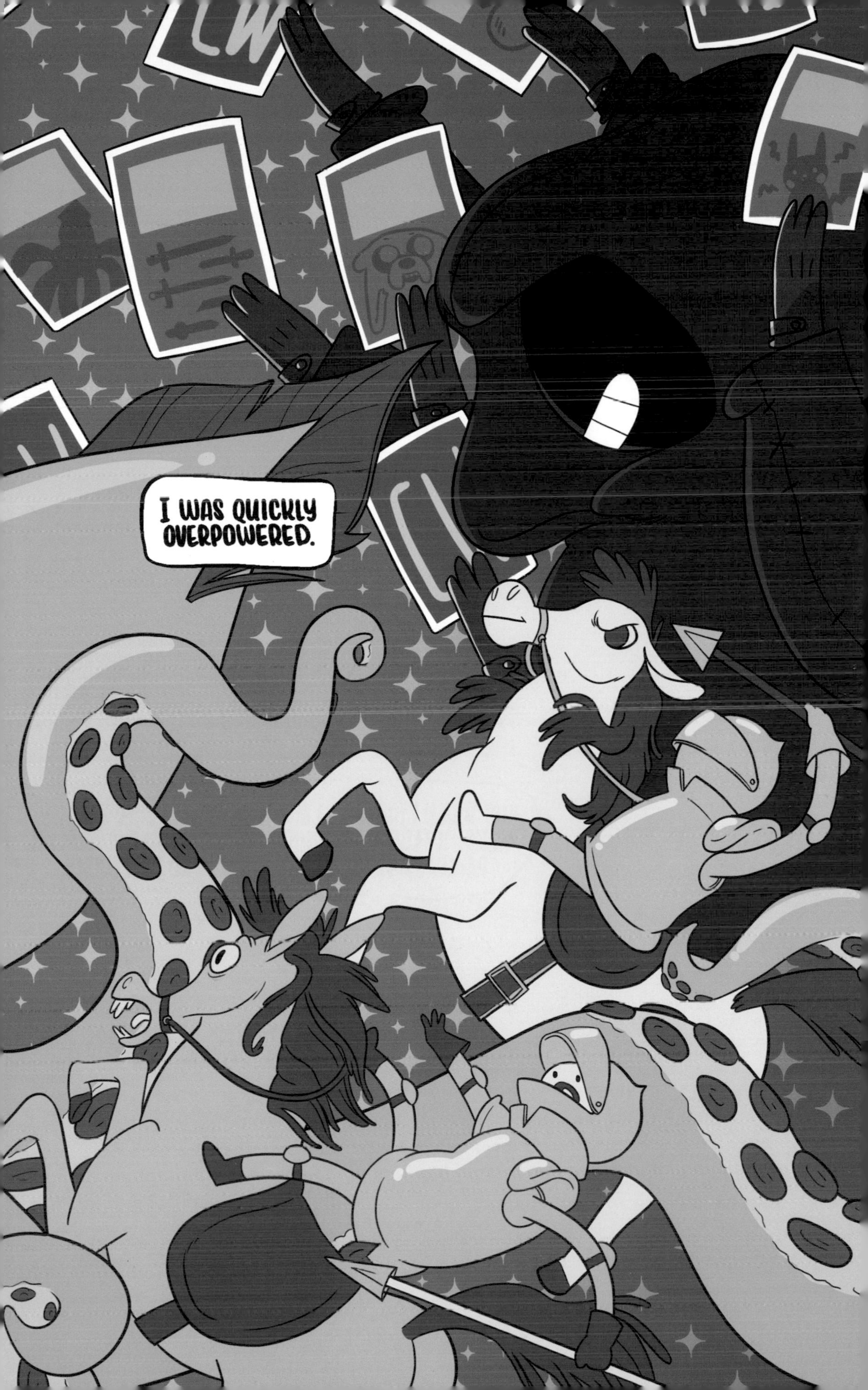
I WAS QUICKLY OVERPOWERED.

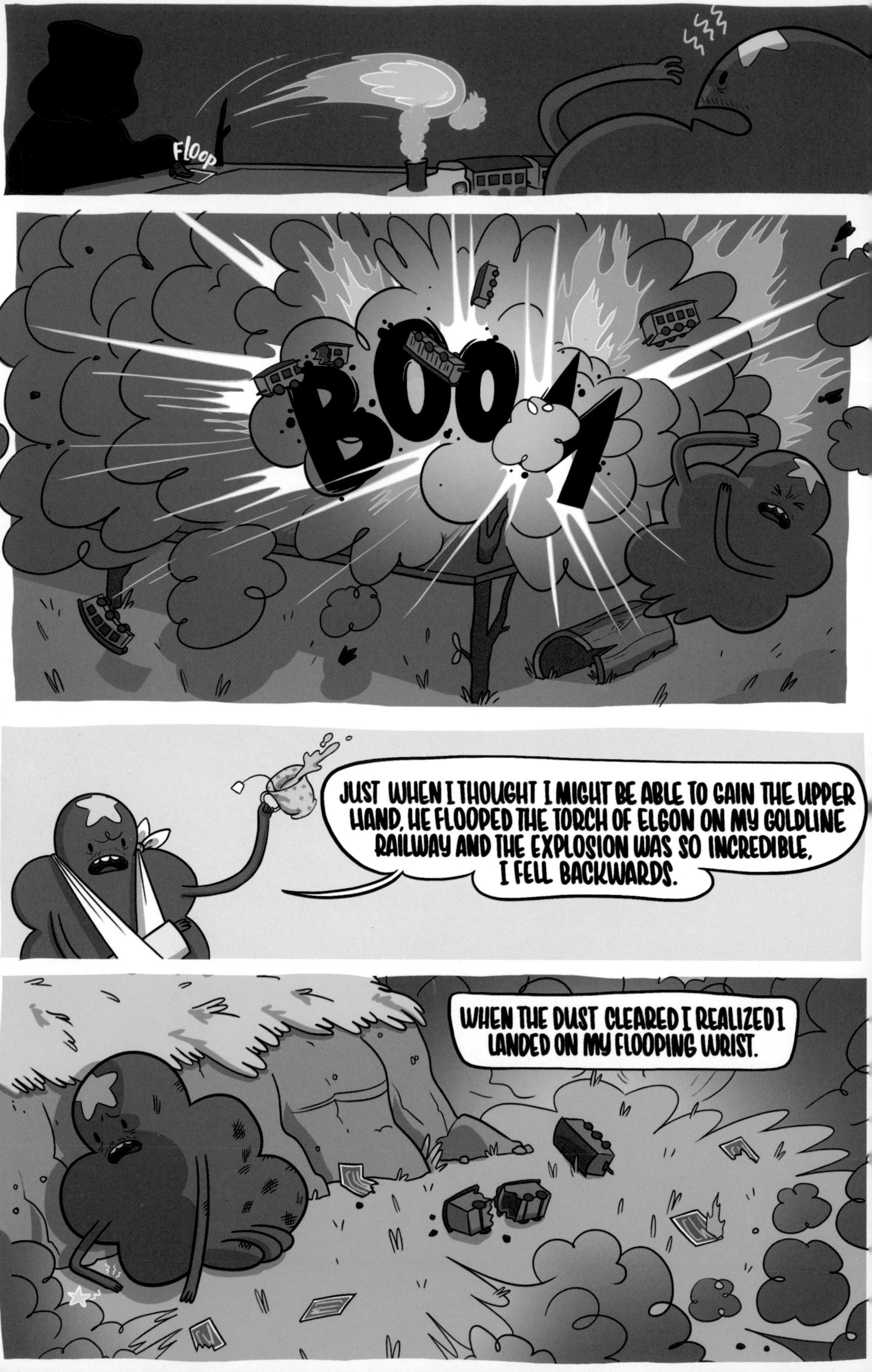
FLOOP
BOOM
JUST WHEN I THOUGHT I MIGHT BE ABLE TO GAIN THE UPPER HAND, HE FLOOPED THE TORCH OF ELGON ON MY GOLDLINE RAILWAY AND THE EXPLOSION WAS SO INCREDIBLE, I FELL BACKWARDS.
WHEN THE DUST CLEARED I REALIZED I LANDED ON MY FLOOPING WRIST.

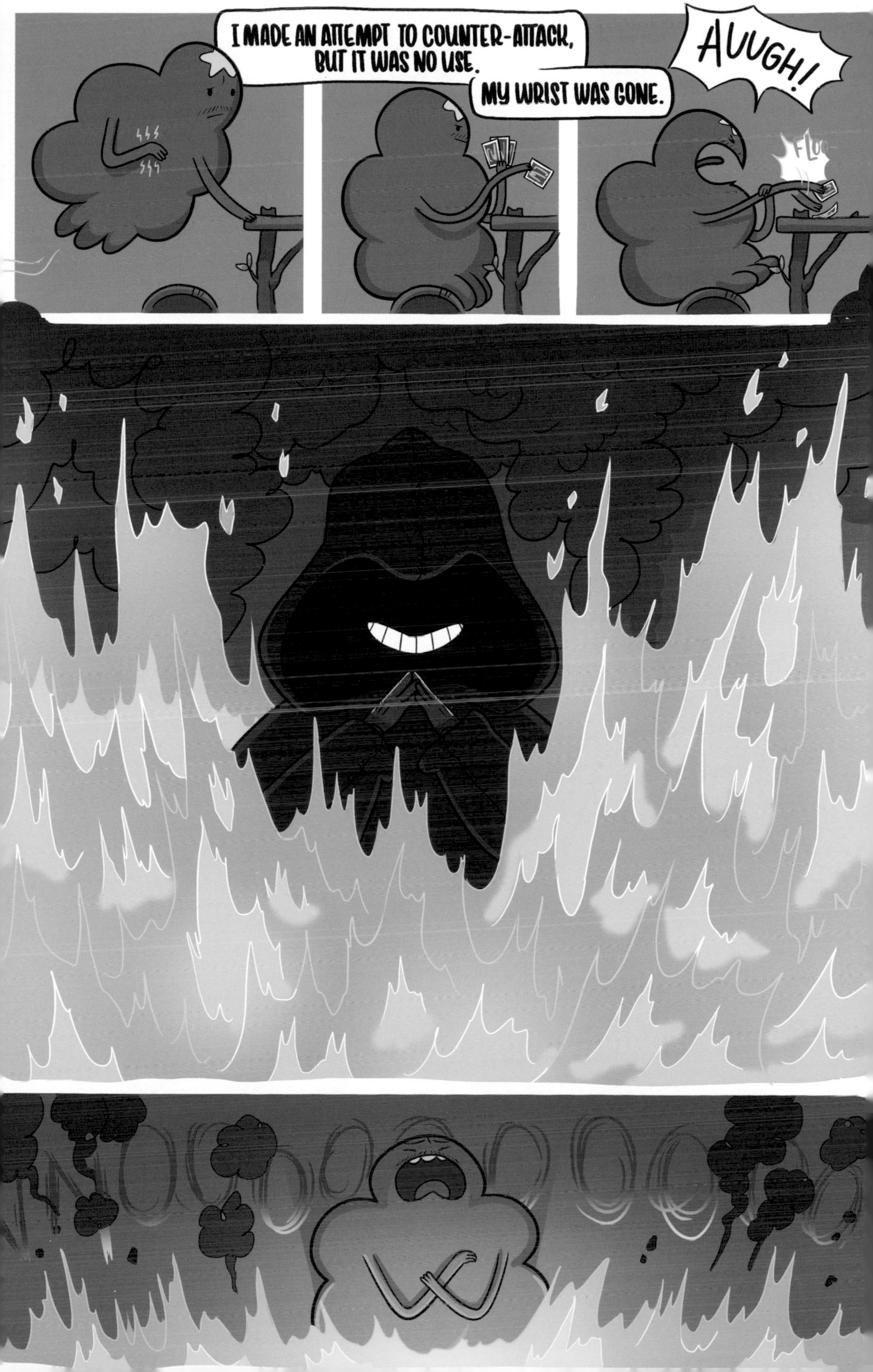
I MADE AN ATTEMPT TO COUNTER-ATTACK, BUT IT WAS NO USE.
MY WRIST WAS GONE.
AUUGH!
FLOO-
NOOOOOOOOOOOOOO

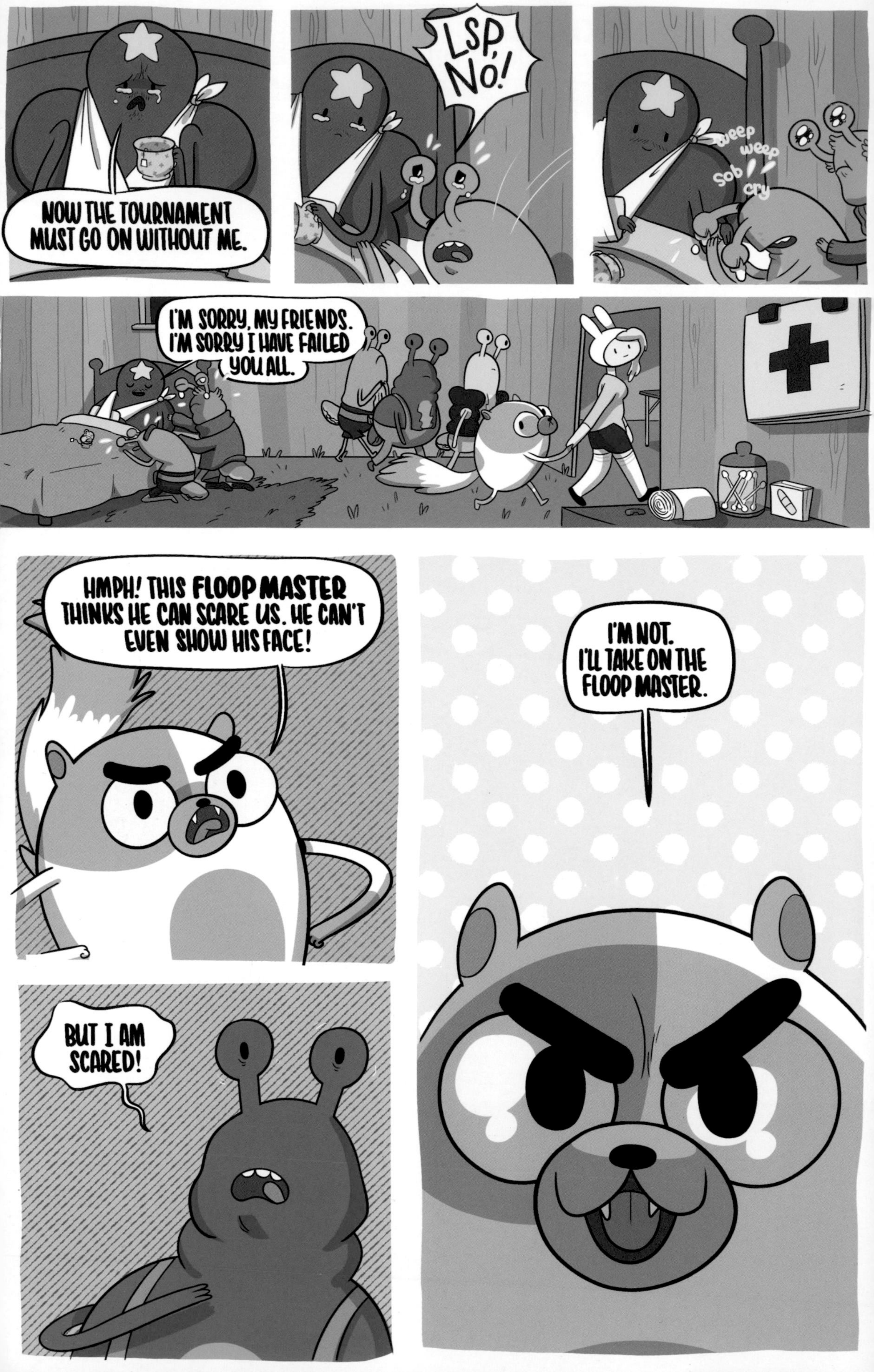
NOW THE TOURNAMENT MUST GO ON WITHOUT ME.
LSP, No!
weep weep
Sob
cry
I'M SORRY, MY FRIENDS. I'M SORRY I HAVE FAILED YOU ALL.
HMPH! THIS FLOOP MASTER THINKS HE CAN SCARE US. HE CAN'T EVEN SHOW HIS FACE!
BUT I AM SCARED!
I'M NOT. I'LL TAKE ON THE FLOOP MASTER.

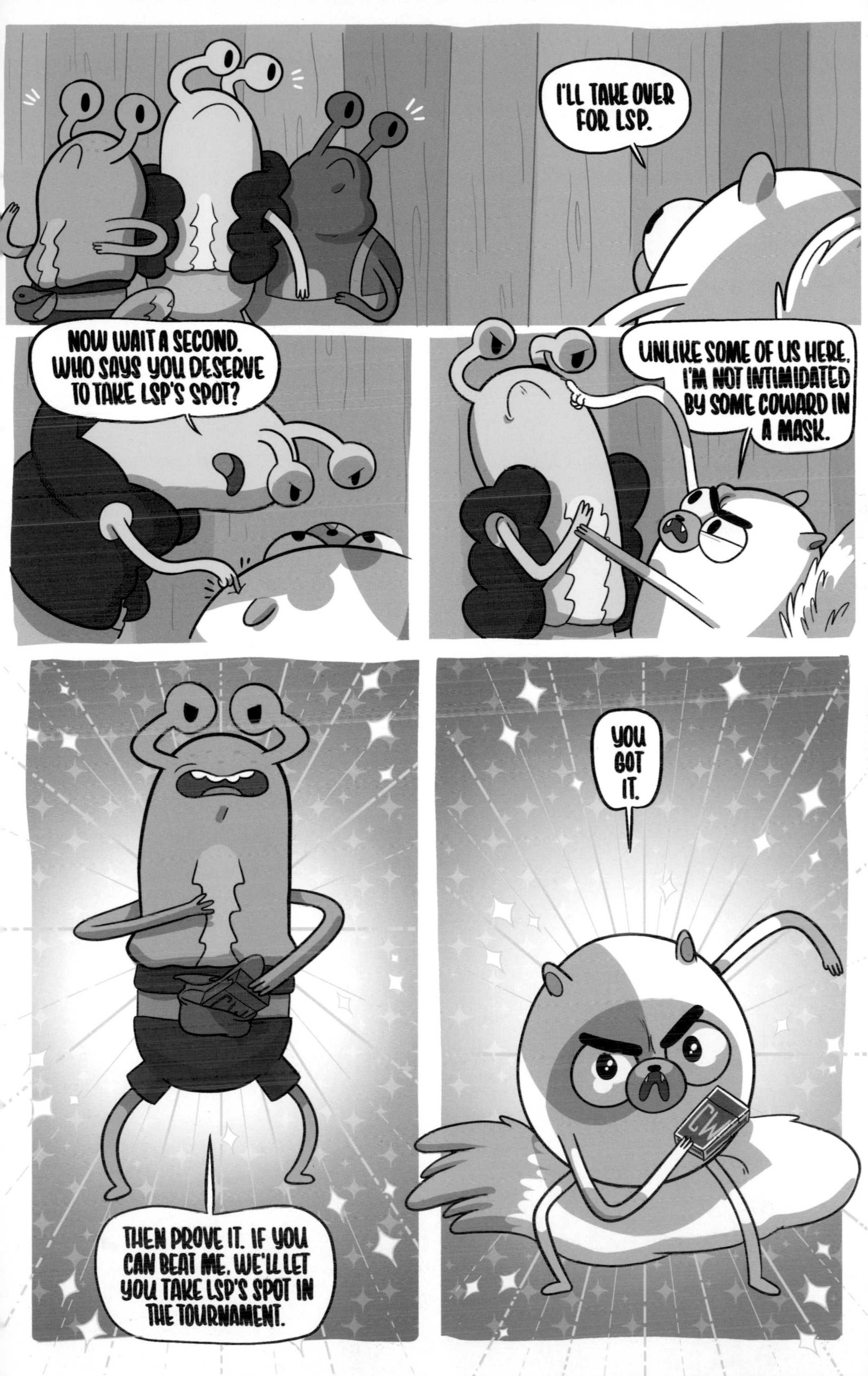
I'LL TAKE OVER FOR LSP.
NOW WAIT A SECOND. WHO SAYS YOU DESERVE TO TAKE LSP'S SPOT?
UNLIKE SOME OF US HERE, I'M NOT INTIMIDATED BY SOME COWARD IN A MASK.
THEN PROVE IT. IF YOU CAN BEAT ME, WE'LL LET YOU TAKE LSP'S SPOT IN THE TOURNAMENT.
YOU GOT IT.

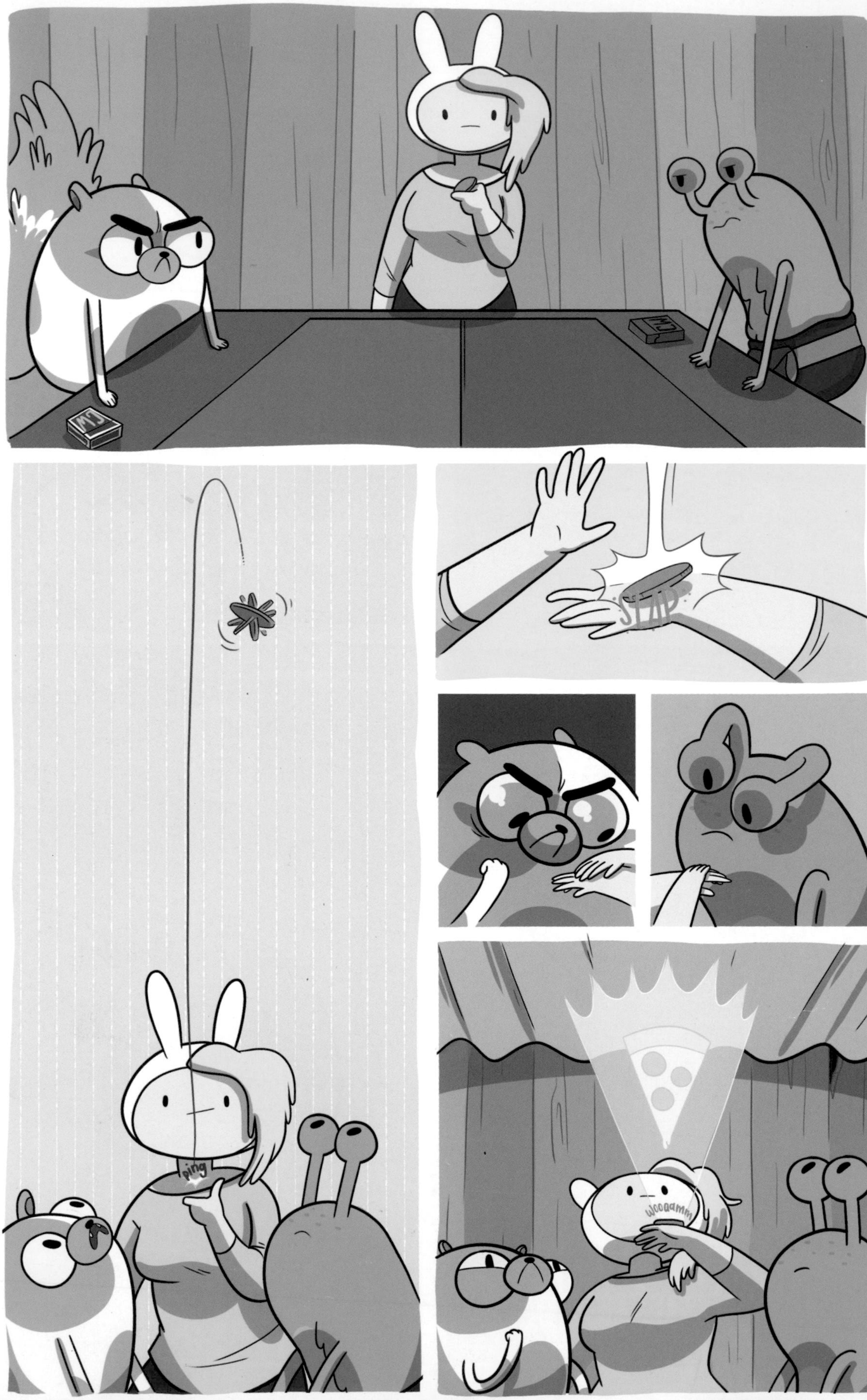
ping
SLAP
wooaamm

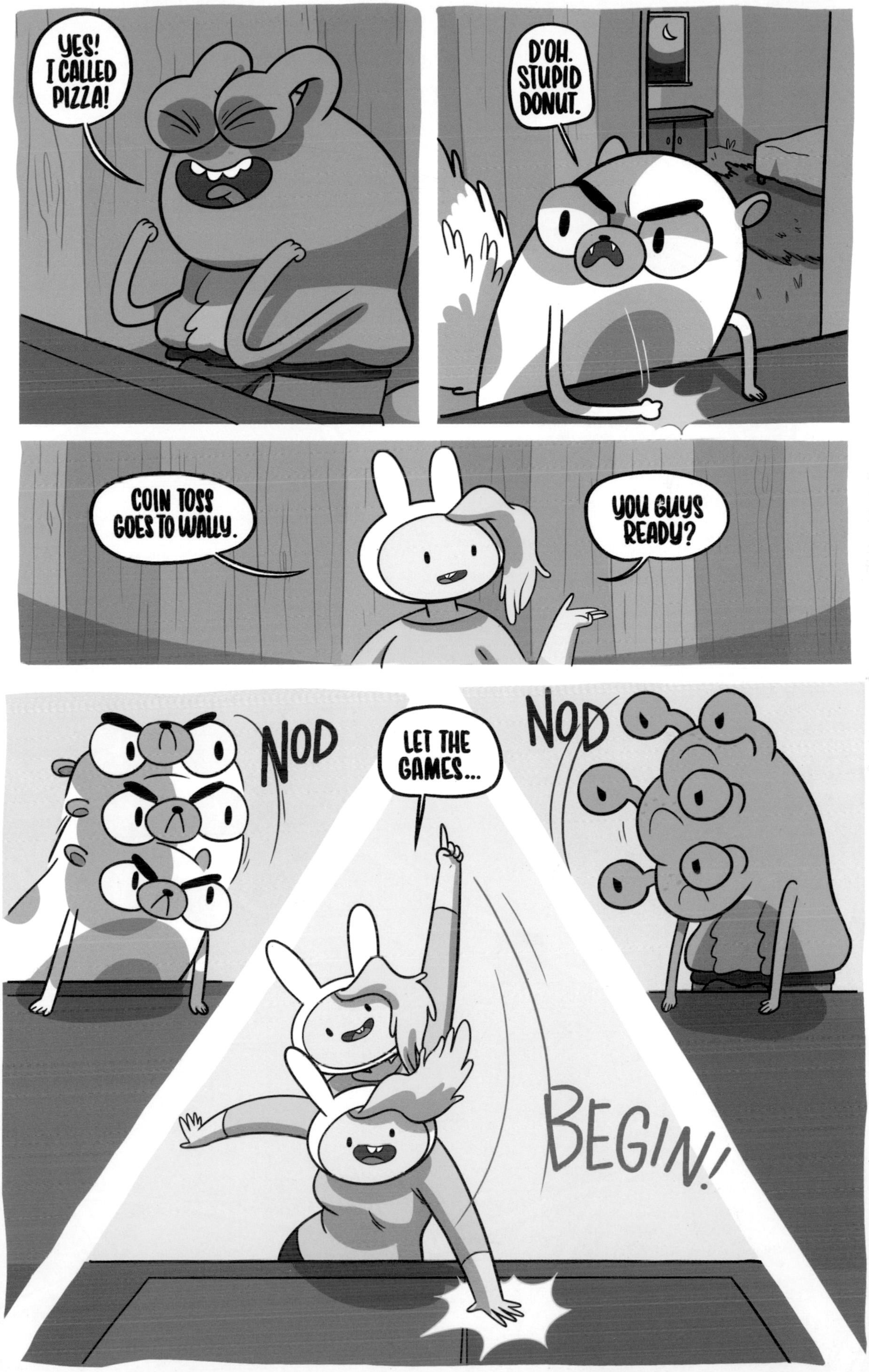
YES! I CALLED PIZZA!
D'OH. STUPID DONUT.
COIN TOSS GOES TO WALLY.
YOU GUYS READY?
NOD
LET THE GAMES...
NOD
BEGIN!

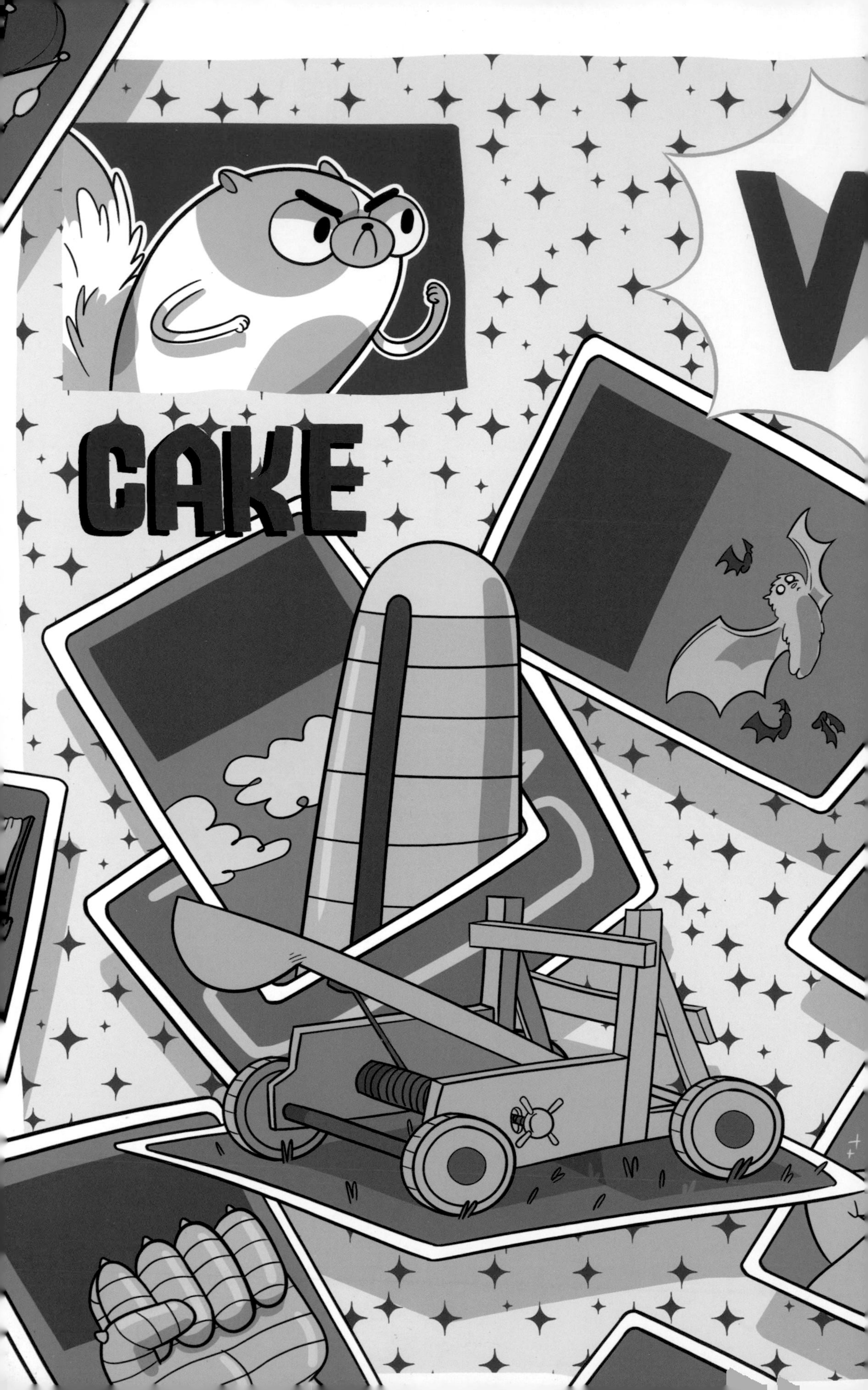
CAKE

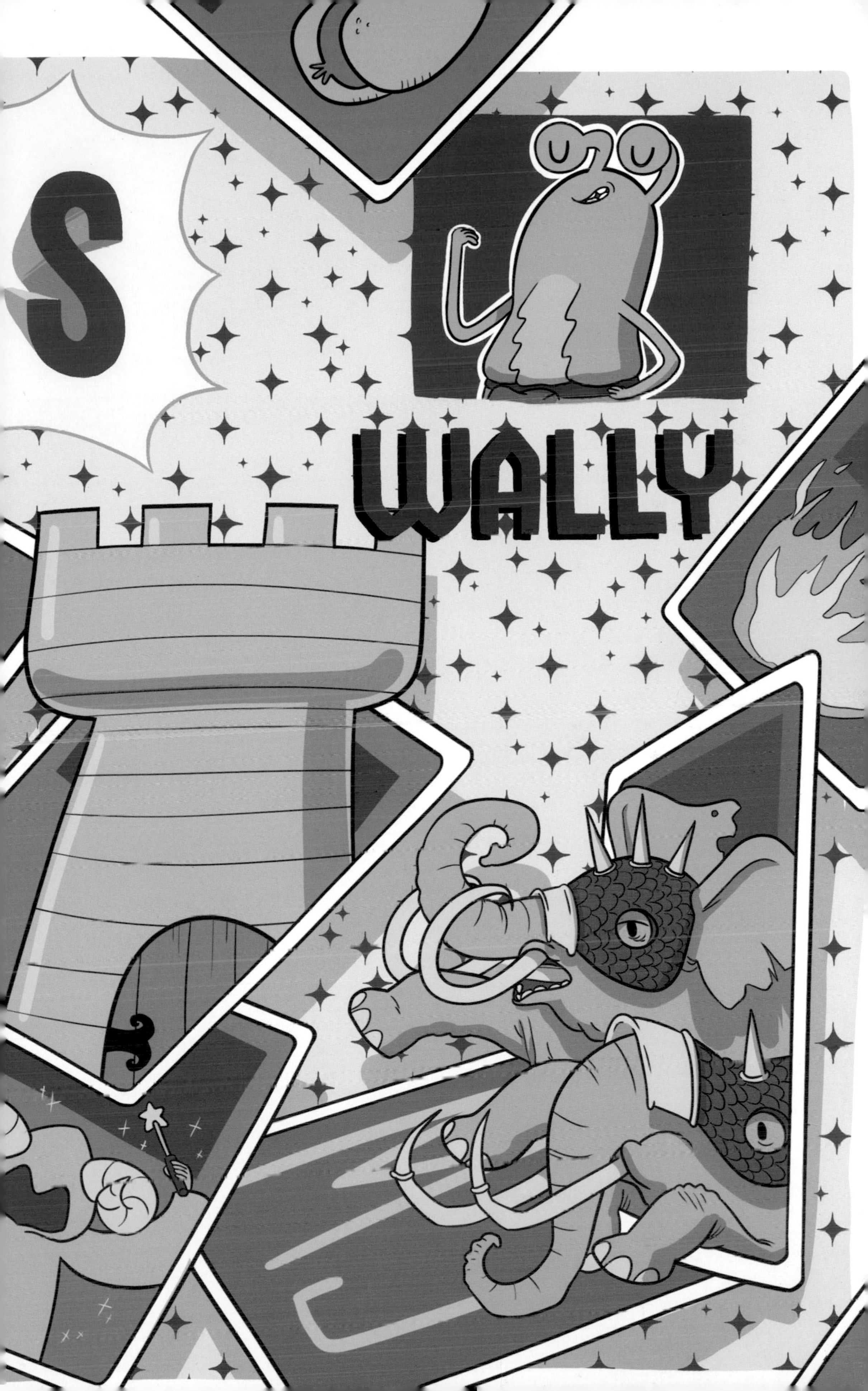
S
WALLY

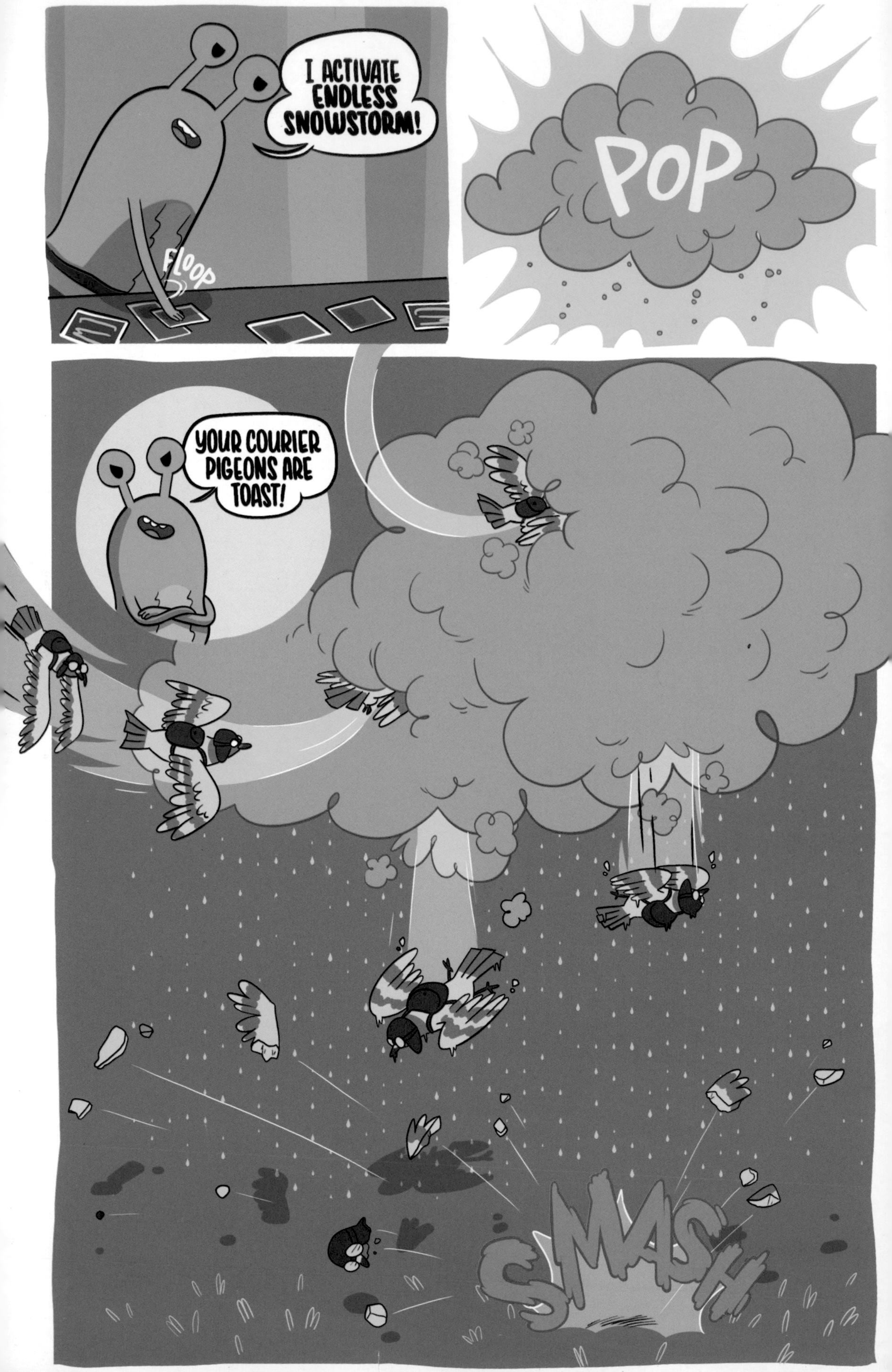
I ACTIVATE ENDLESS SNOWSTORM!
FLOOP
POP
YOUR COURIER PIGEONS ARE TOAST!
SMASH

NO! MY PIGEONS! I TRAINED THEM SO WELL!
OK! POTTY BREAK!
MAYBE NOW'S A GOOD TIME TO RETHINK YOUR STRATEGY. PLAYING A LITTLE DEFENSIVELY, HUH?
HISS
HISS
YOU MIND YOUR OWN! I'M DOING JUST FINE.

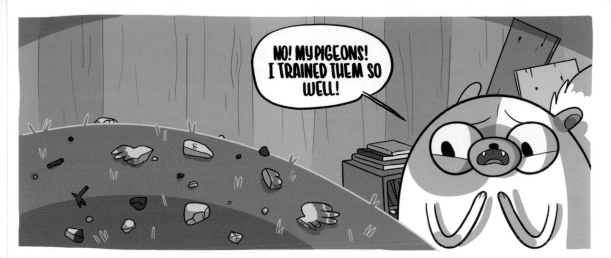

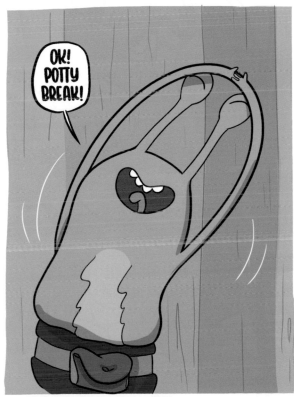

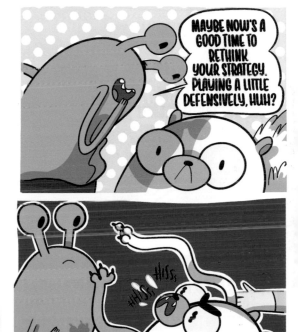

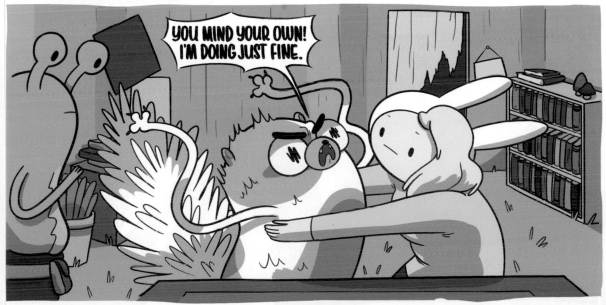

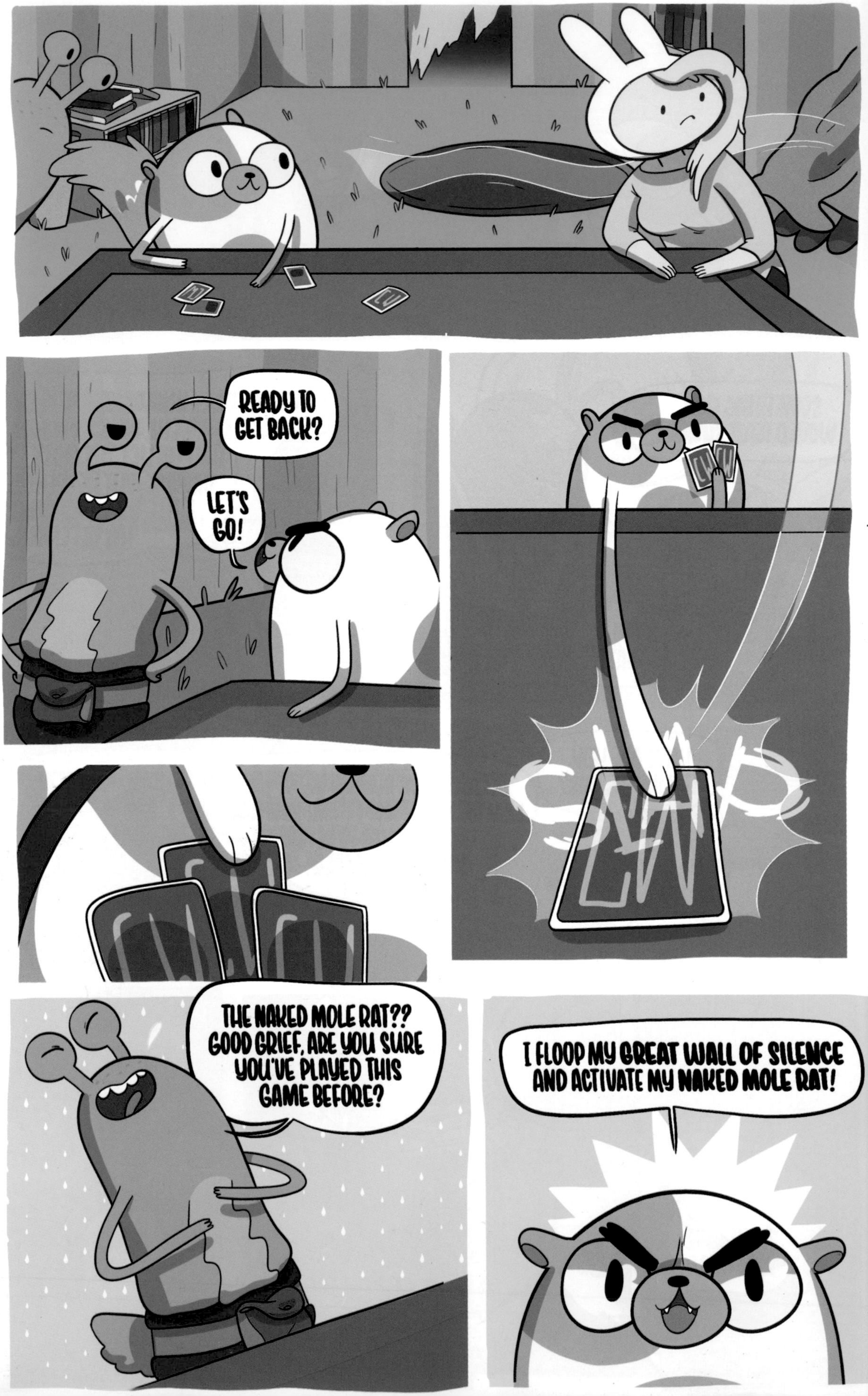
READY TO GET BACK?
LET'S GO!
SLAP
THE NAKED MOLE RAT?? GOOD GRIEF, ARE YOU SURE YOU'VE PLAYED THIS GAME BEFORE?
I FLOOP MY GREAT WALL OF SILENCE AND ACTIVATE MY NAKED MOLE RAT!

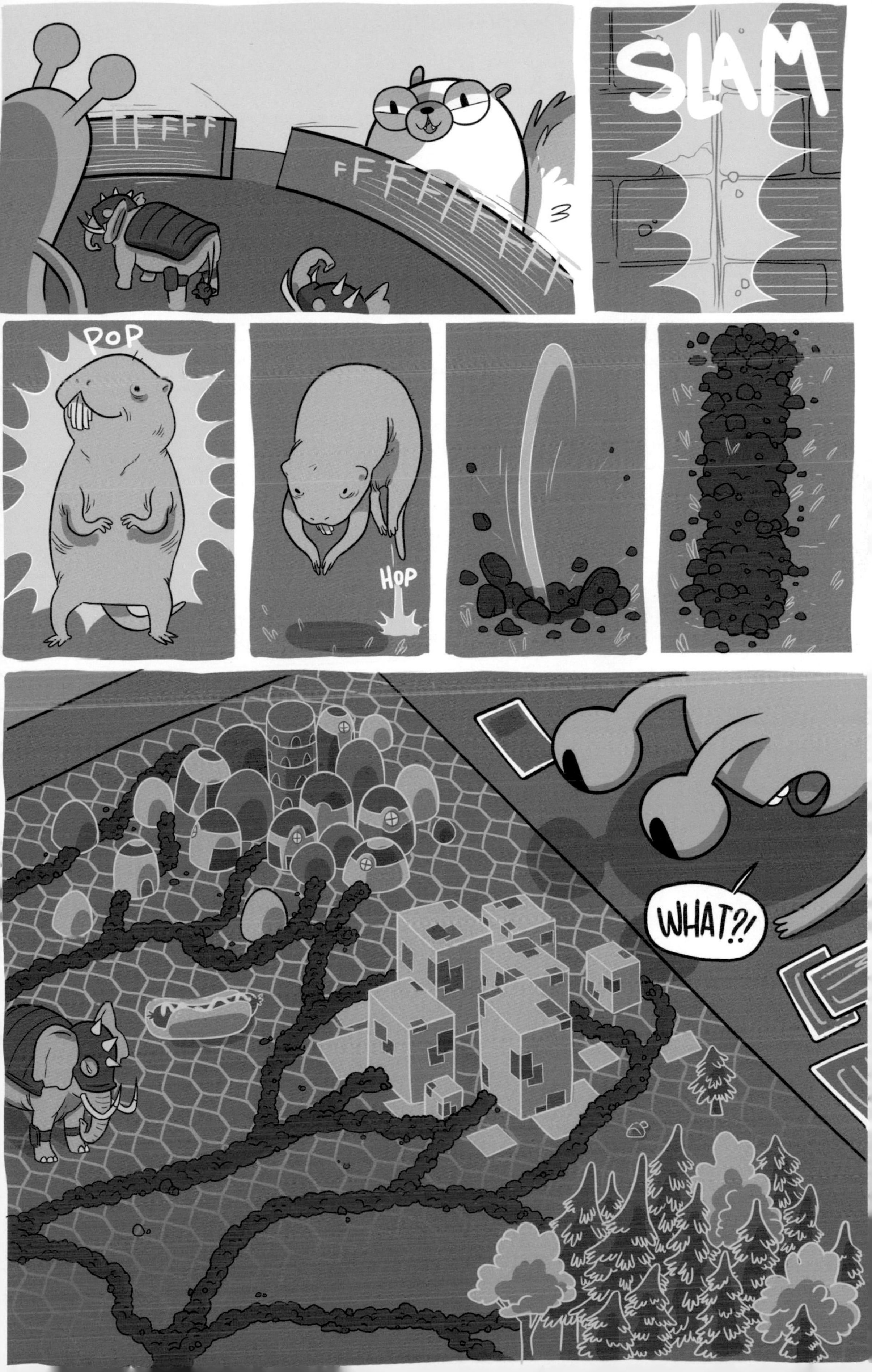
FFFFF
FFFFFFFFFFF
SLAM
POP
HOP
WHAT?!

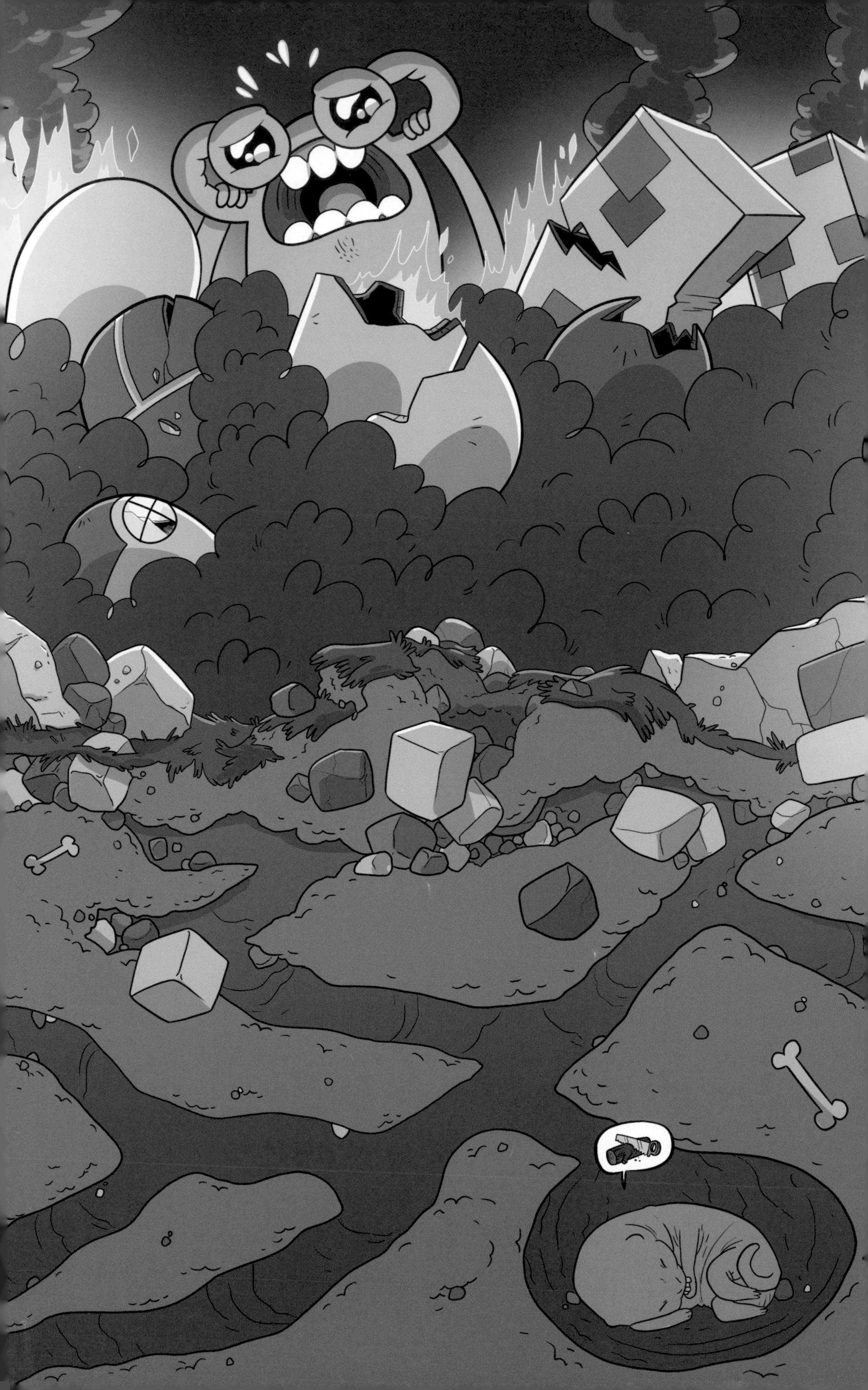

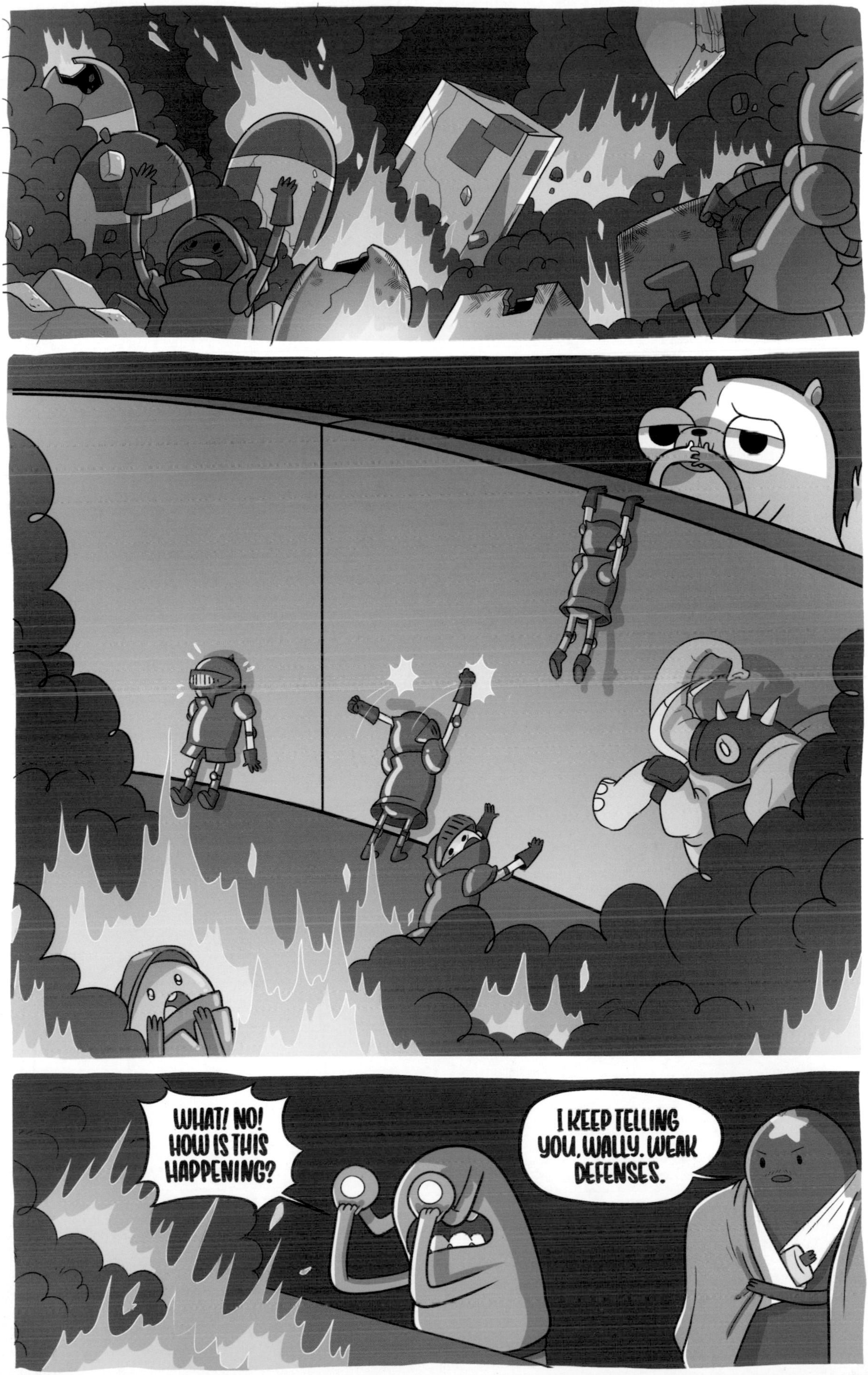
WHAT! NO! HOW IS THIS HAPPENING?
I KEEP TELLING YOU, WALLY. WEAK DEFENSES.

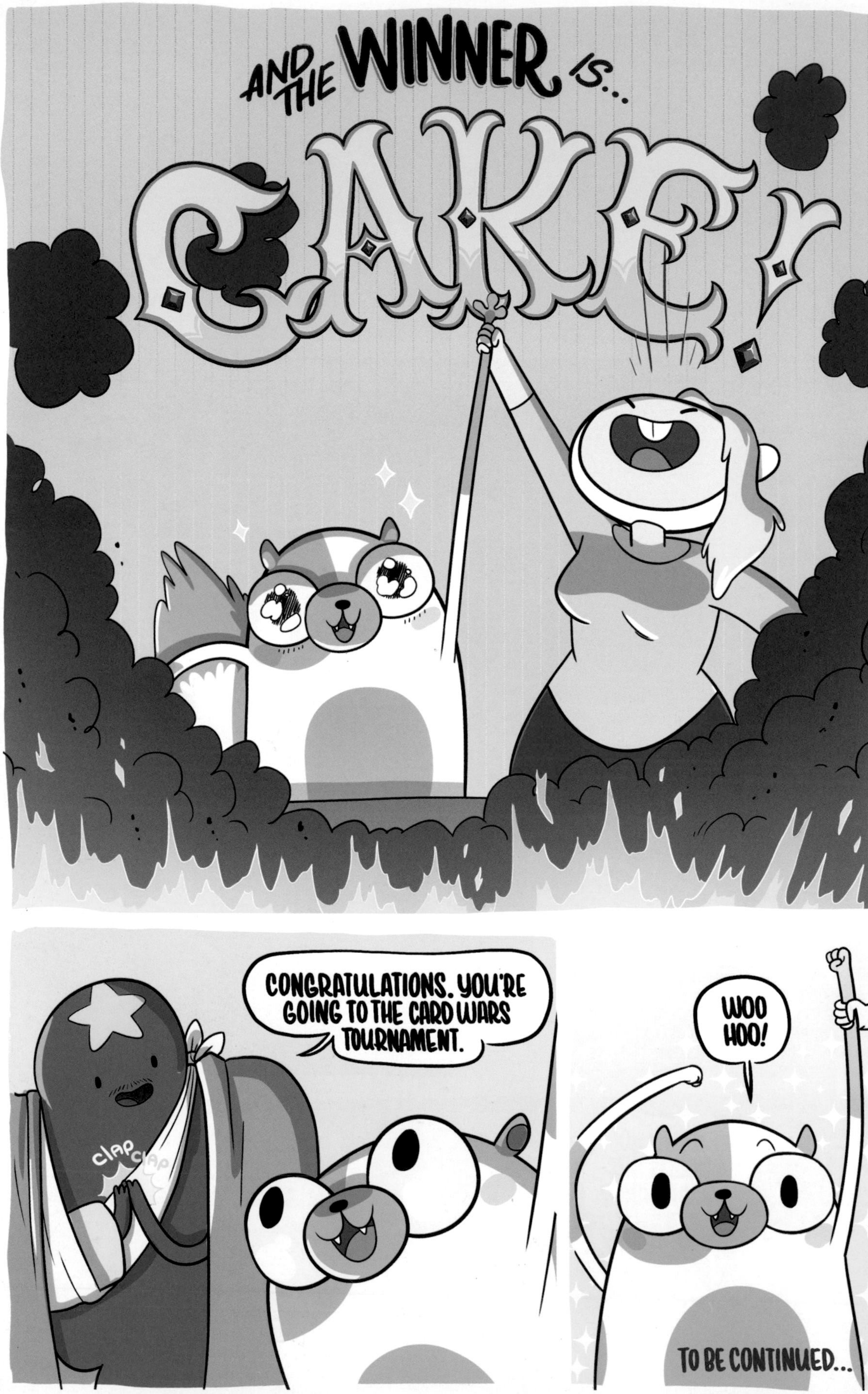
AND THE WINNER IS...
CAKE!
CONGRATULATIONS. YOU'RE GOING TO THE CARD WARS TOURNAMENT.
CLAP CLAP
WOO HOO!
TO BE CONTINUED...

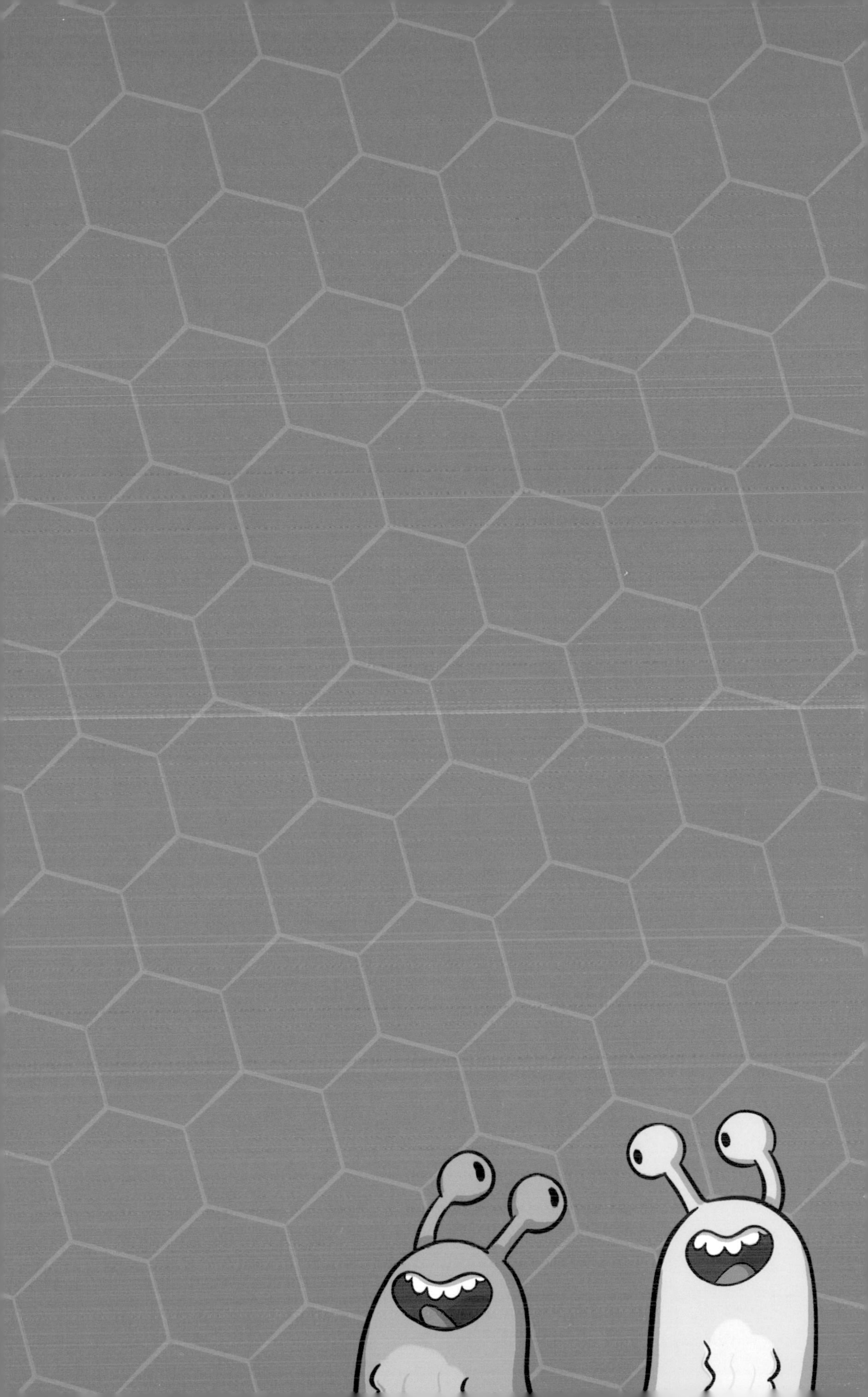

chapter three

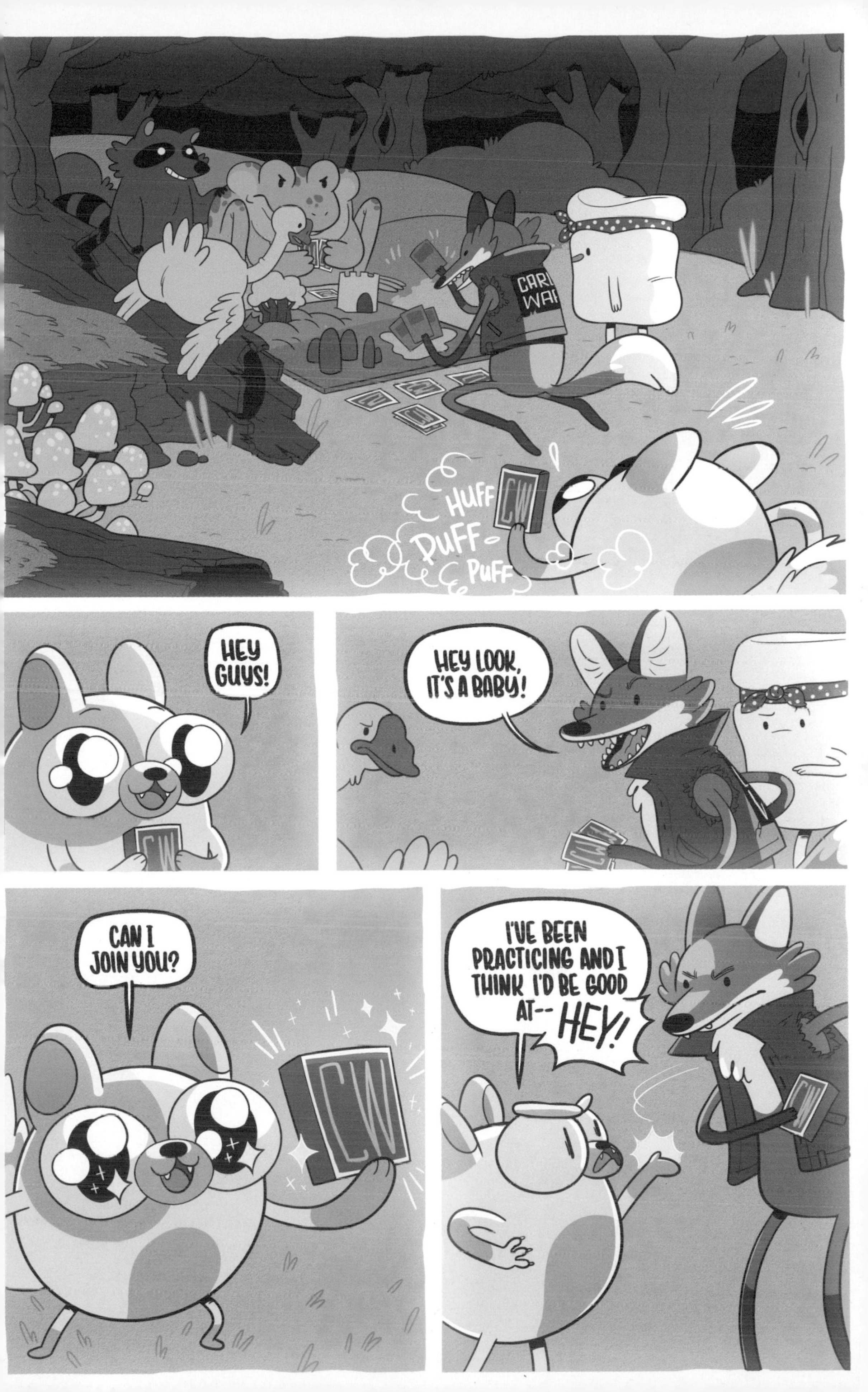
CARD WAR
HUFF
PUFF
PUFF
HEY GUYS!
HEY LOOK, IT'S A BABY!
CAN I JOIN YOU?
I'VE BEEN PRACTICING AND I THINK I'D BE GOOD AT--
HEY!

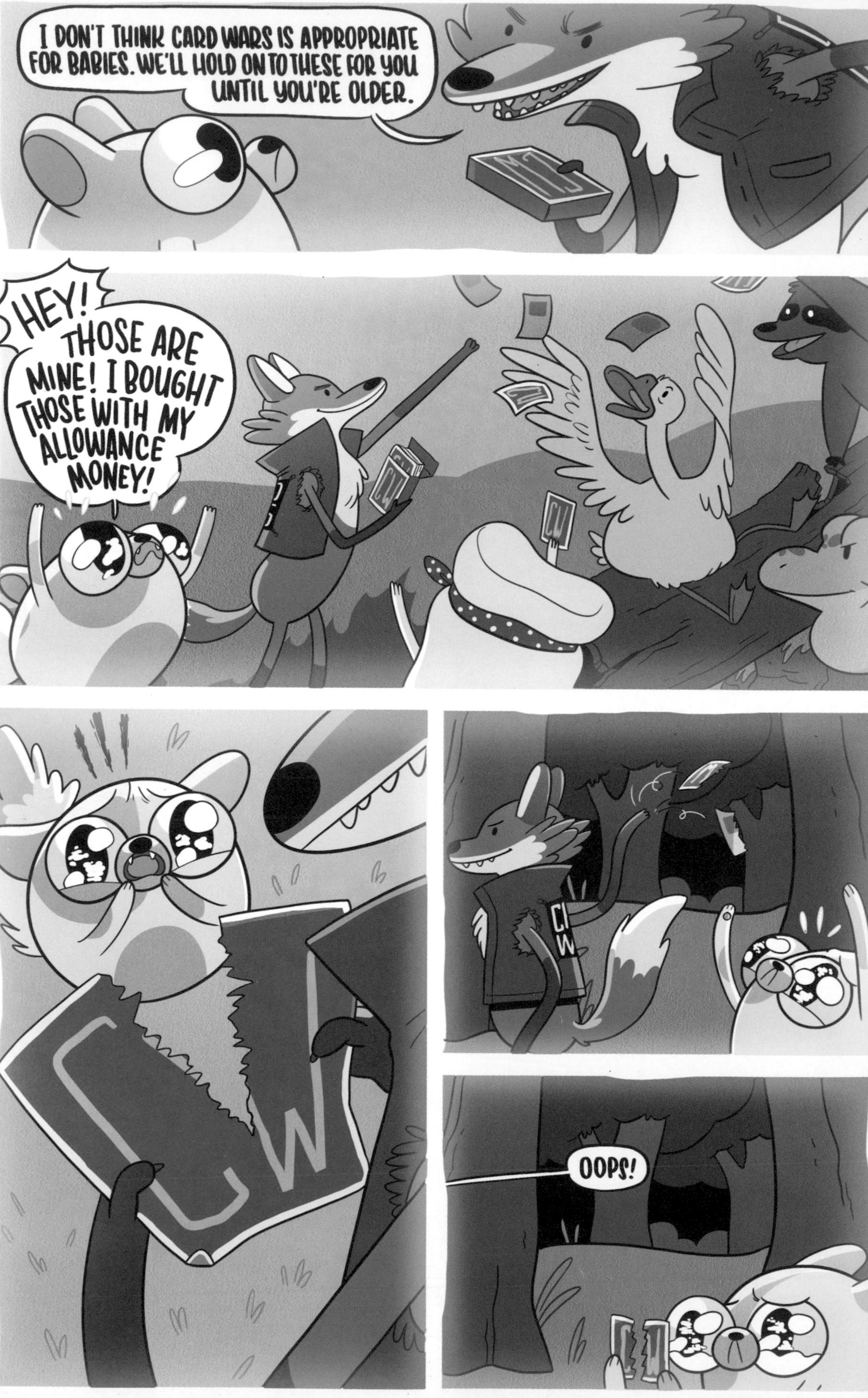

I DON'T THINK CARD WARS IS APPROPRIATE FOR BABIES. WE'LL HOLD ON TO THESE FOR YOU UNTIL YOU'RE OLDER.
HEY! THOSE ARE MINE! I BOUGHT THOSE WITH MY ALLOWANCE MONEY!
OOPS!

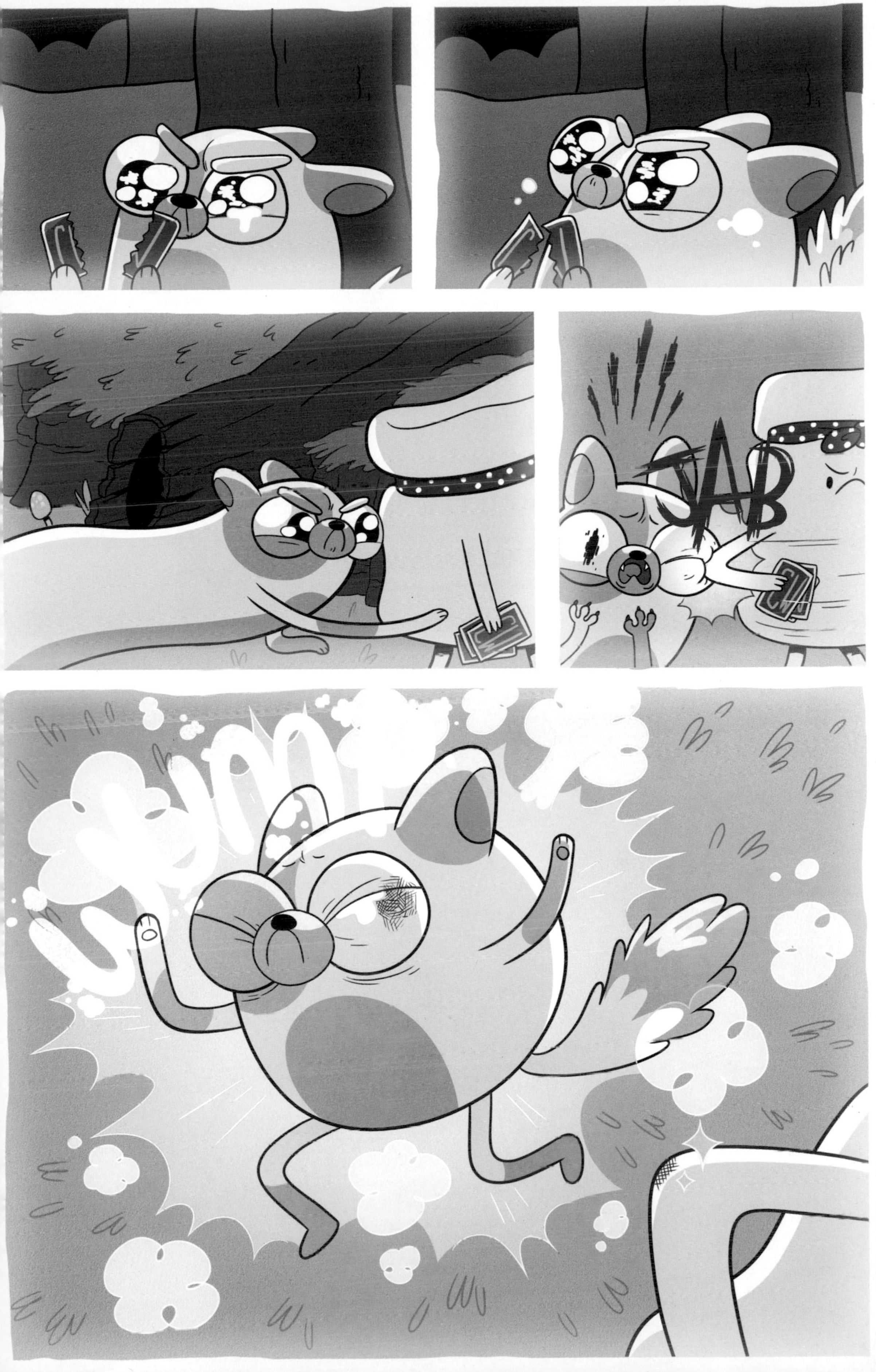
JAB

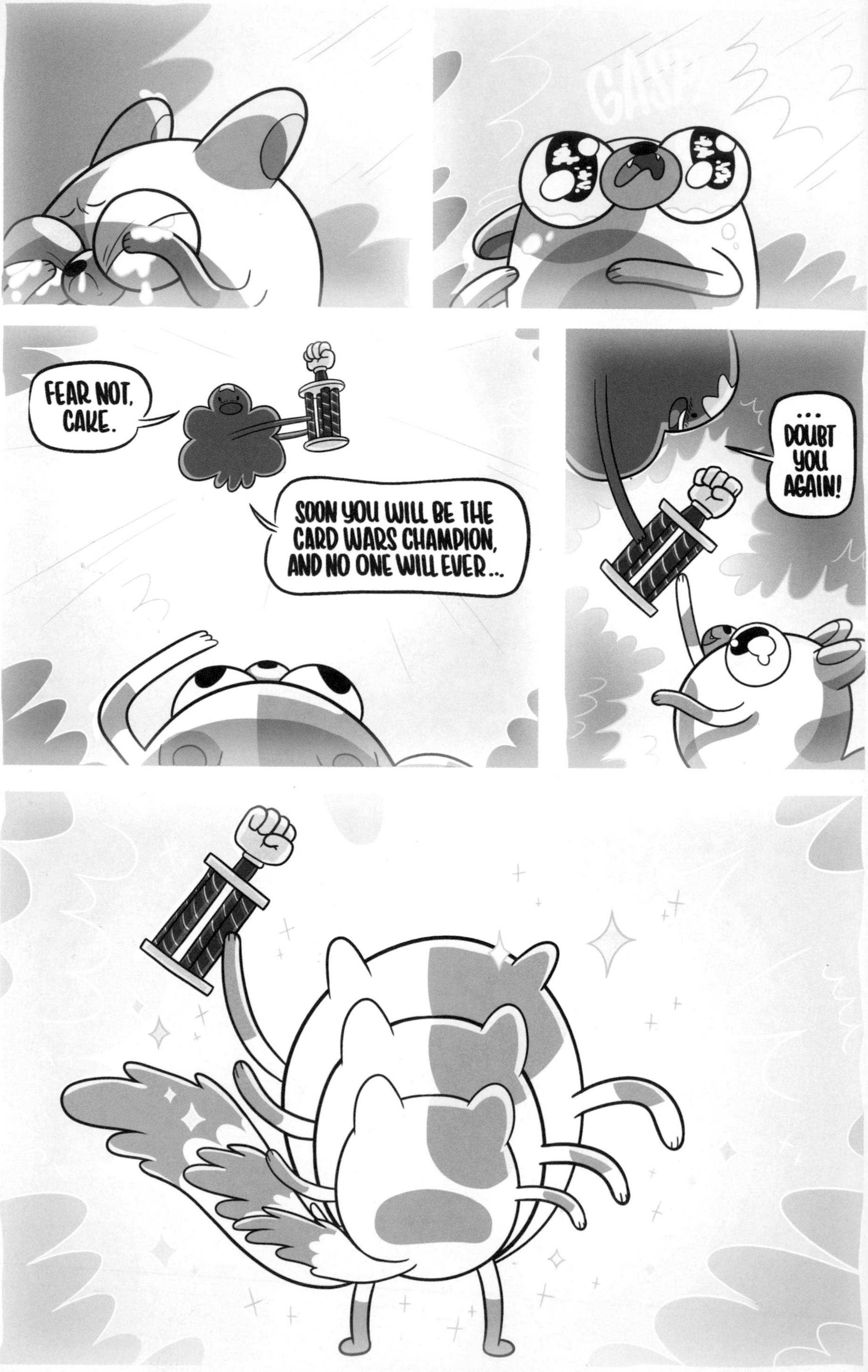
GASP
FEAR NOT, CAKE.
SOON YOU WILL BE THE CARD WARS CHAMPION, AND NO ONE WILL EVER...
...DOUBT YOU AGAIN!

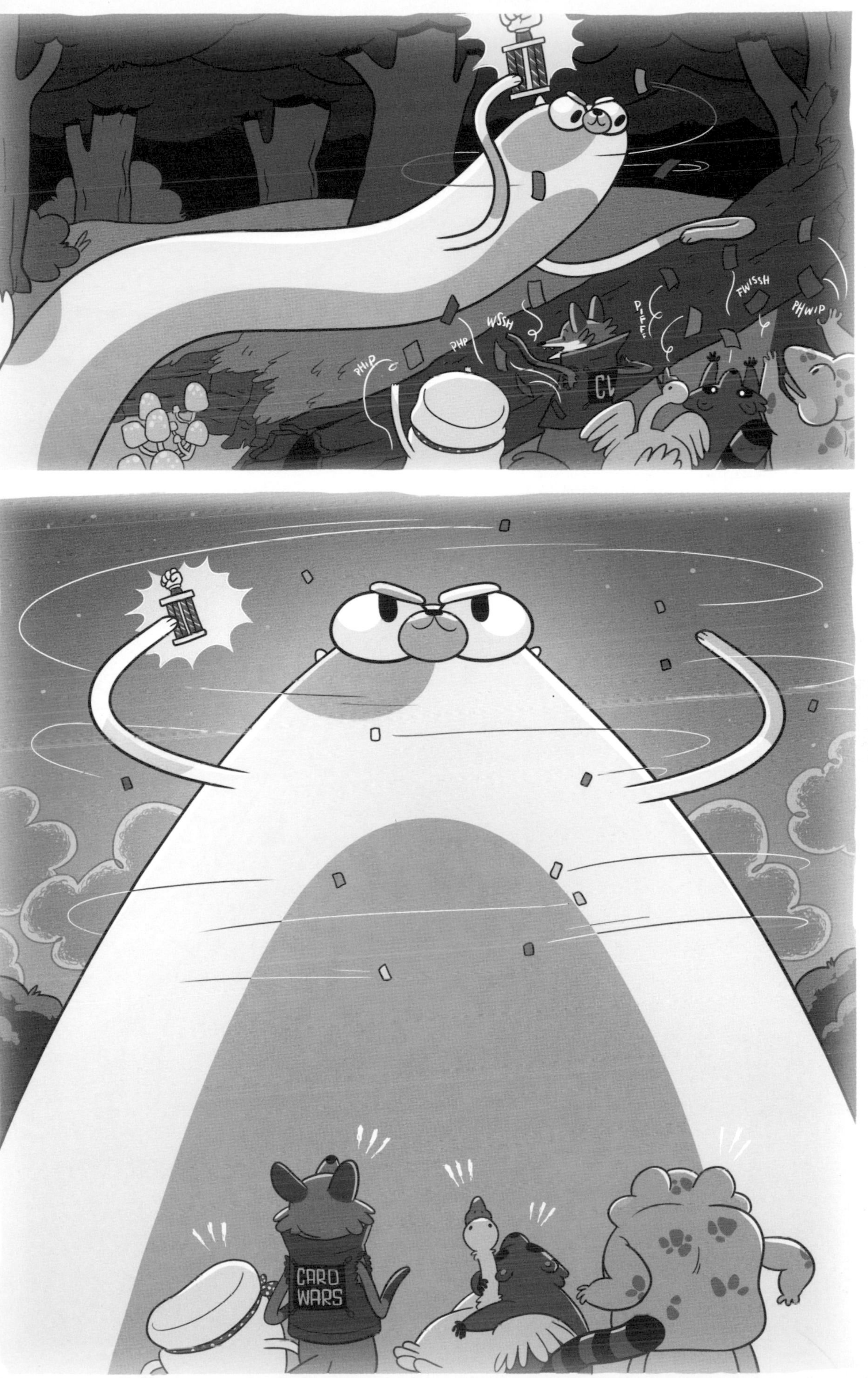
PHIP
PHP
WSSH
PIFFF
FWISSH
PHWIP
CARD WARS

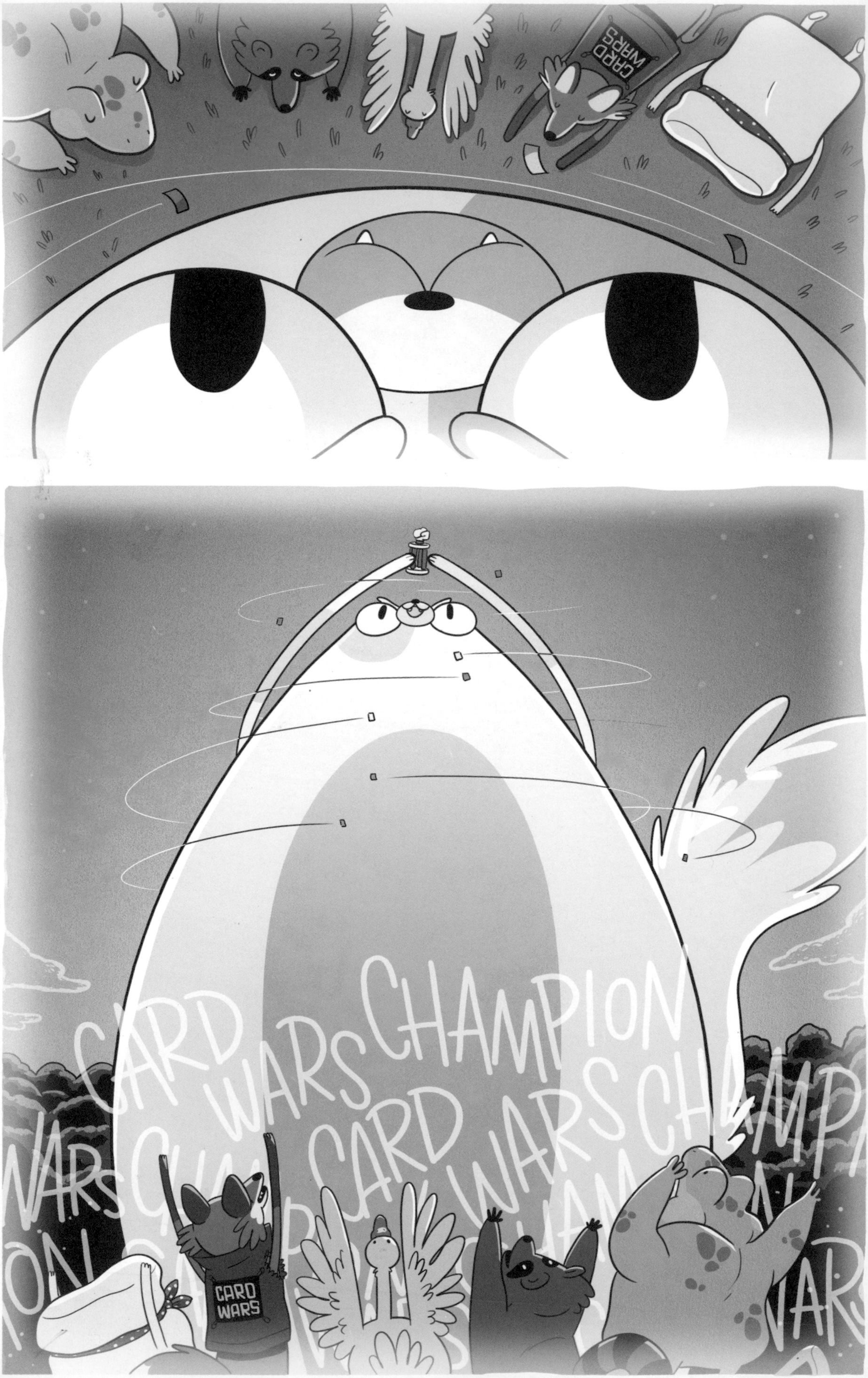
CARD WARS
CARD WARS CHAMPION
CARD WARS CARD WARS CHAMP
CARD WARS

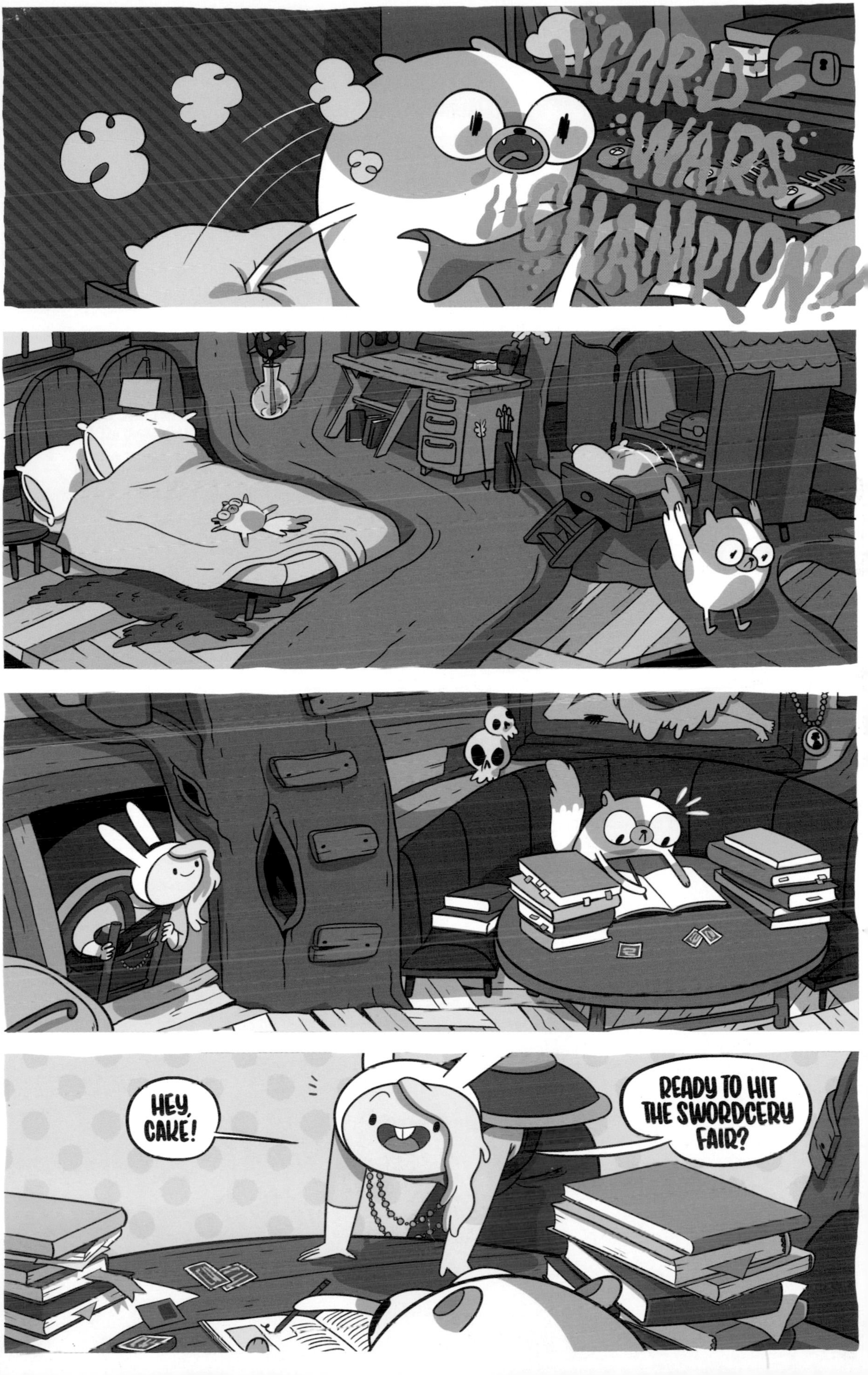
CARD WARS CHAMPION!!
HEY, CAKE!
READY TO HIT THE SWORDCERY FAIR?

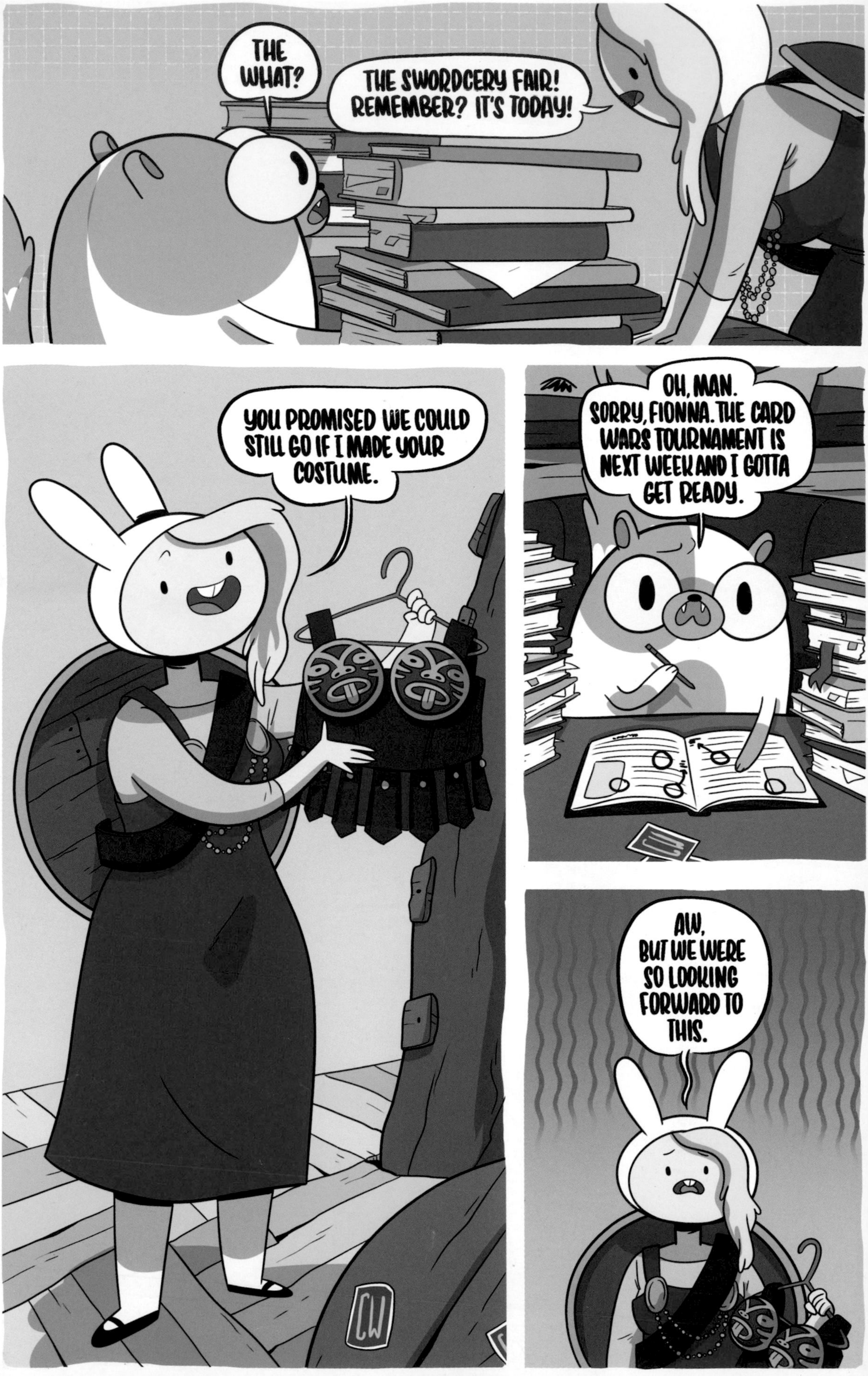
THE WHAT?
THE SWORDCERY FAIR! REMEMBER? IT'S TODAY!
YOU PROMISED WE COULD STILL GO IF I MADE YOUR COSTUME.
OH, MAN. SORRY, FIONNA. THE CARD WARS TOURNAMENT IS NEXT WEEK AND I GOTTA GET READY.
AW, BUT WE WERE SO LOOKING FORWARD TO THIS.
CW

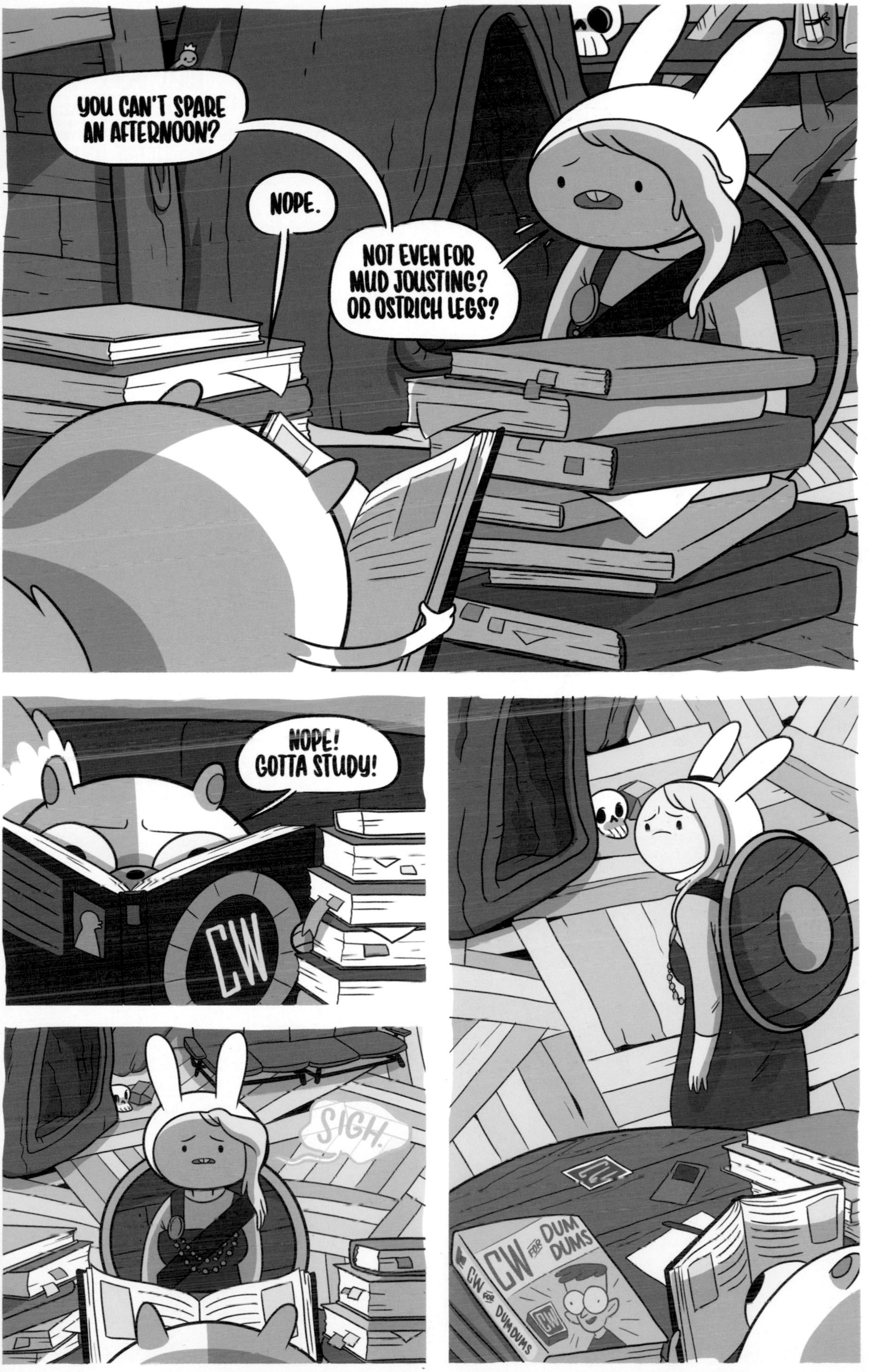
YOU CAN'T SPARE AN AFTERNOON?
NOPE.
NOT EVEN FOR MUD JOUSTING? OR OSTRICH LEGS?
NOPE! GOTTA STUDY!
CW
SIGH.
CW FOR DUM DUMS
CW FOR DUMDUMS

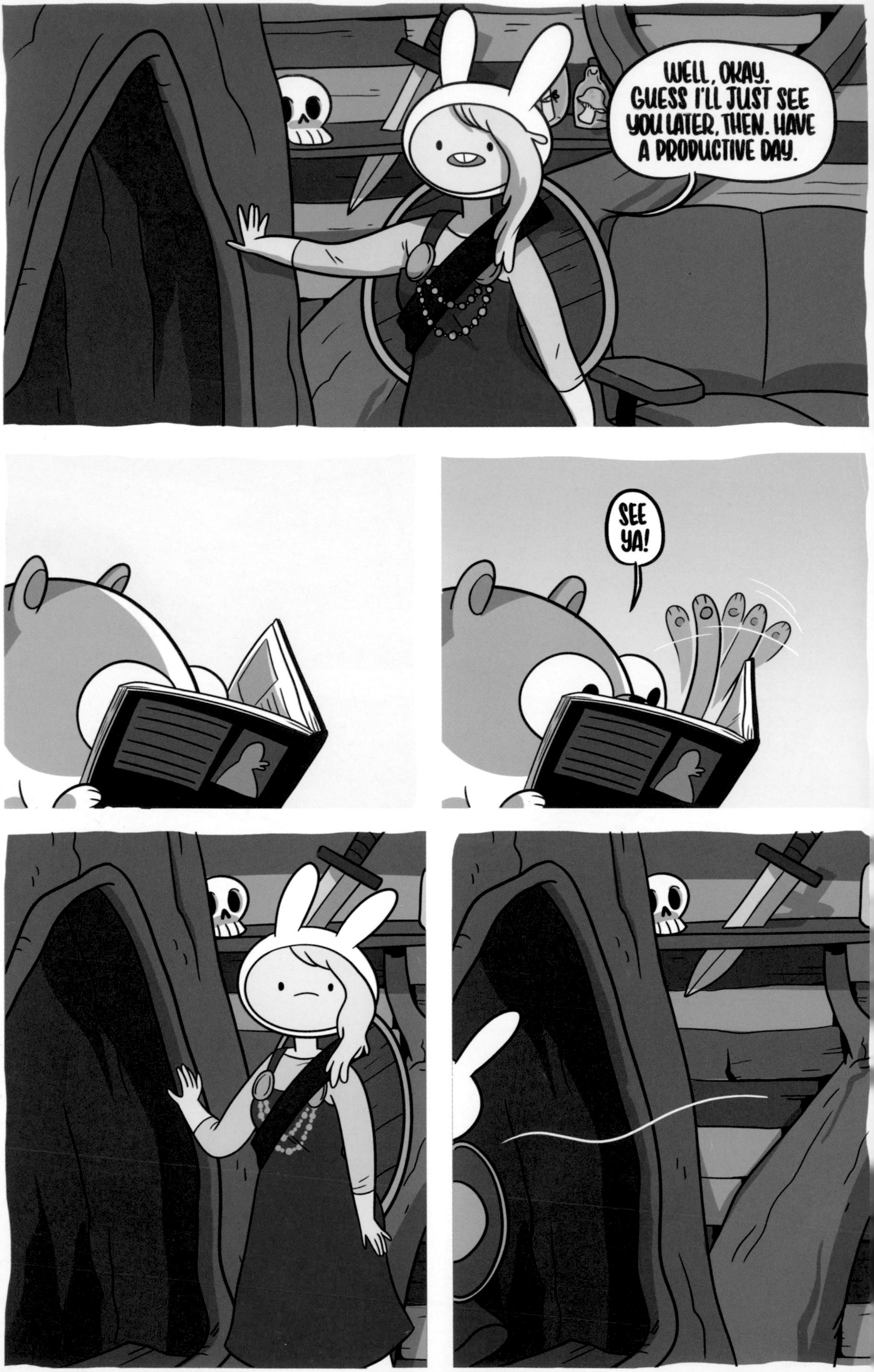
WELL, OKAY. GUESS I'LL JUST SEE YOU LATER, THEN. HAVE A PRODUCTIVE DAY.
SEE YA!

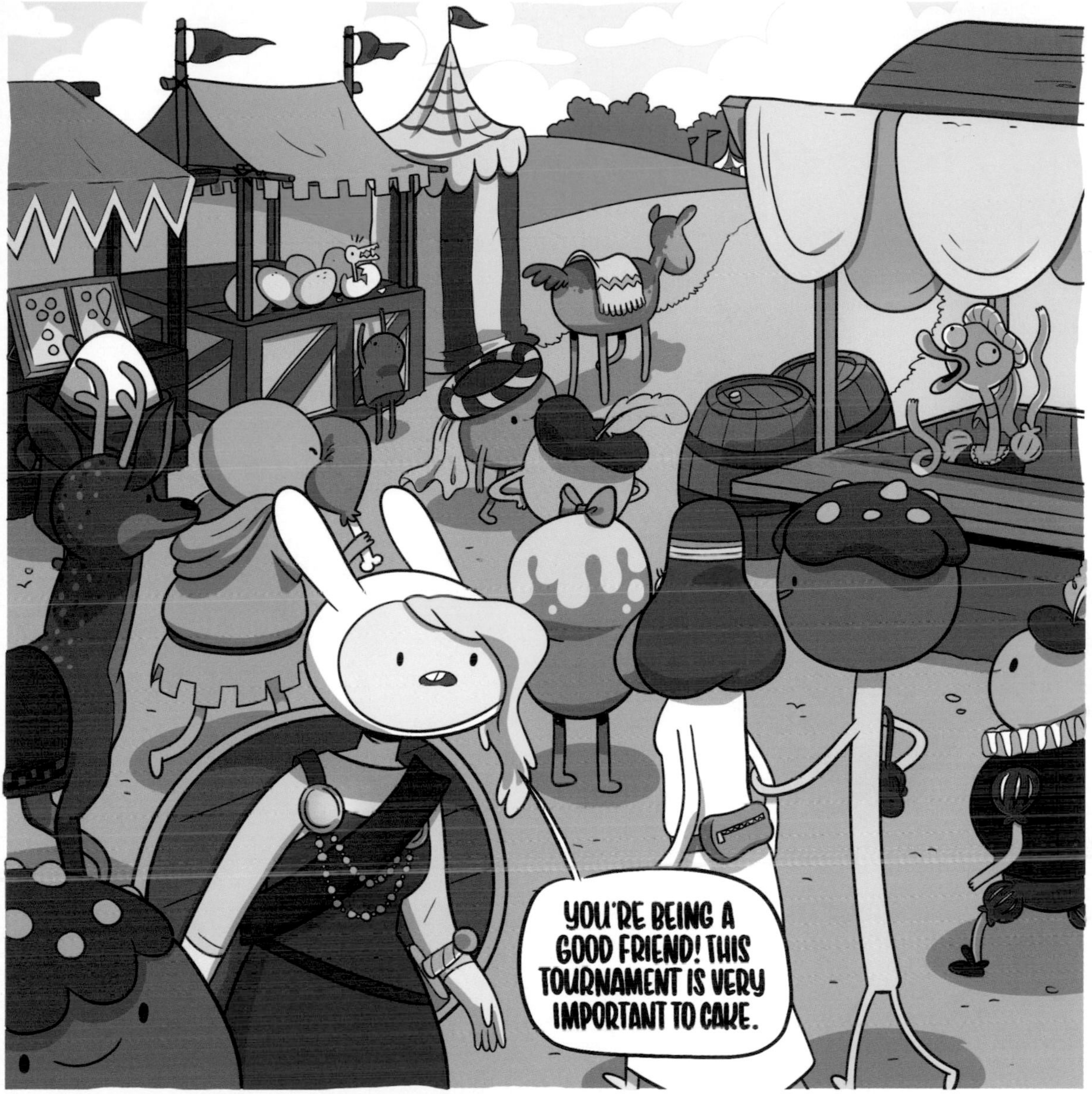
YOU'RE BEING A GOOD FRIEND! THIS TOURNAMENT IS VERY IMPORTANT TO CAKE.

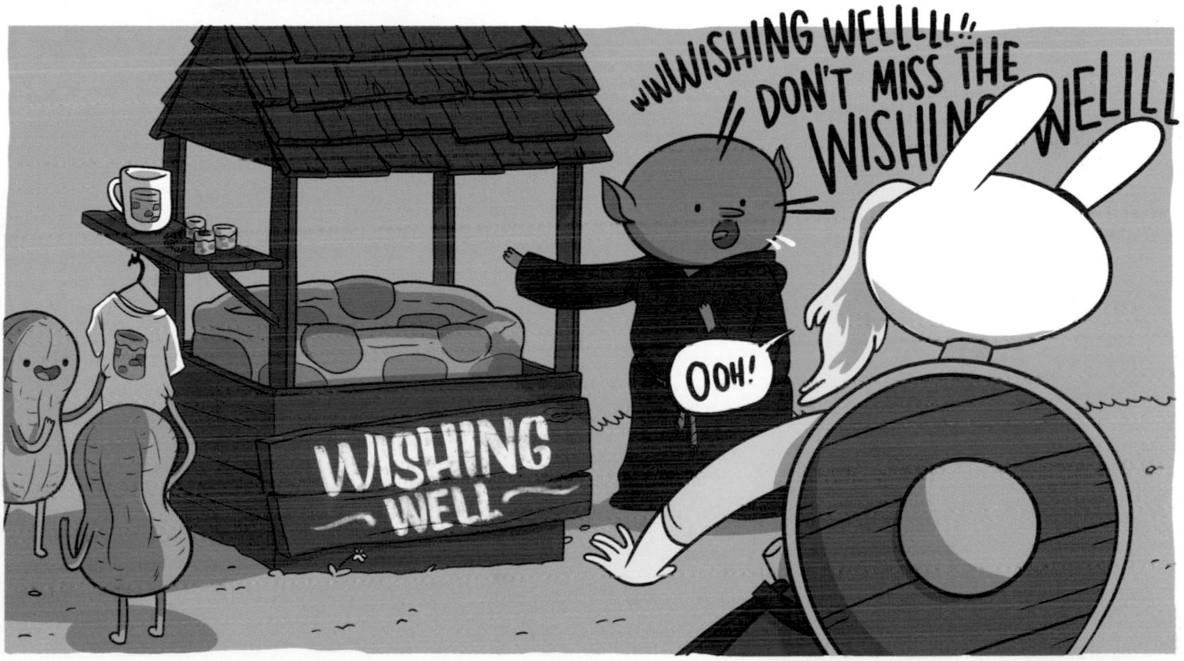
wwWISHING WELLLLL!!
DON'T MISS THE WISHIN WELLLL
WISHING WELL
OOH!

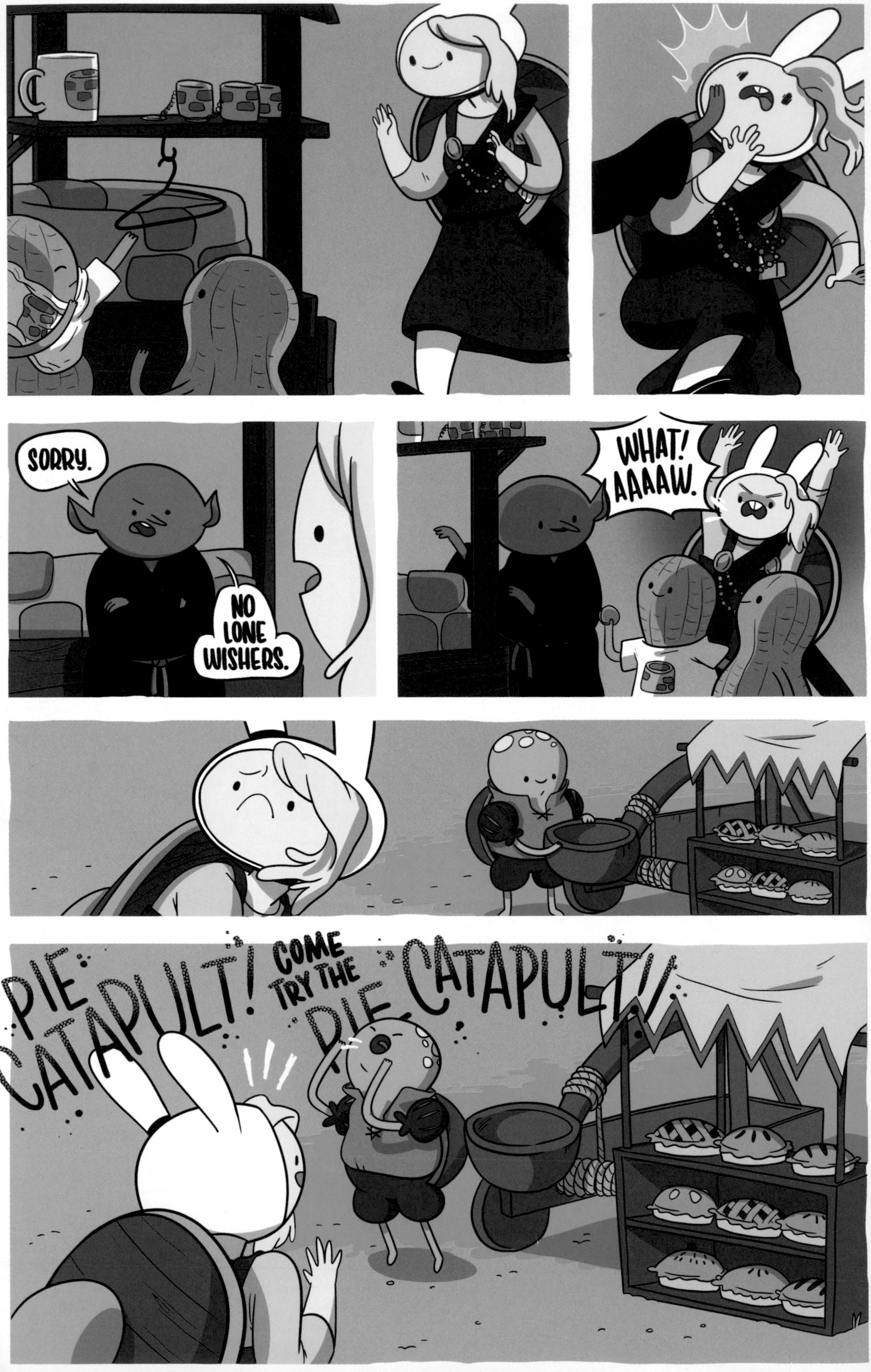
SORRY.
NO LONE WISHERS.
WHAT! AAAAW.
PIE CATAPULT! COME TRY THE PIE CATAPULT!

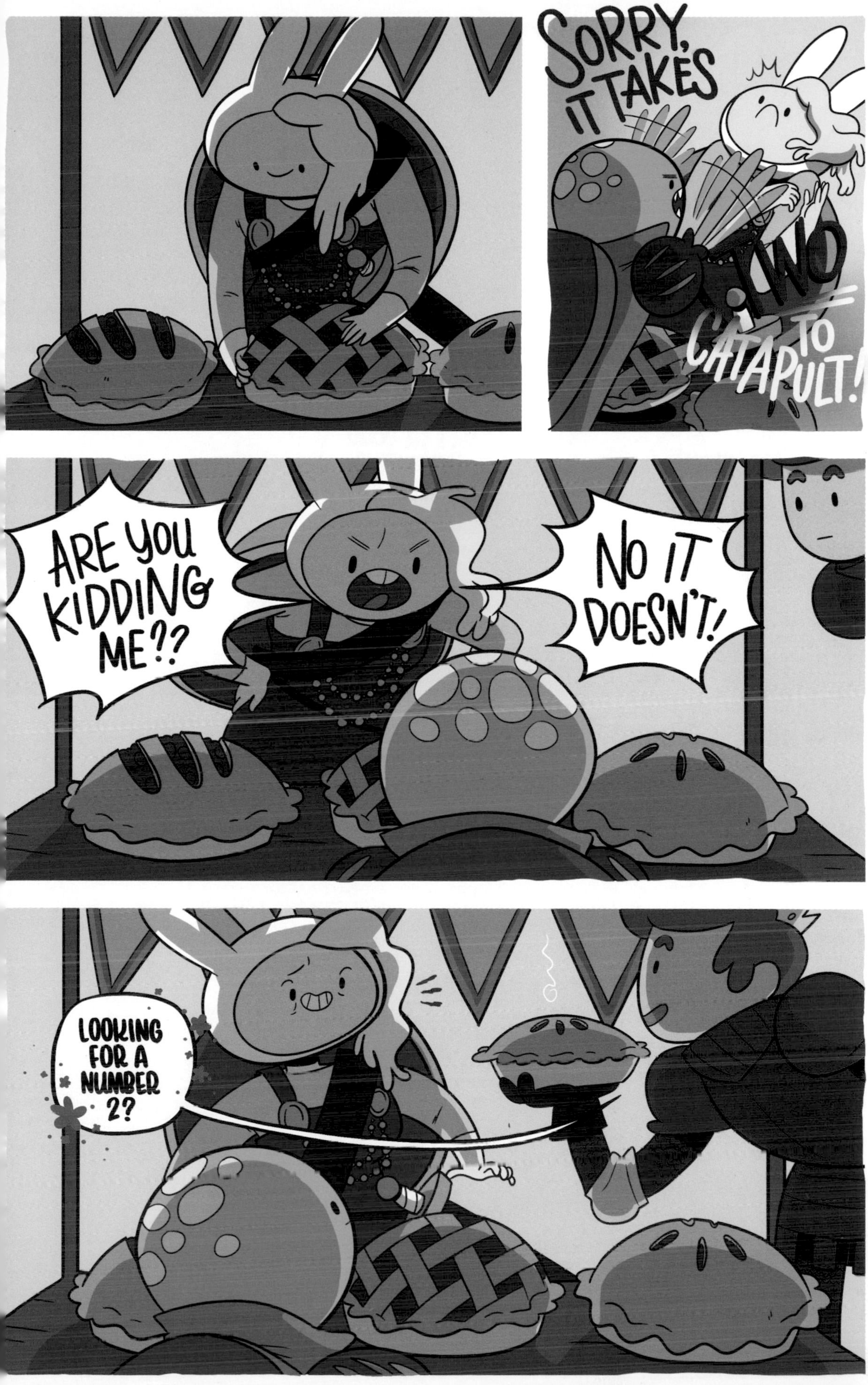
SORRY, IT TAKES TWO TO CATAPULT!
ARE YOU KIDDING ME??
NO IT DOESN'T!
LOOKING FOR A NUMBER 2?

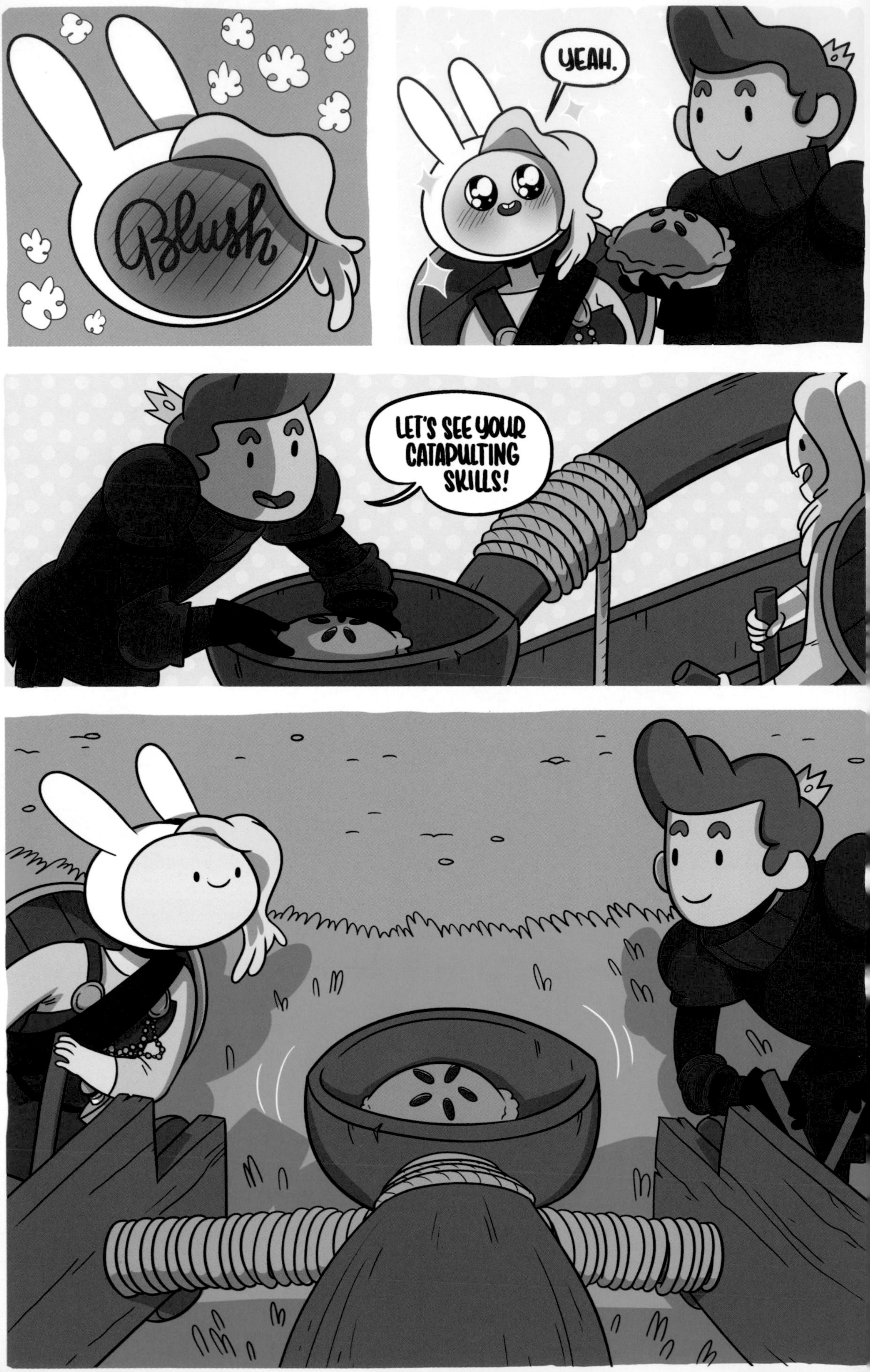
Blush
YEAH.
LET'S SEE YOUR CATAPULTING SKILLS!

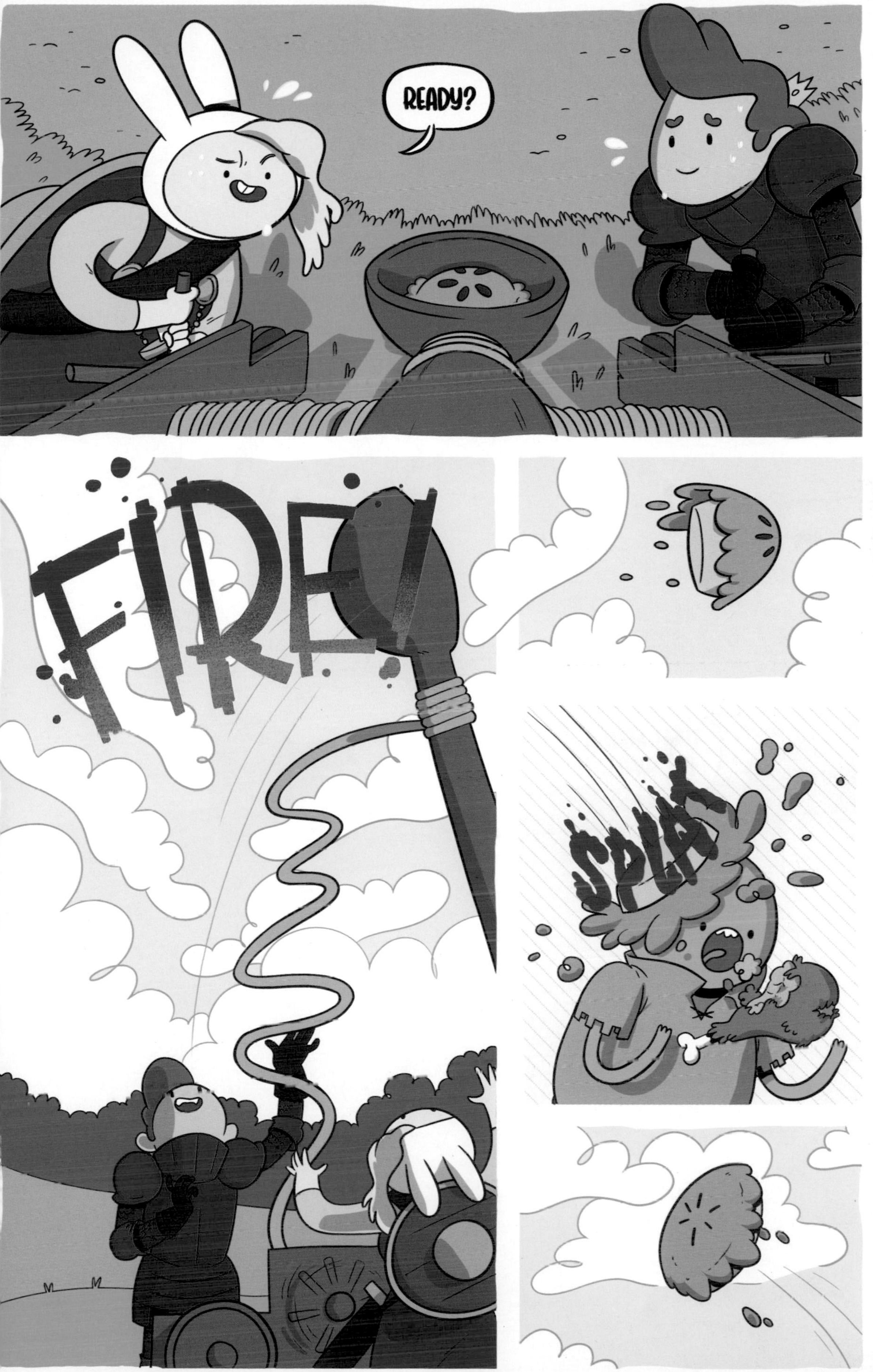
READY?
FIRE!
SPLAT

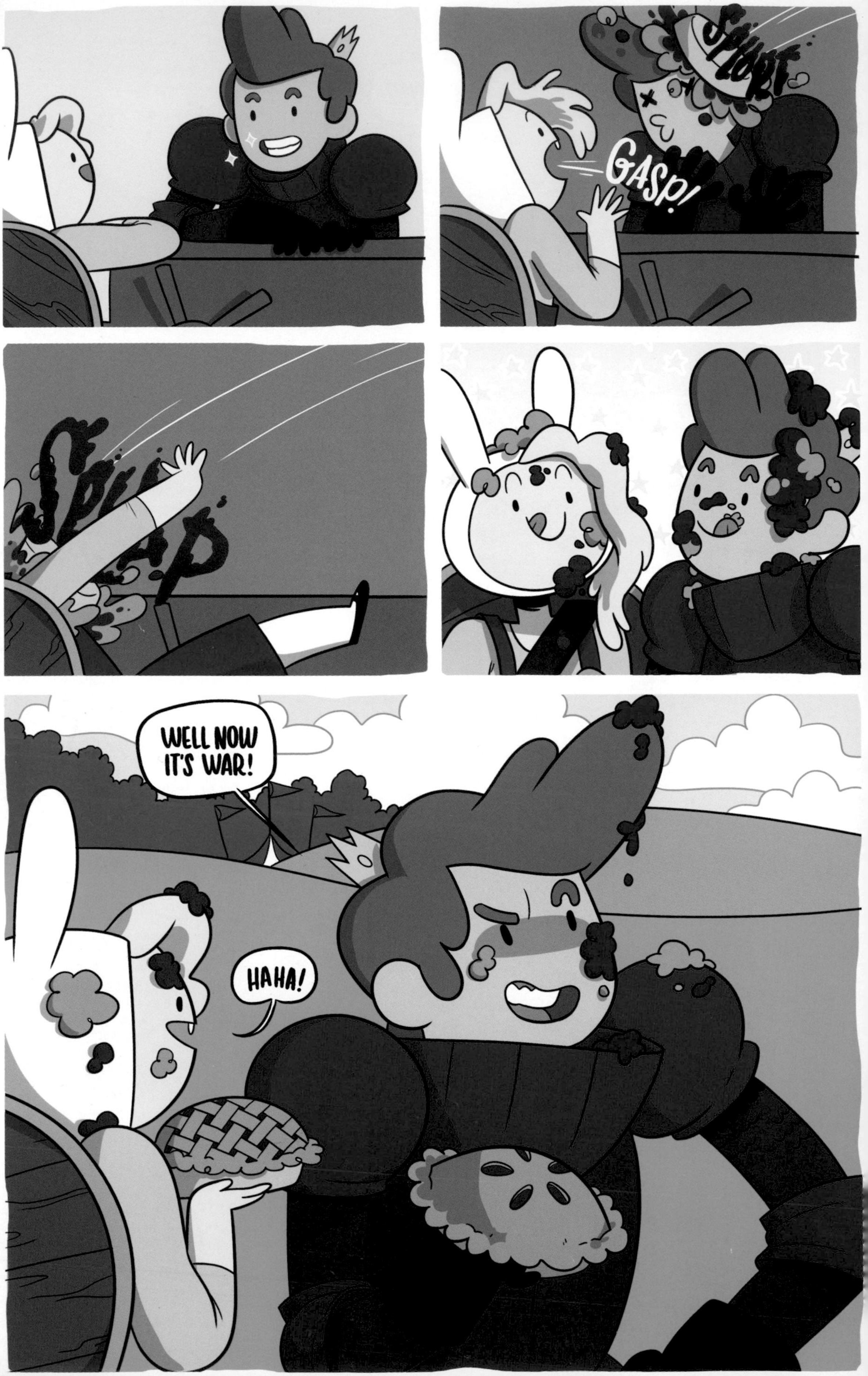
SPLORT
GASP!
SPLAP
WELL NOW IT'S WAR!
HAHA!

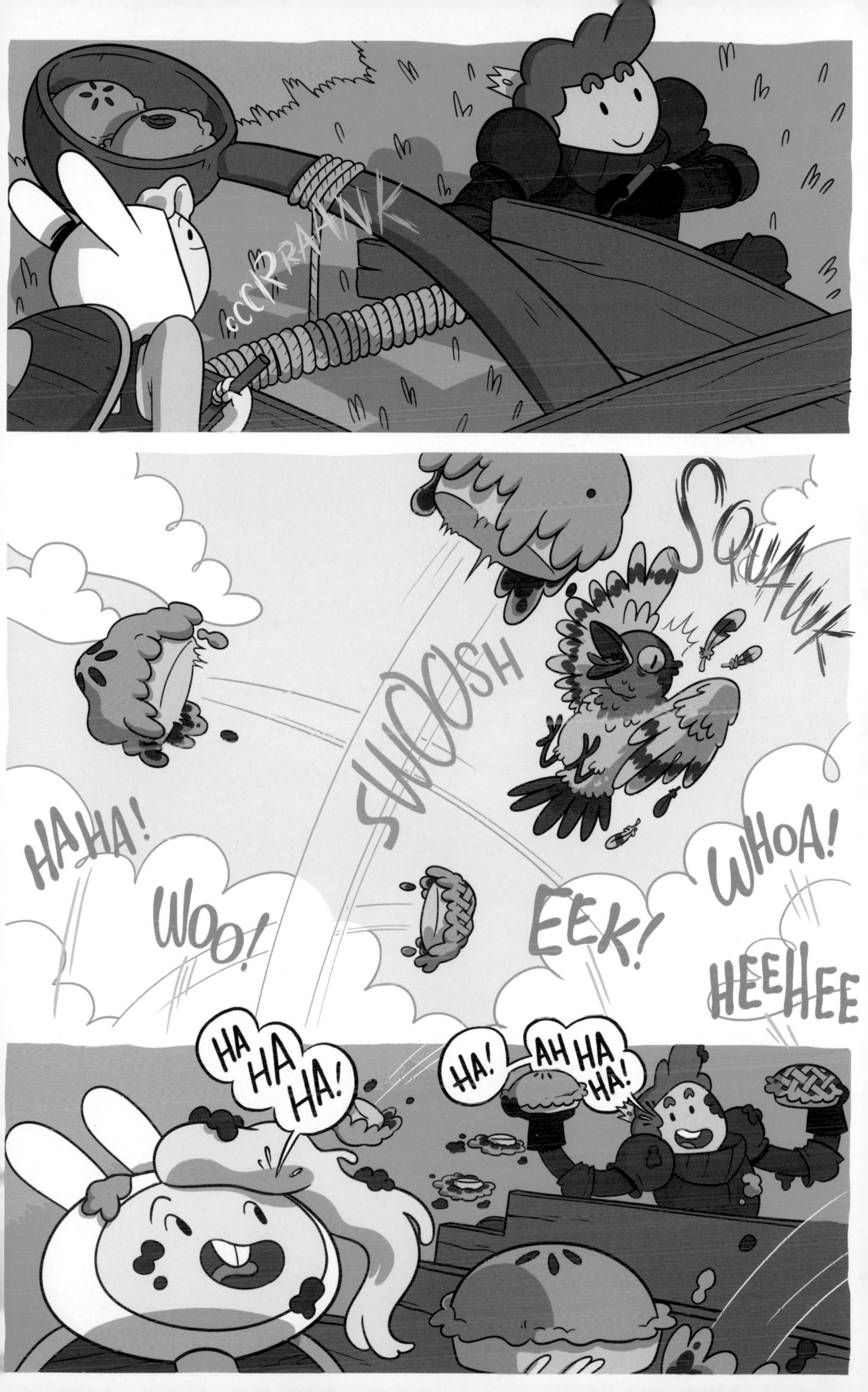
CCCRRAANK
SWOOSH
SQUAWK
HAHA!
WOO!
EEK!
WHOA!
HEEHEE
HA HA HA!
HA!
AH HA HA!

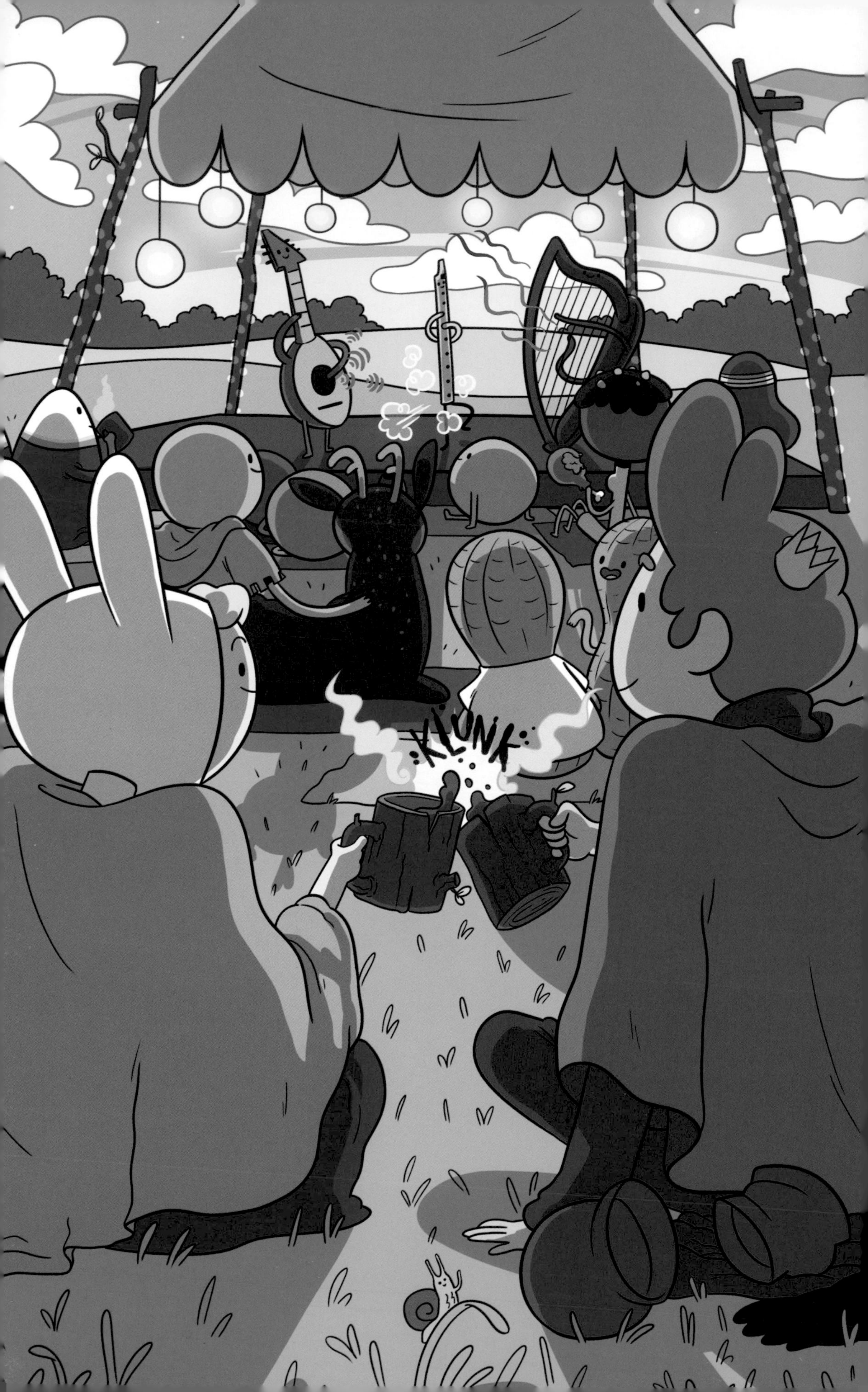
KLUNK

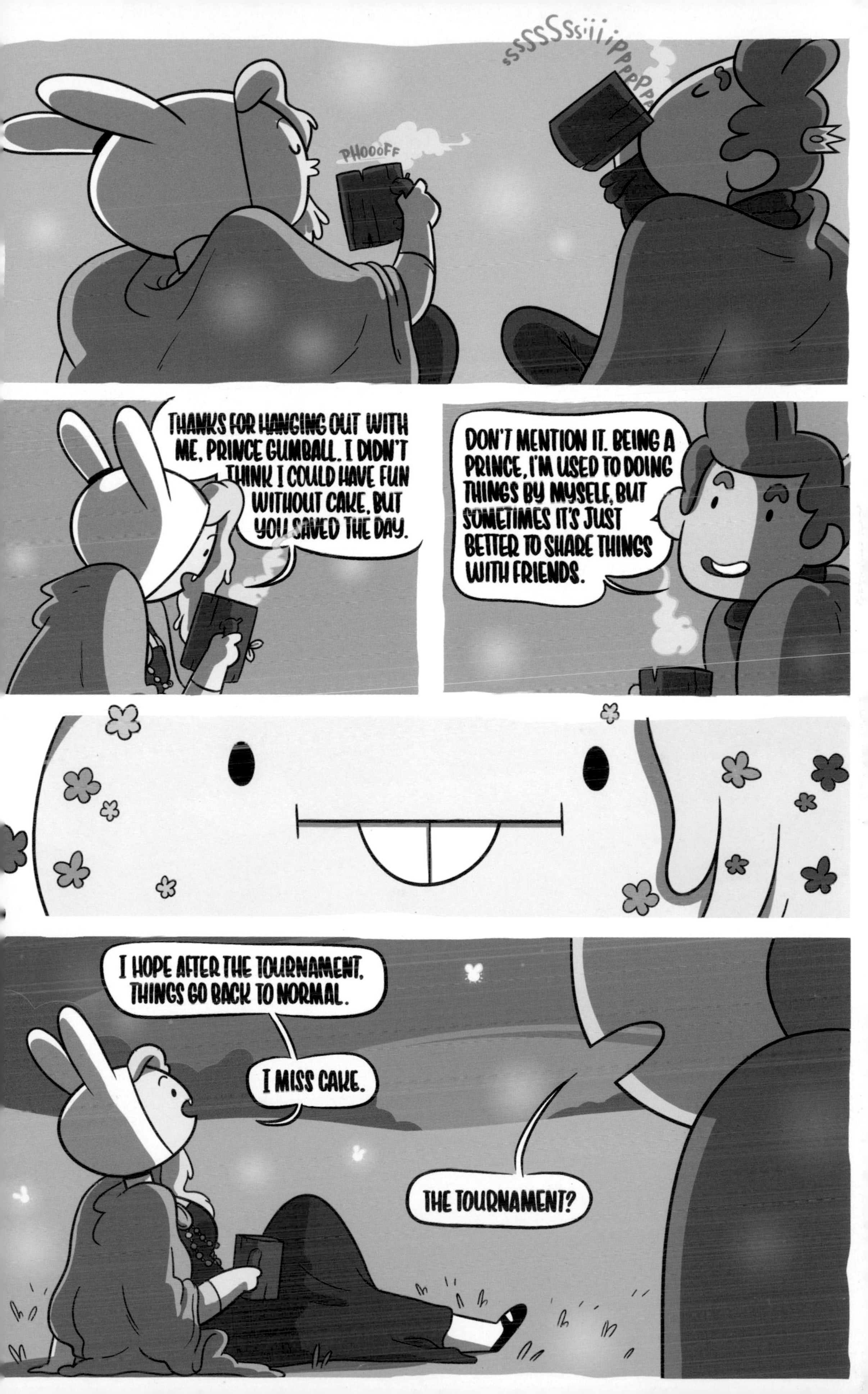
PHOOOFF
sSSSSSsiiiiPPPPP
THANKS FOR HANGING OUT WITH ME, PRINCE GUMBALL. I DIDN'T THINK I COULD HAVE FUN WITHOUT CAKE, BUT YOU SAVED THE DAY.
DON'T MENTION IT. BEING A PRINCE, I'M USED TO DOING THINGS BY MYSELF, BUT SOMETIMES IT'S JUST BETTER TO SHARE THINGS WITH FRIENDS.
I HOPE AFTER THE TOURNAMENT, THINGS GO BACK TO NORMAL.
I MISS CAKE.
THE TOURNAMENT?

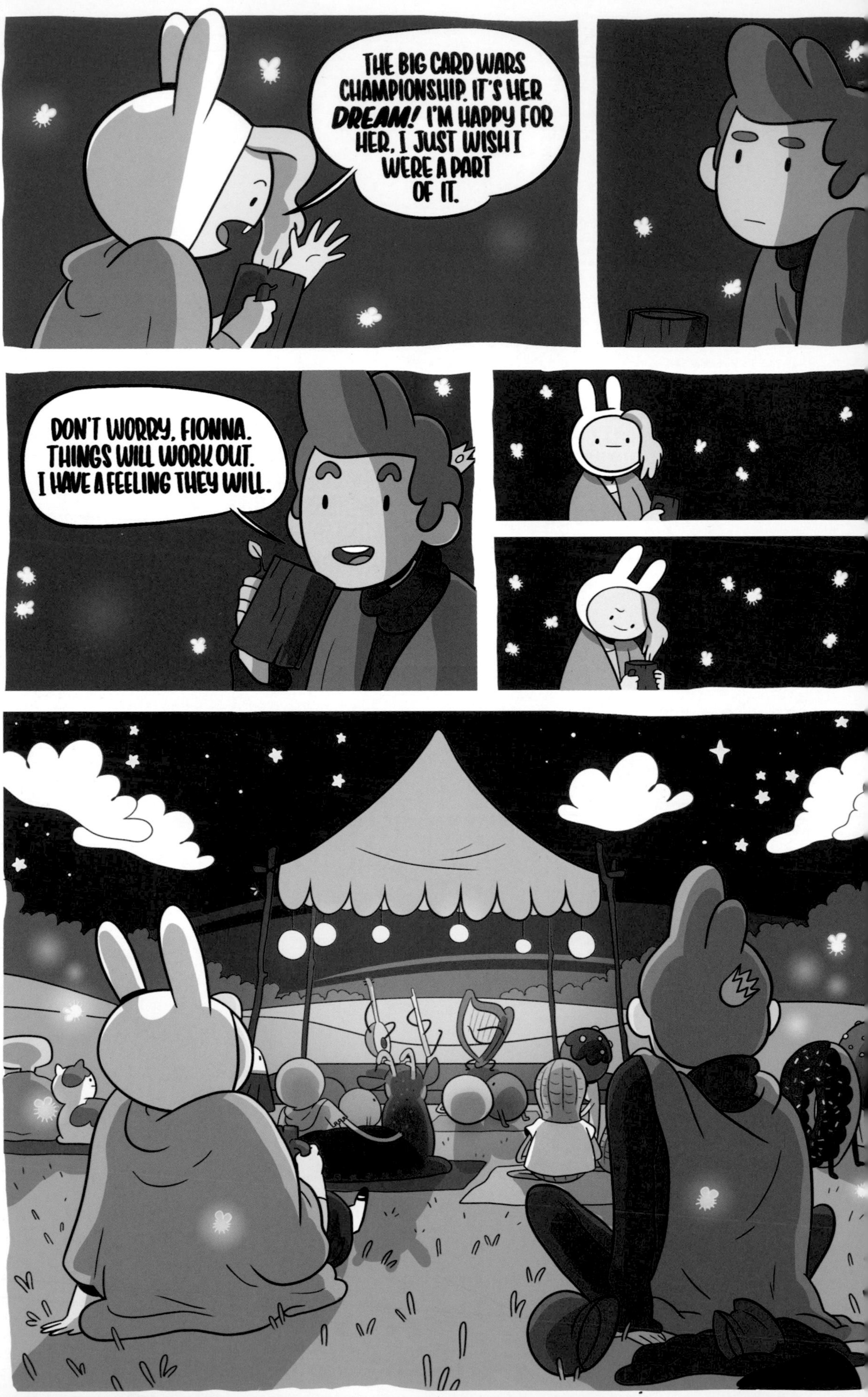
THE BIG CARD WARS CHAMPIONSHIP. IT'S HER DREAM! I'M HAPPY FOR HER, I JUST WISH I WERE A PART OF IT.
DON'T WORRY, FIONNA. THINGS WILL WORK OUT. I HAVE A FEELING THEY WILL.

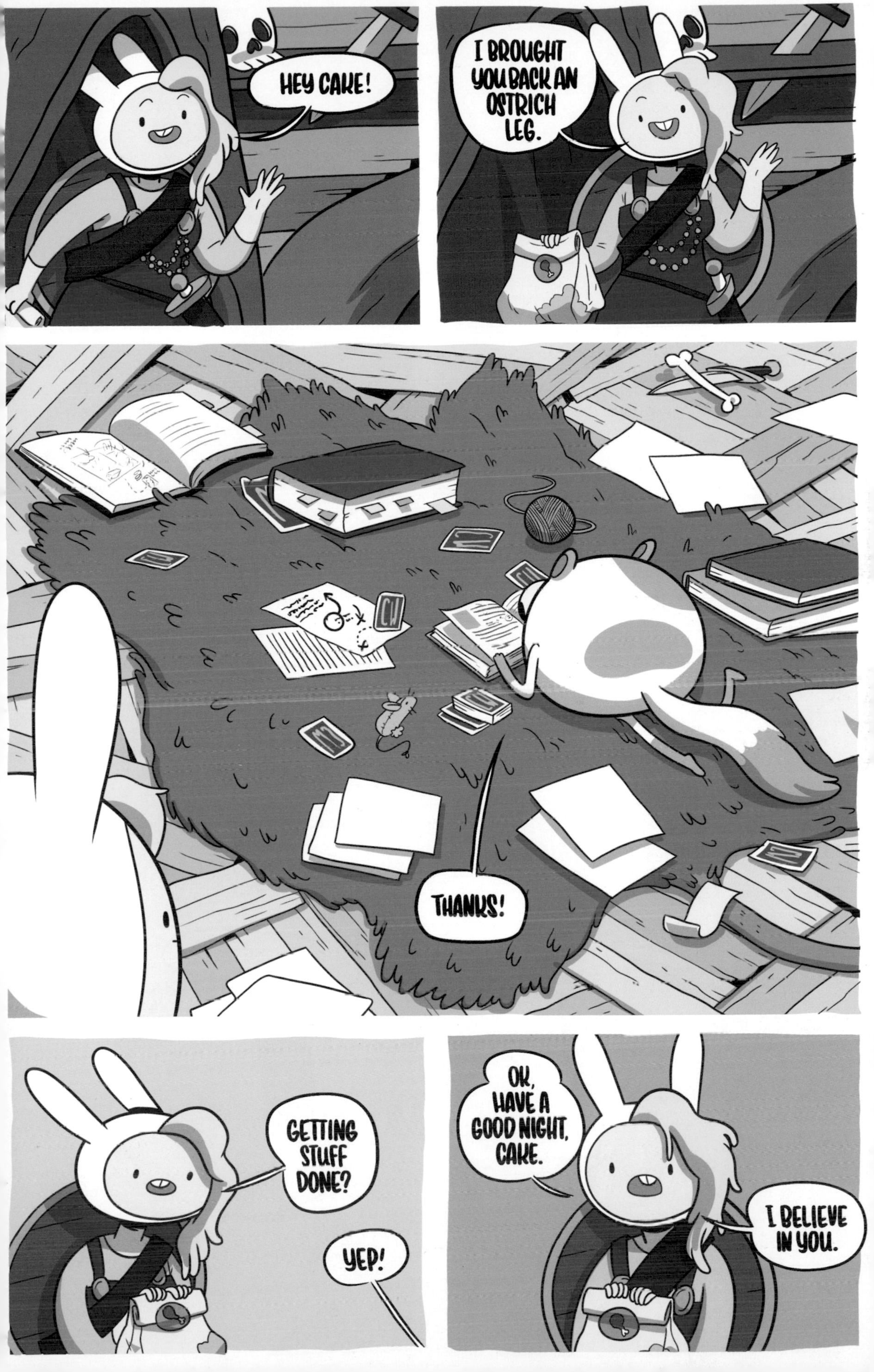
HEY CAKE!
I BROUGHT YOU BACK AN OSTRICH LEG.
THANKS!
GETTING STUFF DONE?
YEP!
OK, HAVE A GOOD NIGHT, CAKE.
I BELIEVE IN YOU.

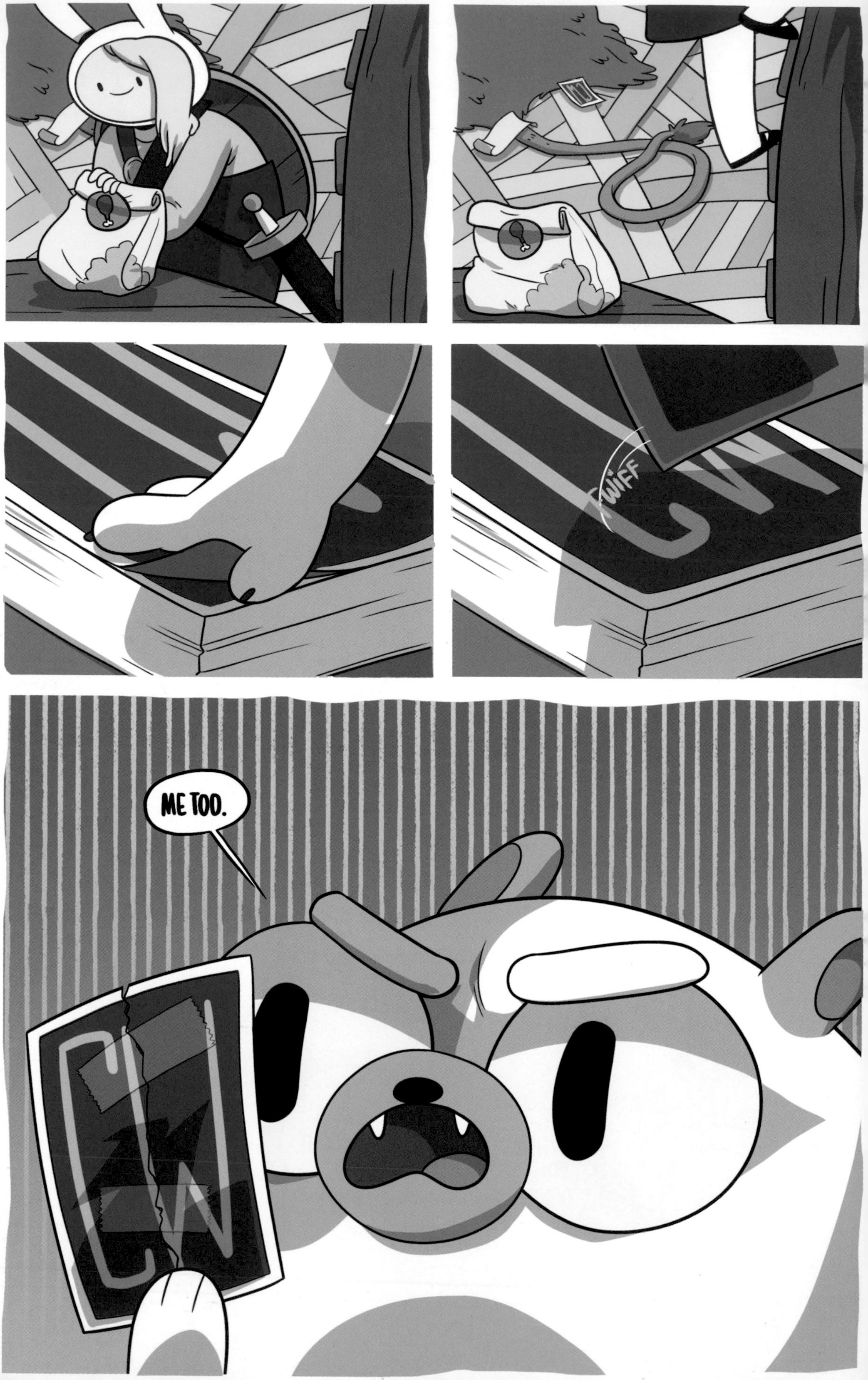
FWIFF
ME TOO.

chapter four

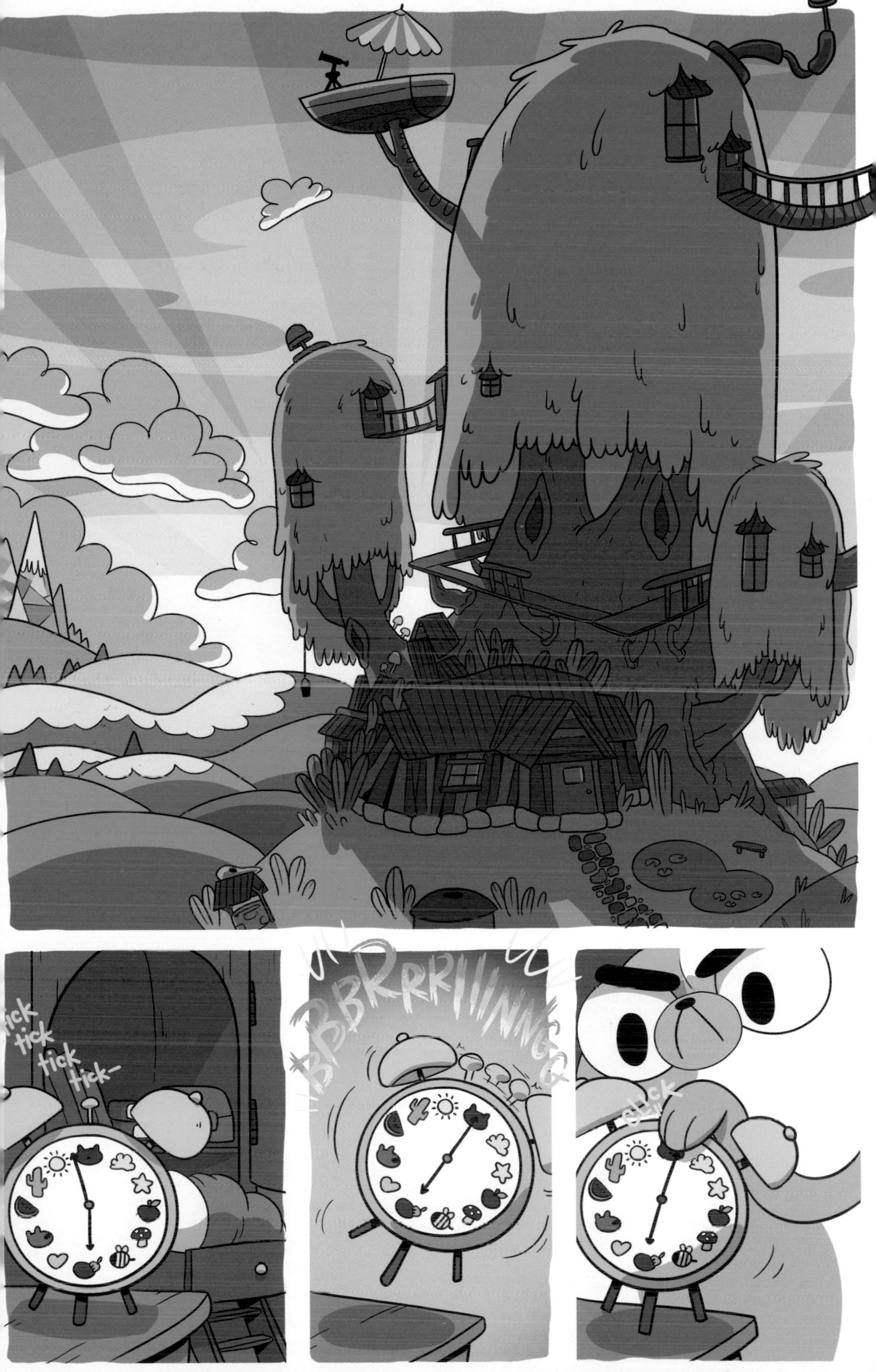
tick
tick
tick-
BBRRRIIINNGG

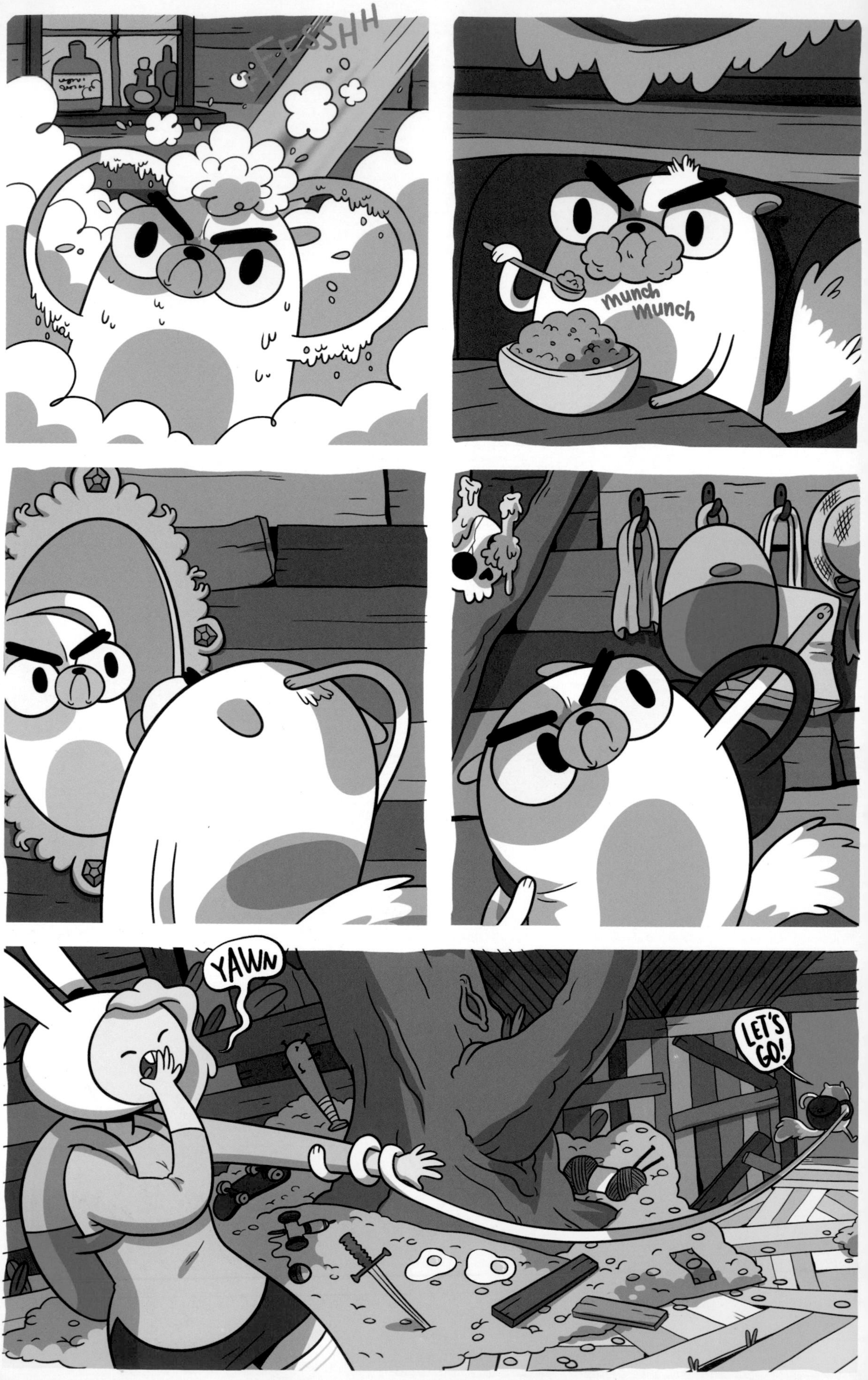
FFSSHH
munch munch
YAWN
LET'S GO!

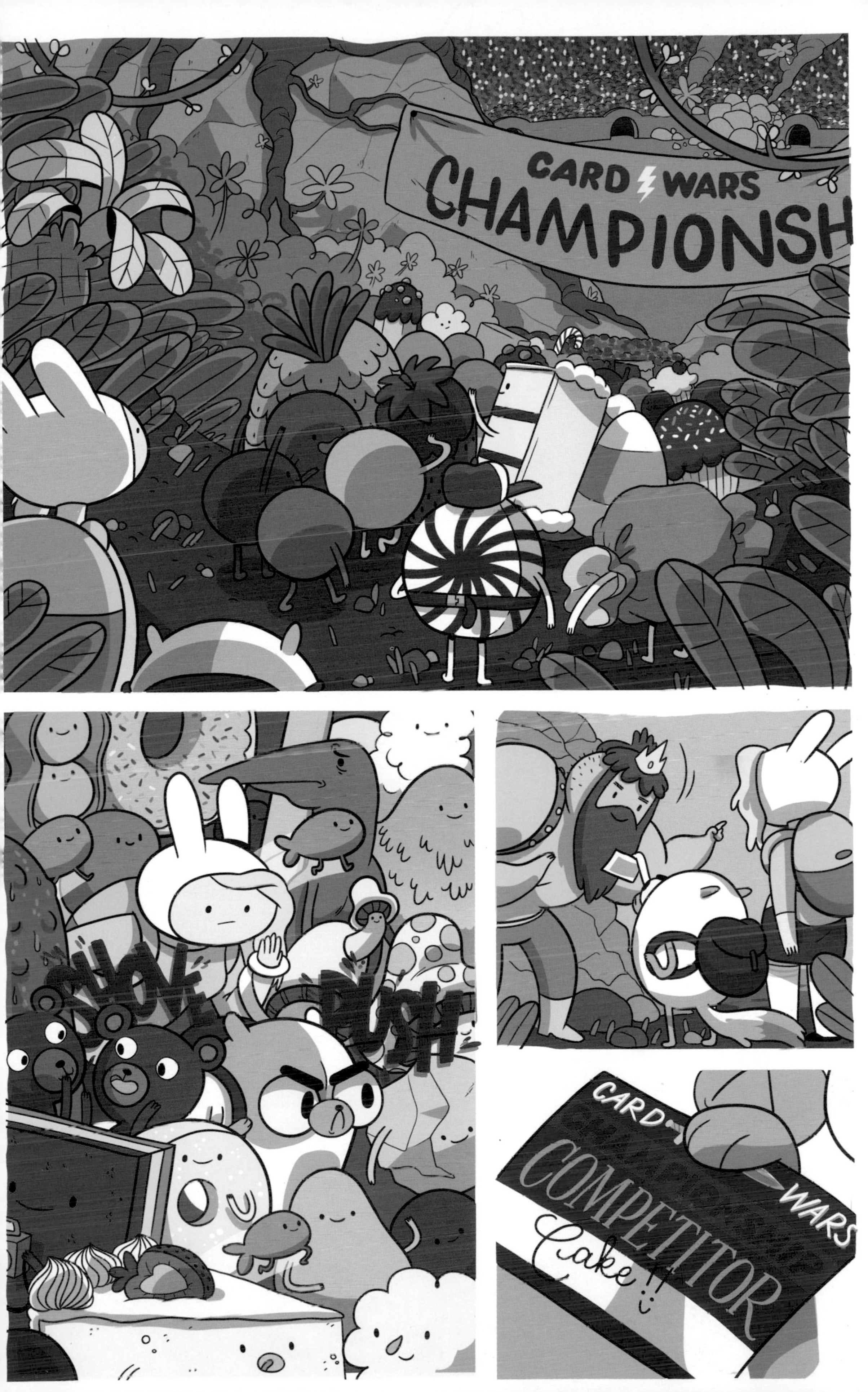
CARD WARS
CHAMPIONSH
SHOVE
PUSH
CARD WARS
COMPETITOR
Cake!!

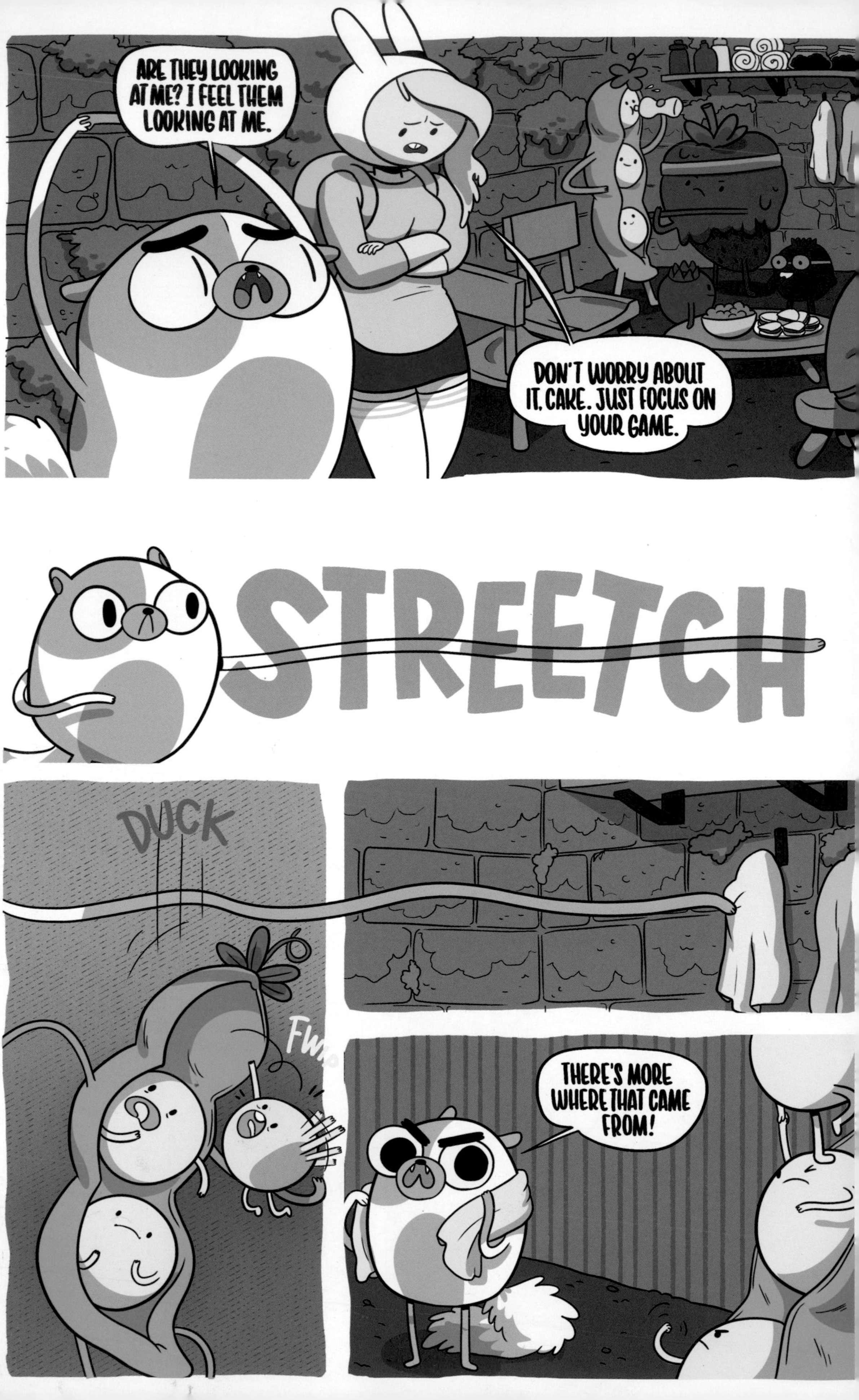
ARE THEY LOOKING AT ME? I FEEL THEM LOOKING AT ME.
DON'T WORRY ABOUT IT, CAKE. JUST FOCUS ON YOUR GAME.
STREETCH
DUCK
THERE'S MORE WHERE THAT CAME FROM!

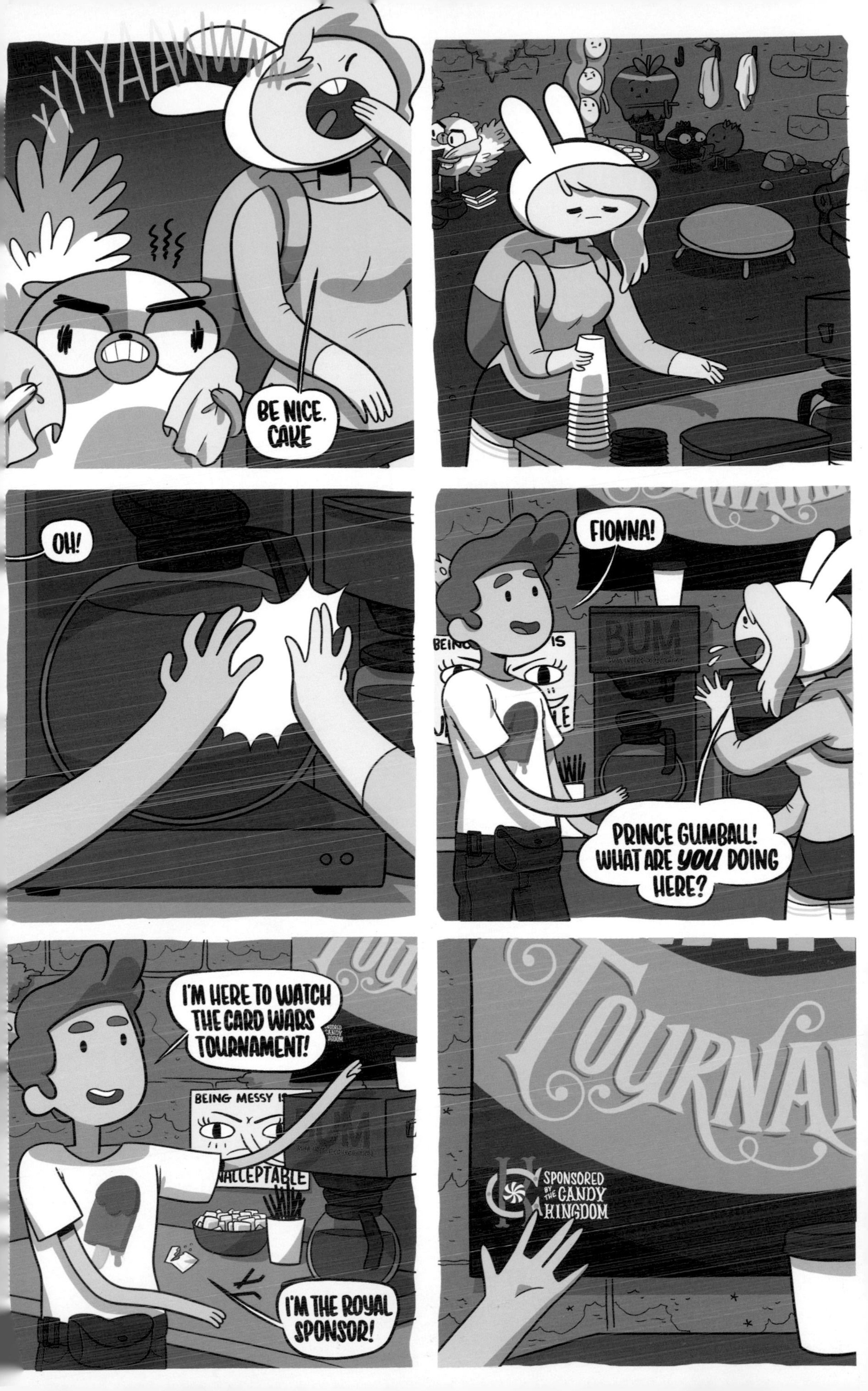

YYYAAWWWN
BE NICE, CAKE
OH!
FIONNA!
BUM
PRINCE GUMBALL! WHAT ARE *YOU* DOING HERE?
I'M HERE TO WATCH THE CARD WARS TOURNAMENT!
BEING MESSY IS
UNACCEPTABLE
I'M THE ROYAL SPONSOR!
TOURNAM
SPONSORED BY THE CANDY KINGDOM

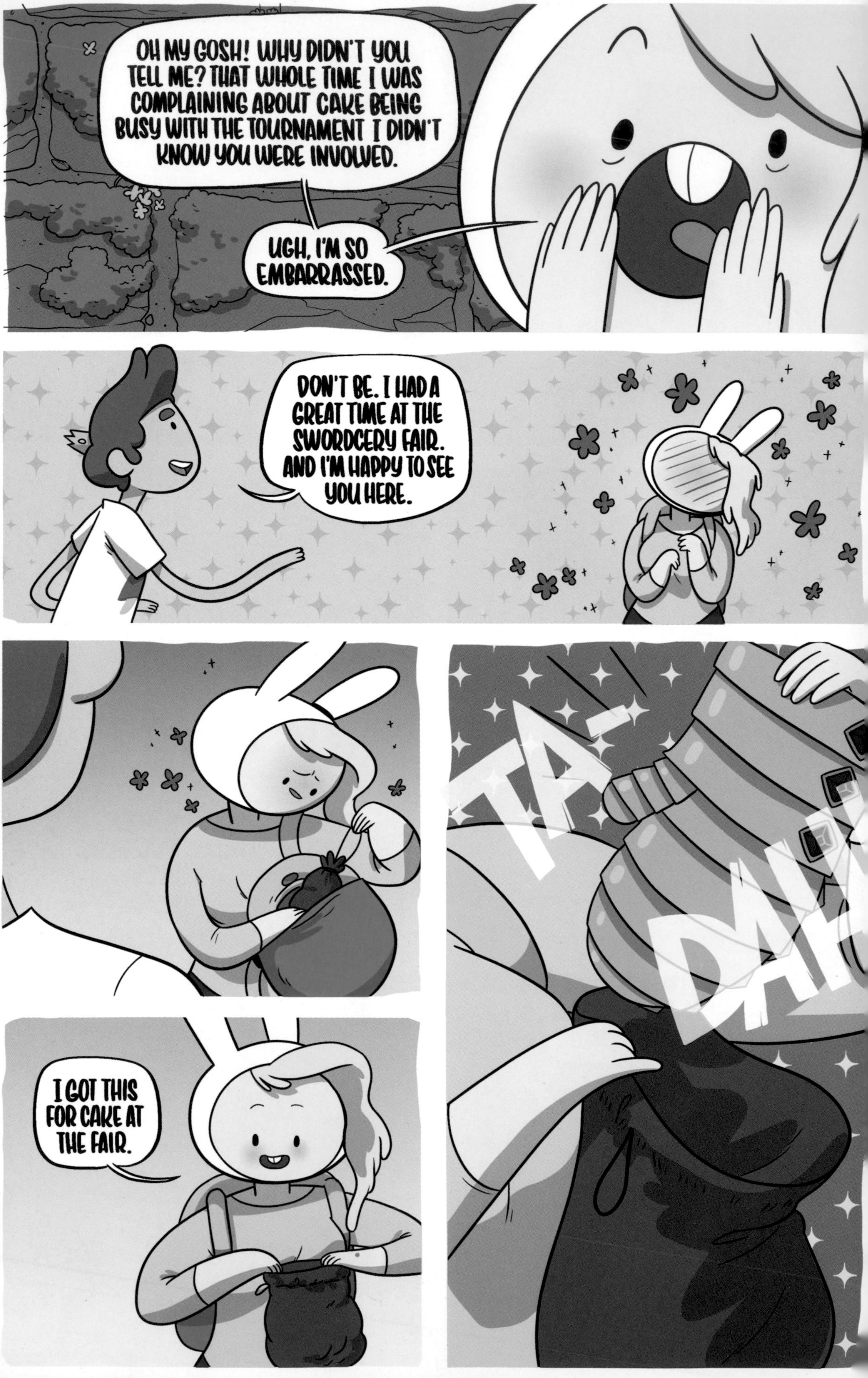
OH MY GOSH! WHY DIDN'T YOU TELL ME? THAT WHOLE TIME I WAS COMPLAINING ABOUT CAKE BEING BUSY WITH THE TOURNAMENT I DIDN'T KNOW YOU WERE INVOLVED.
UGH, I'M SO EMBARRASSED.
DON'T BE. I HAD A GREAT TIME AT THE SWORDCERY FAIR. AND I'M HAPPY TO SEE YOU HERE.
I GOT THIS FOR CAKE AT THE FAIR.
TA-
DAH

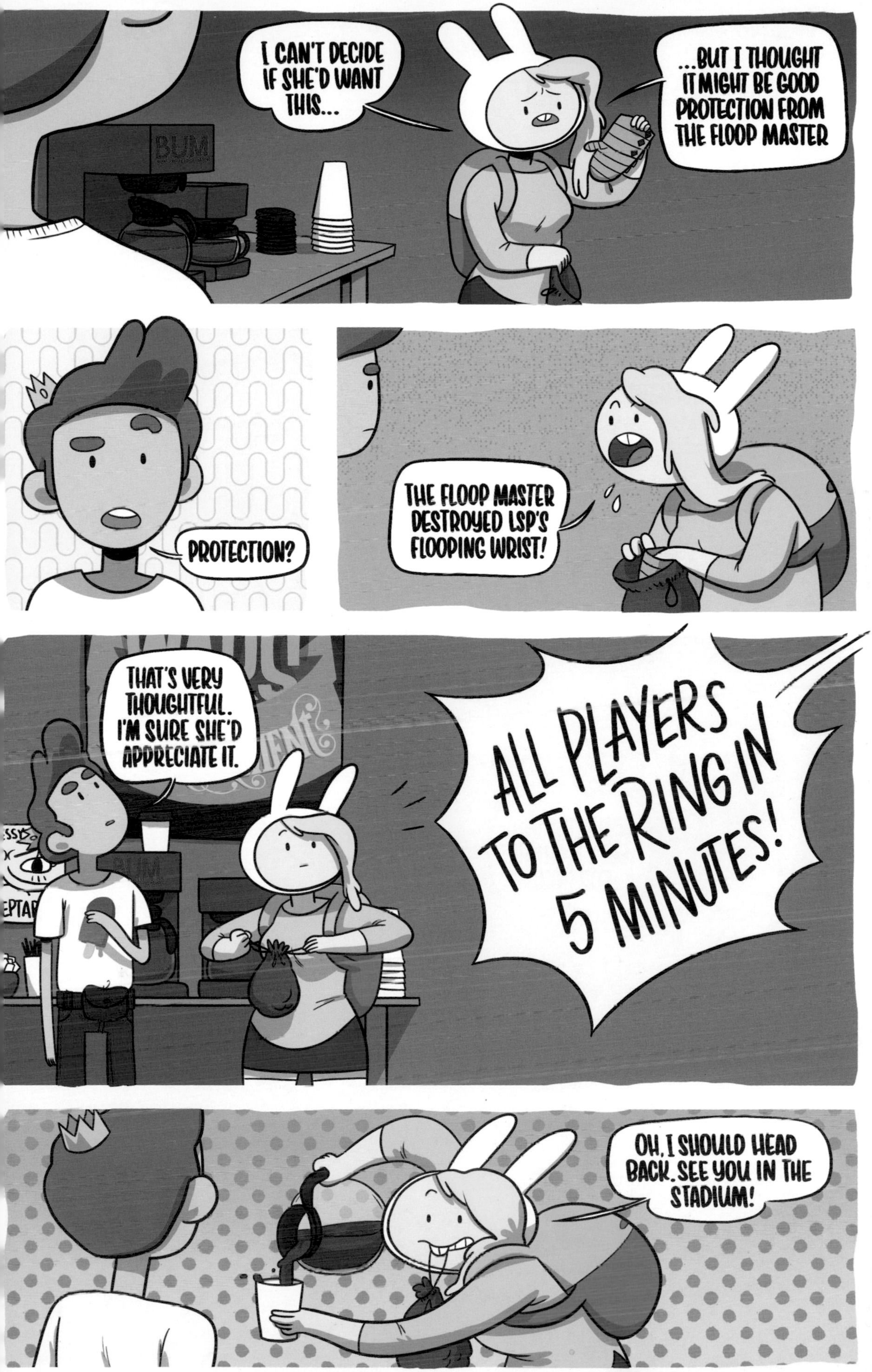
I CAN'T DECIDE IF SHE'D WANT THIS...
...BUT I THOUGHT IT MIGHT BE GOOD PROTECTION FROM THE FLOOP MASTER
PROTECTION?
THE FLOOP MASTER DESTROYED LSP'S FLOOPING WRIST!
THAT'S VERY THOUGHTFUL. I'M SURE SHE'D APPRECIATE IT.
ALL PLAYERS TO THE RING IN 5 MINUTES!
OH, I SHOULD HEAD BACK. SEE YOU IN THE STADIUM!

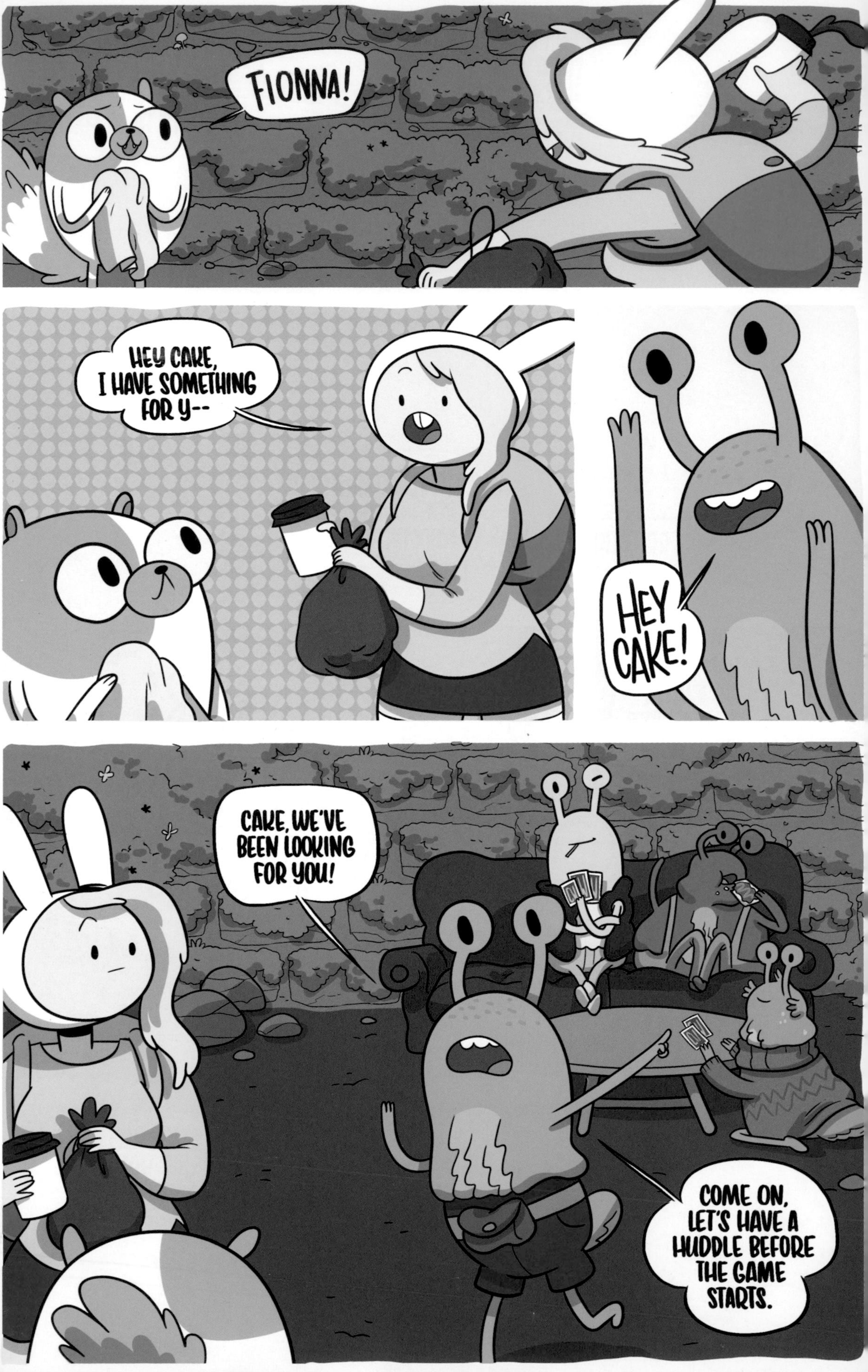
FIONNA!
HEY CAKE, I HAVE SOMETHING FOR Y--
HEY CAKE!
CAKE, WE'VE BEEN LOOKING FOR YOU!
COME ON, LET'S HAVE A HUDDLE BEFORE THE GAME STARTS.

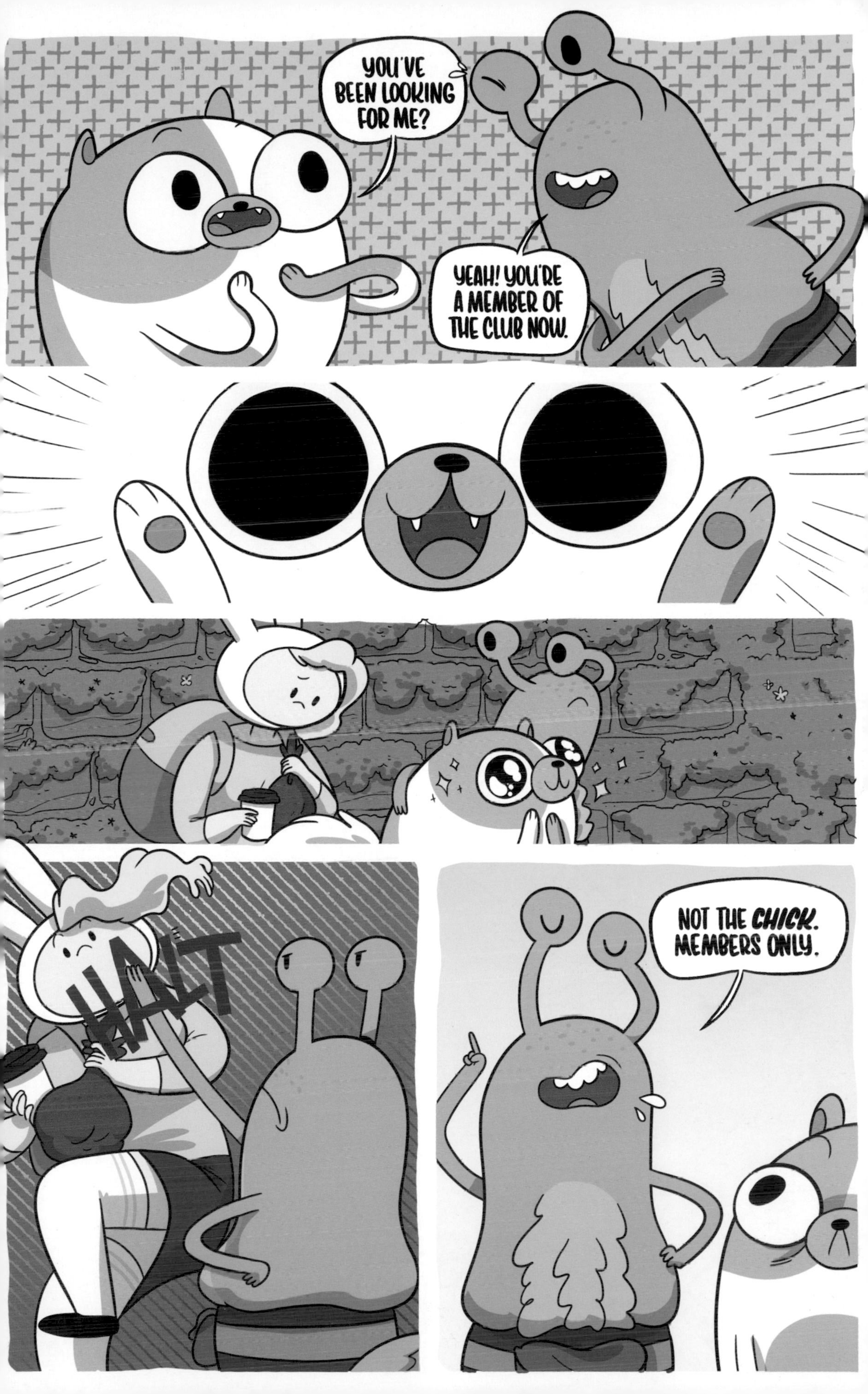
YOU'VE BEEN LOOKING FOR ME?
YEAH! YOU'RE A MEMBER OF THE CLUB NOW.
HALT
NOT THE CHICK. MEMBERS ONLY.

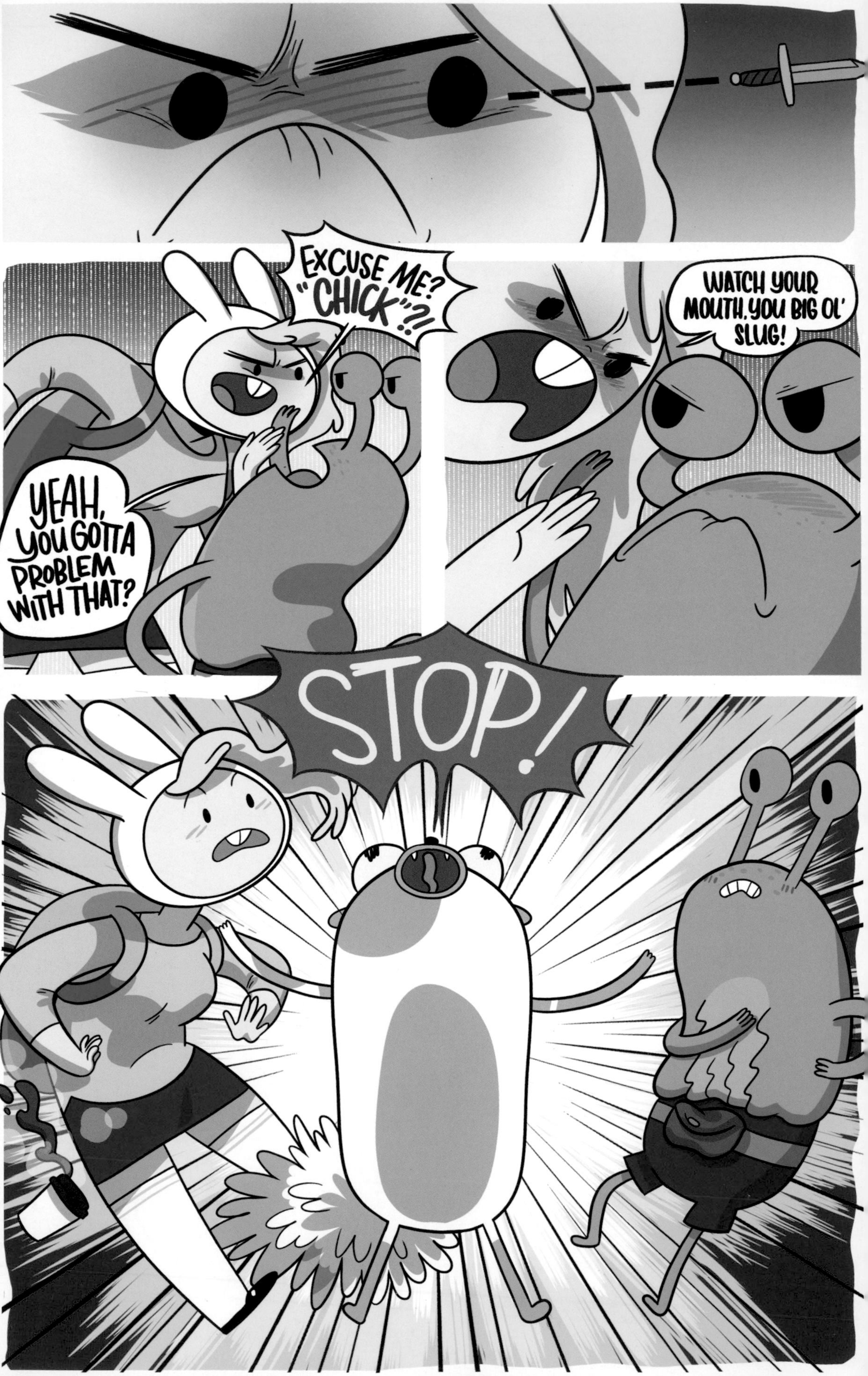
EXCUSE ME? "CHICK"?!
YEAH, YOU GOTTA PROBLEM WITH THAT?
WATCH YOUR MOUTH, YOU BIG OL' SLUG!
STOP!

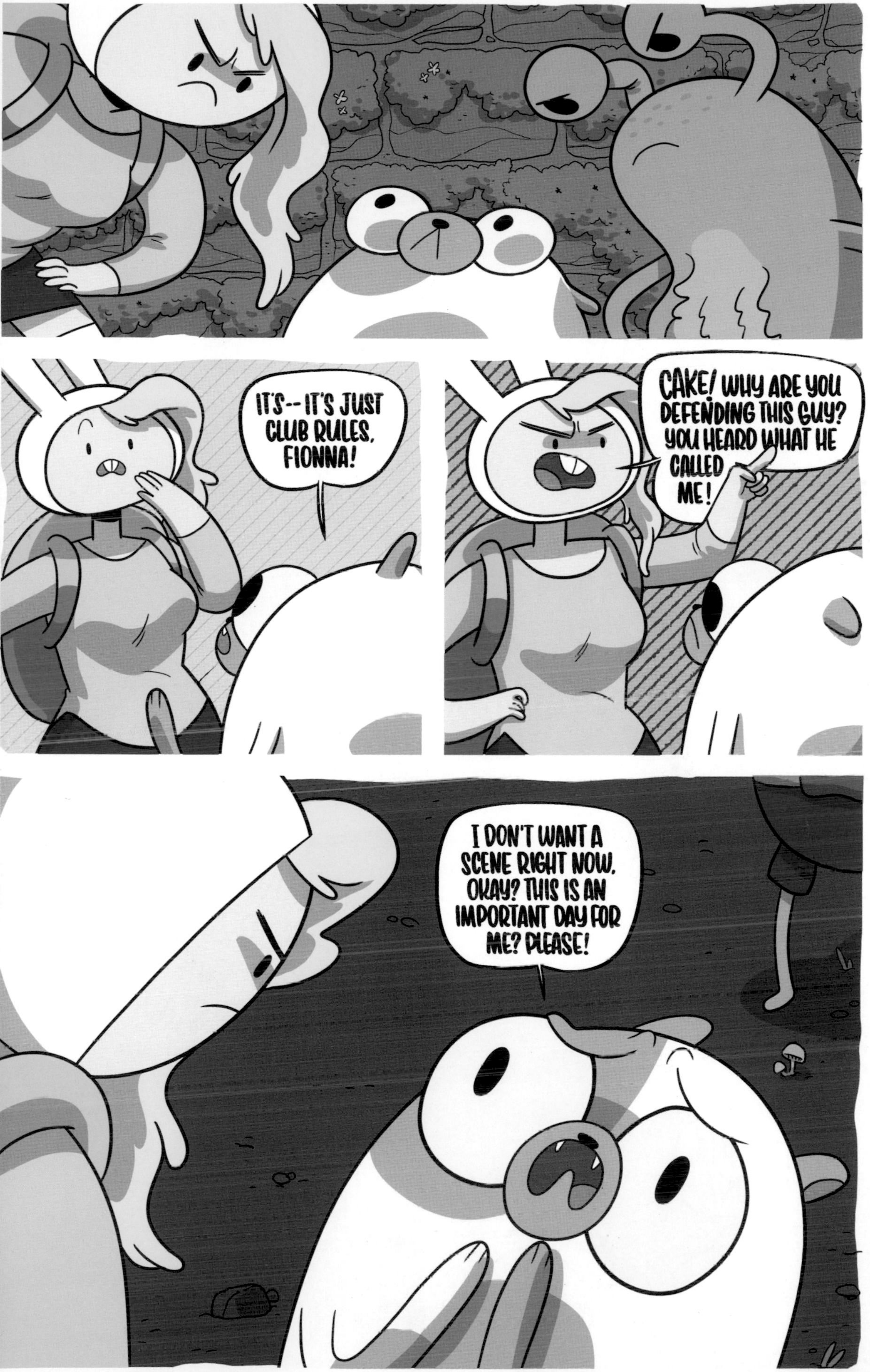
IT'S-- IT'S JUST CLUB RULES, FIONNA!
CAKE! WHY ARE YOU DEFENDING THIS GUY? YOU HEARD WHAT HE CALLED ME!
I DON'T WANT A SCENE RIGHT NOW, OKAY? THIS IS AN IMPORTANT DAY FOR ME? PLEASE!

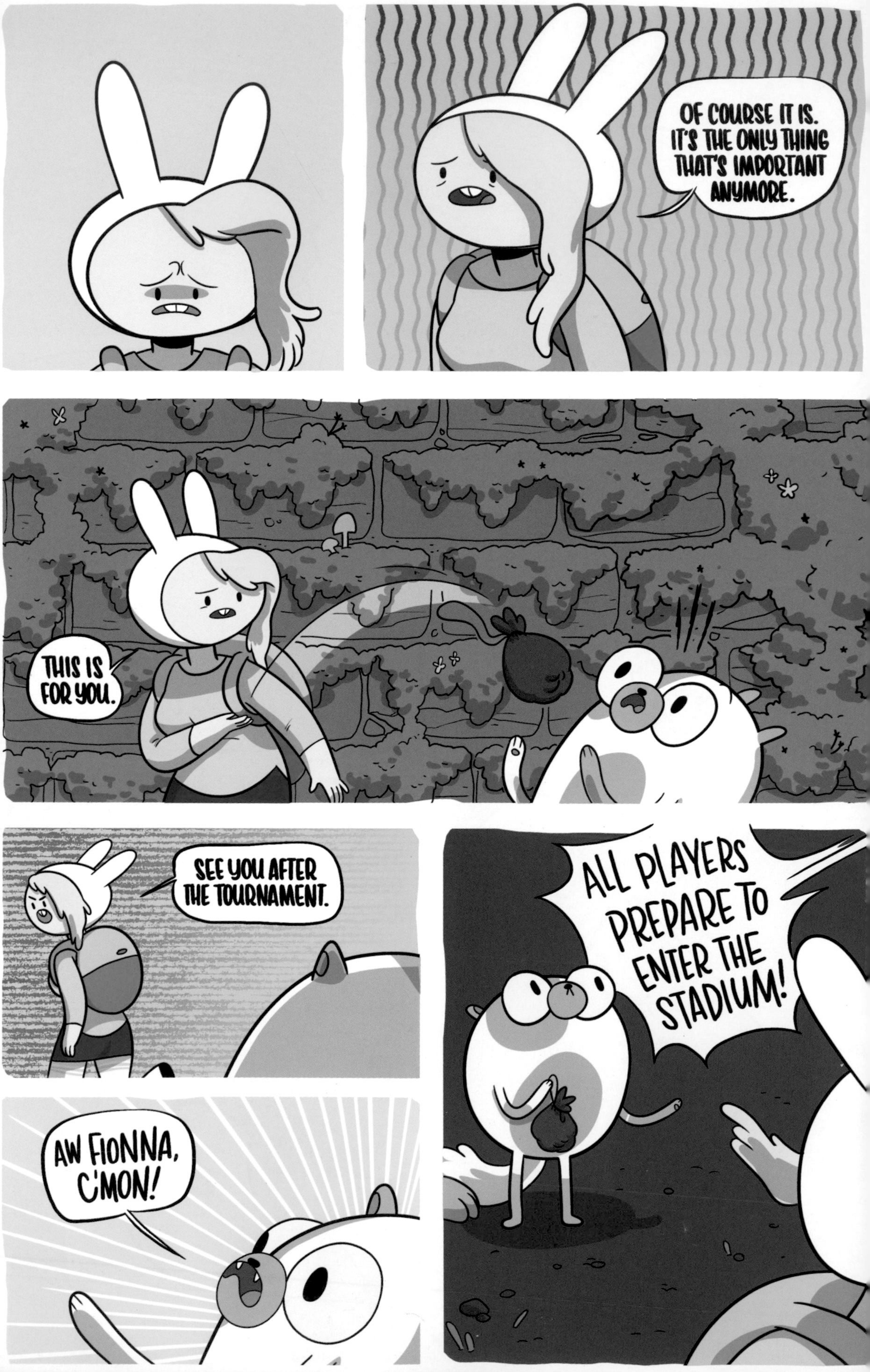
OF COURSE IT IS. IT'S THE ONLY THING THAT'S IMPORTANT ANYMORE.
THIS IS FOR YOU.
SEE YOU AFTER THE TOURNAMENT.
AW FIONNA, C'MON!
ALL PLAYERS PREPARE TO ENTER THE STADIUM!

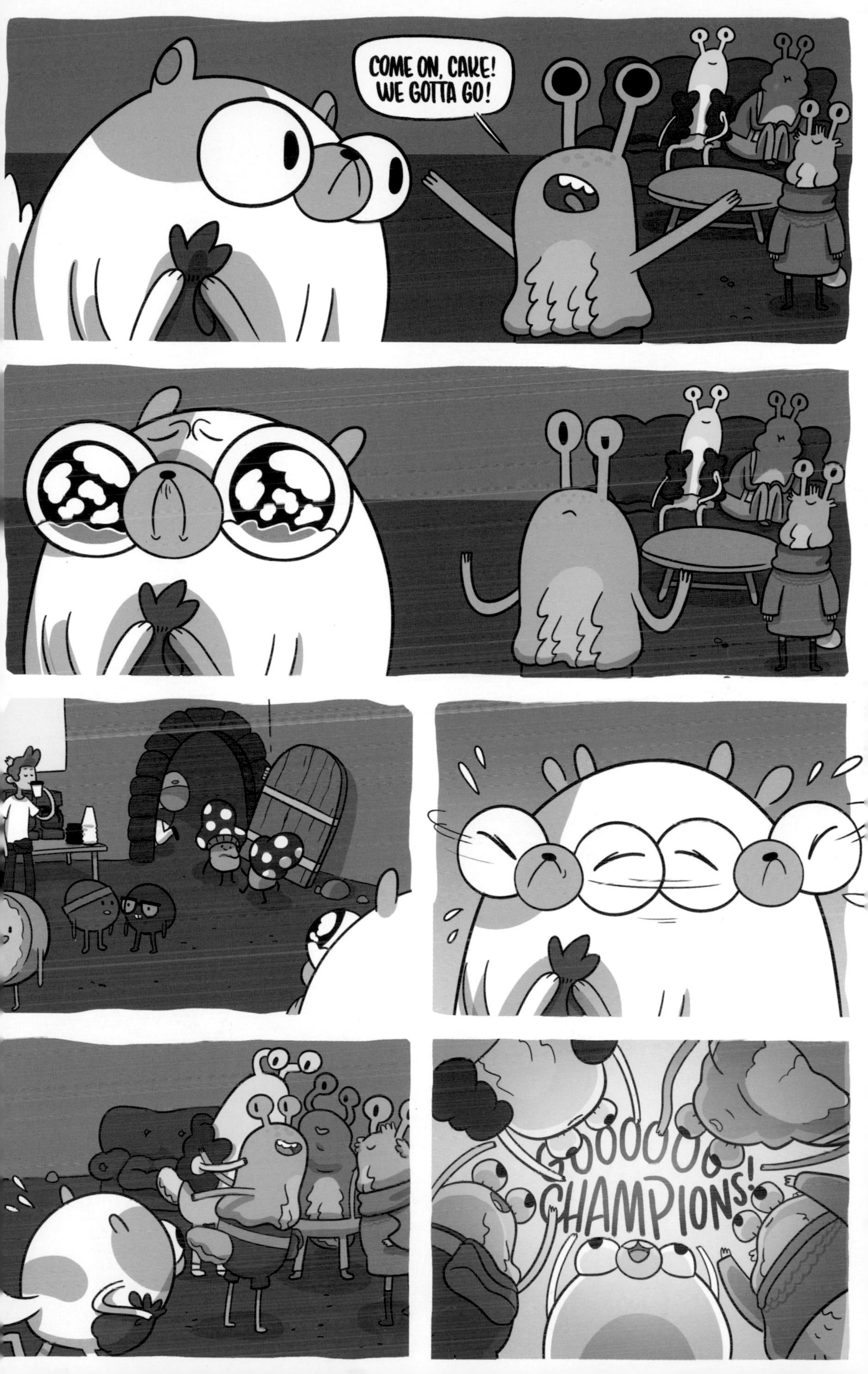
COME ON, CAKE! WE GOTTA GO!
GOOOOOO CHAMPIONS!

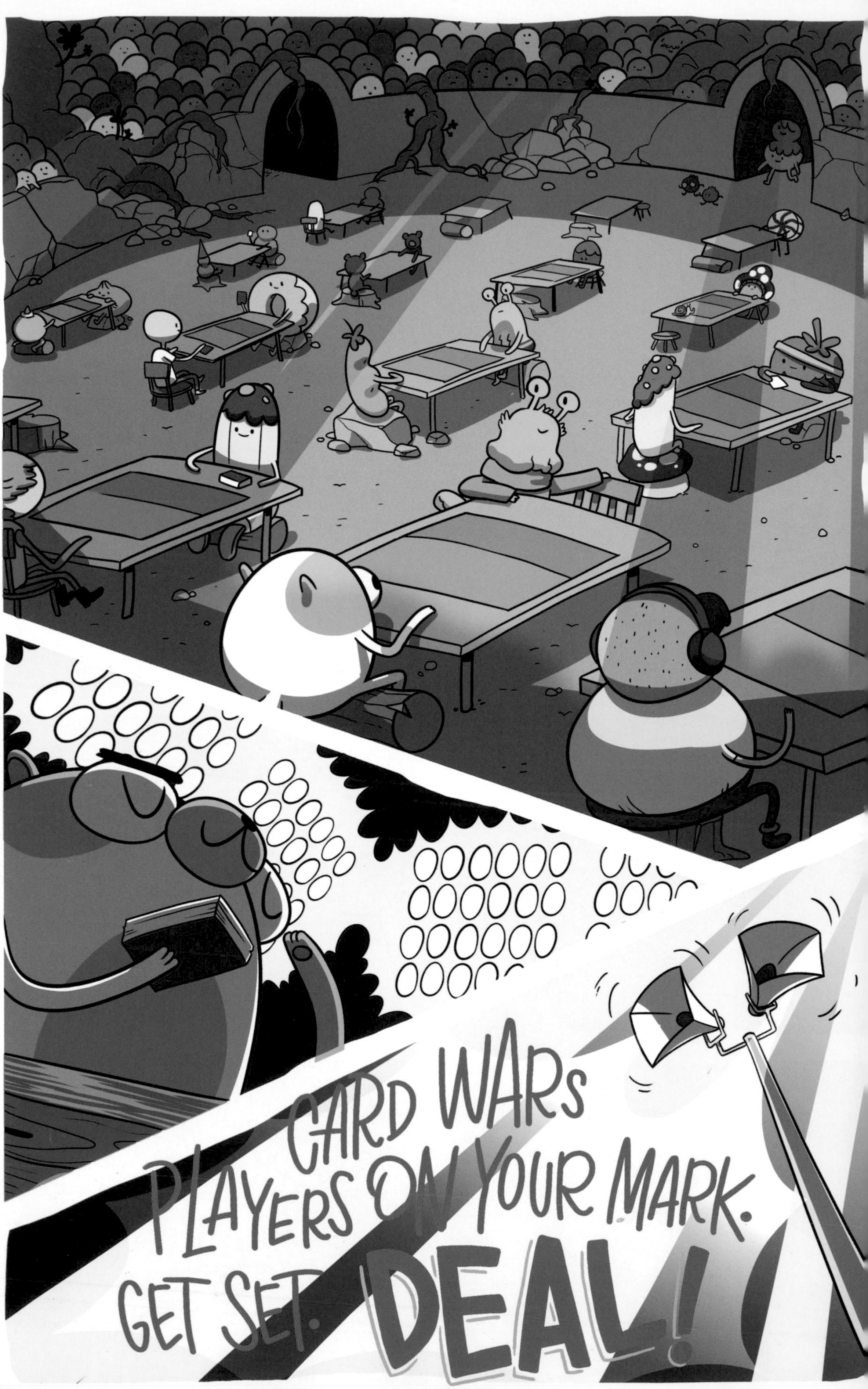
CARD WARS
PLAYERS ON YOUR MARK.
GET SET. DEAL!

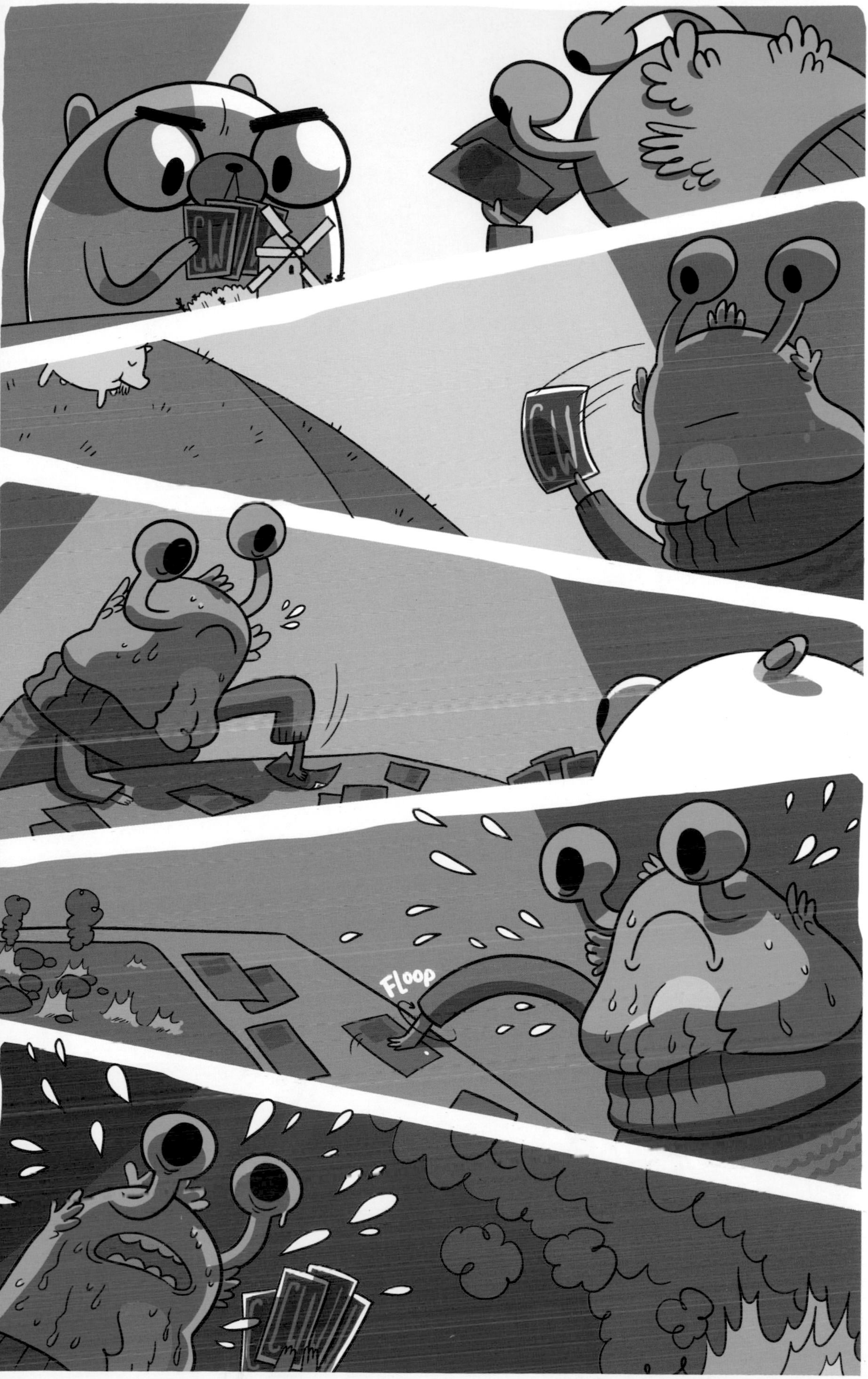
FLOOP

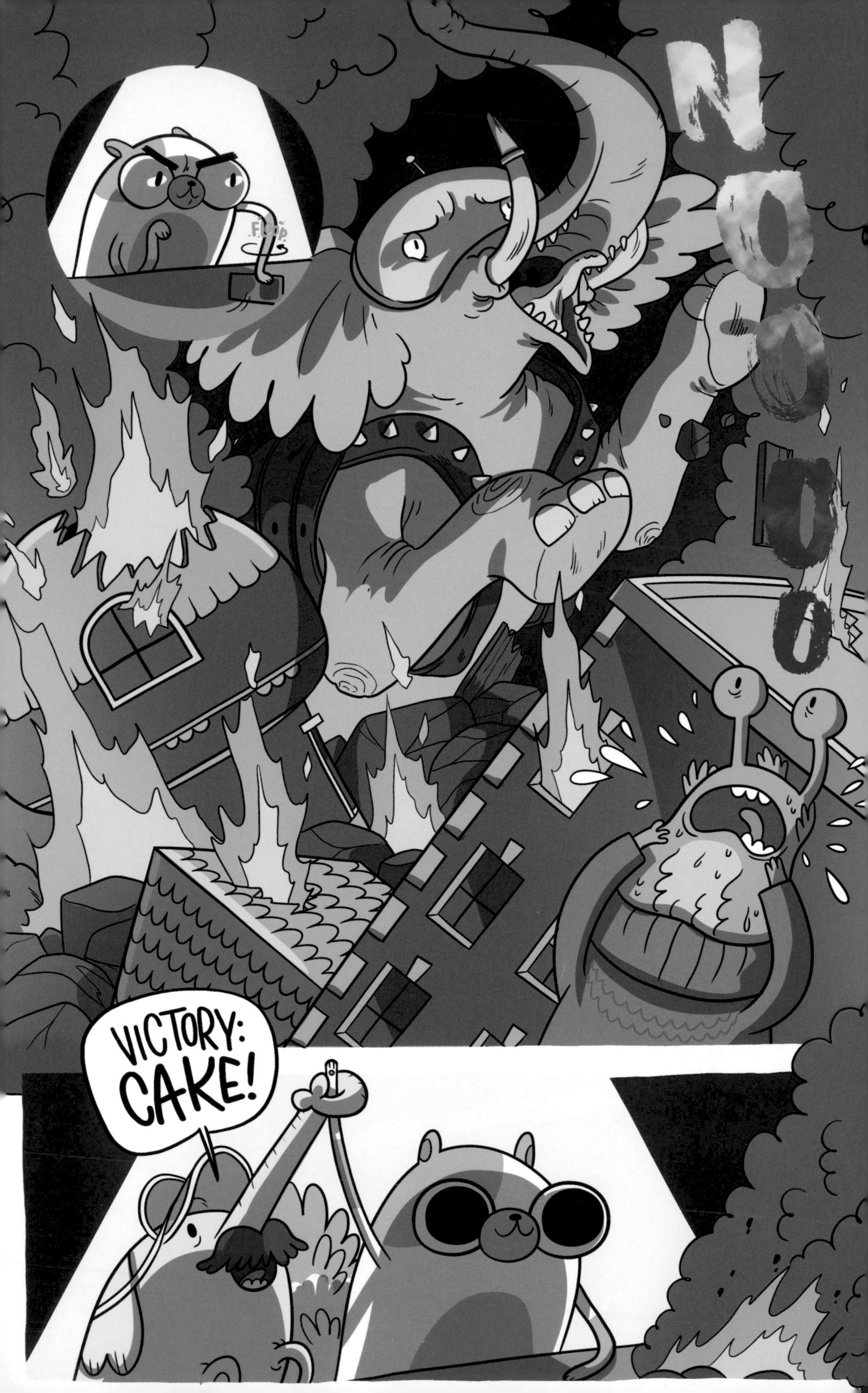
FLOOP
NOOOOO
VICTORY: CAKE!

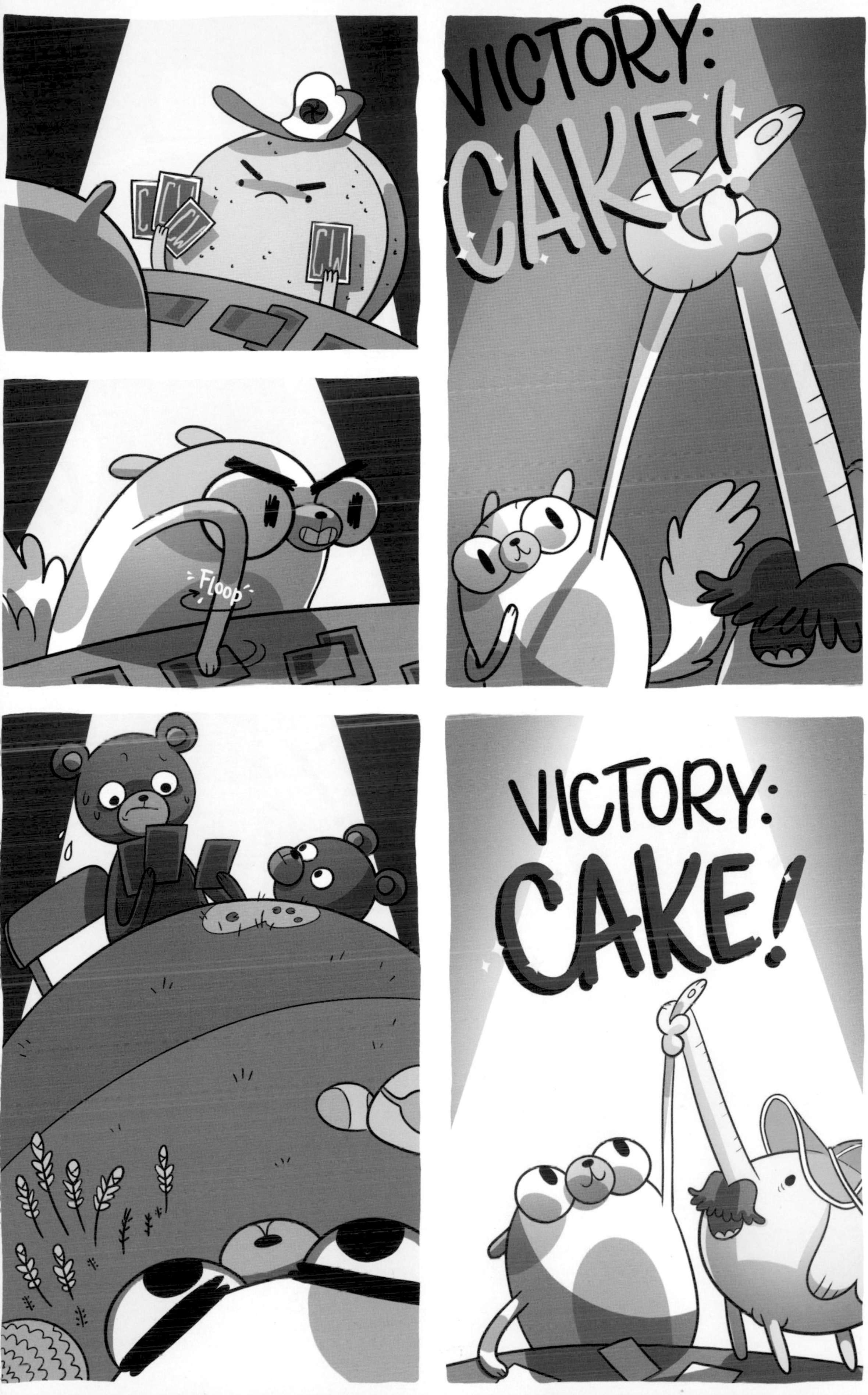
FLOOP
VICTORY: CAKE!
VICTORY: CAKE!

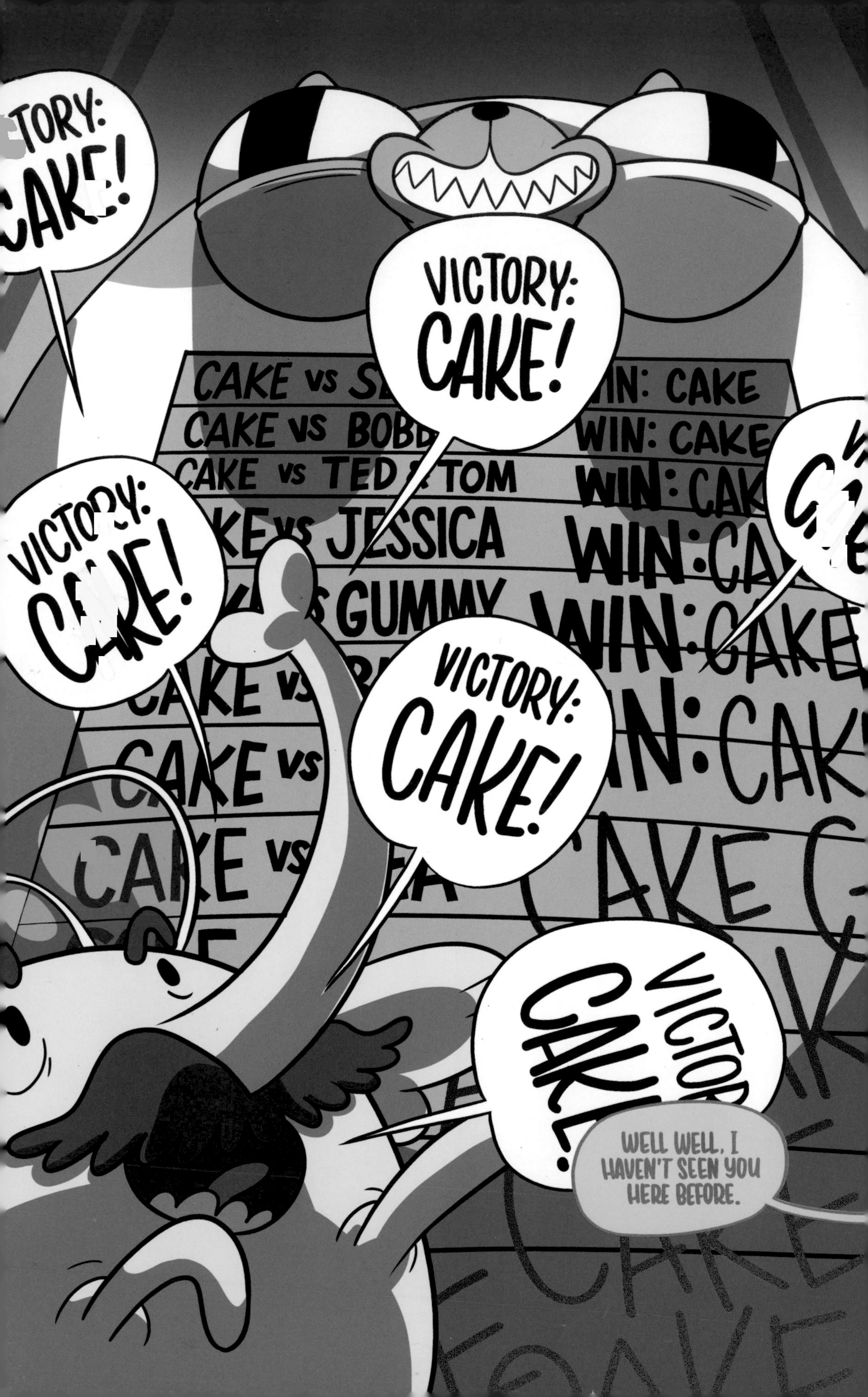

TORY: CAKE!
VICTORY: CAKE!
CAKE vs WIN: CAKE
CAKE vs BOBB WIN: CAKE
CAKE vs TED & TOM WIN: CAKE
VICTORY: CAKE!
JESSICA WIN: CAKE
GUMMY WIN: CAKE
CAKE vs WIN: CAKE
CAKE vs
CAKE vs
VICTORY: CAKE!
VICTORY: CAKE!
WELL WELL. I HAVEN'T SEEN YOU HERE BEFORE.

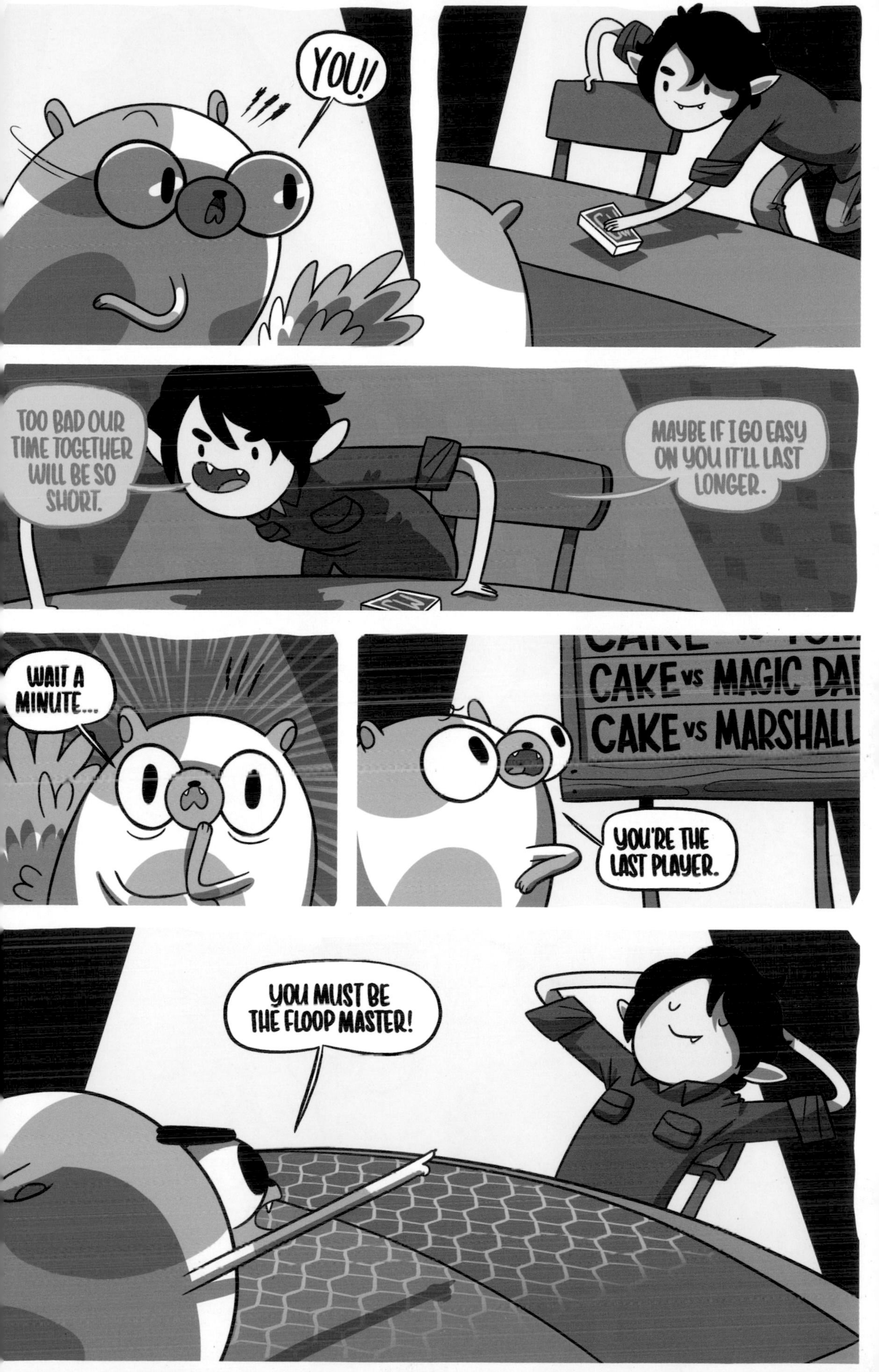
YOU!
TOO BAD OUR TIME TOGETHER WILL BE SO SHORT.
MAYBE IF I GO EASY ON YOU IT'LL LAST LONGER.
WAIT A MINUTE...
CAKE vs MAGIC DA
CAKE vs MARSHALL
YOU'RE THE LAST PLAYER.
YOU MUST BE THE FLOOP MASTER!

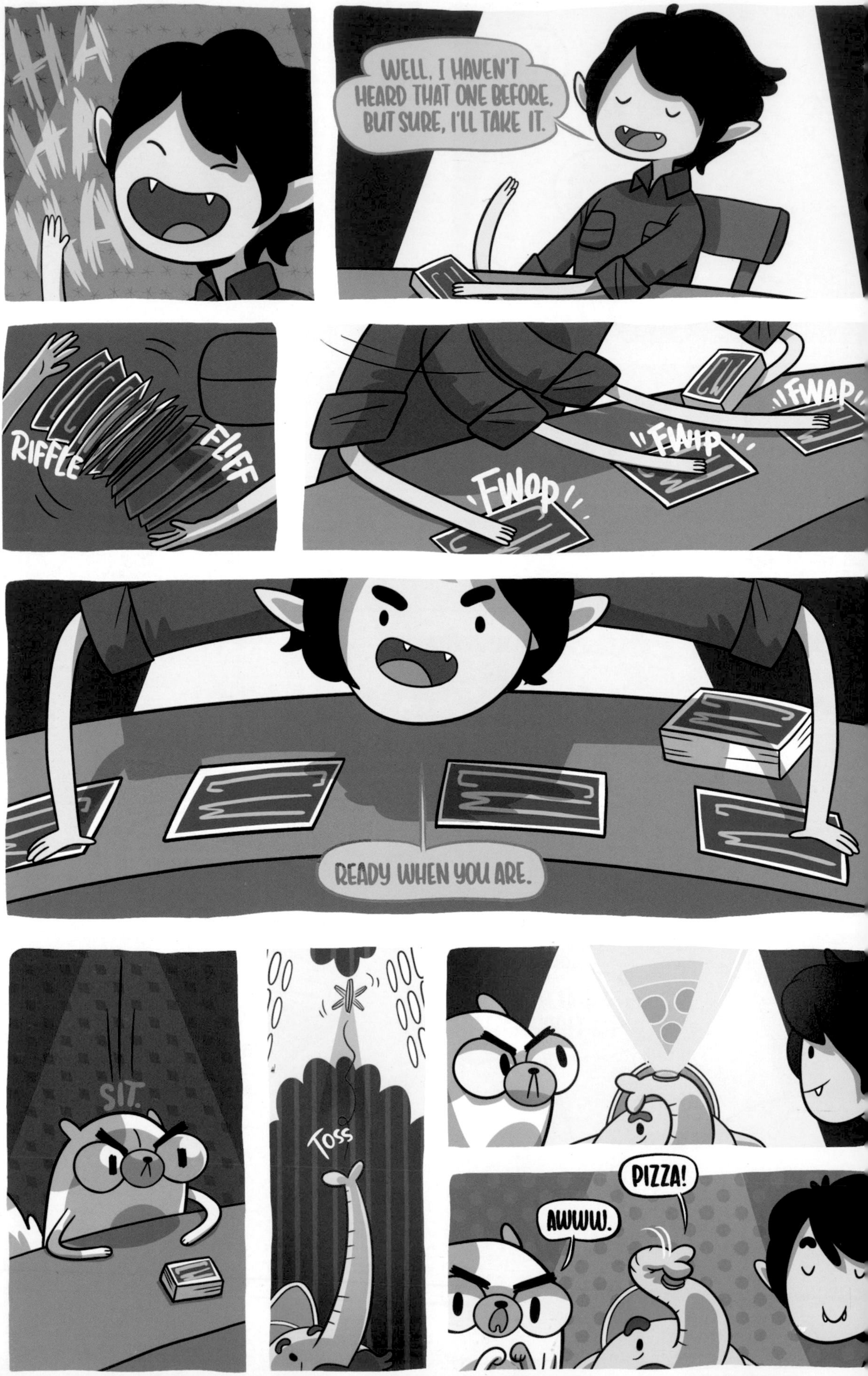
HA HA HA
WELL, I HAVEN'T HEARD THAT ONE BEFORE, BUT SURE, I'LL TAKE IT.
RIFFLE
FLIFF
FWAP
FWIP
FWOP
READY WHEN YOU ARE.
SIT.
TOSS
AWWW.
PIZZA!

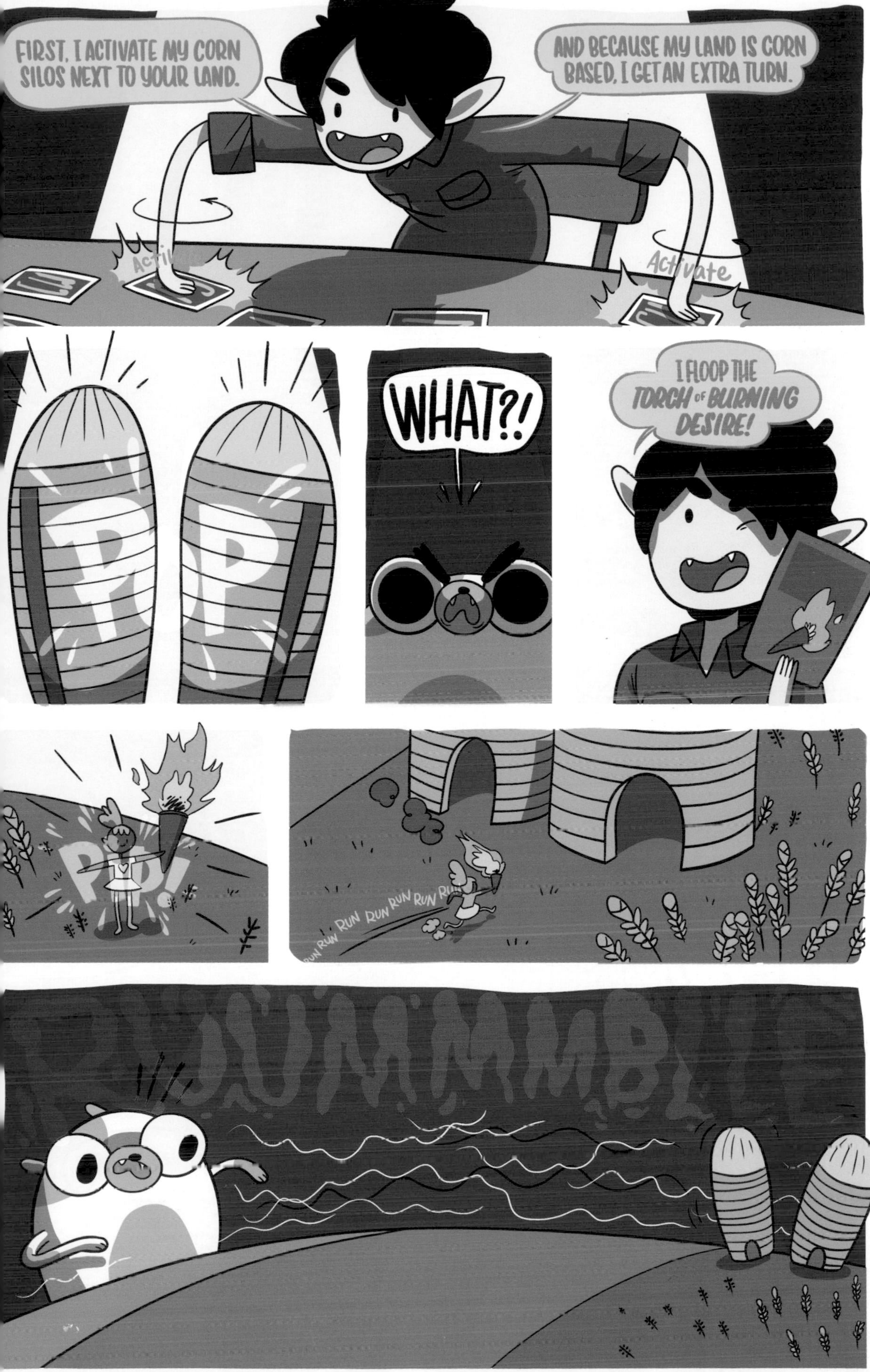
FIRST, I ACTIVATE MY CORN SILOS NEXT TO YOUR LAND.
AND BECAUSE MY LAND IS CORN BASED, I GET AN EXTRA TURN.
Activate
POP
WHAT?!
I FLOOP THE TORCH OF BURNING DESIRE!
RUN RUN RUN RUN RUN RUN

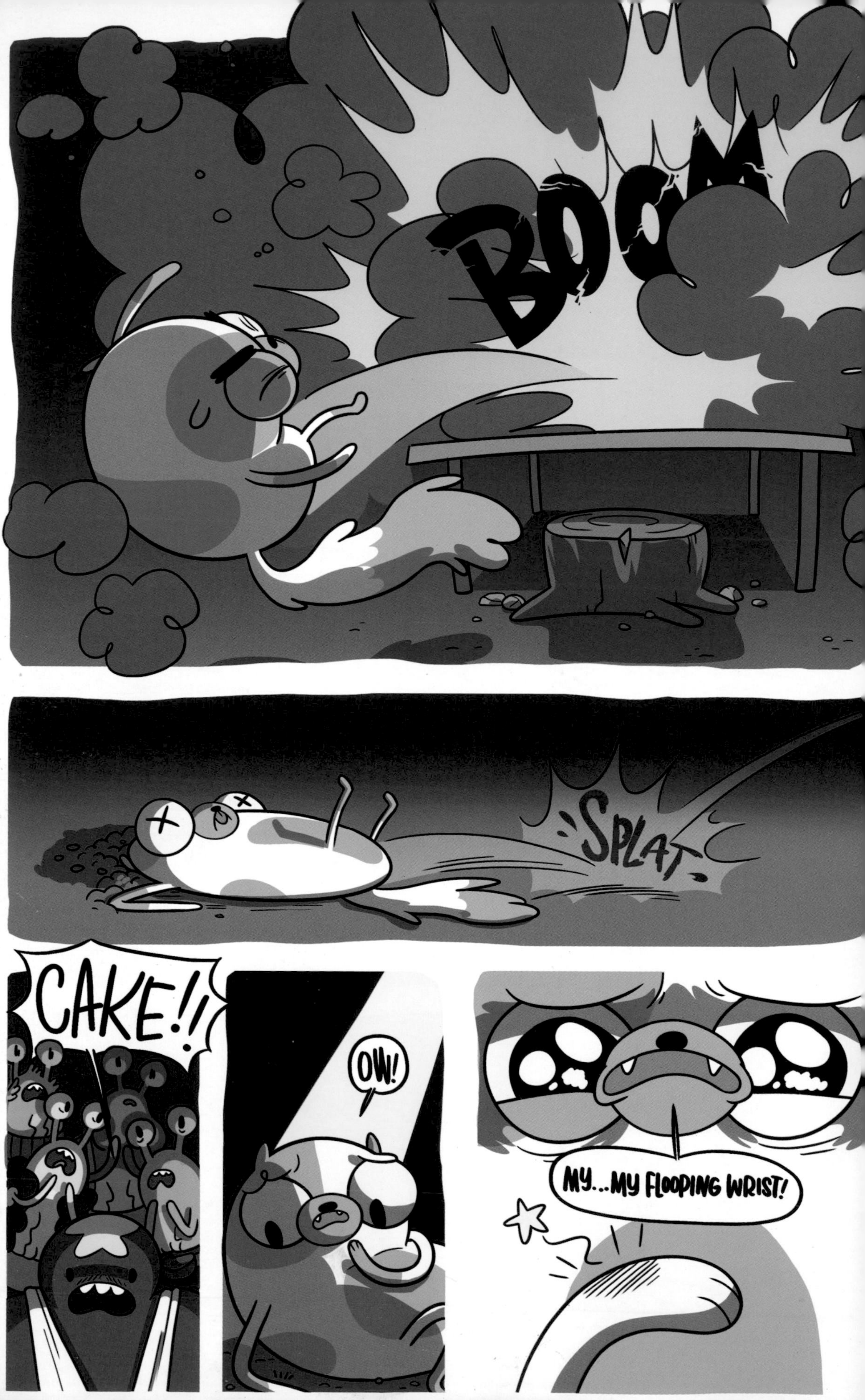
BOOM
SPLAT
CAKE!!
OW!
MY...MY FLOOPING WRIST!

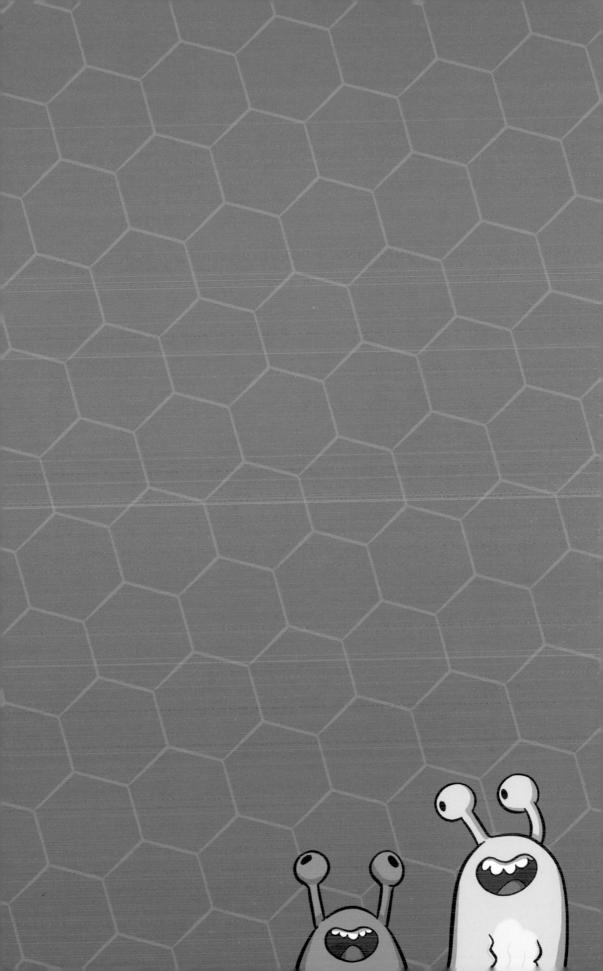

chapter five

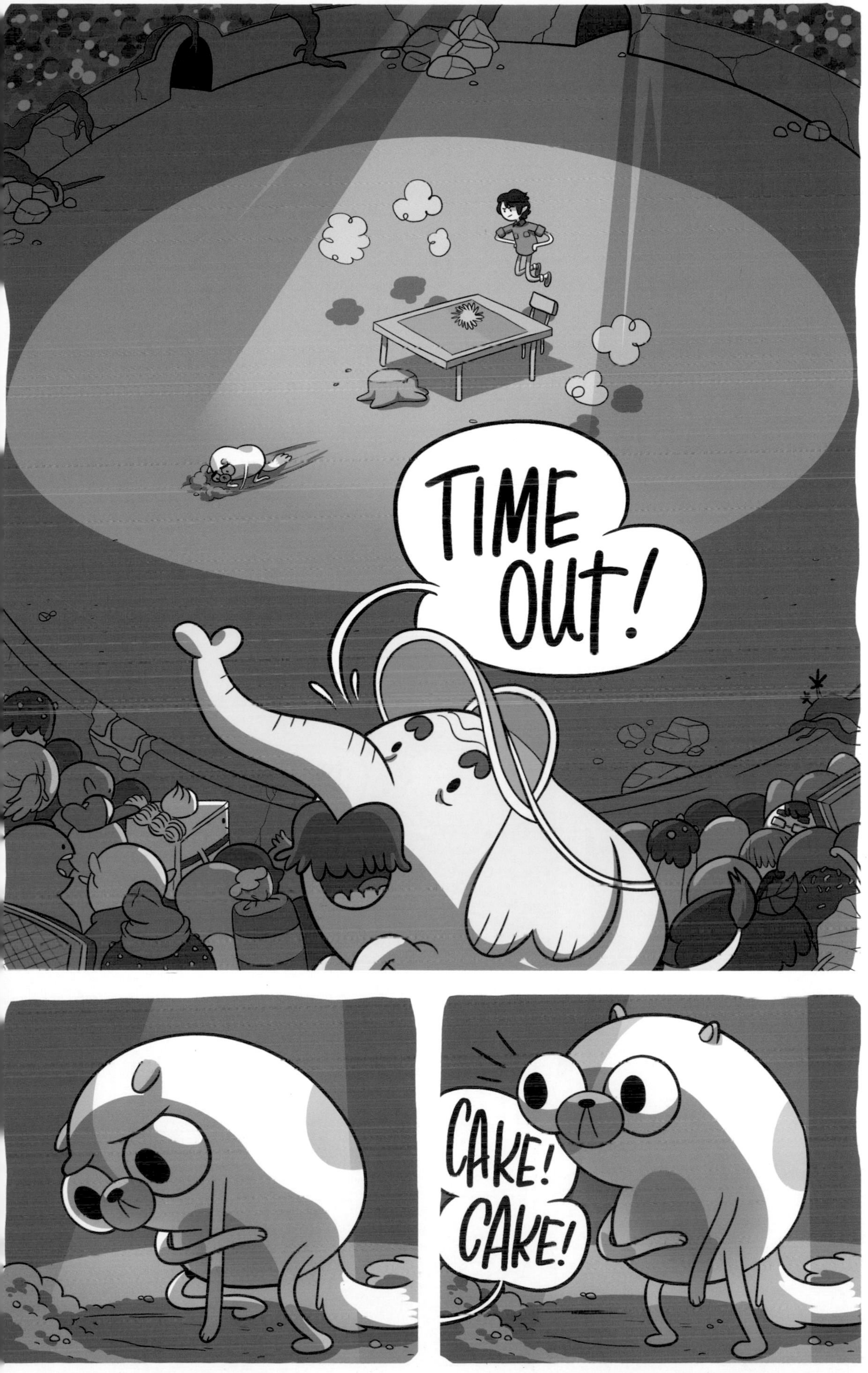
TIME OUT!
CAKE! CAKE!

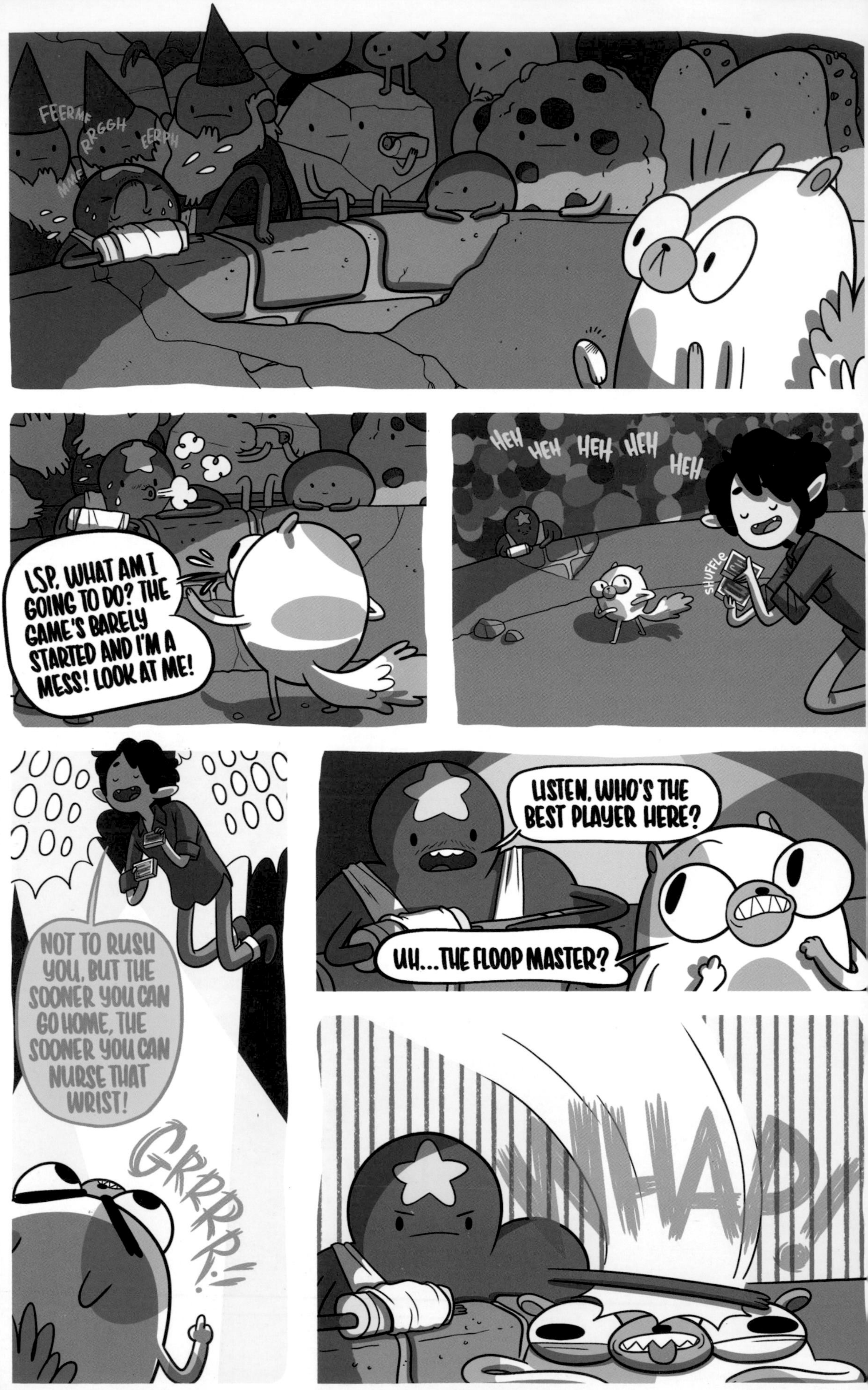
FEERMF
RRGGH
EERPH
MMF
LSP, WHAT AM I GOING TO DO? THE GAME'S BARELY STARTED AND I'M A MESS! LOOK AT ME!
HEH HEH HEH HEH HEH
SHUFFLE
NOT TO RUSH YOU, BUT THE SOONER YOU CAN GO HOME, THE SOONER YOU CAN NURSE THAT WRIST!
GRRRR!!
LISTEN, WHO'S THE BEST PLAYER HERE?
UH...THE FLOOP MASTER?
WHAP!

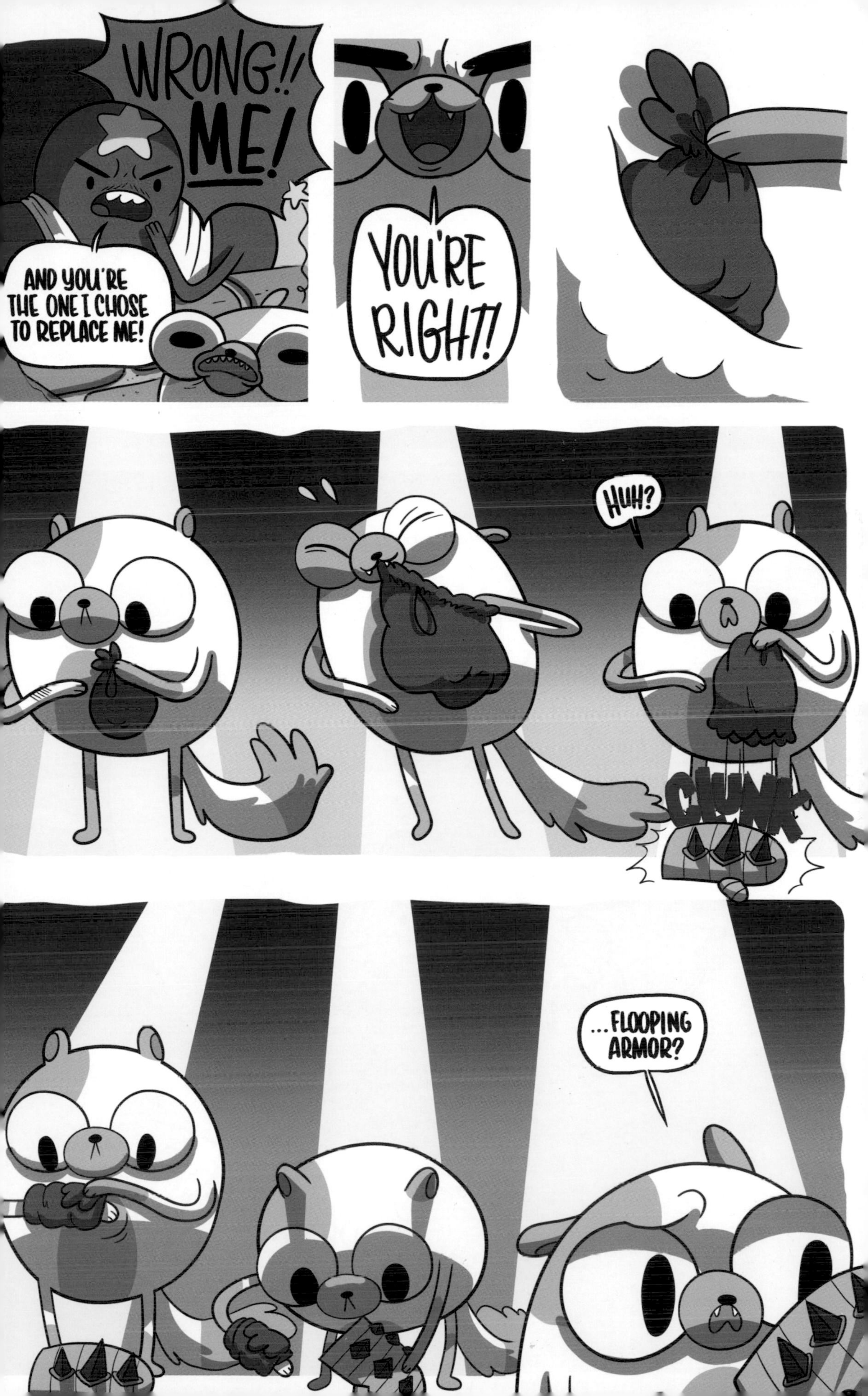
WRONG!! ME!
AND YOU'RE THE ONE I CHOSE TO REPLACE ME!
YOU'RE RIGHT!!
HUH?
CLUNK
...FLOOPING ARMOR?

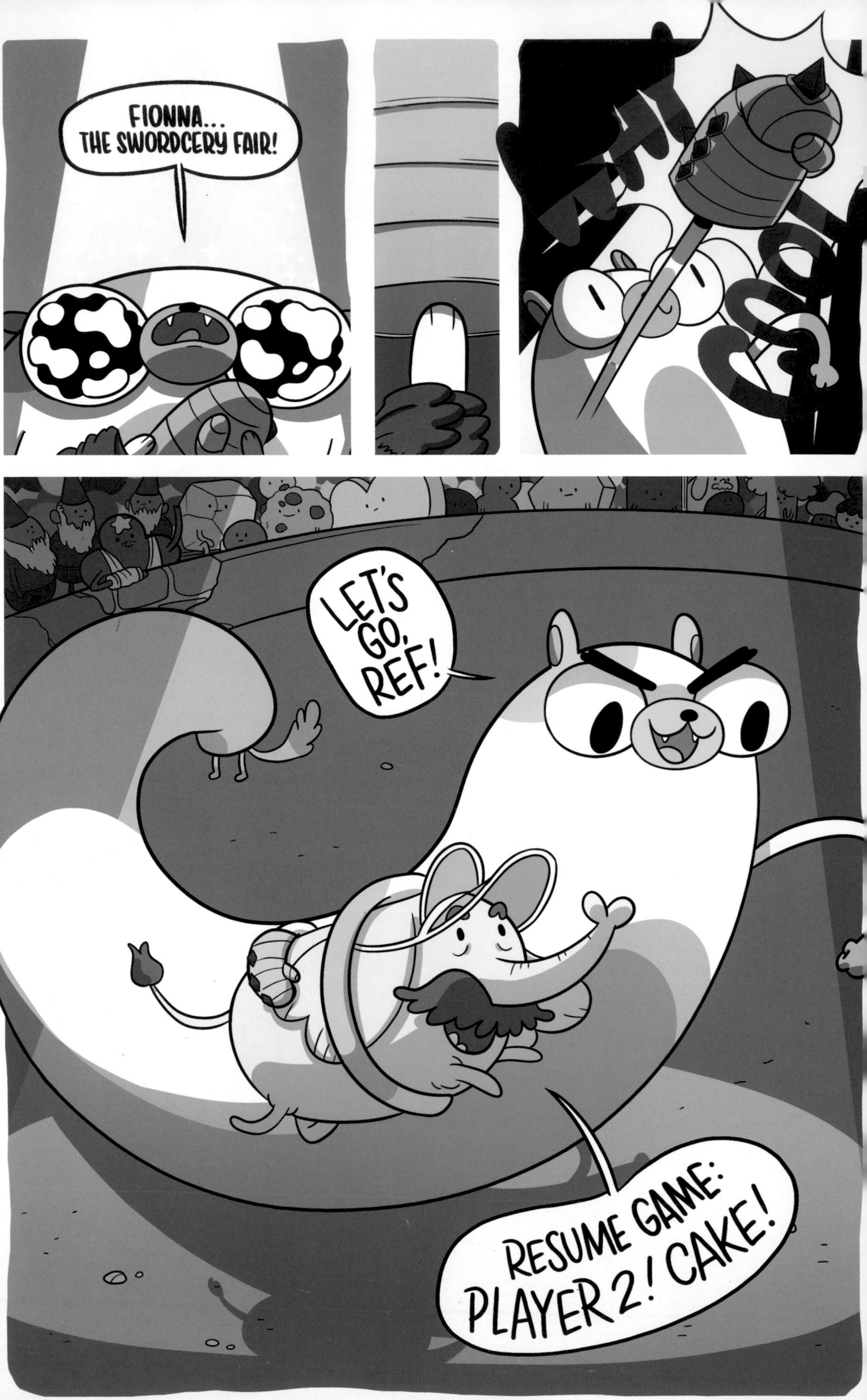
FIONNA... THE SWORDCERY FAIR!
LET'S GO, REF!
RESUME GAME: PLAYER 2! CAKE!

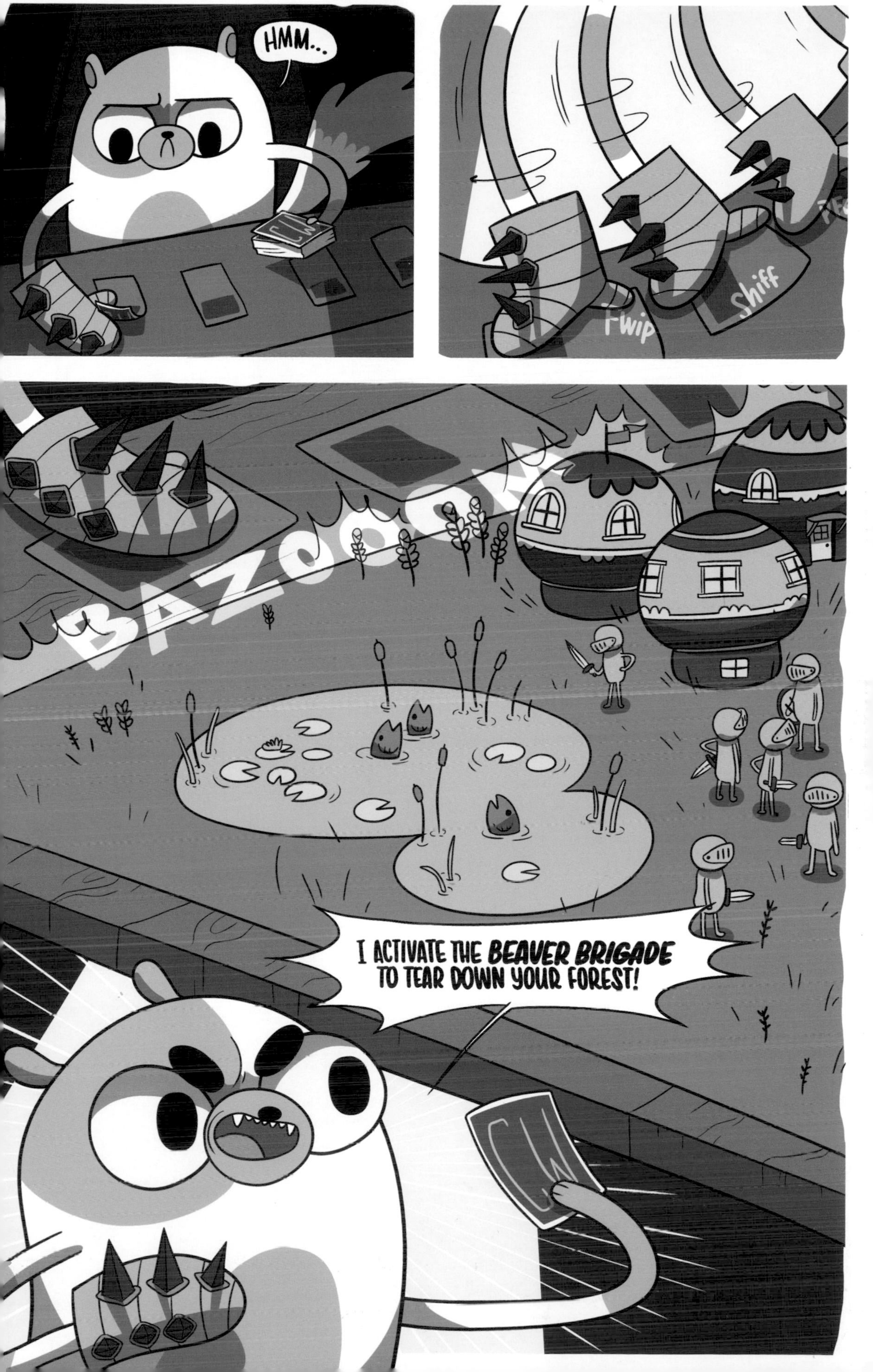
HMM...
Fwip
Shiff
BAZOOOM
I ACTIVATE THE *BEAVER BRIGADE* TO TEAR DOWN YOUR FOREST!

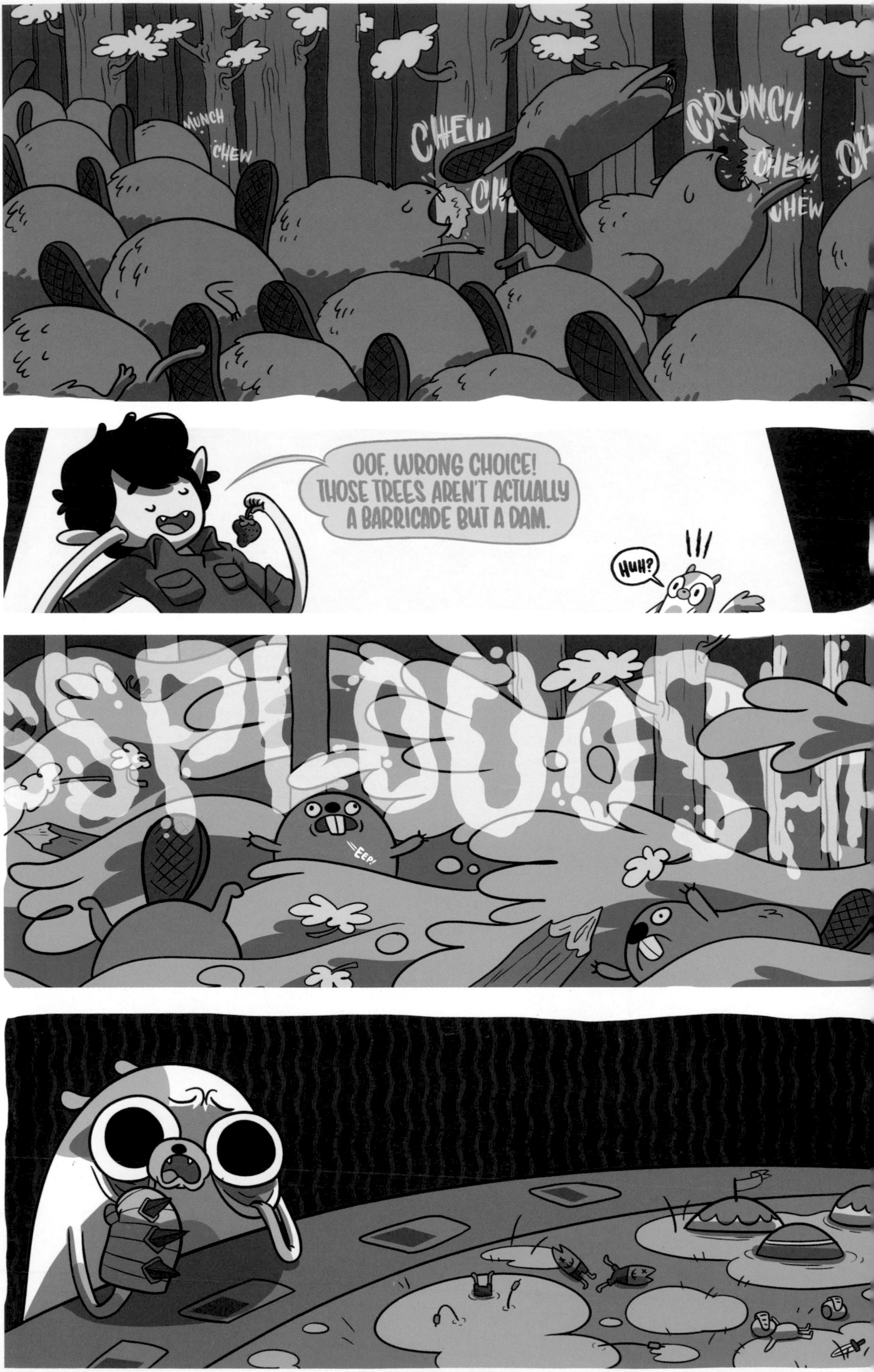
MUNCH
CHEW
CHEW
CRUNCH
CHEW
CHEW
OOF, WRONG CHOICE! THOSE TREES AREN'T ACTUALLY A BARRICADE BUT A DAM.
HUH?
SPLOOOSH
EEP!

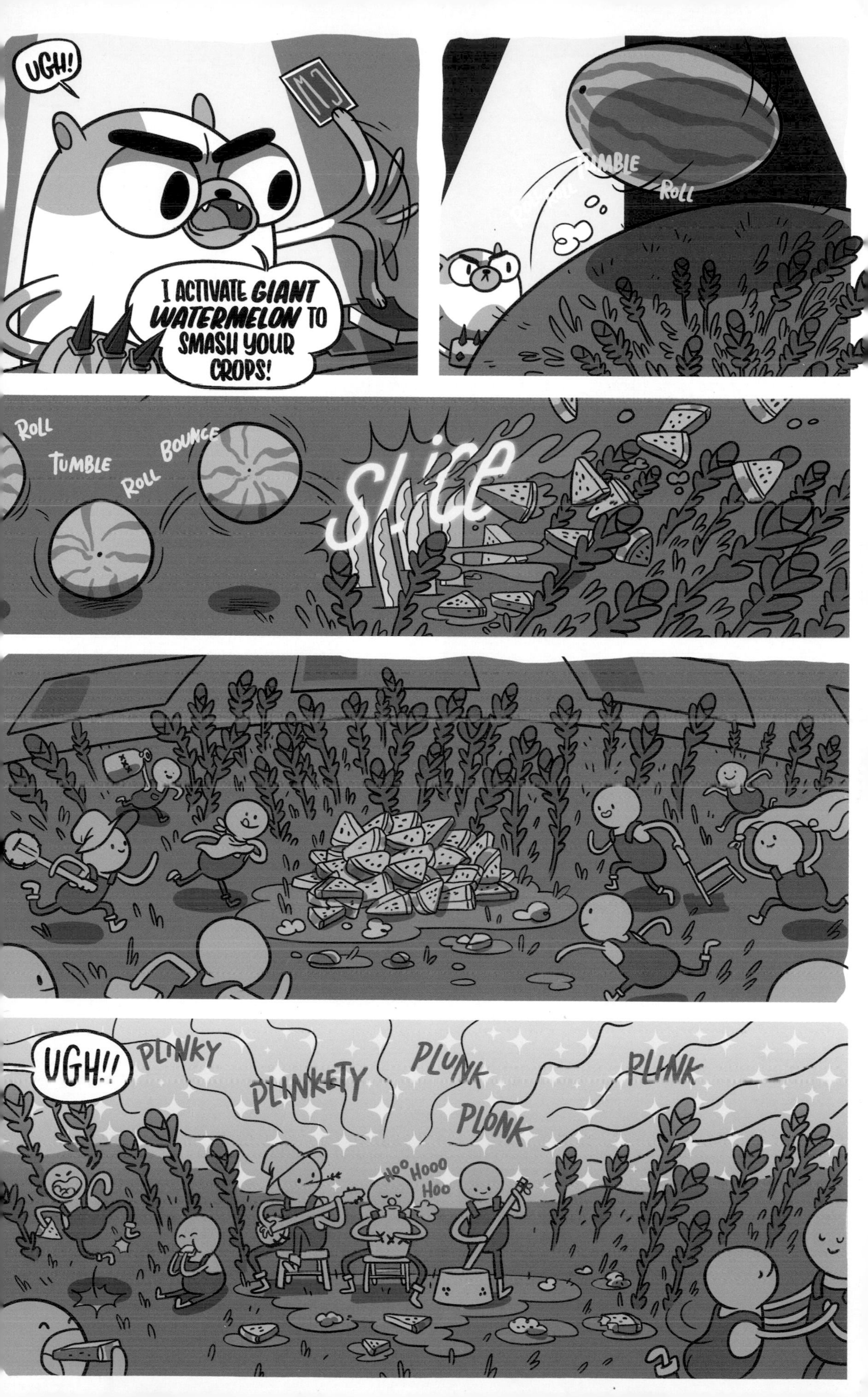
UGH!
I ACTIVATE GIANT WATERMELON TO SMASH YOUR CROPS!
TUMBLE
ROLL
ROLL
TUMBLE
ROLL
BOUNCE
SLICE
UGH!!
PLINKY
PLINKETY
PLUNK
PLINK
PLONK
HOO HOOO HOO

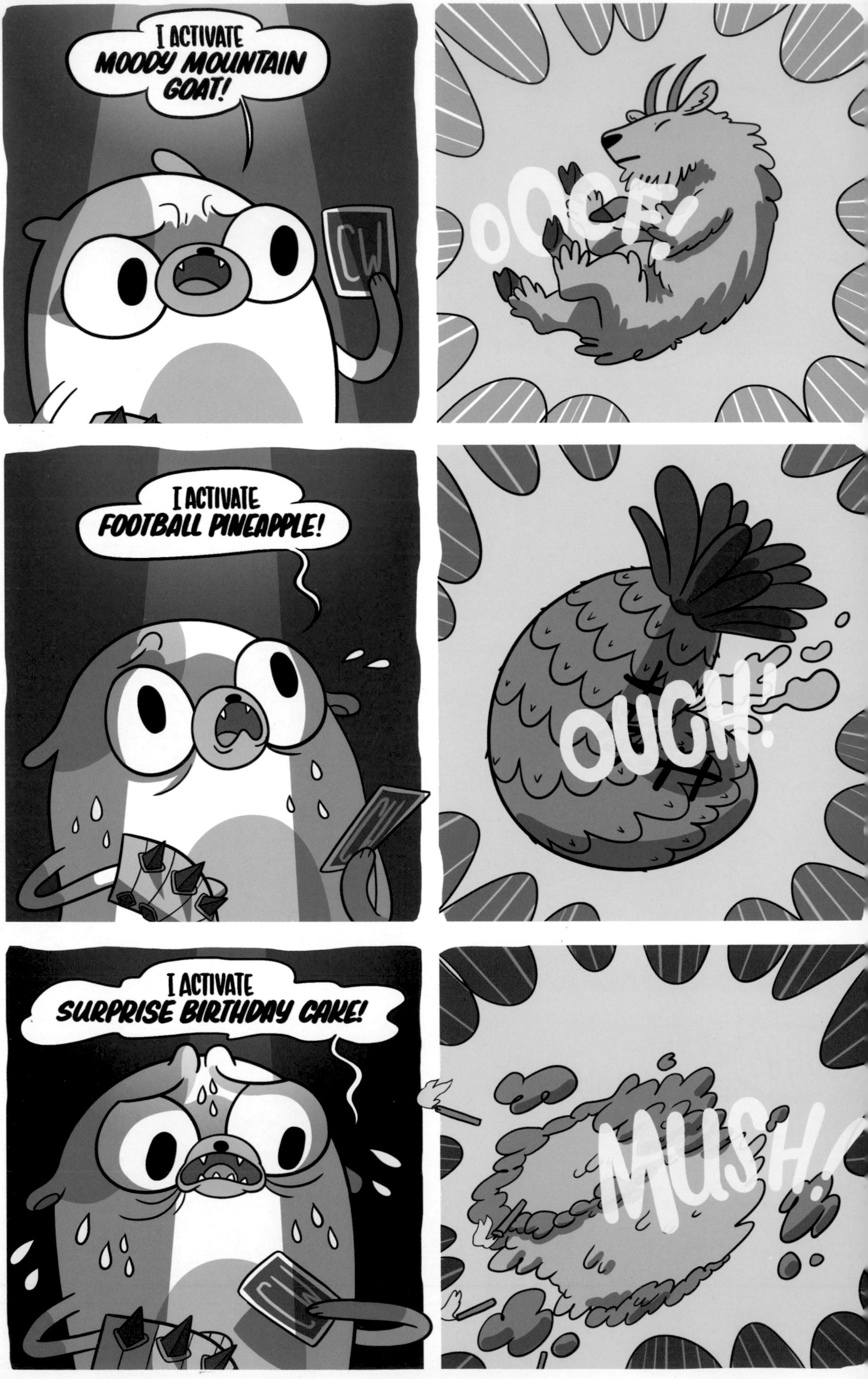

I ACTIVATE MOODY MOUNTAIN GOAT!
OOOF!
I ACTIVATE FOOTBALL PINEAPPLE!
OUCH!
I ACTIVATE SURPRISE BIRTHDAY CAKE!
MUSH!

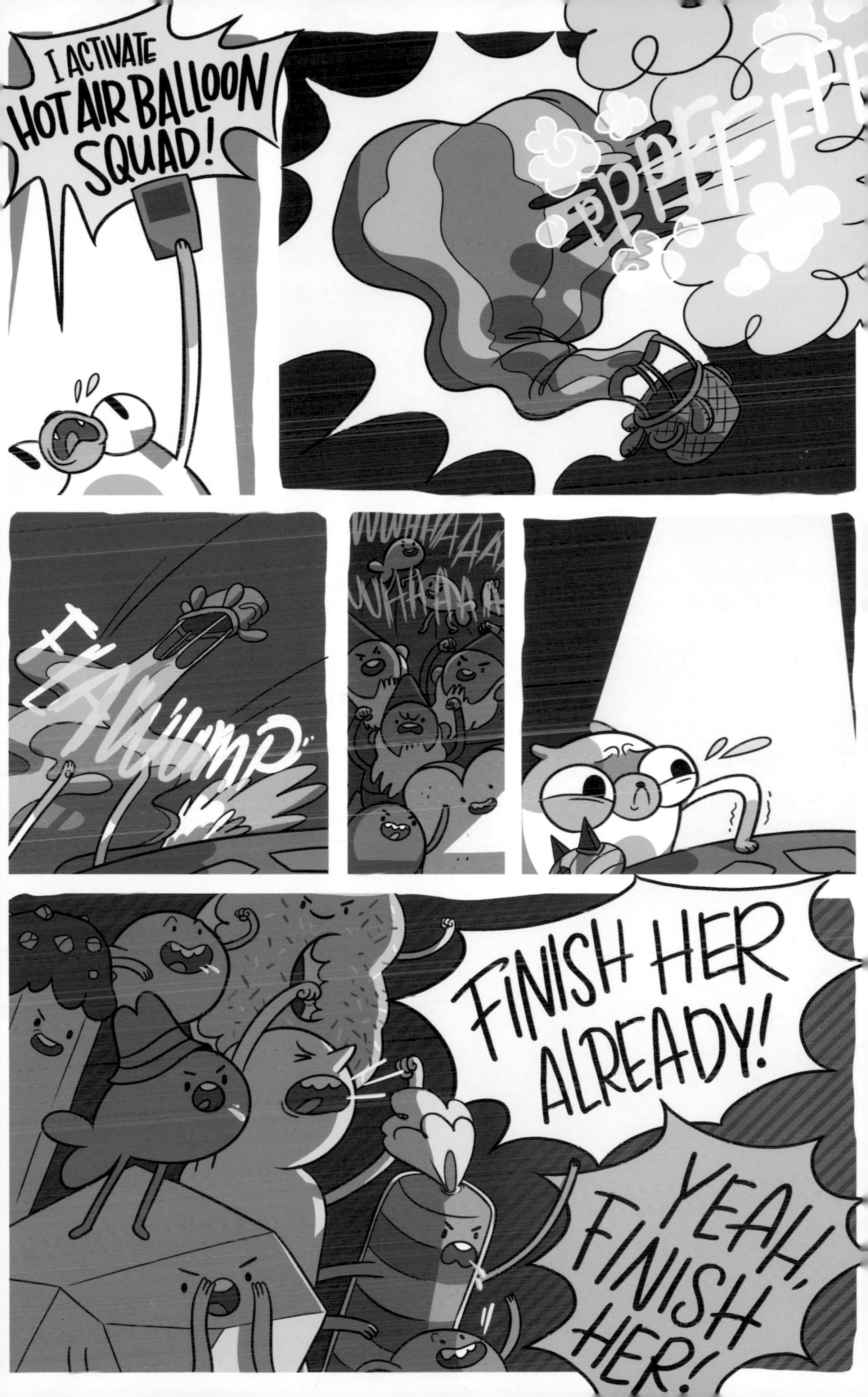
I ACTIVATE HOT AIR BALLOON SQUAD!
PPPFFFFF
FWUMP
WHHAAAA
WHHAAAA
FINISH HER ALREADY!
YEAH, FINISH HER!

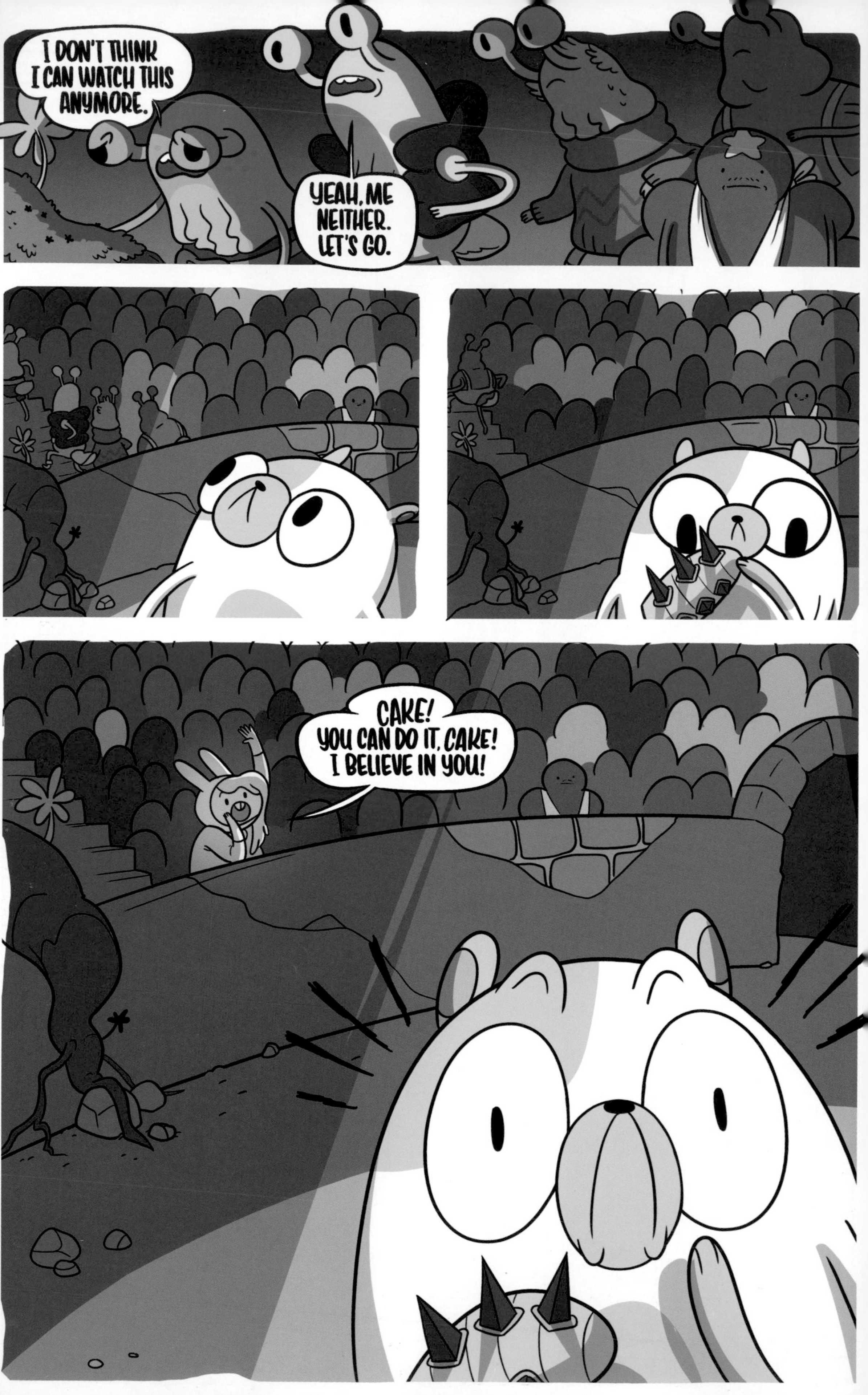
I DON'T THINK I CAN WATCH THIS ANYMORE.
YEAH, ME NEITHER. LET'S GO.
CAKE! YOU CAN DO IT, CAKE! I BELIEVE IN YOU!

OH, FIONNA, I'M SO SORRY. YOU'RE THE ONE WHO HAD FAITH IN ME ALL ALONG.

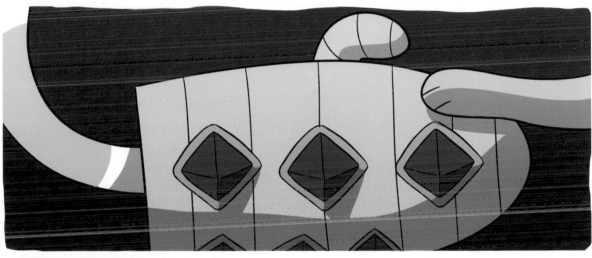

SNIFFLe

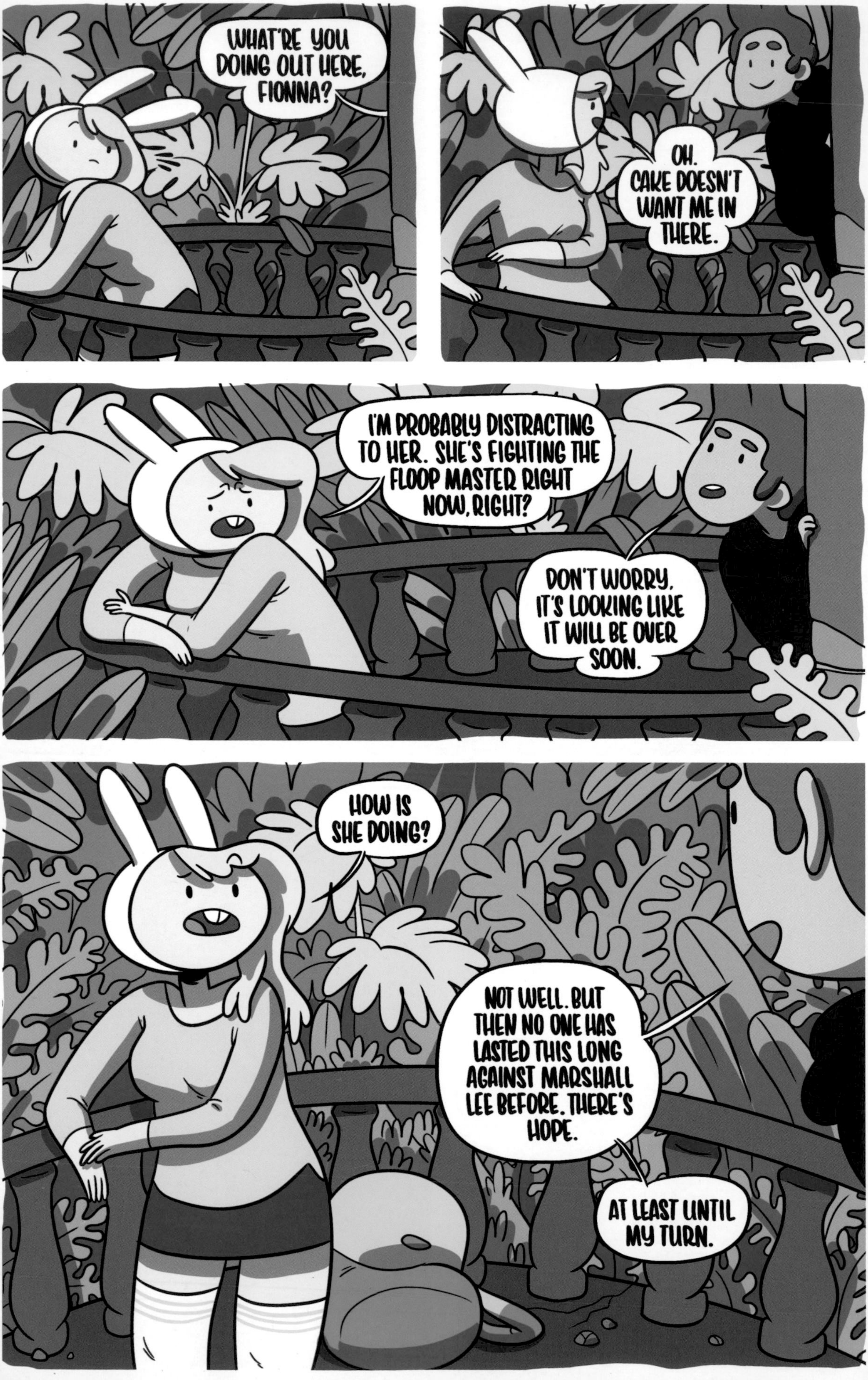
WHAT'RE YOU DOING OUT HERE, FIONNA?
OH. CAKE DOESN'T WANT ME IN THERE.
I'M PROBABLY DISTRACTING TO HER. SHE'S FIGHTING THE FLOOP MASTER RIGHT NOW, RIGHT?
DON'T WORRY, IT'S LOOKING LIKE IT WILL BE OVER SOON.
HOW IS SHE DOING?
NOT WELL. BUT THEN NO ONE HAS LASTED THIS LONG AGAINST MARSHALL LEE BEFORE. THERE'S HOPE.
AT LEAST UNTIL MY TURN.

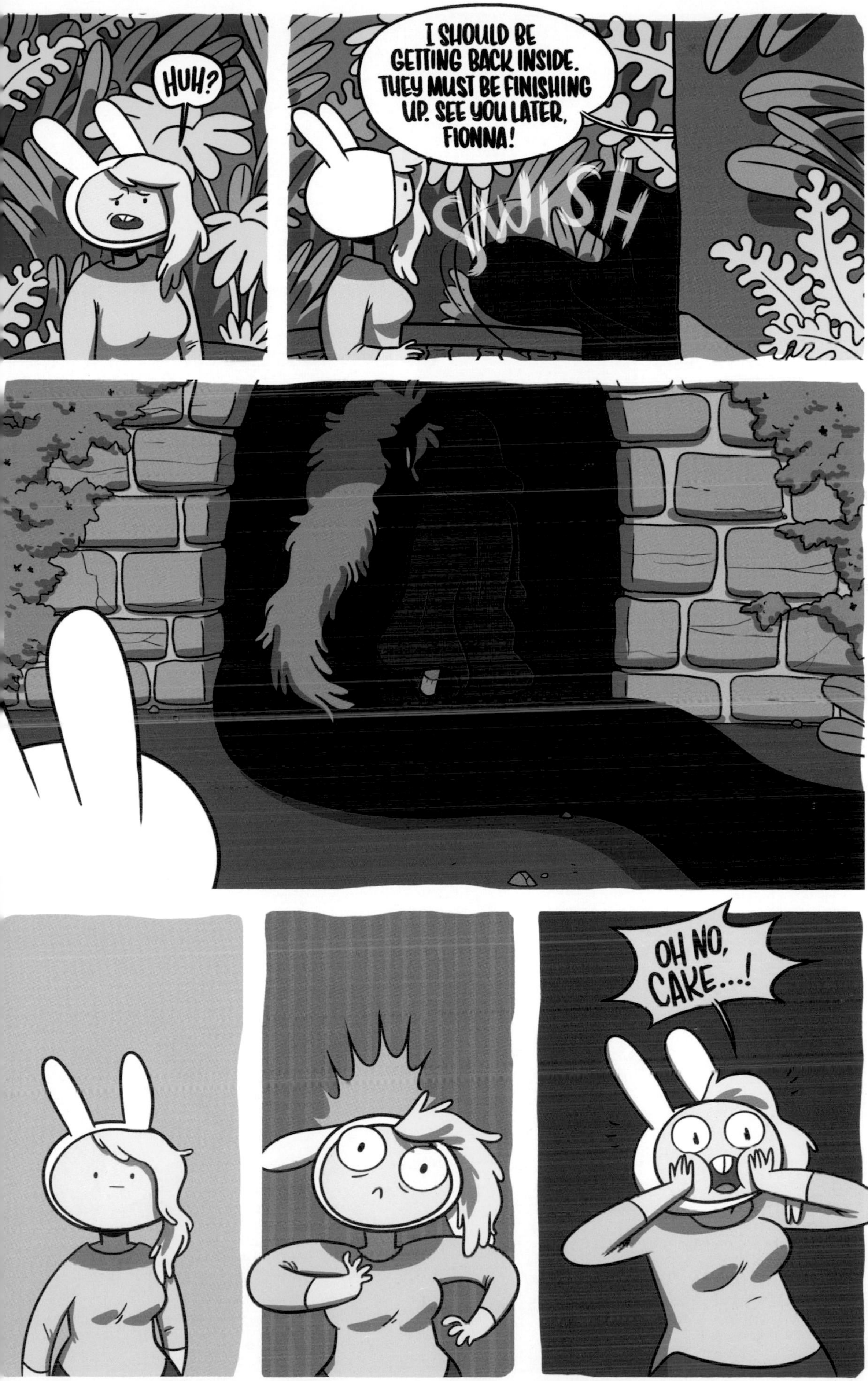
HUH?
I SHOULD BE GETTING BACK INSIDE. THEY MUST BE FINISHING UP. SEE YOU LATER, FIONNA!
SWISH
OH NO, CAKE...!

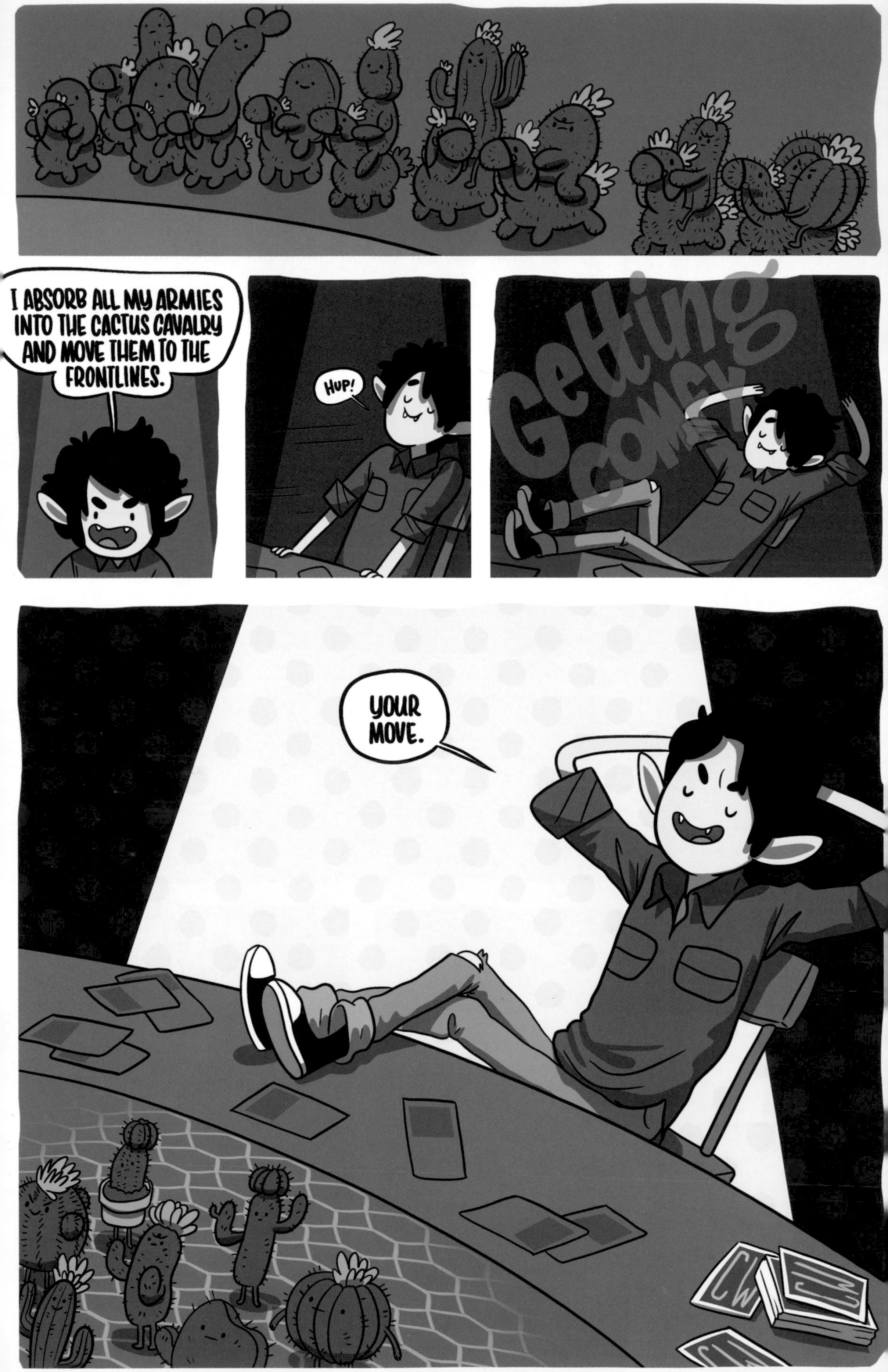

I ABSORB ALL MY ARMIES INTO THE CACTUS CAVALRY AND MOVE THEM TO THE FRONTLINES.
HUP!
Getting Comfy
YOUR MOVE.

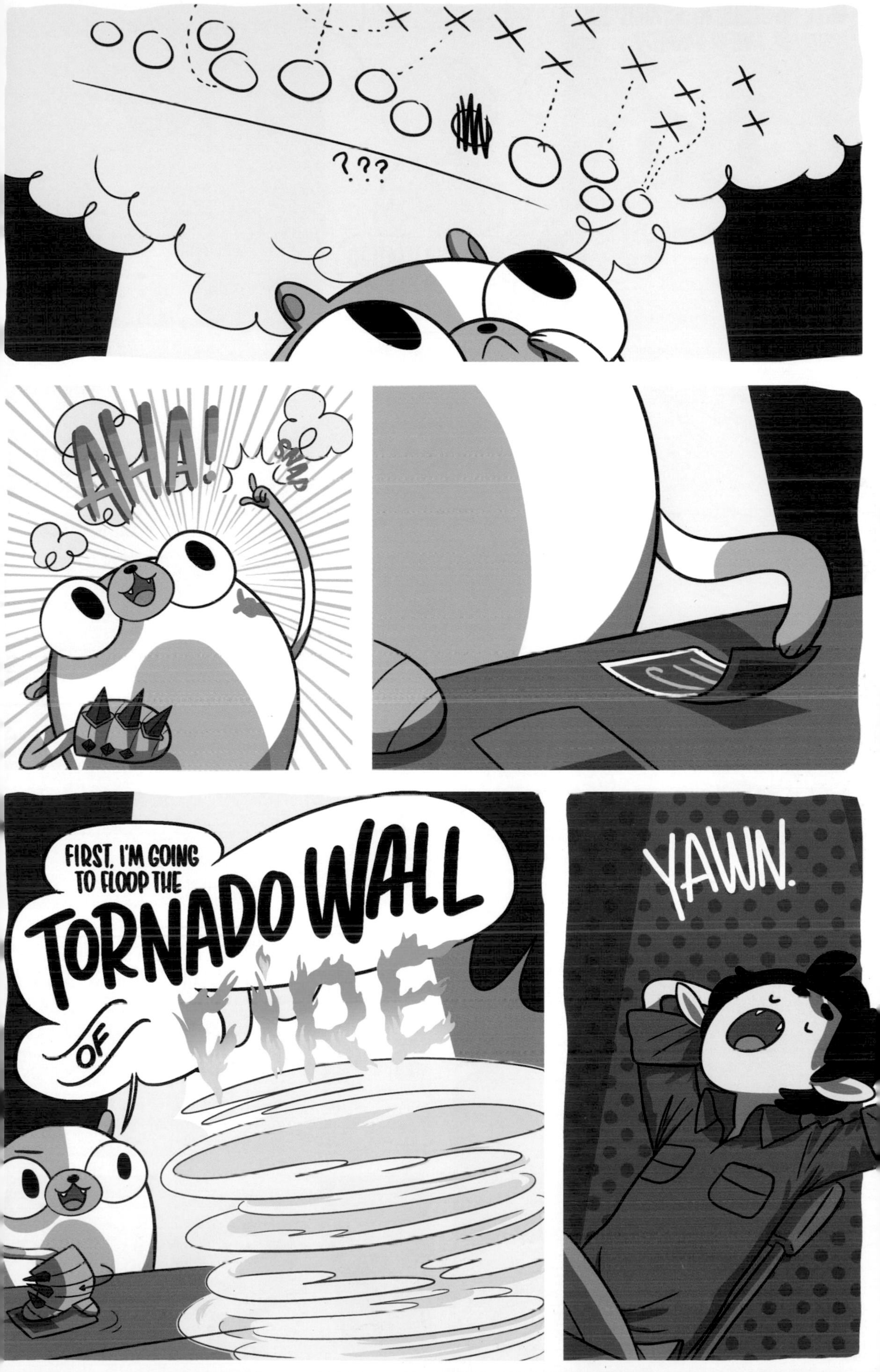
???
AHA!
SNAP
FIRST, I'M GOING TO FLOOP THE TORNADO WALL OF FIRE
YAWN.

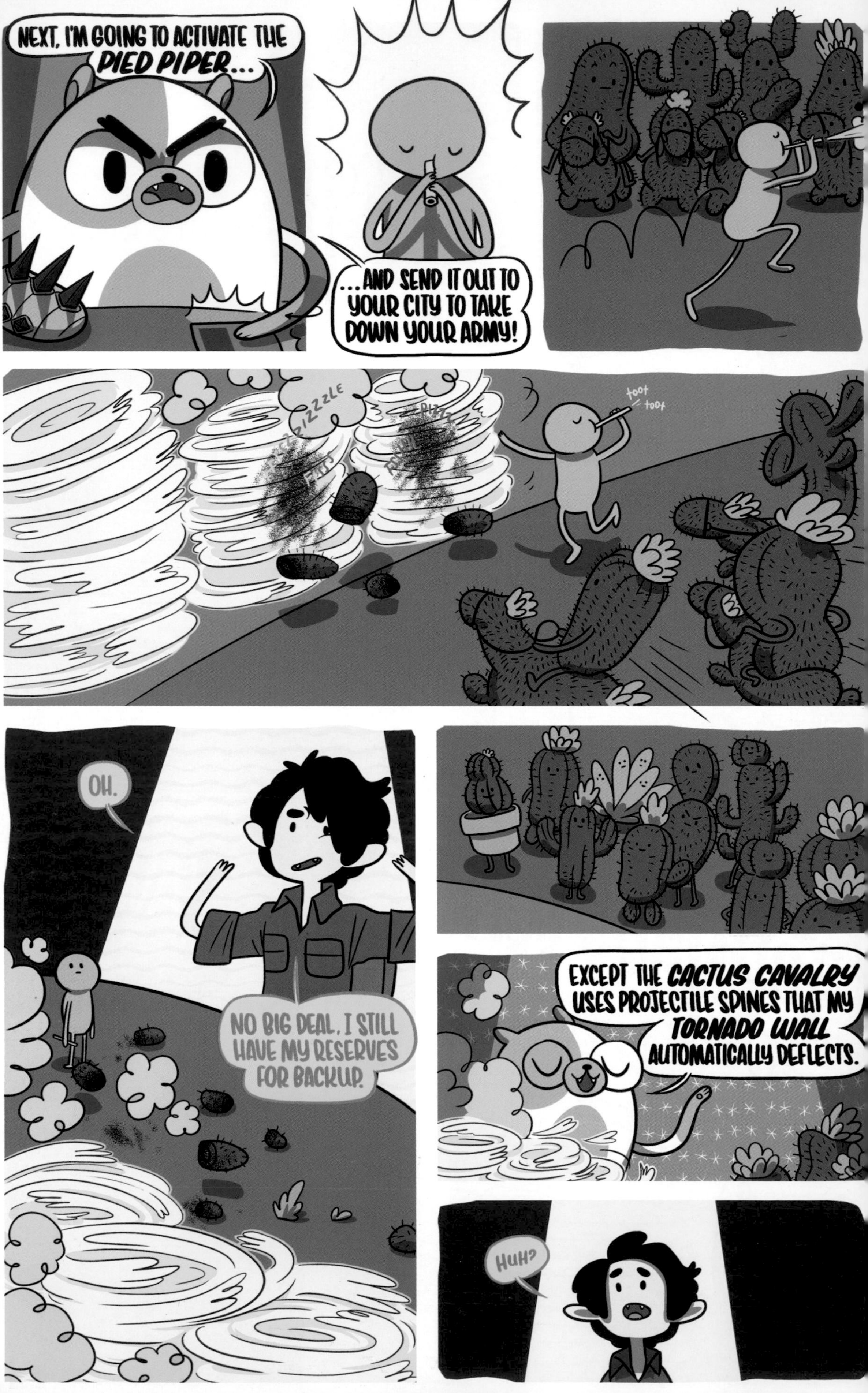

NEXT, I'M GOING TO ACTIVATE THE PIED PIPER...
...AND SEND IT OUT TO YOUR CITY TO TAKE DOWN YOUR ARMY!
toot toot
OH.
NO BIG DEAL, I STILL HAVE MY RESERVES FOR BACKUP.
EXCEPT THE CACTUS CAVALRY USES PROJECTILE SPINES THAT MY TORNADO WALL AUTOMATICALLY DEFLECTS.
HUH?

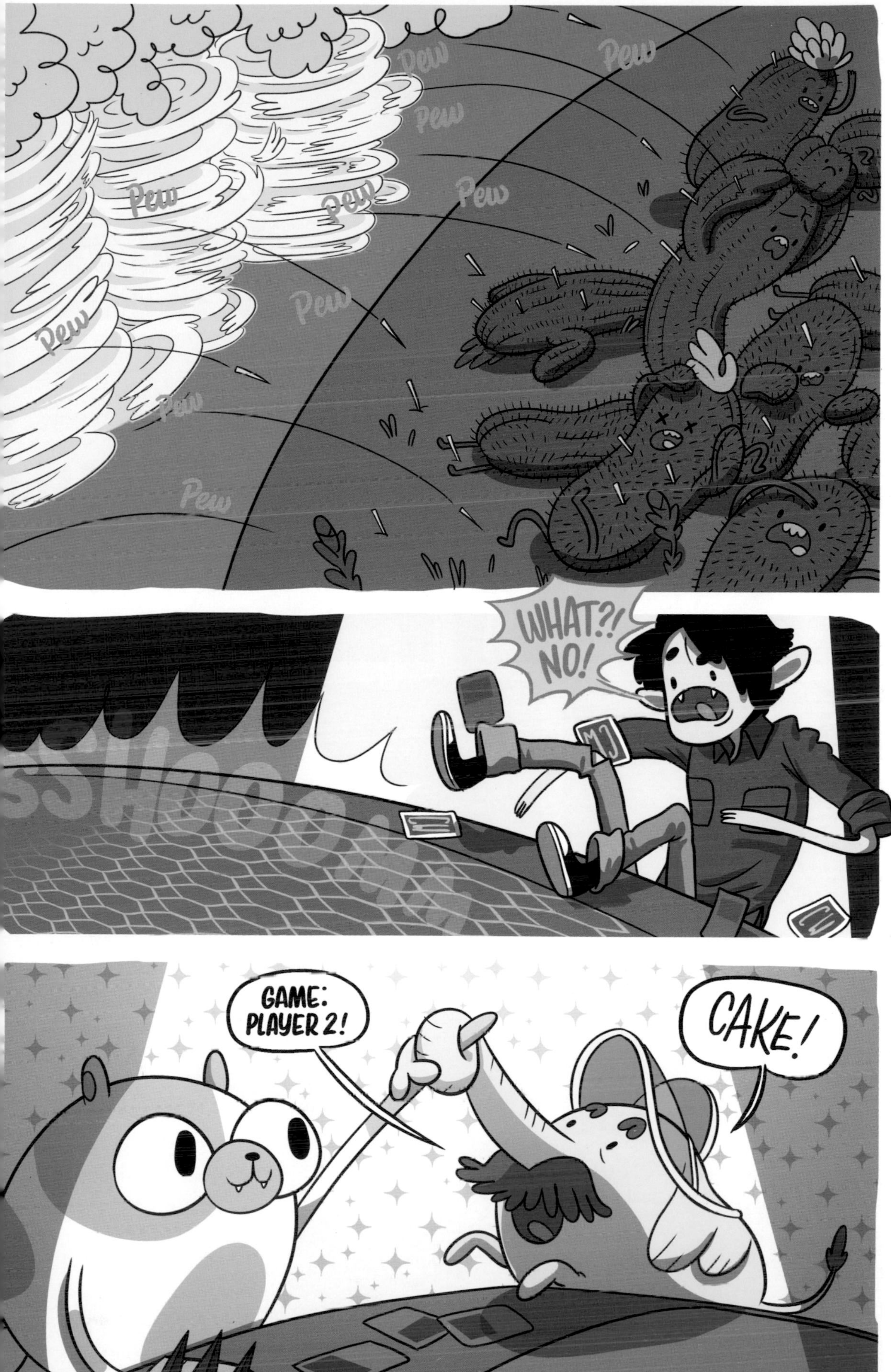
Pew
Pew
Pew
Pew
Pew
Pew
Pew
Pew
Pew
WHAT?!
NO!
SSHOOO
GAME: PLAYER 2!
CAKE!

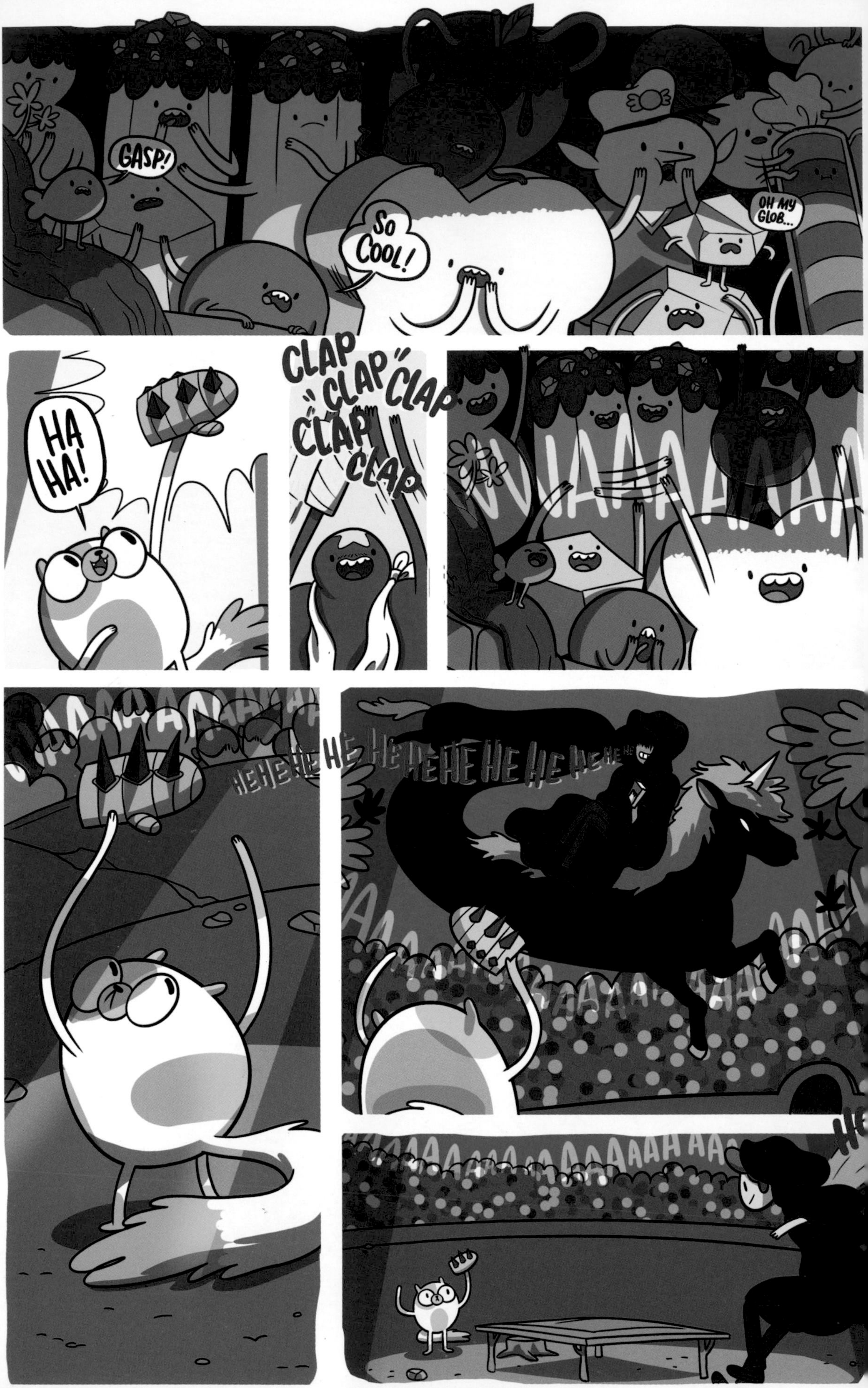
GASP!
SO COOL!
OH MY GLOB...
HA HA!
CLAP
CLAP
CLAP
CLAP
CLAP
HE HE HE HE HE HE HE HE HE HE

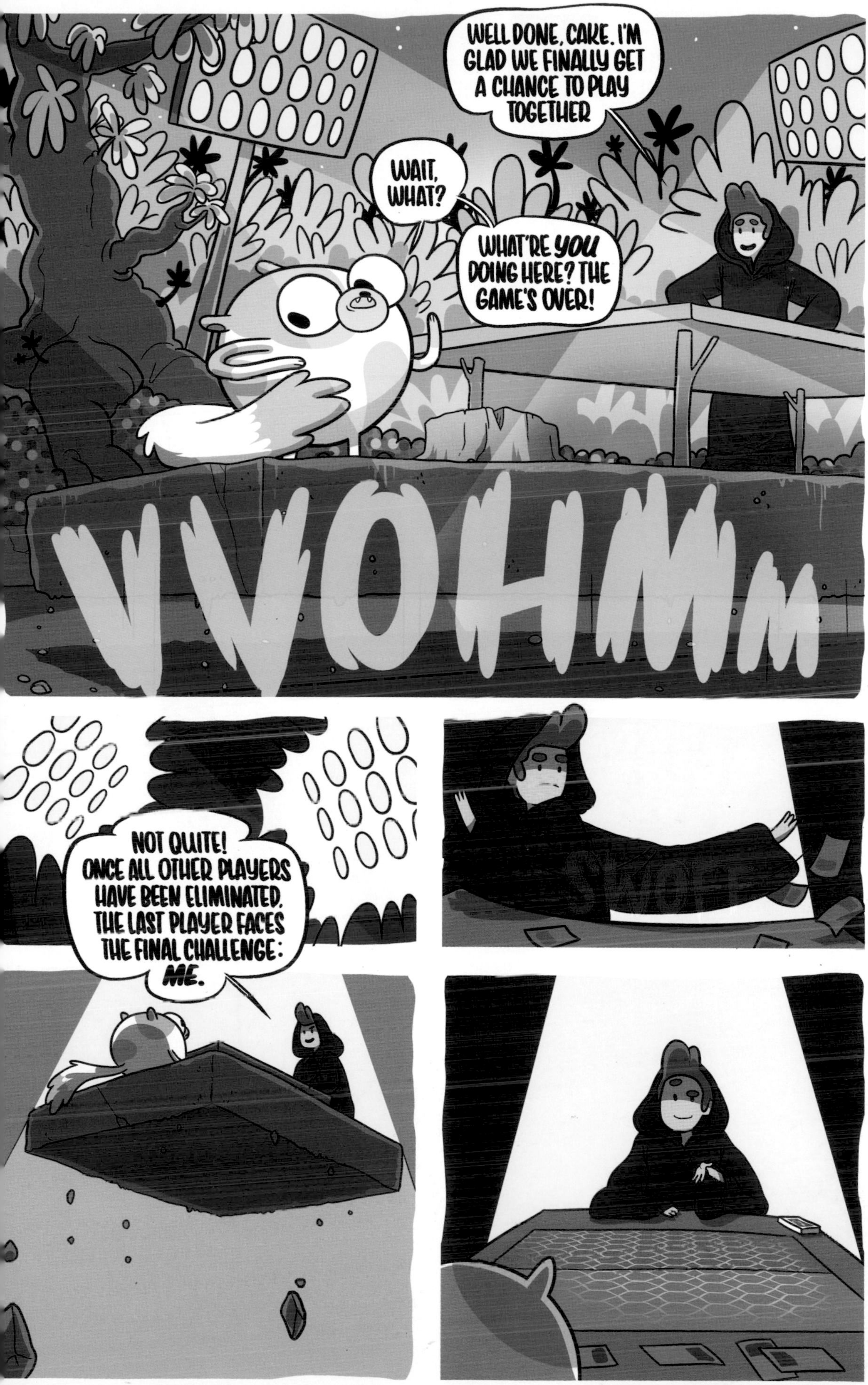
WELL DONE, CAKE. I'M GLAD WE FINALLY GET A CHANCE TO PLAY TOGETHER
WAIT, WHAT?
WHAT'RE YOU DOING HERE? THE GAME'S OVER!
VVOHMM
NOT QUITE! ONCE ALL OTHER PLAYERS HAVE BEEN ELIMINATED, THE LAST PLAYER FACES THE FINAL CHALLENGE: ME.
SWOFF

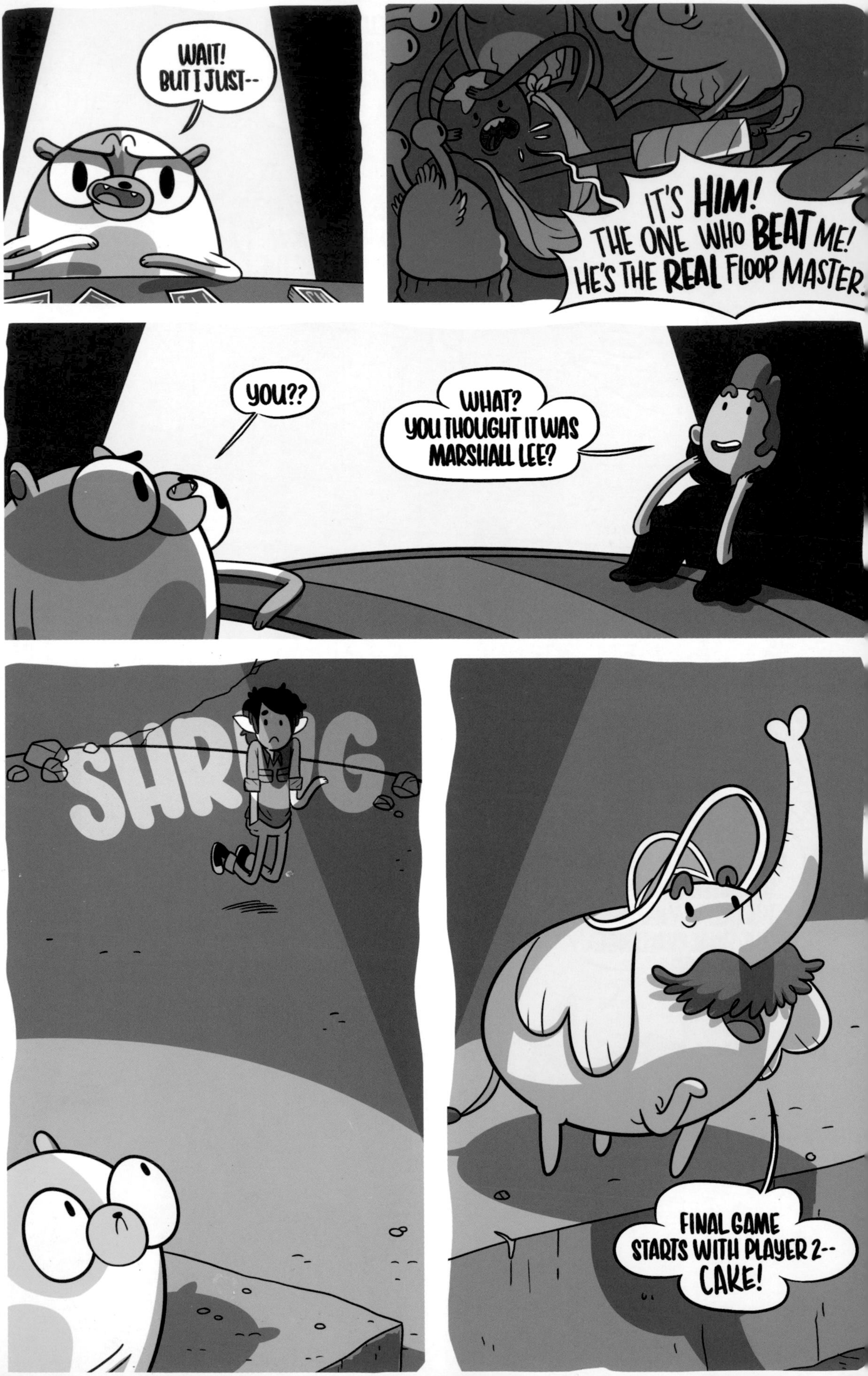
WAIT!
BUT I JUST--
IT'S HIM!
THE ONE WHO BEAT ME!
HE'S THE REAL FLOOP MASTER.
YOU??
WHAT?
YOU THOUGHT IT WAS
MARSHALL LEE?
SHRUG
FINAL GAME
STARTS WITH PLAYER 2--
CAKE!

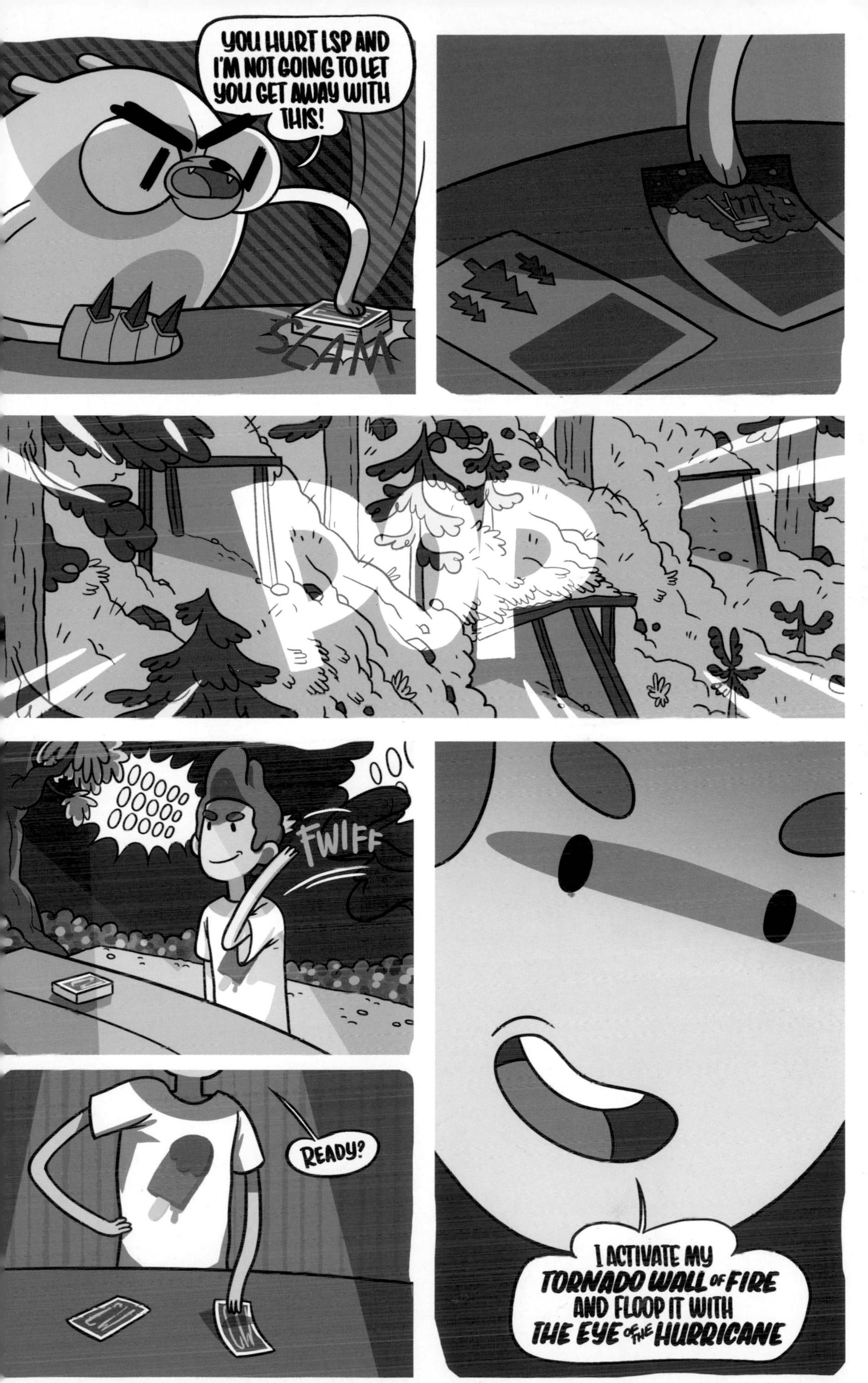
YOU HURT LSP AND I'M NOT GOING TO LET YOU GET AWAY WITH THIS!
SLAM
POP
OOOOOO OOOOOO OOOOOO
OOO
FWIFF
READY?
I ACTIVATE MY TORNADO WALL OF FIRE AND FLOOP IT WITH THE EYE OF THE HURRICANE

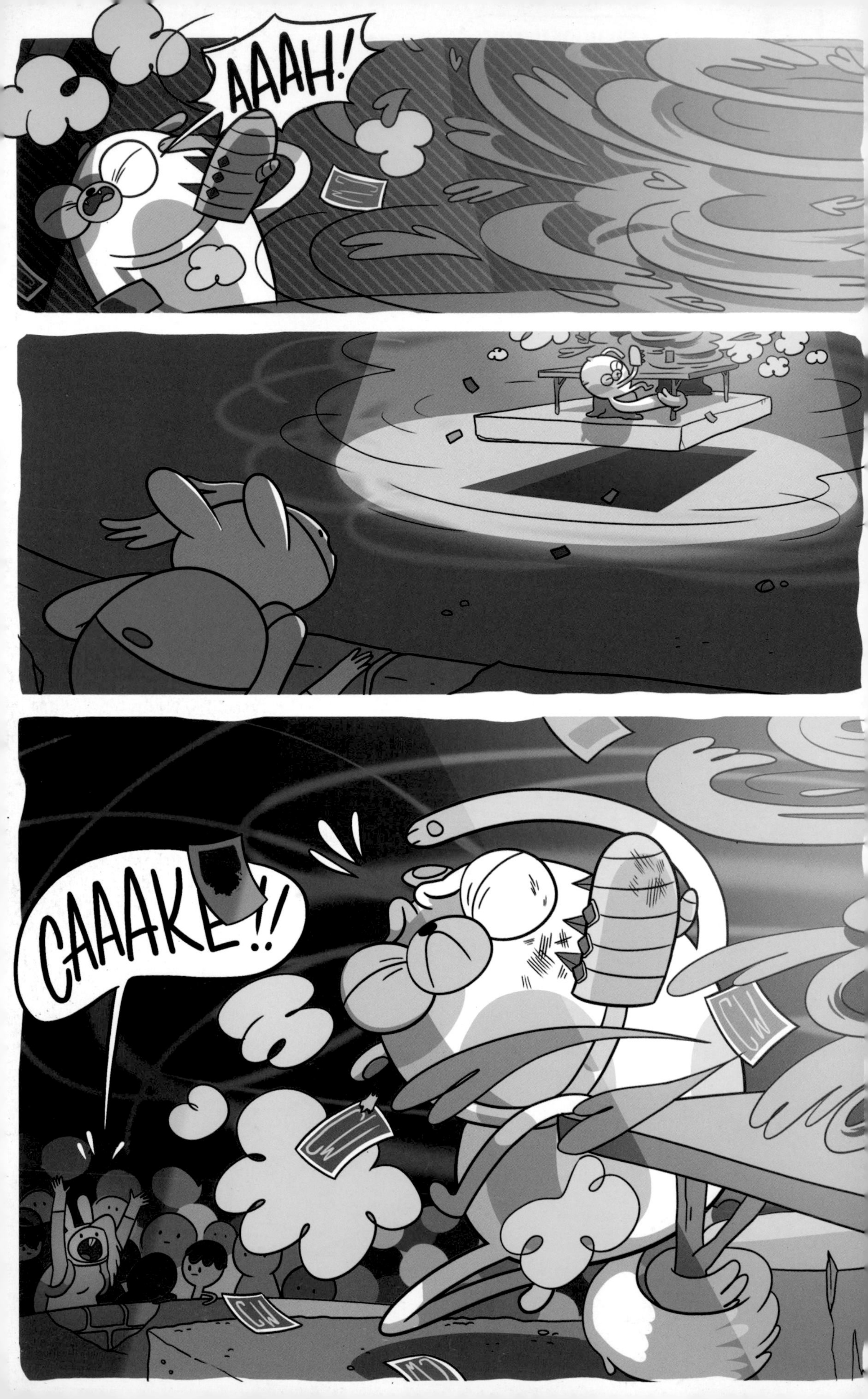
AAAH!
CAAAKE!!

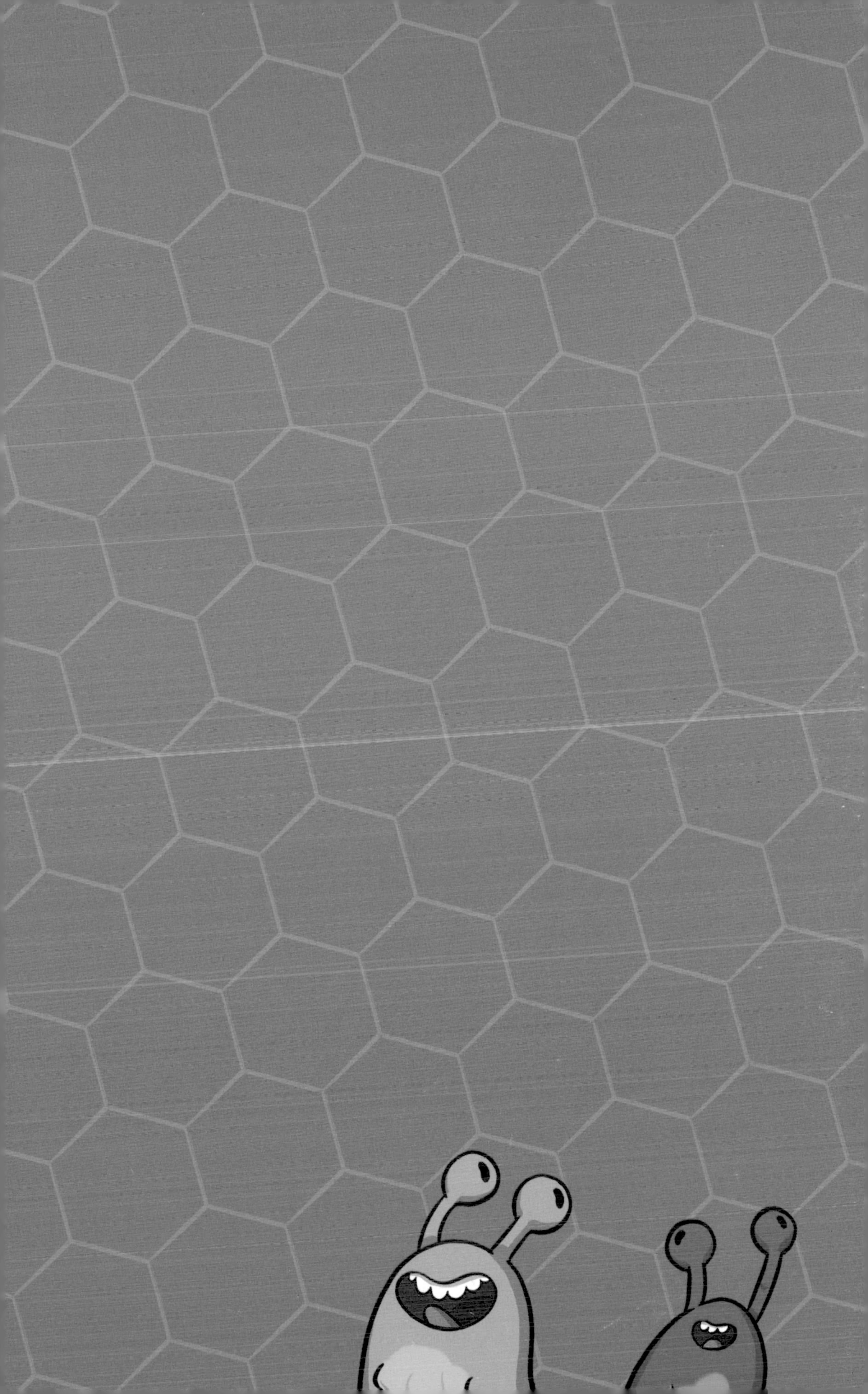

chapter six

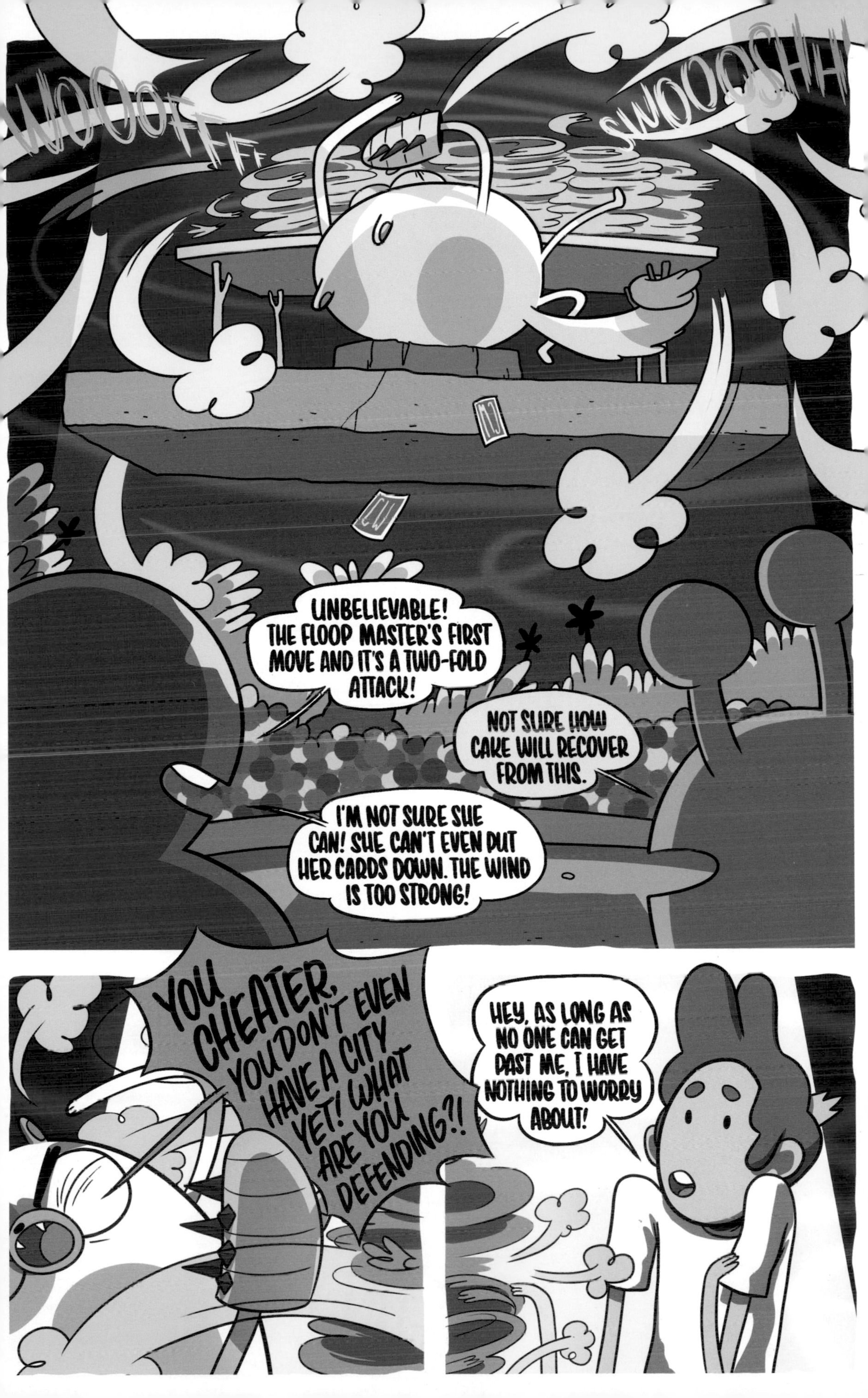
WOOOFFFF
SWOOOSHH
UNBELIEVABLE! THE FLOOP MASTER'S FIRST MOVE AND IT'S A TWO-FOLD ATTACK!
NOT SURE HOW CAKE WILL RECOVER FROM THIS.
I'M NOT SURE SHE CAN! SHE CAN'T EVEN PUT HER CARDS DOWN. THE WIND IS TOO STRONG!
YOU CHEATER, YOU DON'T EVEN HAVE A CITY YET! WHAT ARE YOU DEFENDING?!
HEY, AS LONG AS NO ONE CAN GET PAST ME, I HAVE NOTHING TO WORRY ABOUT!

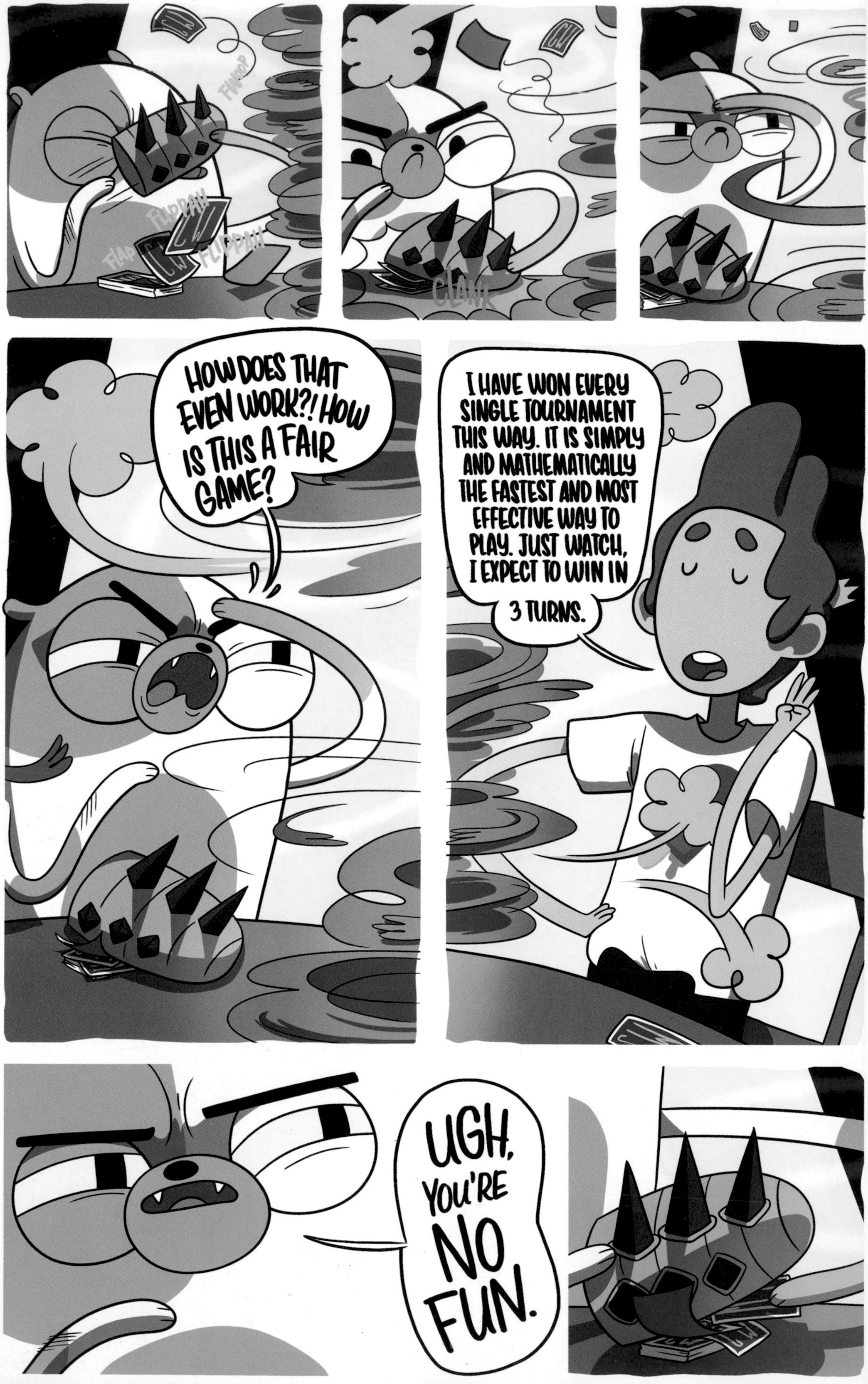
FWOOP
FLIPPAH
FLAP
FLIPPAH
CLANK
HOW DOES THAT EVEN WORK?! HOW IS THIS A FAIR GAME?
I HAVE WON EVERY SINGLE TOURNAMENT THIS WAY. IT IS SIMPLY AND MATHEMATICALLY THE FASTEST AND MOST EFFECTIVE WAY TO PLAY. JUST WATCH, I EXPECT TO WIN IN
3 TURNS.
UGH, YOU'RE NO FUN.

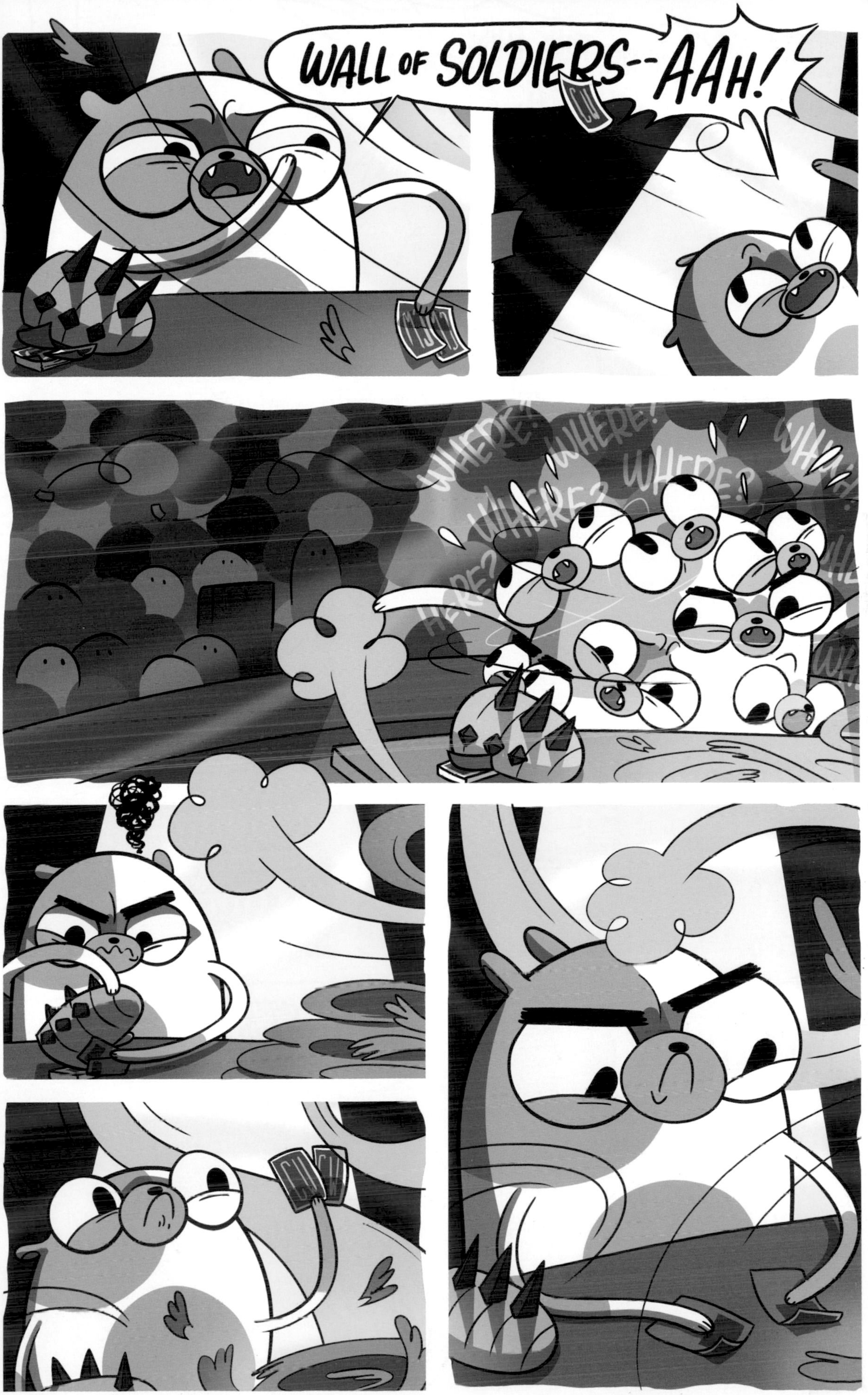
WALL OF SOLDIERS--AAH!
WHERE?
WHERE!
WHERE?
WHERE?
WHERE?

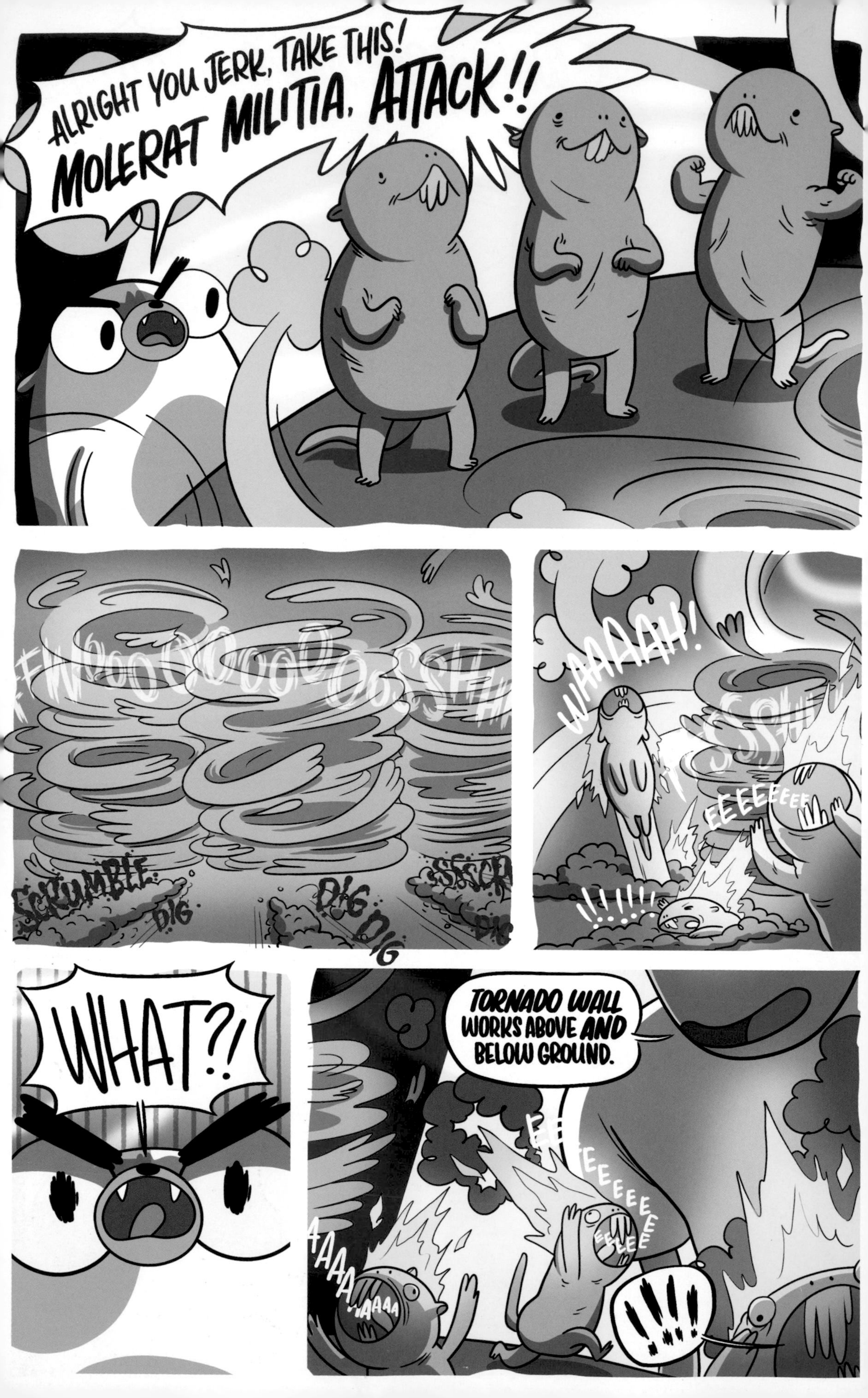
ALRIGHT YOU JERK, TAKE THIS!
MOLERAT MILITIA, ATTACK!!
SCRUMBLE
DIG
DIG DIG
WAAAAH!
EEEEEEEE
!!!!!!
WHAT?!
TORNADO WALL WORKS ABOVE AND BELOW GROUND.
!!!

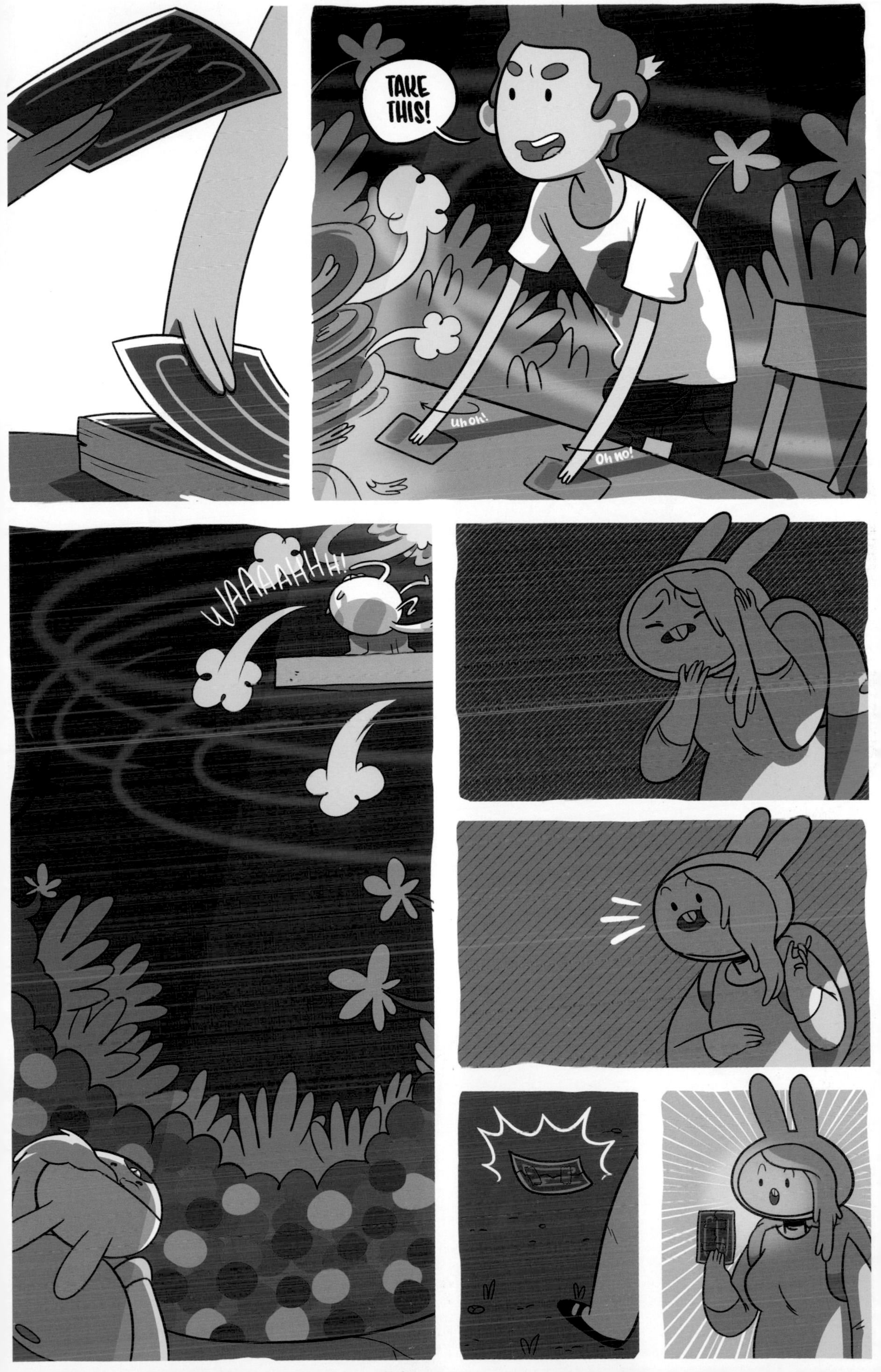
TAKE THIS!
Uh oh!
Oh no!
WAAAAAHHH!

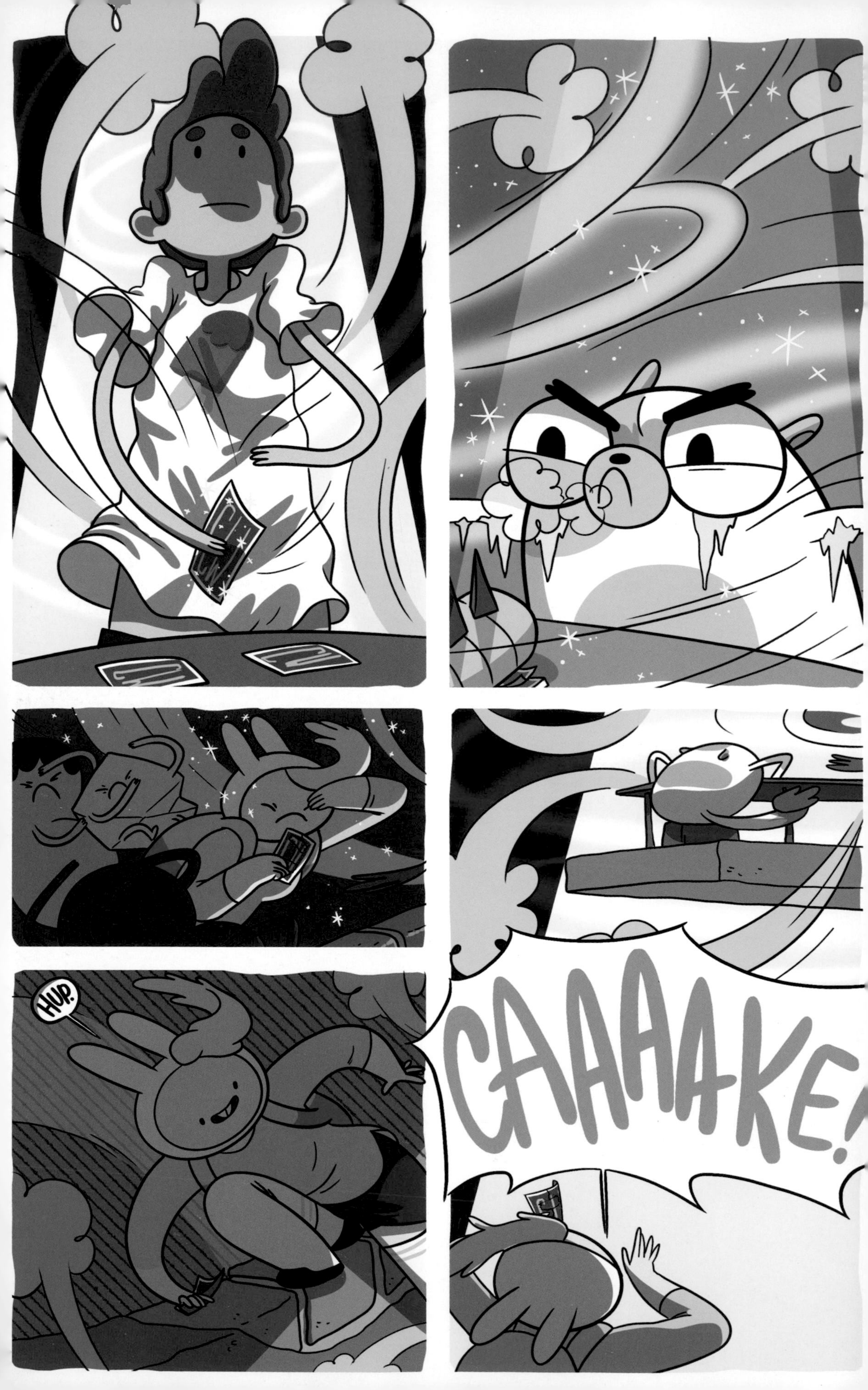
HUP.
CAAAAKE!

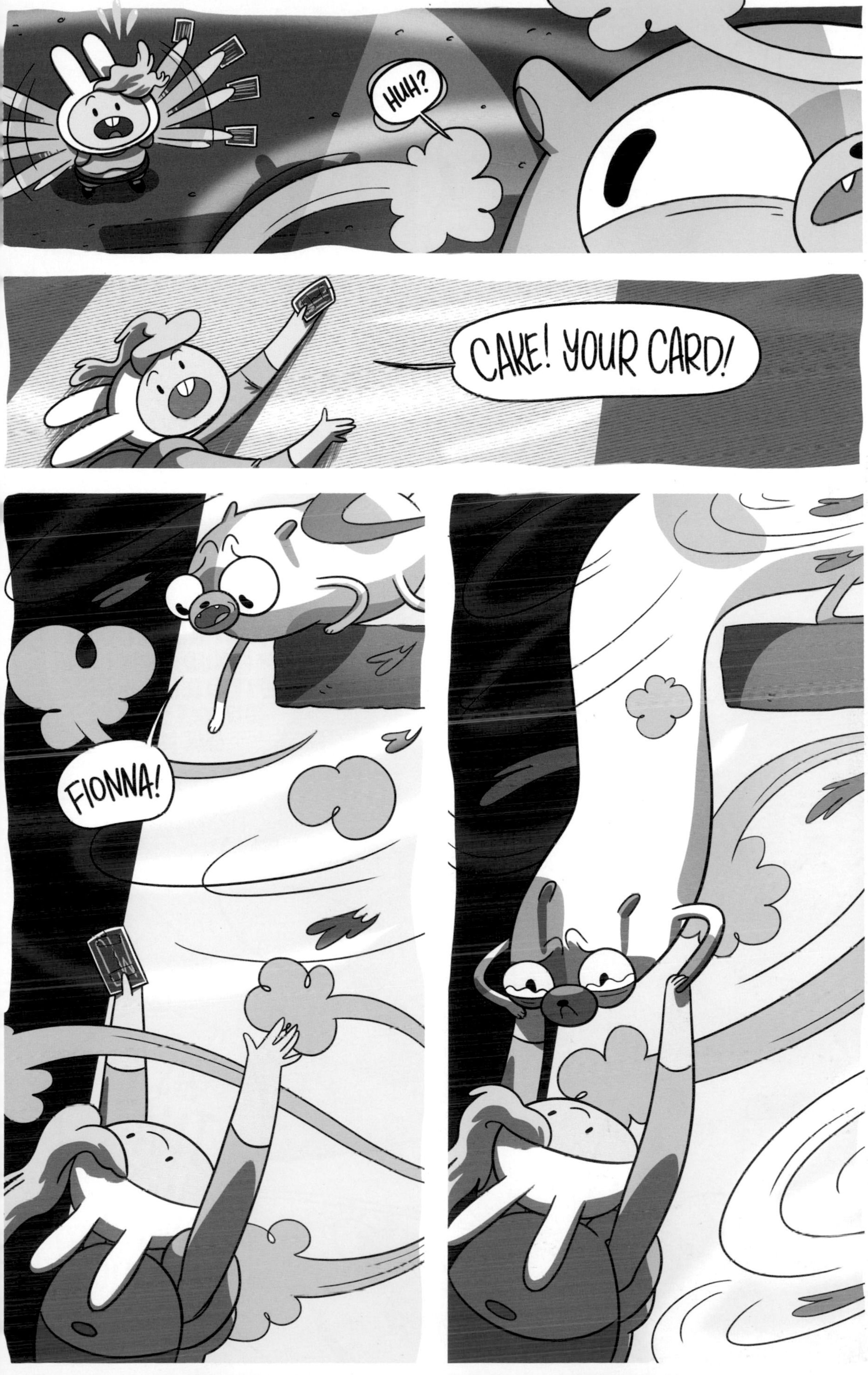
HUH?
CAKE! YOUR CARD!
FIONNA!

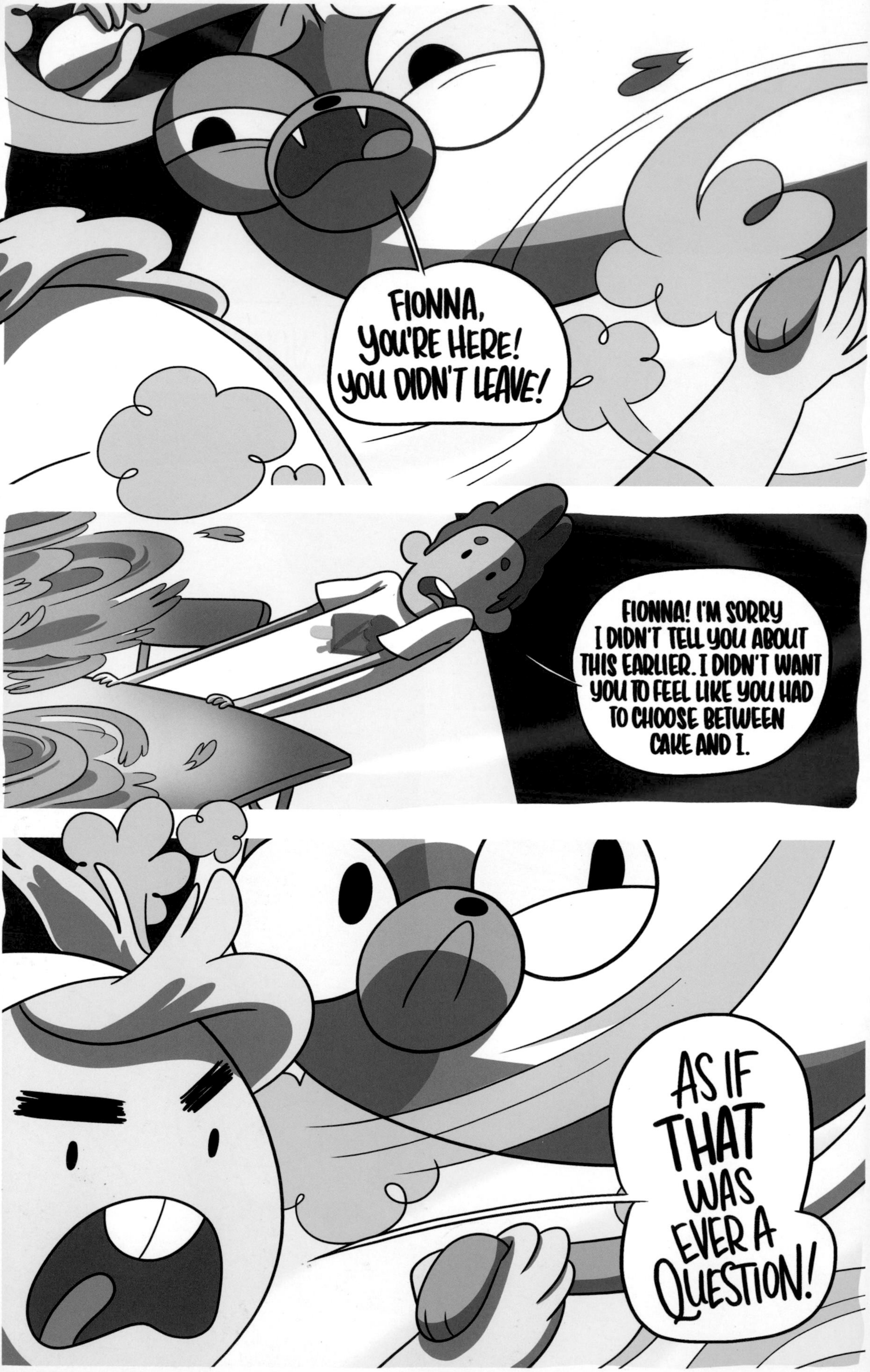
FIONNA, YOU'RE HERE! YOU DIDN'T LEAVE!
FIONNA! I'M SORRY I DIDN'T TELL YOU ABOUT THIS EARLIER. I DIDN'T WANT YOU TO FEEL LIKE YOU HAD TO CHOOSE BETWEEN CAKE AND I.
AS IF THAT WAS EVER A QUESTION!

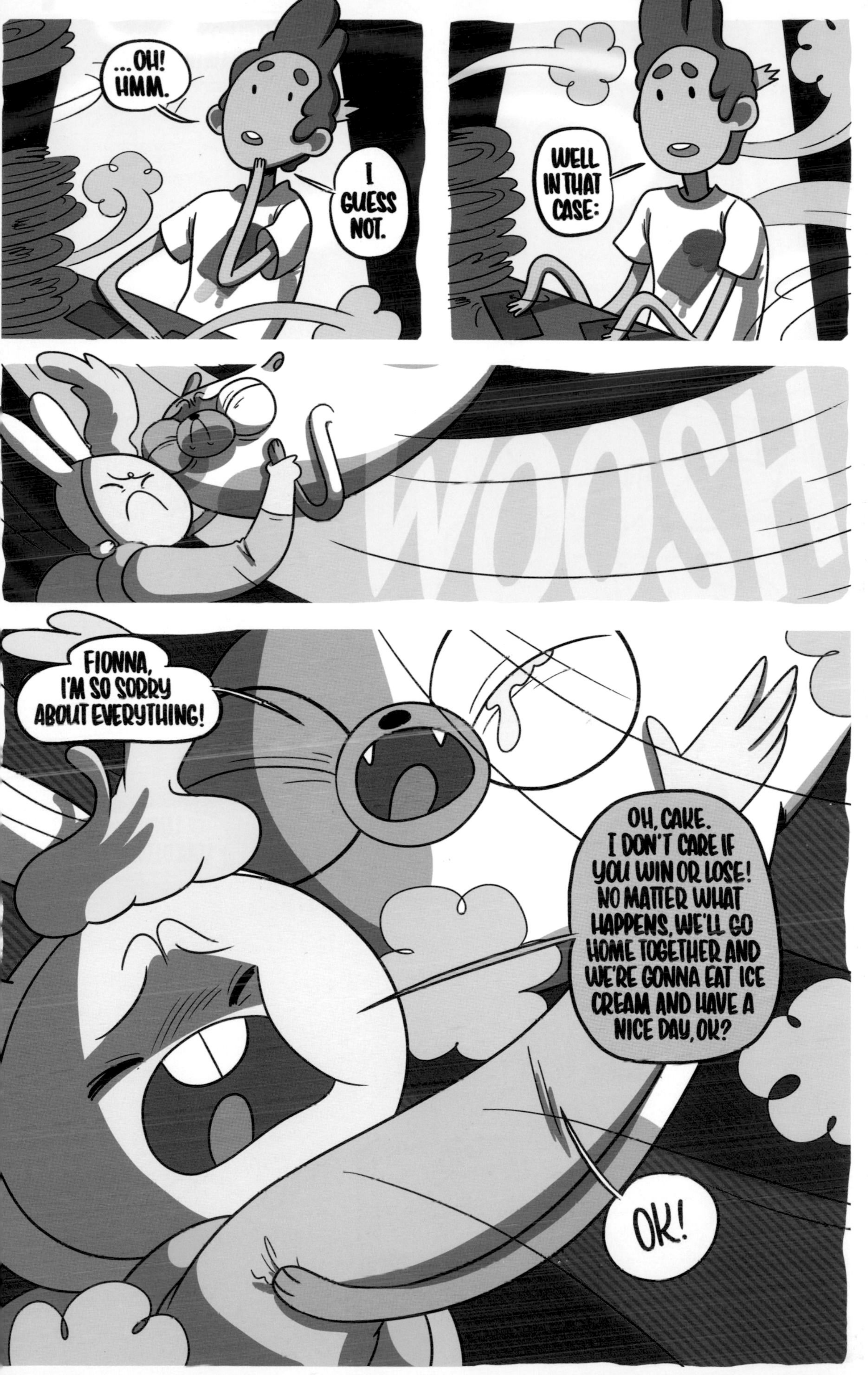
...OH! HMM.
I GUESS NOT.
WELL IN THAT CASE:
WOOSH!
FIONNA, I'M SO SORRY ABOUT EVERYTHING!
OH, CAKE. I DON'T CARE IF YOU WIN OR LOSE! NO MATTER WHAT HAPPENS, WE'LL GO HOME TOGETHER AND WE'RE GONNA EAT ICE CREAM AND HAVE A NICE DAY, OK?
OK!

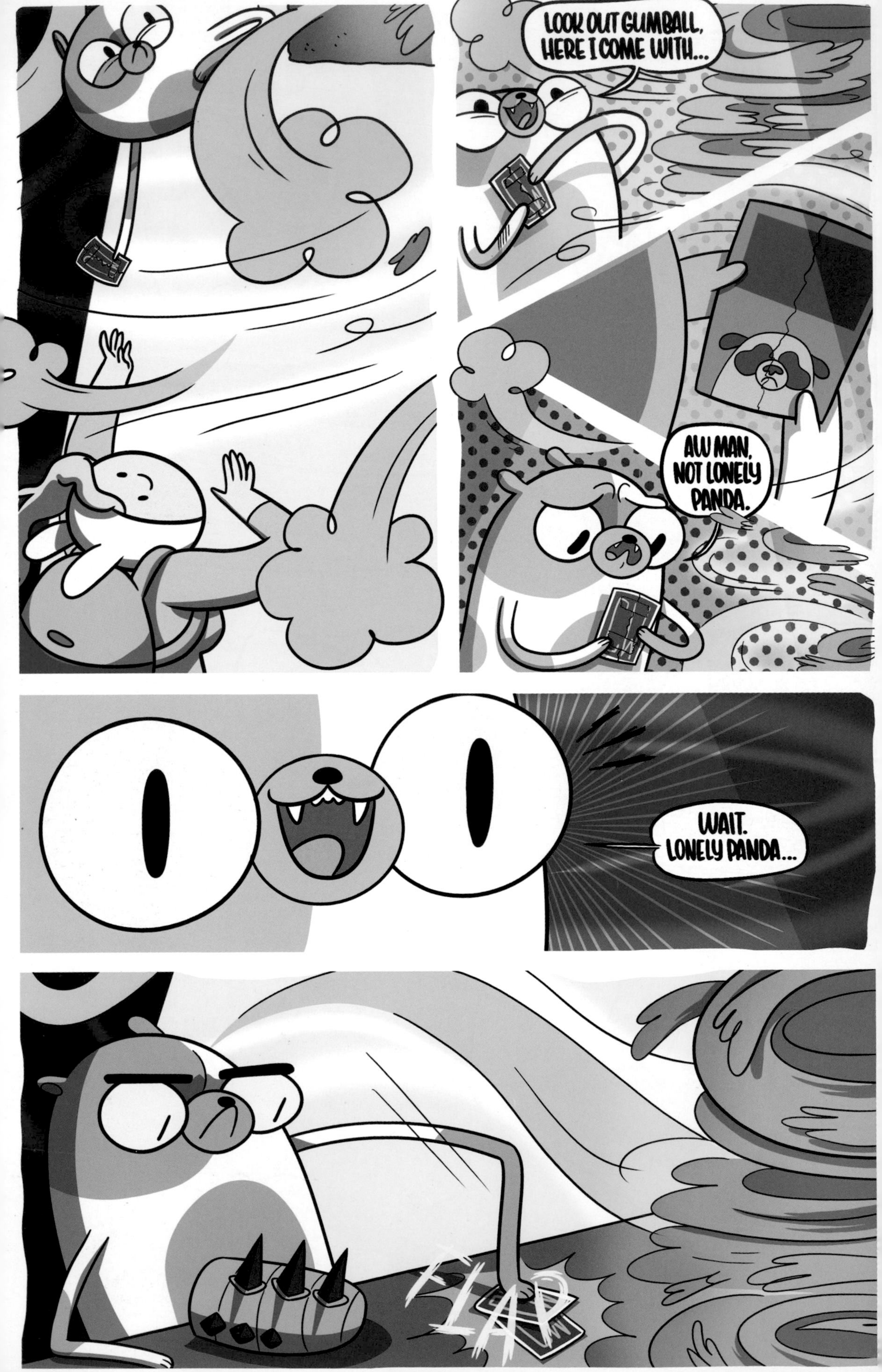
LOOK OUT GUMBALL, HERE I COME WITH...
AW MAN, NOT LONELY PANDA.
WAIT. LONELY PANDA...
FLAP

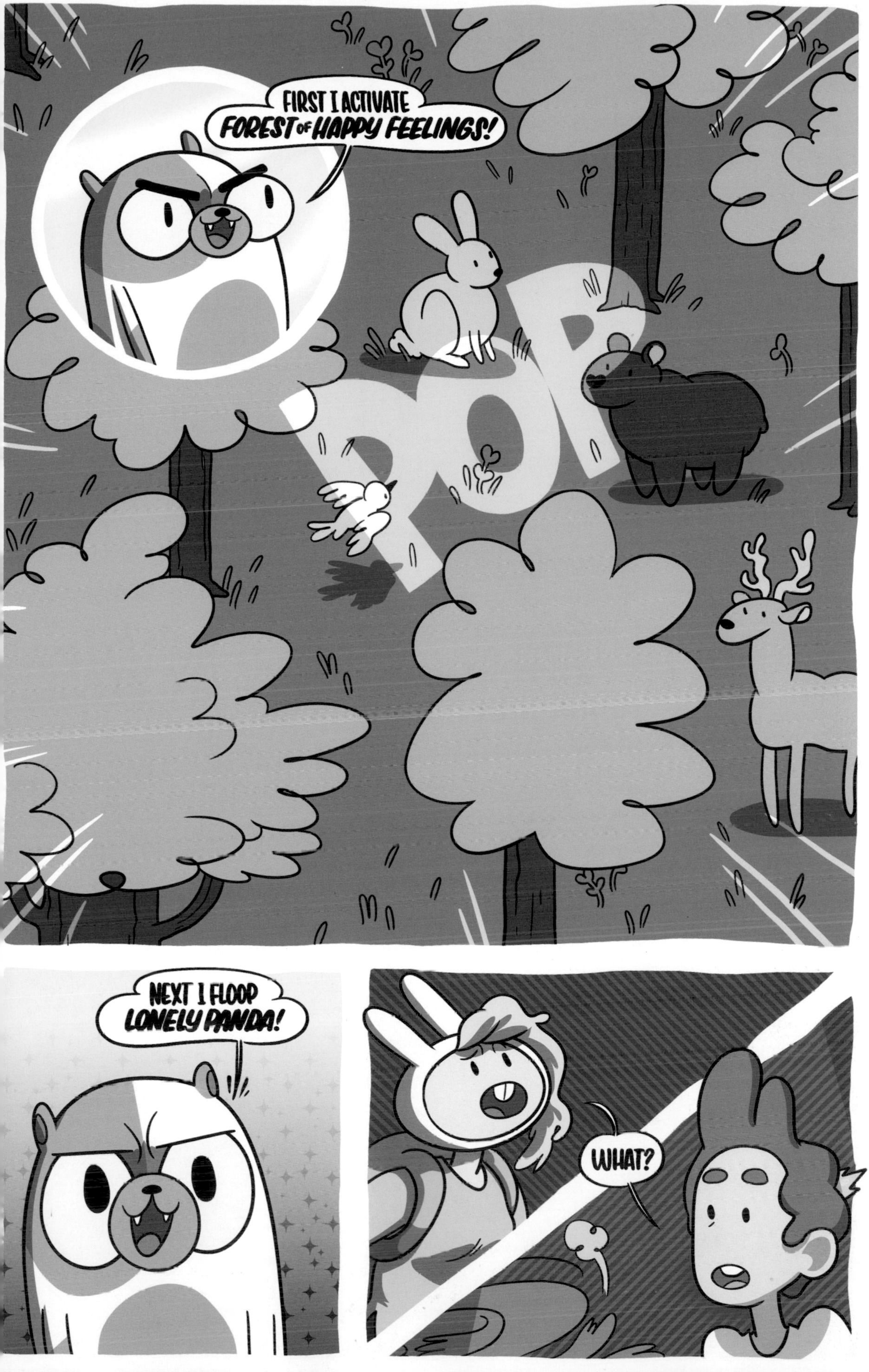
FIRST I ACTIVATE FOREST of HAPPY FEELINGS!
POP
NEXT I FLOOP LONELY PANDA!
WHAT?

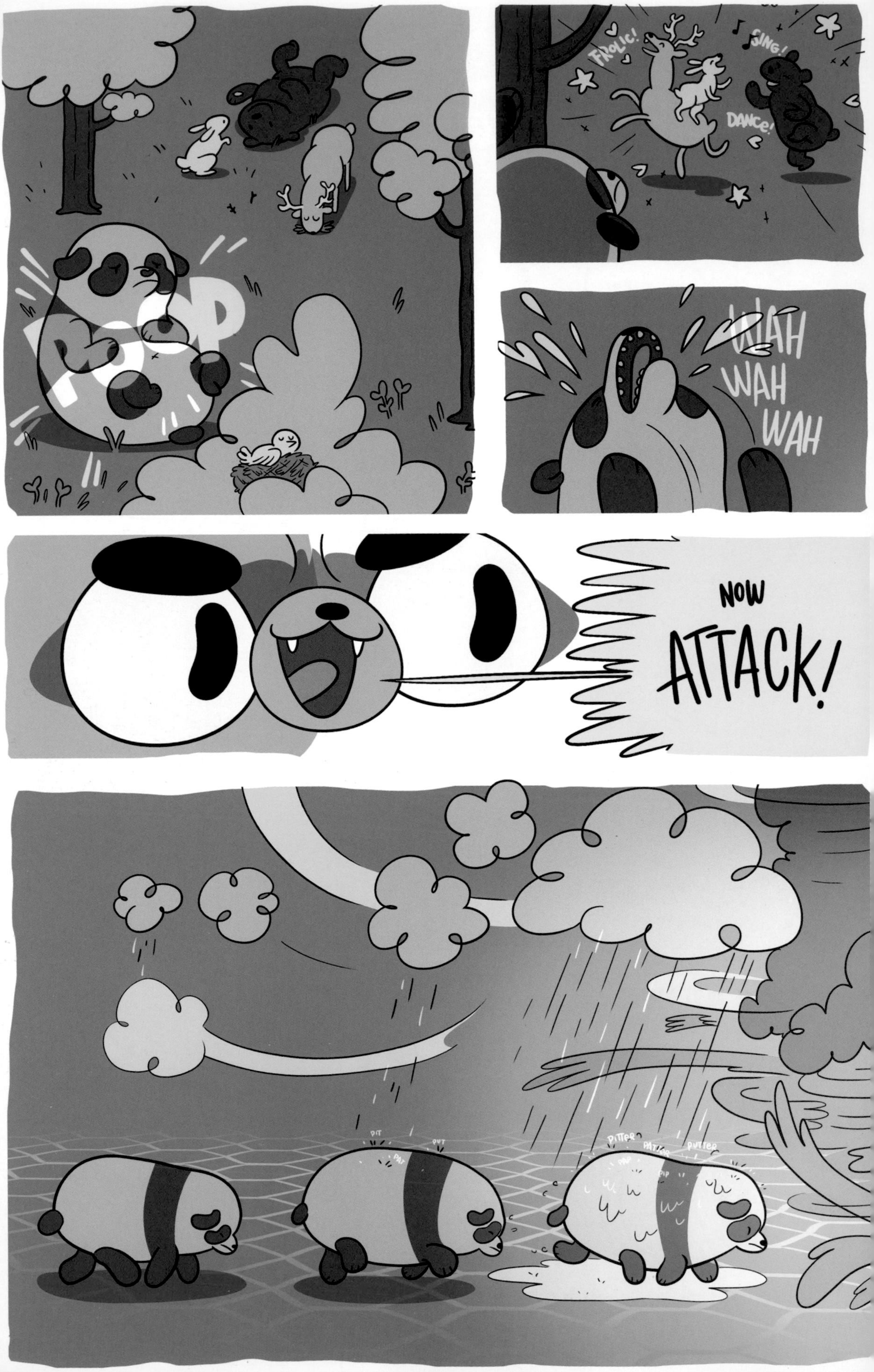
POOF
FROLIC!
SING!
DANCE!
WAH WAH WAH
NOW ATTACK!
PIT
PAT
PUT
PITTER
PAP
PATTER
PIP
PUTTER

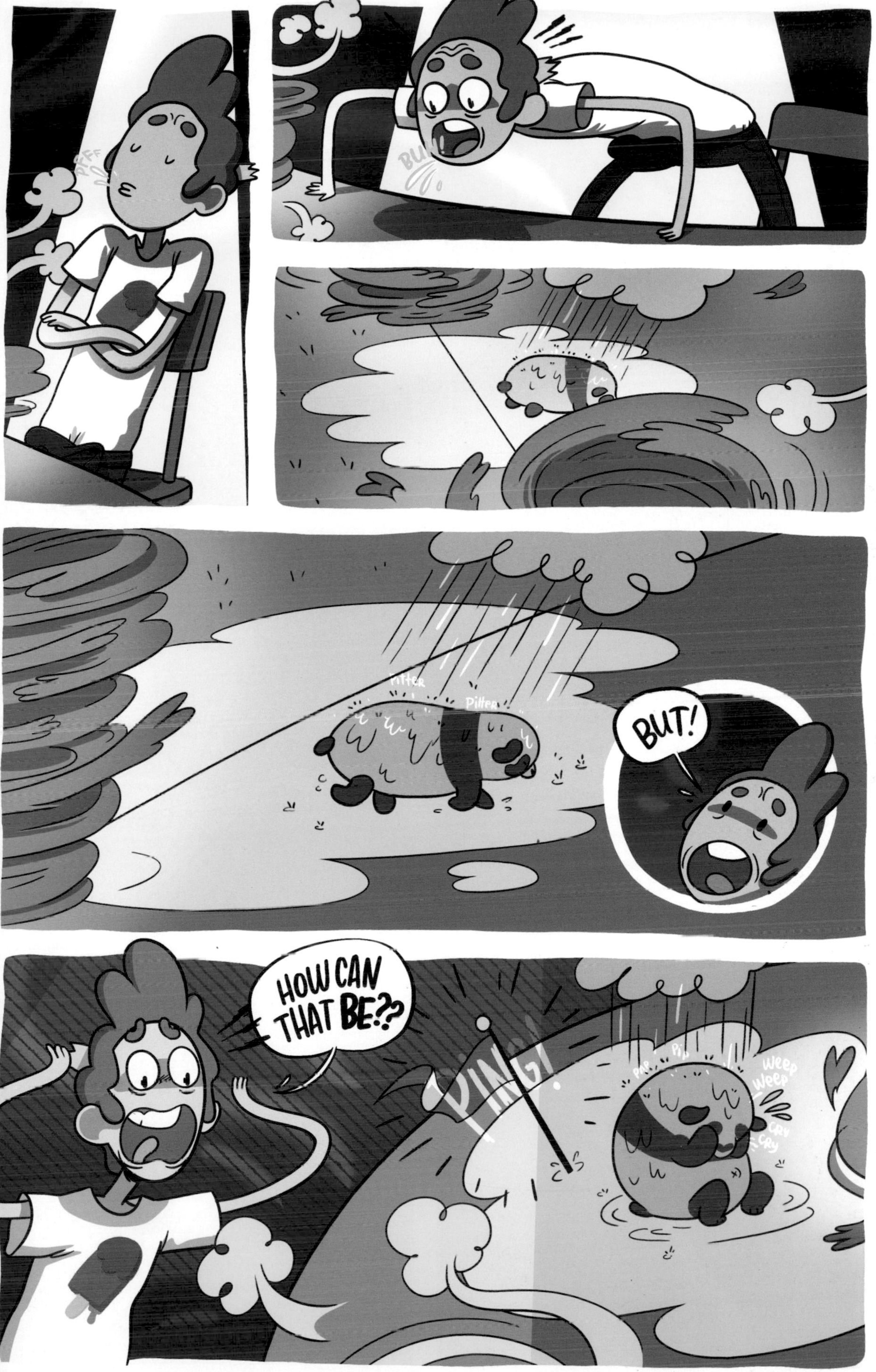
PFFF
Pitter
Pitter
BUT!
HOW CAN THAT BE??
PING!
PAP
Pip
WEEP
WEEP
CRY
CRY

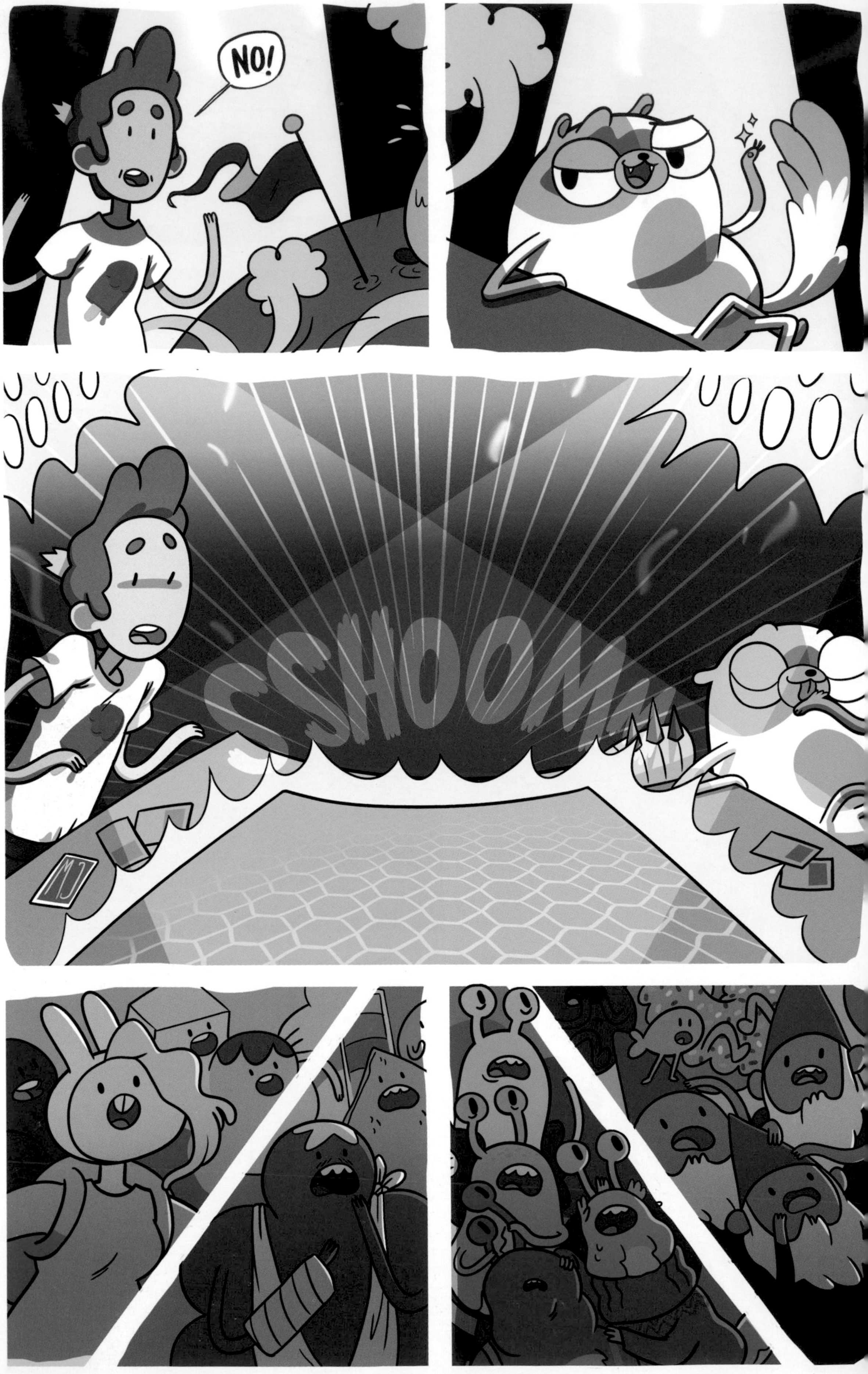
NO!
SSHOOM

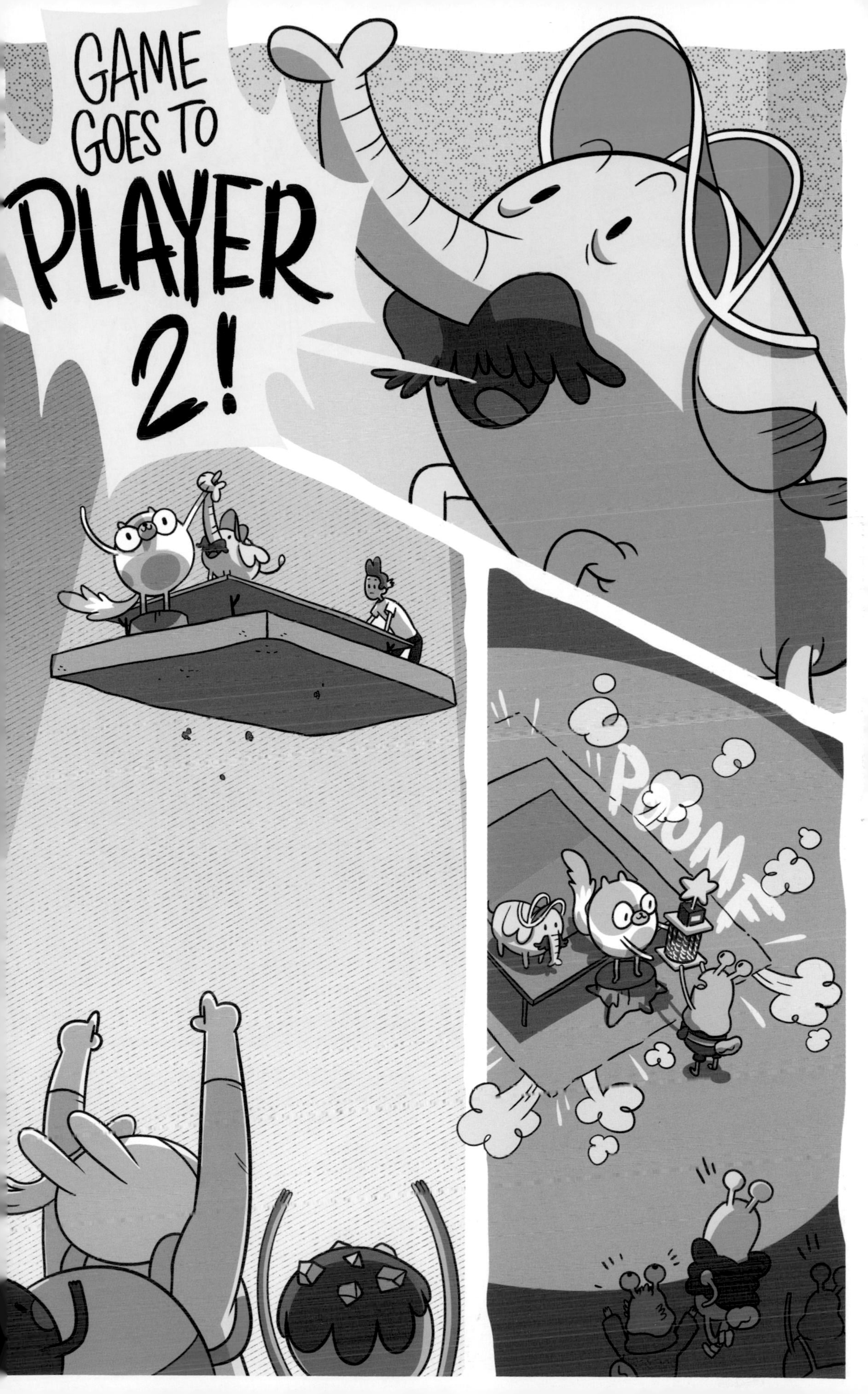
GAME GOES TO PLAYER 2!
POOMF

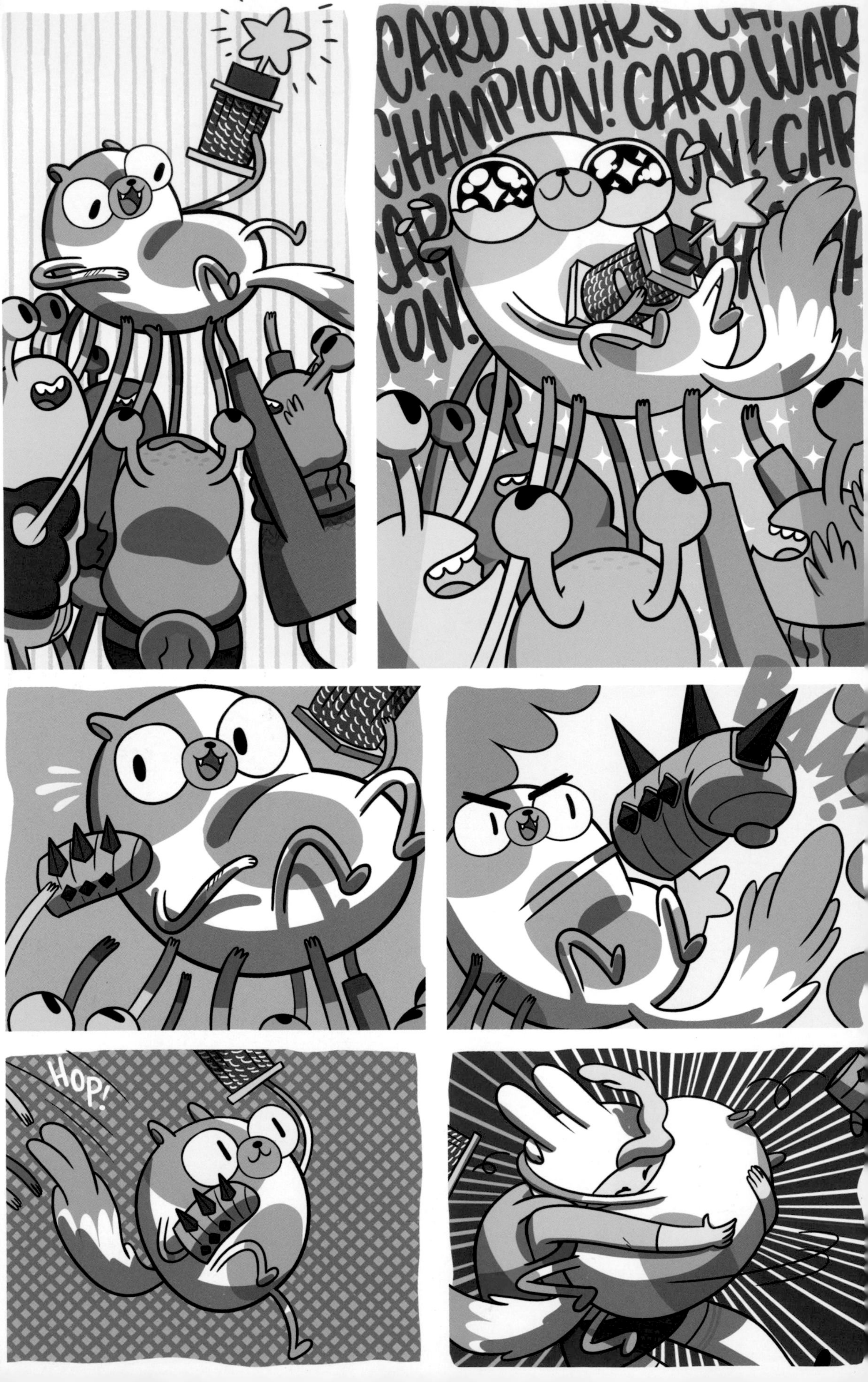
CARD WARS CA
CHAMPION! CARD WAR
HOP!

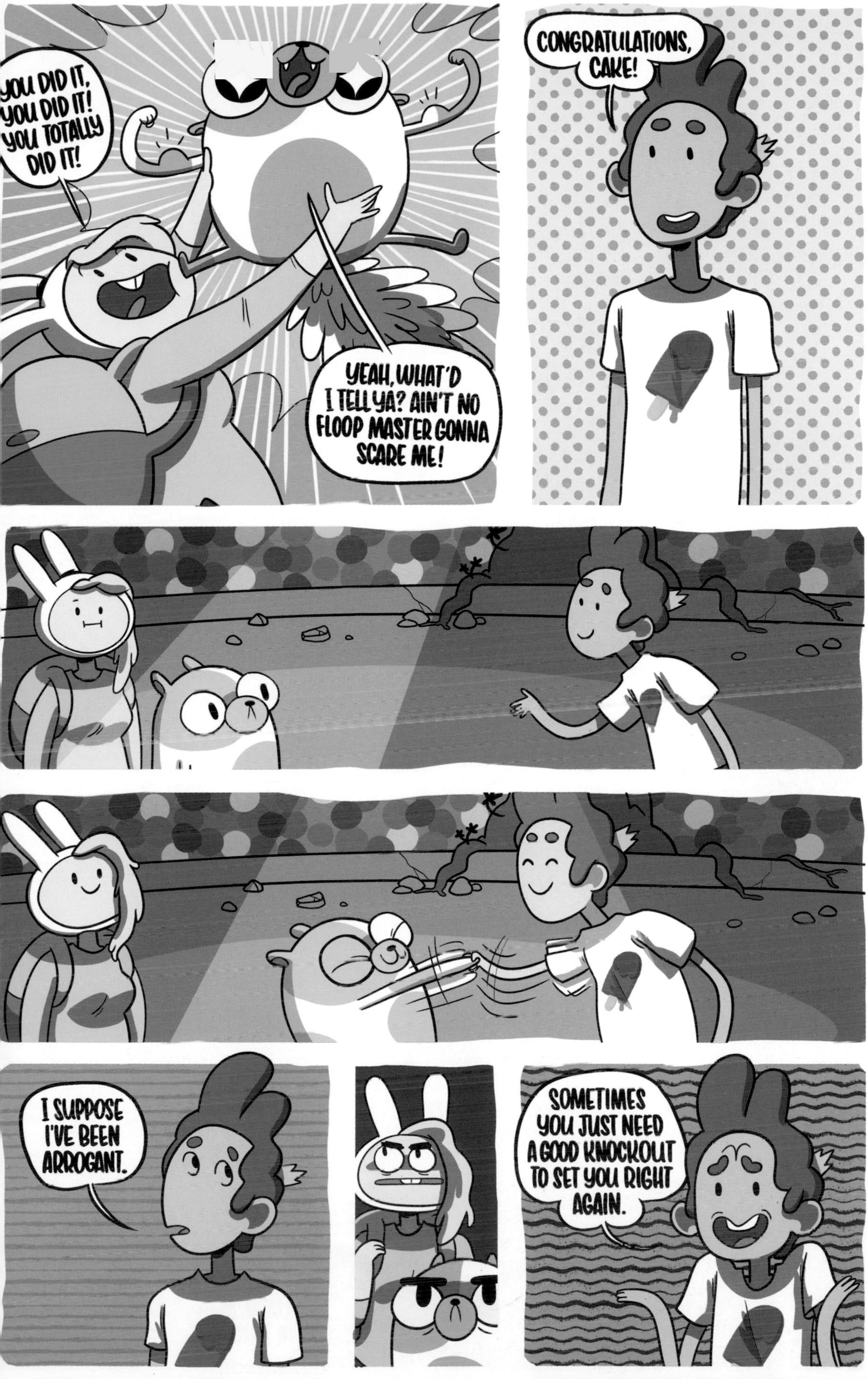
YOU DID IT, YOU DID IT! YOU TOTALLY DID IT!
YEAH, WHAT'D I TELL YA? AIN'T NO FLOOP MASTER GONNA SCARE ME!
CONGRATULATIONS, CAKE!
I SUPPOSE I'VE BEEN ARROGANT.
SOMETIMES YOU JUST NEED A GOOD KNOCKOUT TO SET YOU RIGHT AGAIN.

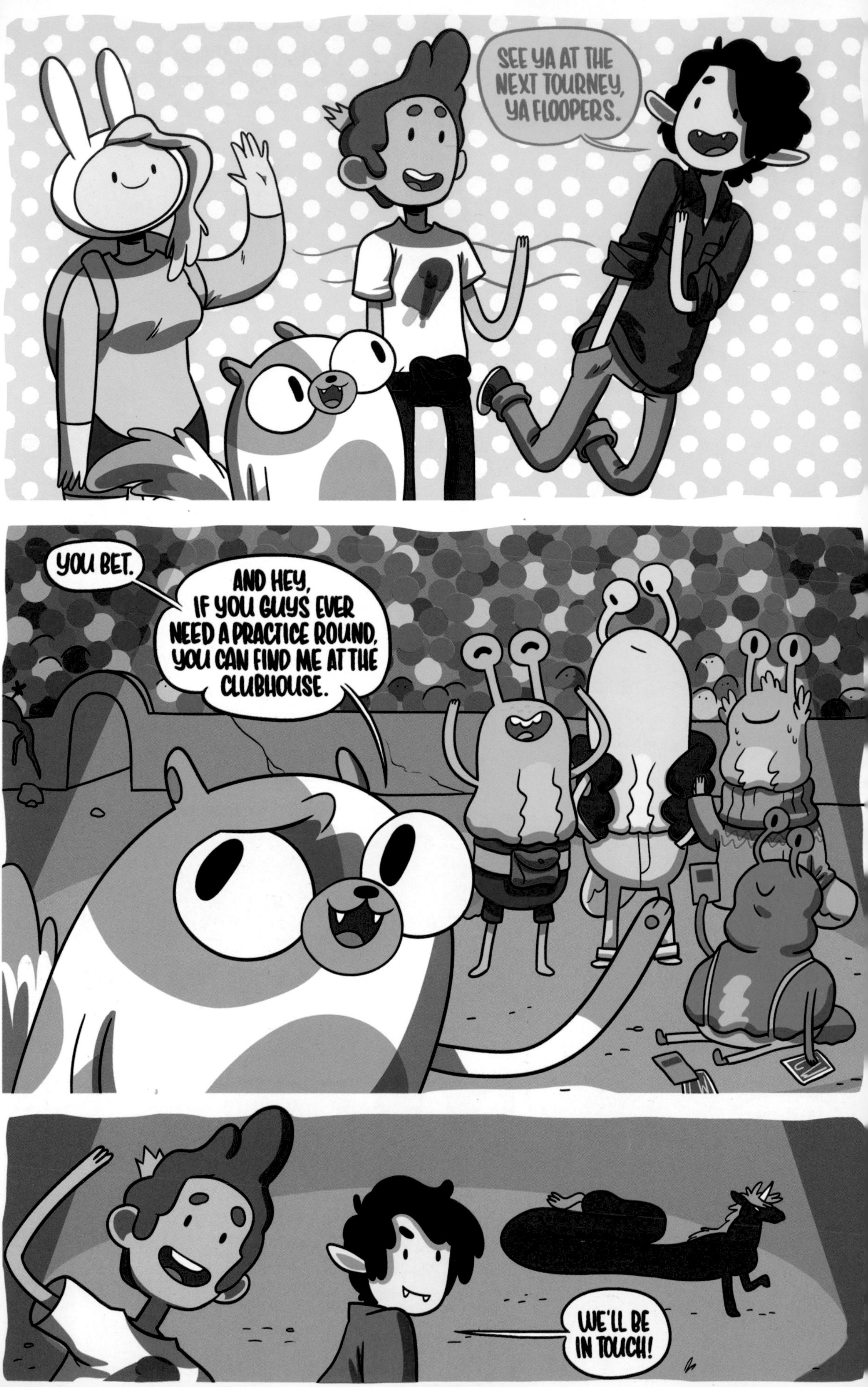
SEE YA AT THE NEXT TOURNEY, YA FLOOPERS.
YOU BET.
AND HEY, IF YOU GUYS EVER NEED A PRACTICE ROUND, YOU CAN FIND ME AT THE CLUBHOUSE.
WE'LL BE IN TOUCH!

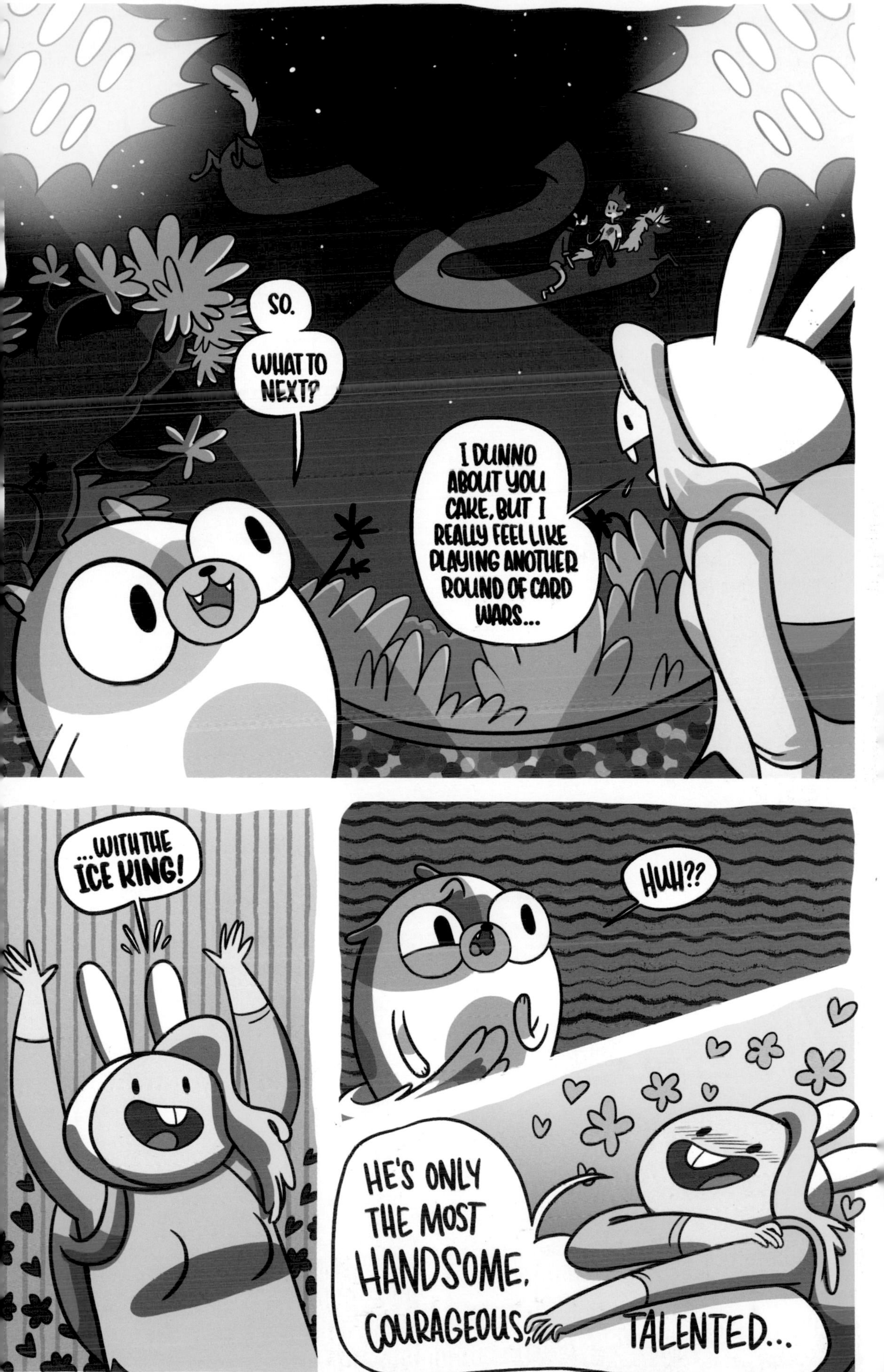
SO.
WHAT TO NEXT?
I DUNNO ABOUT YOU CAKE, BUT I REALLY FEEL LIKE PLAYING ANOTHER ROUND OF CARD WARS...
...WITH THE ICE KING!
HUH??
HE'S ONLY THE MOST HANDSOME, COURAGEOUS, TALENTED...

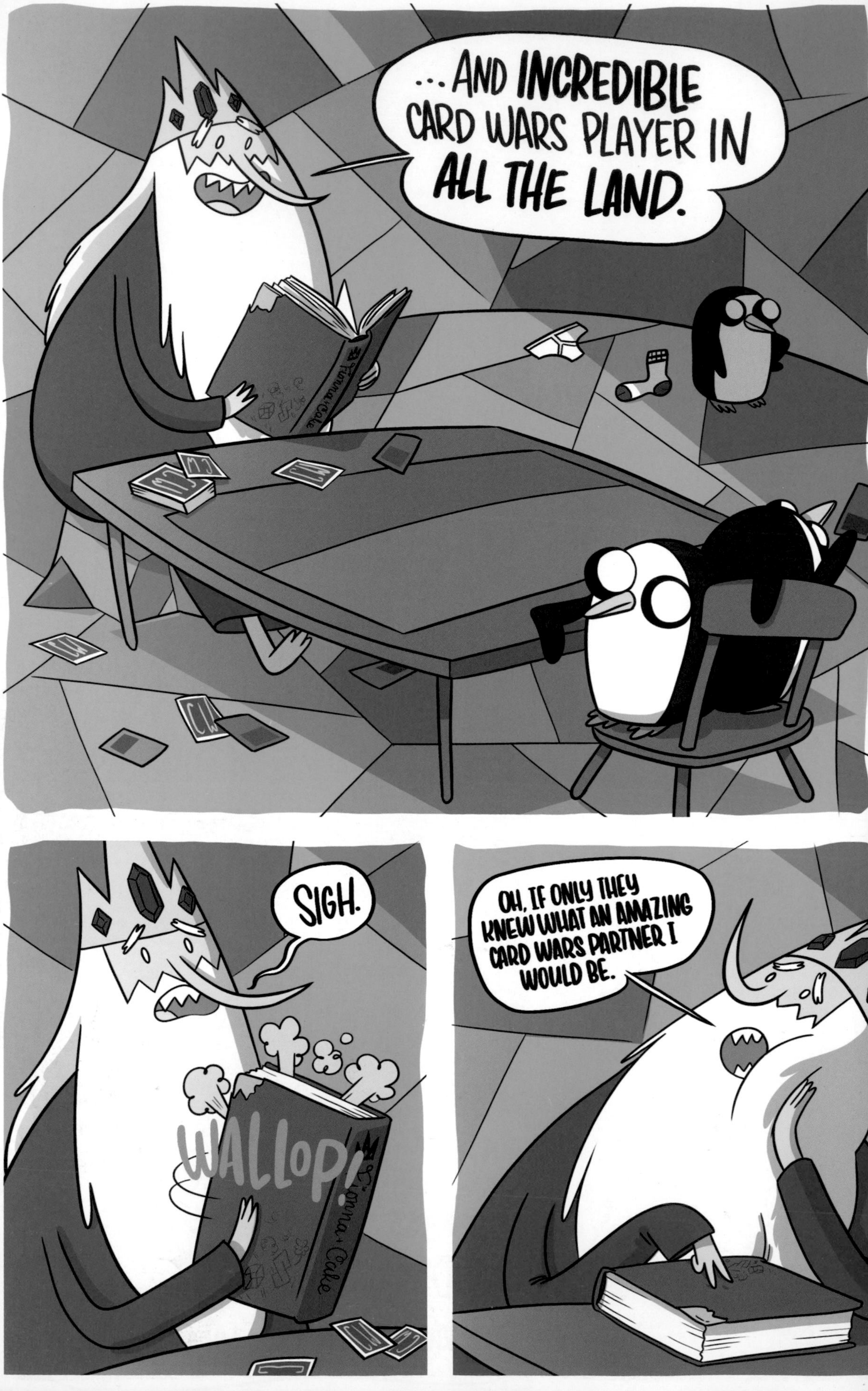
...AND INCREDIBLE CARD WARS PLAYER IN ALL THE LAND.
SIGH.
WALLOP!
OH, IF ONLY THEY KNEW WHAT AN AMAZING CARD WARS PARTNER I WOULD BE.

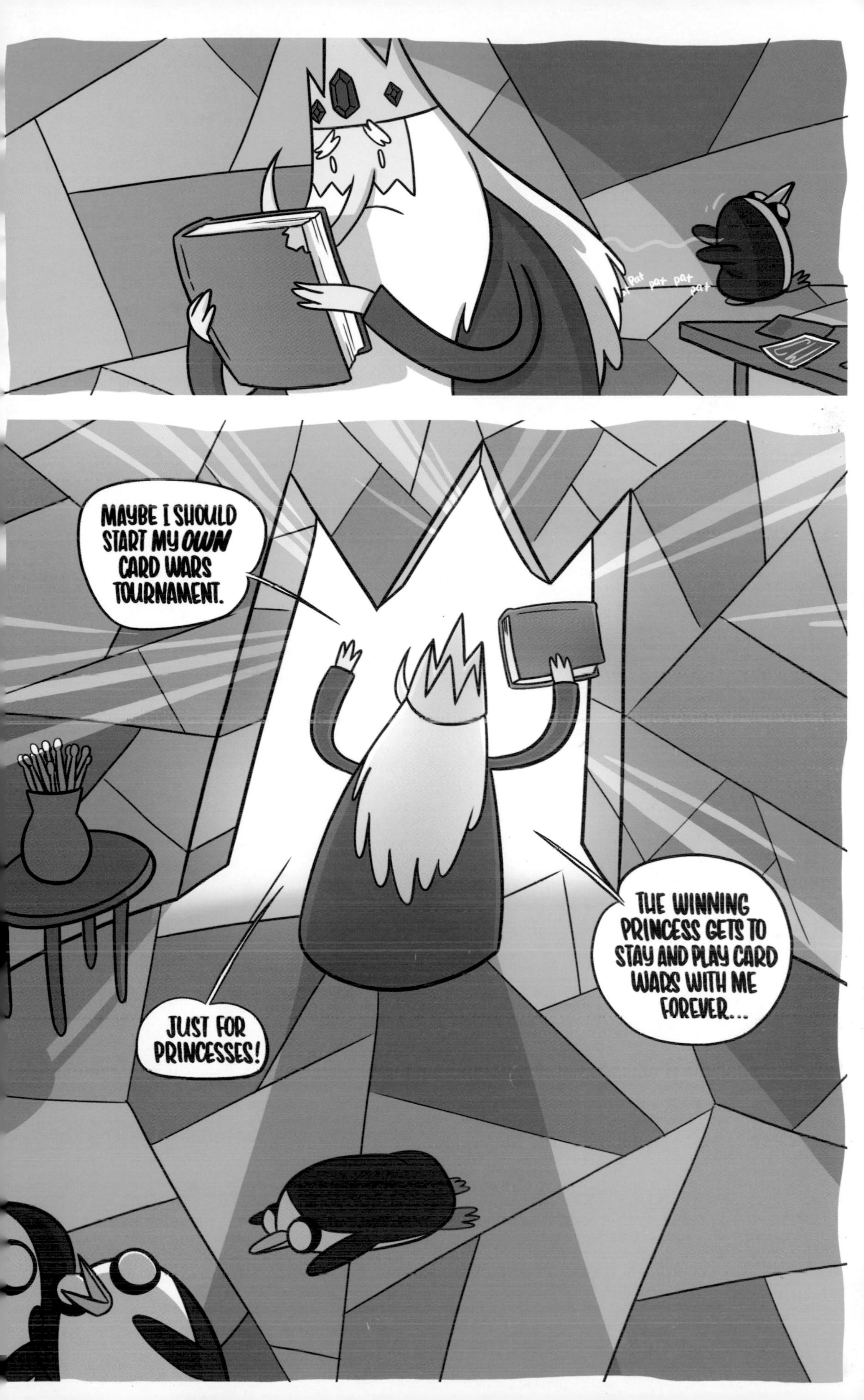
pat pat pat pat pat
MAYBE I SHOULD START MY *OWN* CARD WARS TOURNAMENT.
JUST FOR PRINCESSES!
THE WINNING PRINCESS GETS TO STAY AND PLAY CARD WARS WITH ME FOREVER...

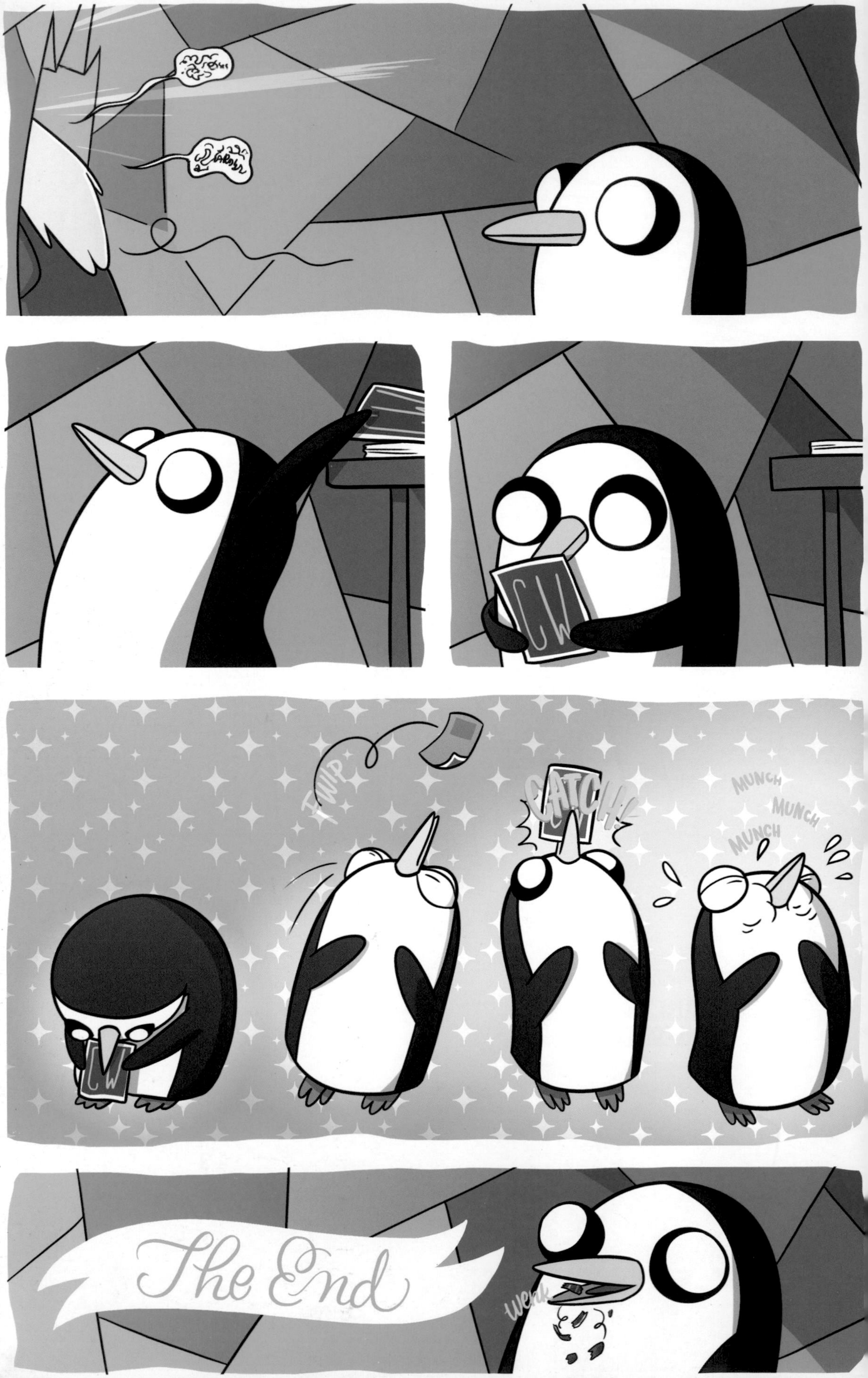

TWIP
CATCH!
MUNCH
MUNCH
MUNCH
The End
WENK

COVER GALLERY

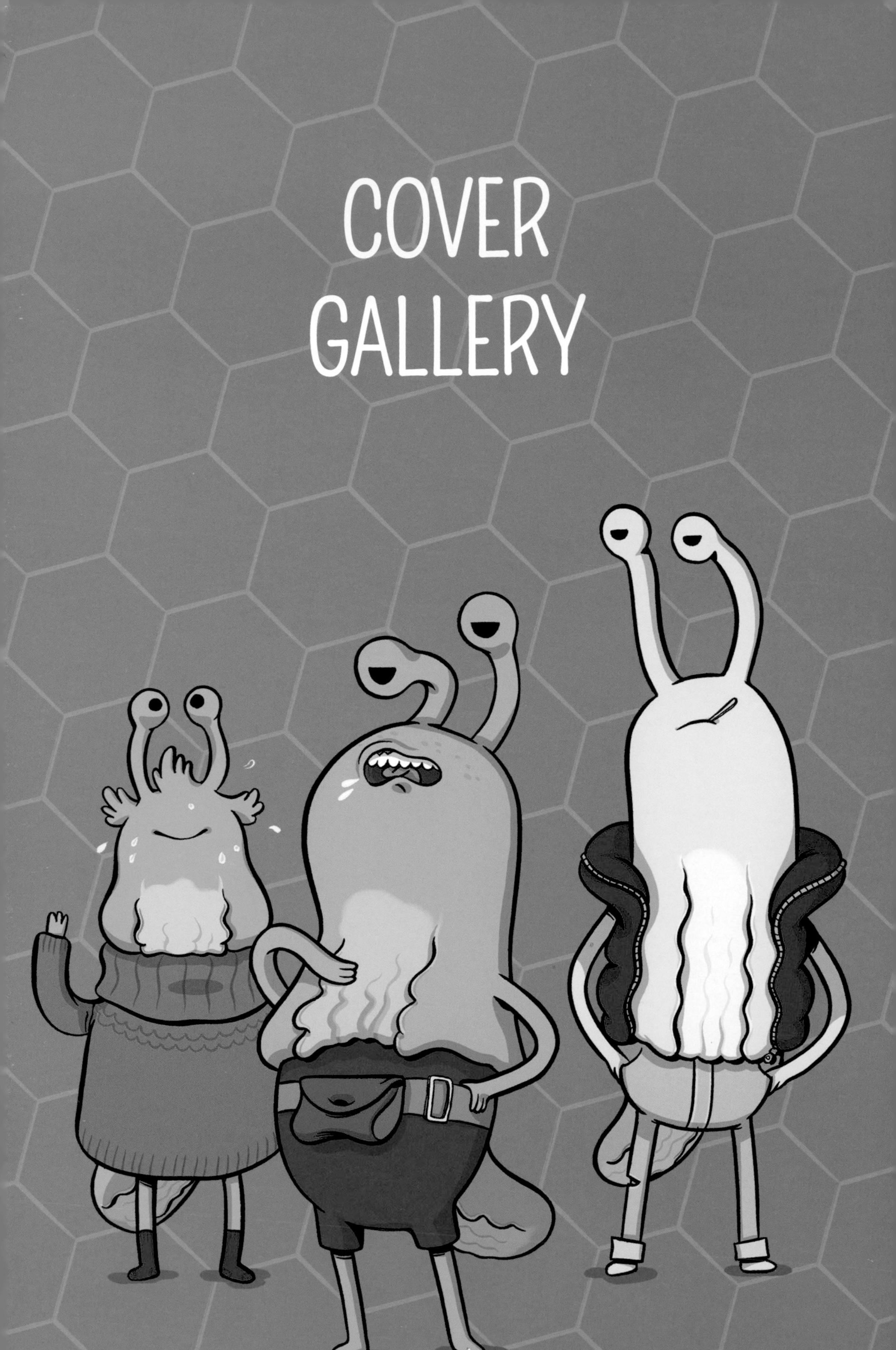

issue one cover

JEN WANG

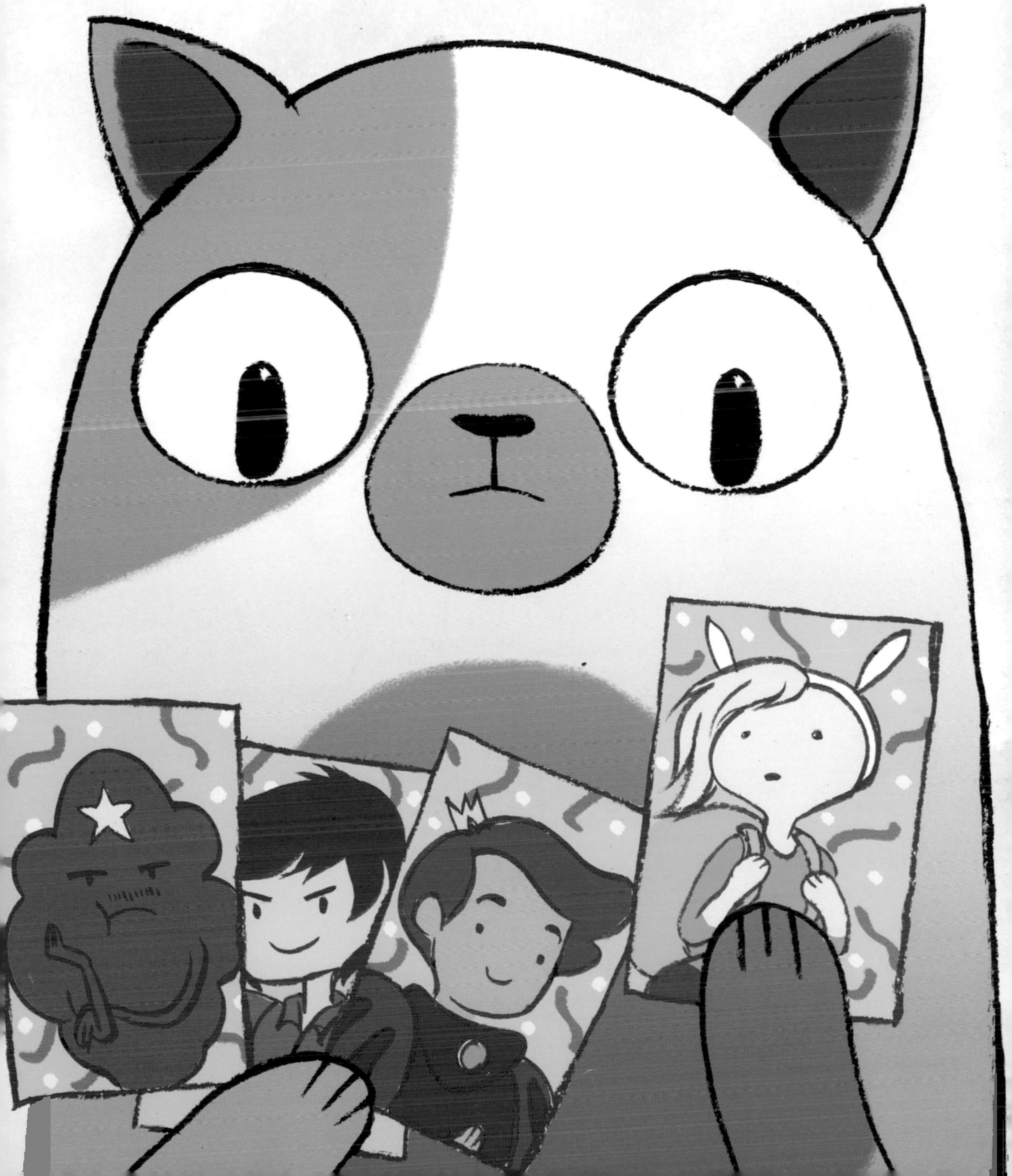

issue two cover
JEN WANG

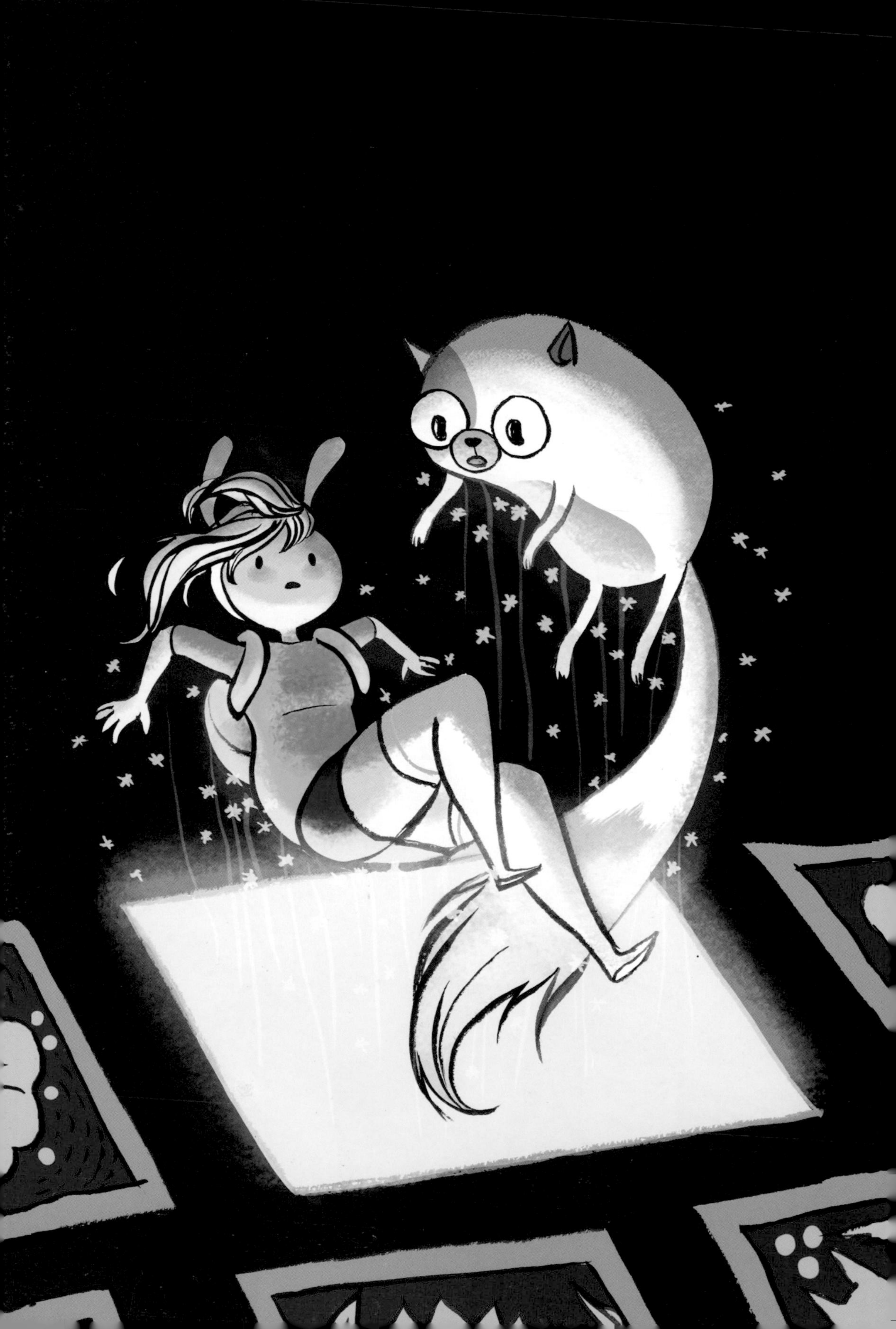

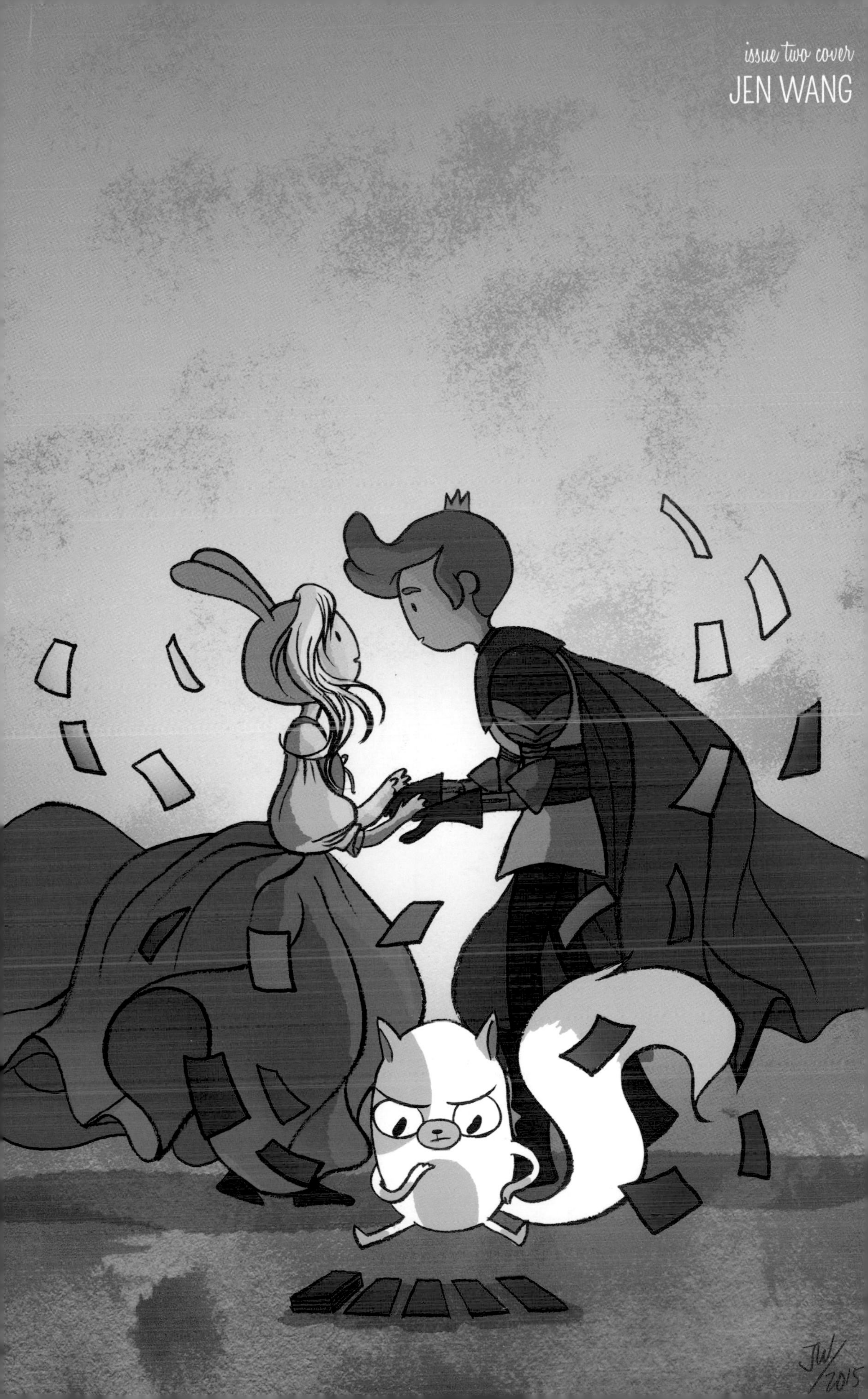
JW/2015
issue two cover
JEN WANG

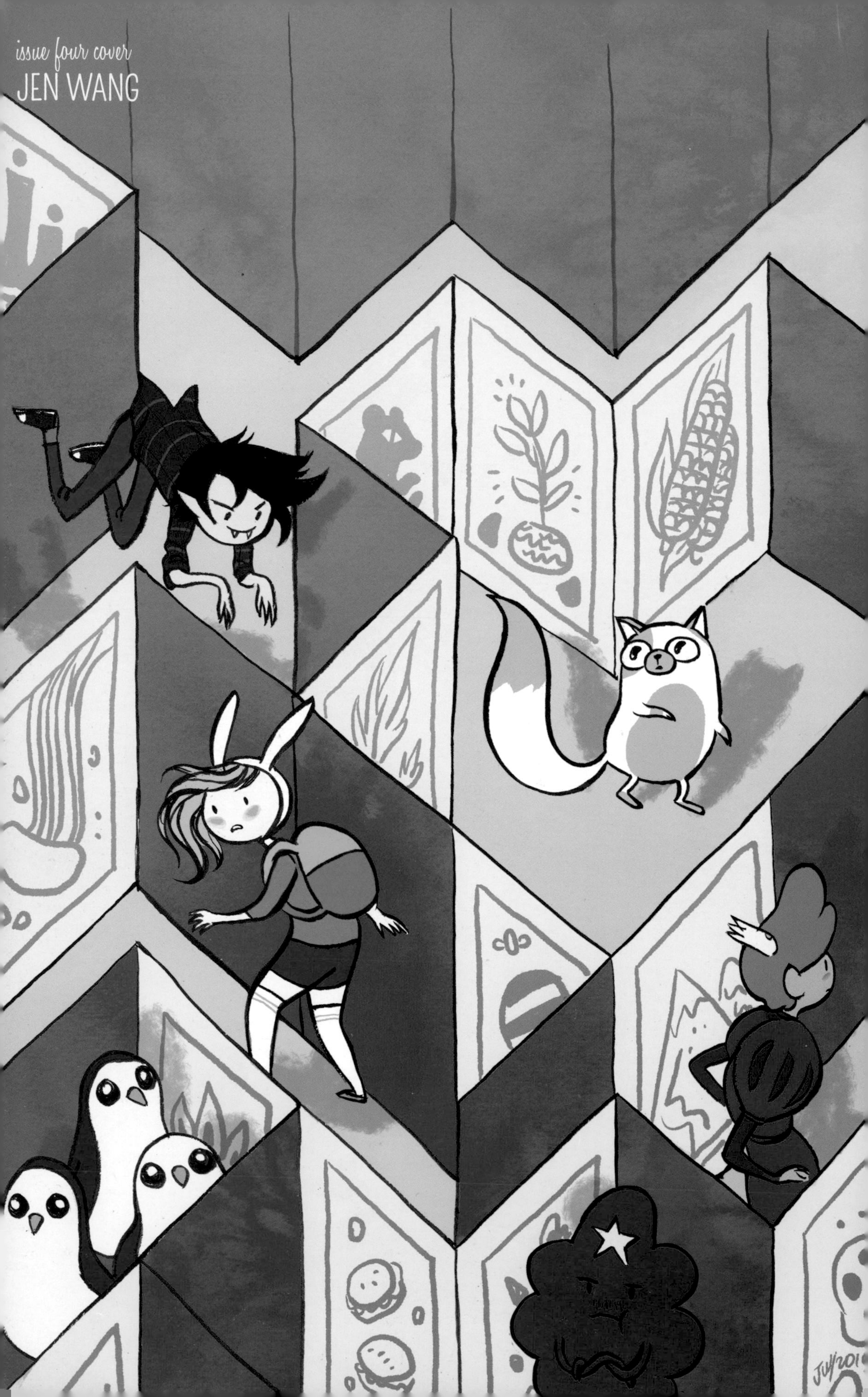

issue four cover
JEN WANG

issue five cover
JEN WANG

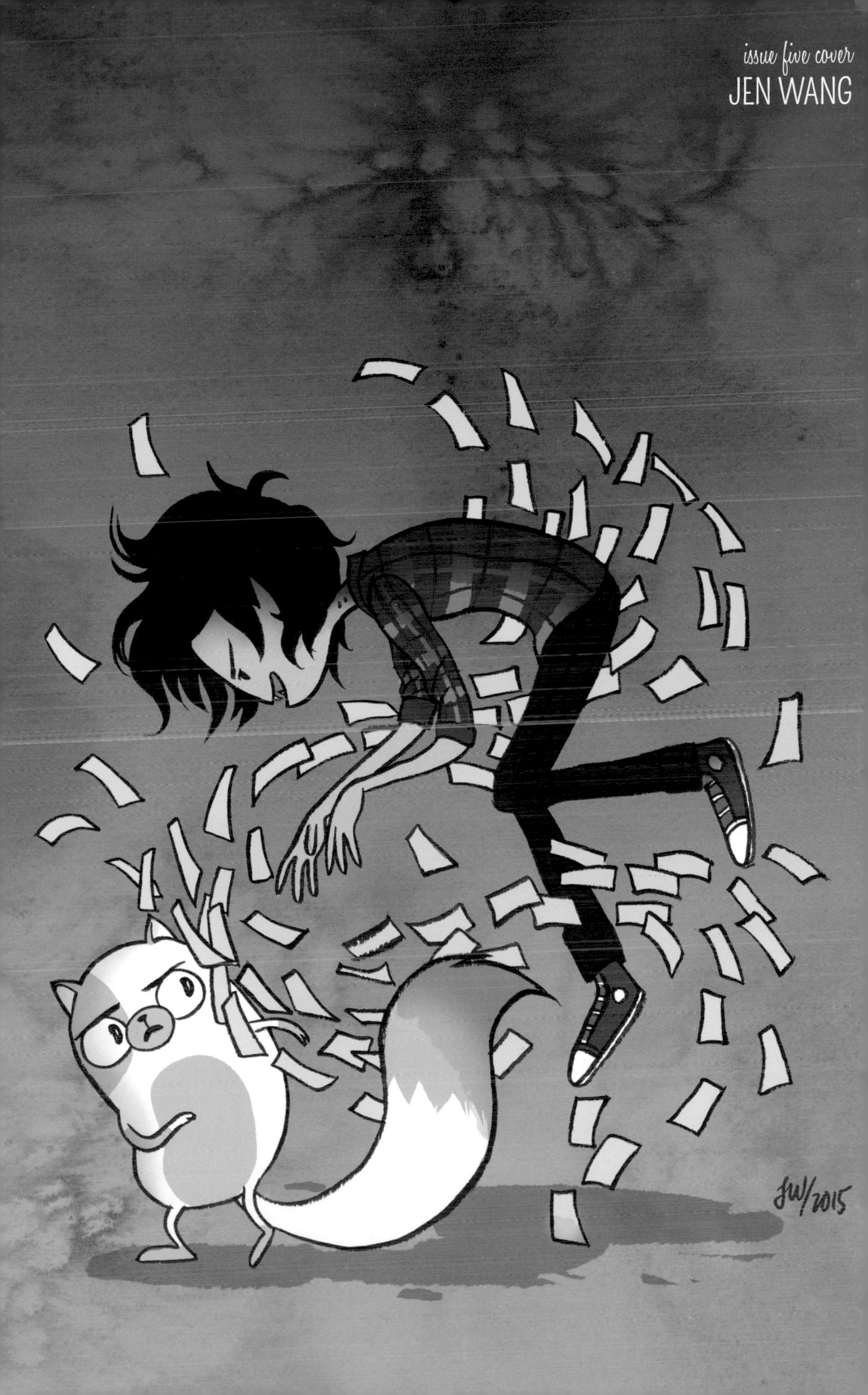
JW/2015

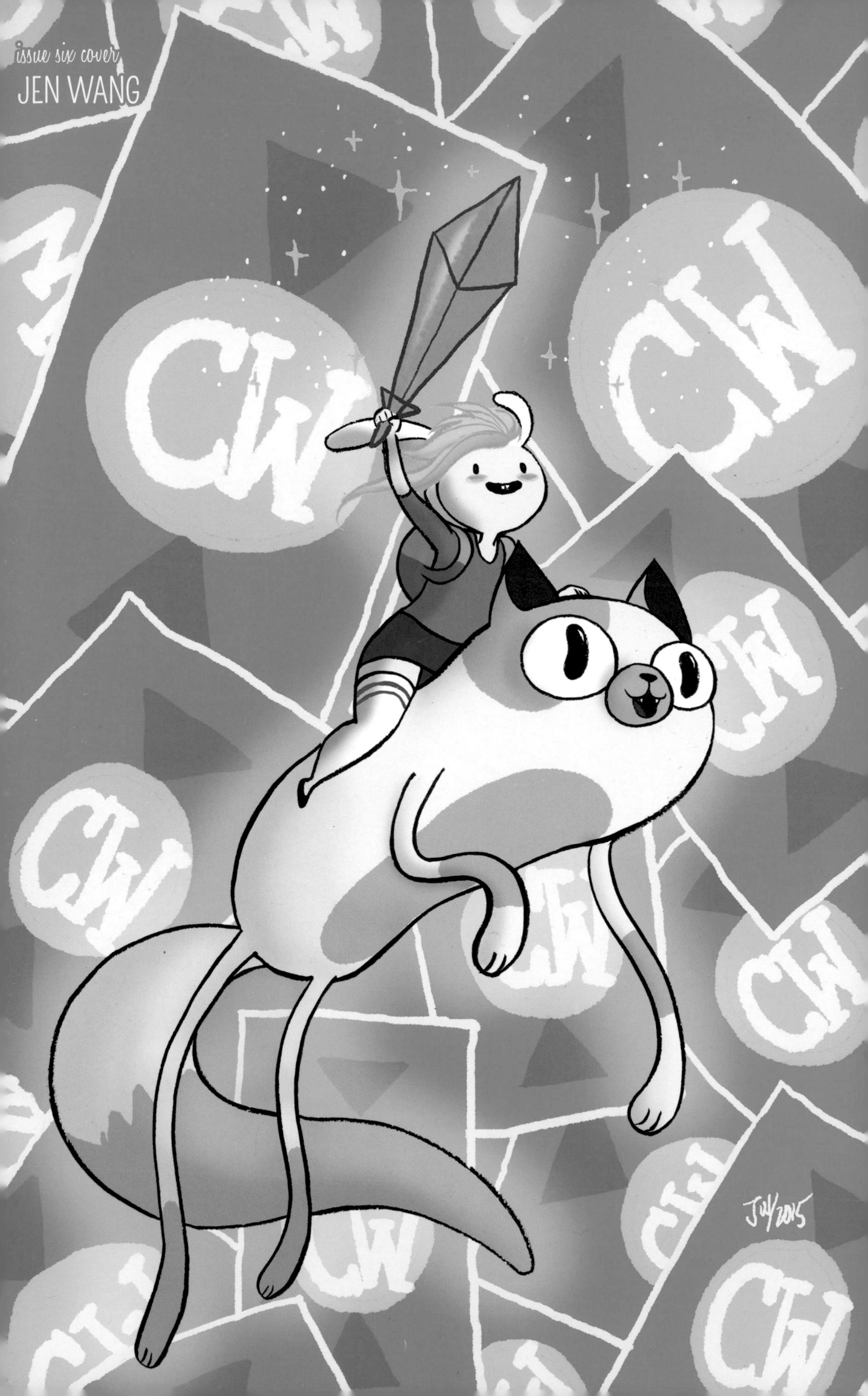
JW/2015

issue six cover
JEN WANG

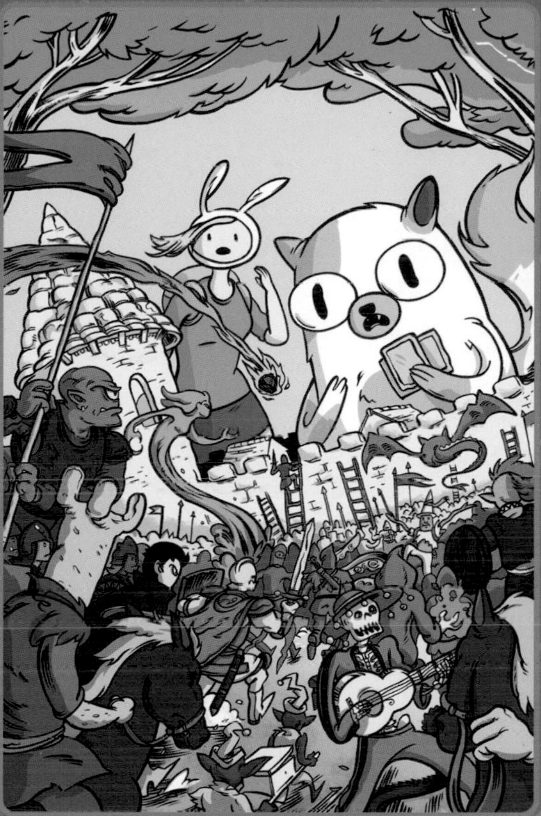

issue one subscription
WYETH YATES

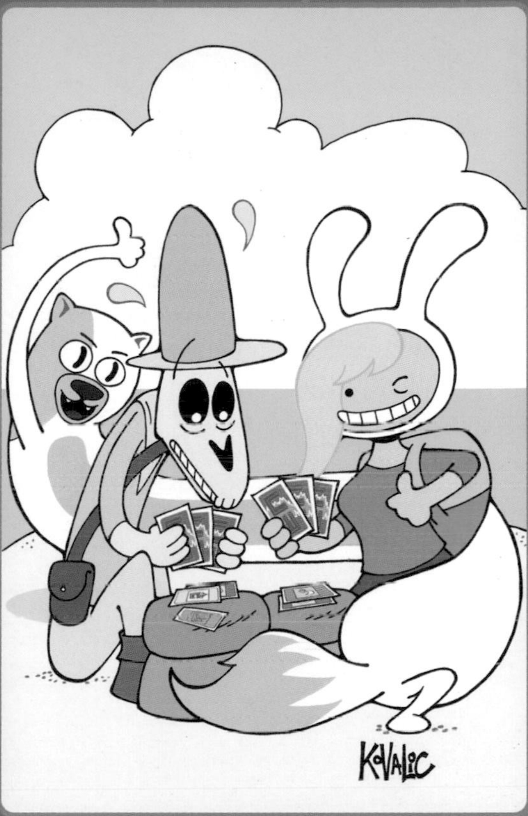
KOVALIC

issue one variant
JOHN KOVALIC

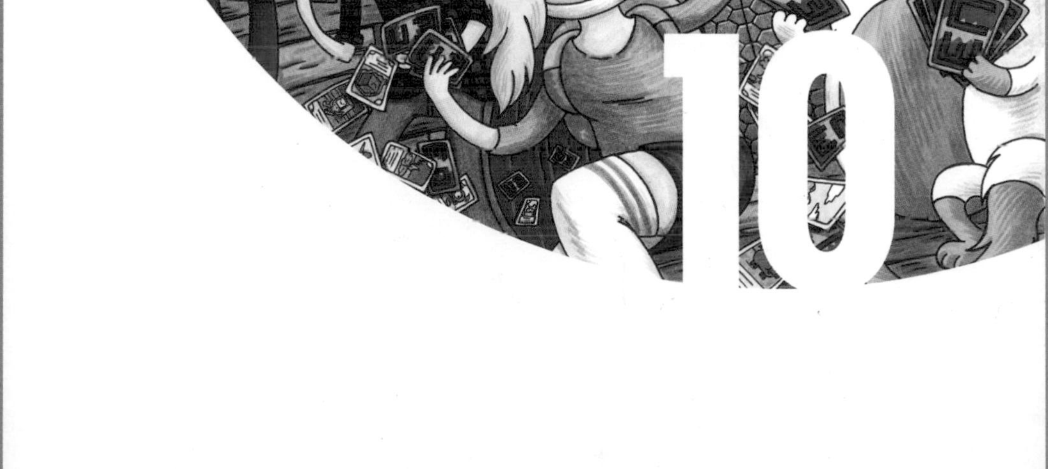
10

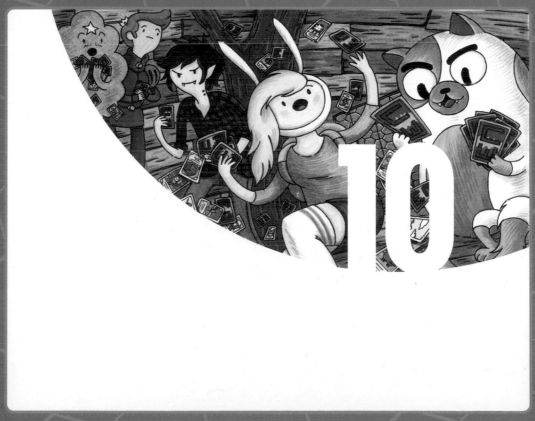

issue one boom! ten years variant
JEFFREY BROWN

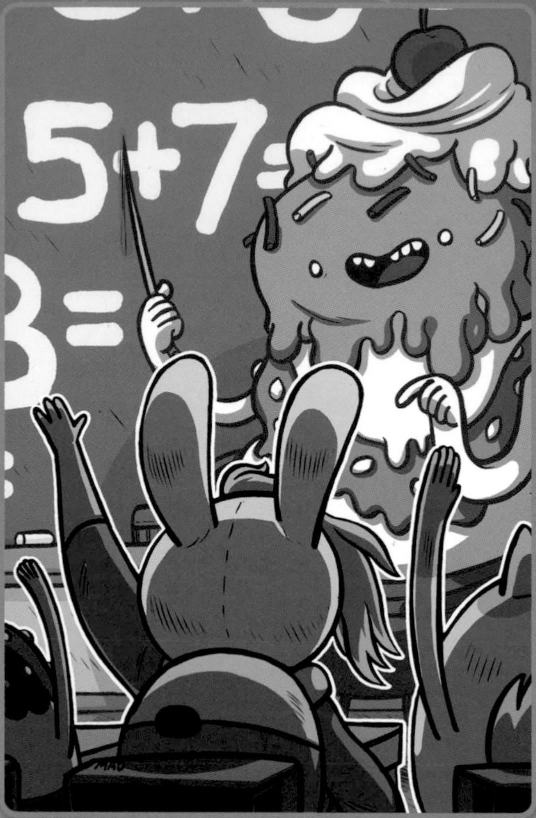
5+7=

issue one san diego comic-con exclusive
MAD RUPERT

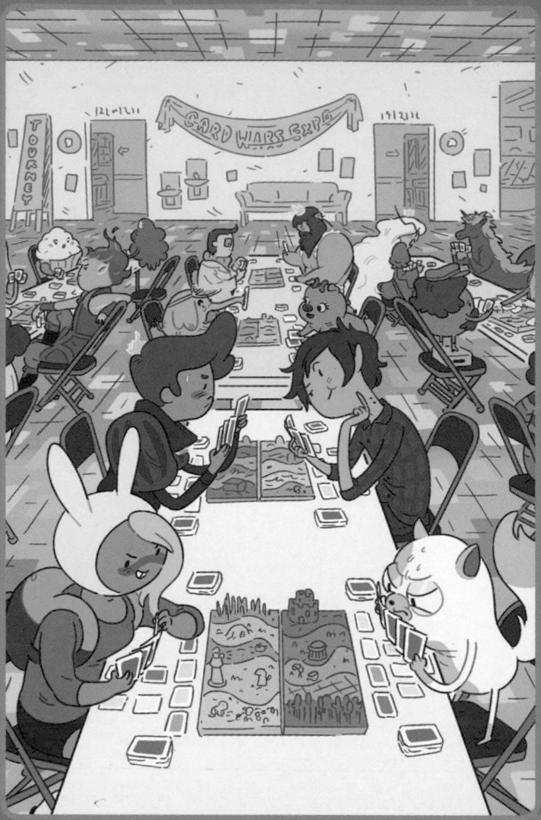
CARD WARS EXPO
TOURNEY

issue one a shop called quest exclusive
JESSIE WONG

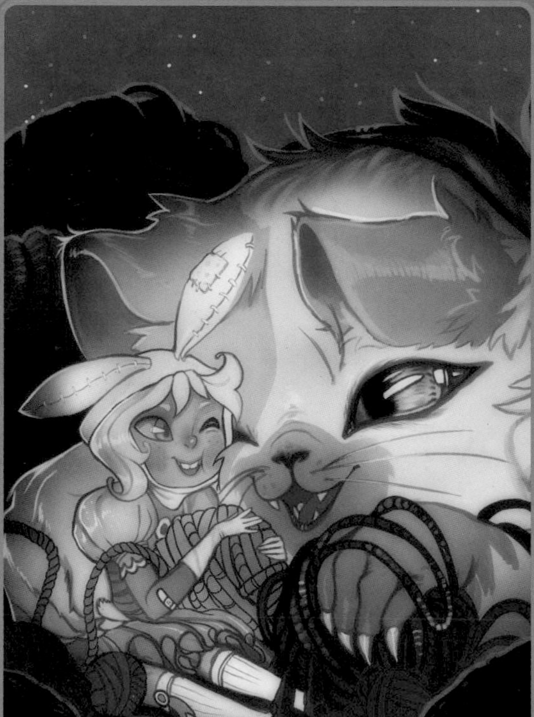

issue one diamond san diego comic-con exclusive
MICHELLE CZAJKOWSKI

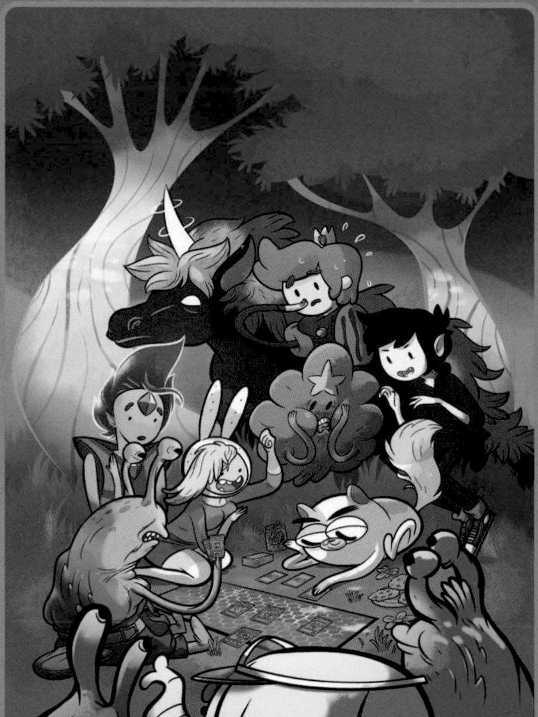

issue two subscription
NICOLE HAMILTON

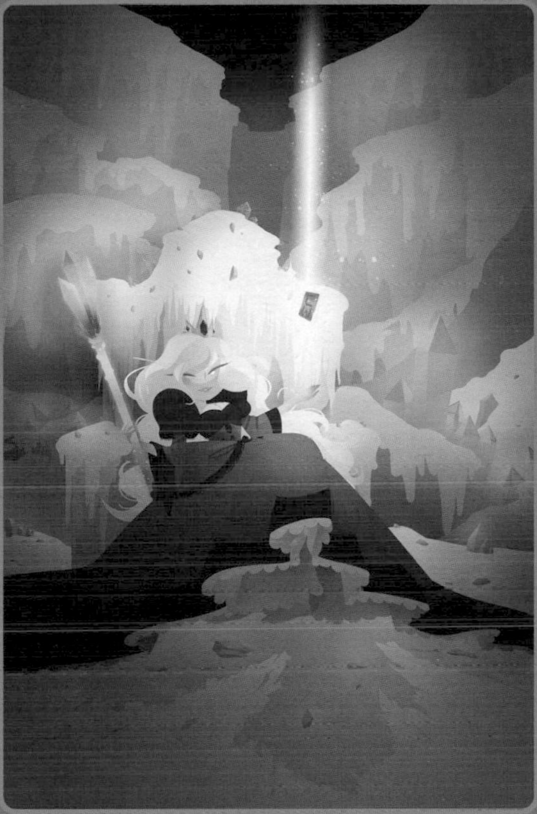

issue two variant
MAYA KERN

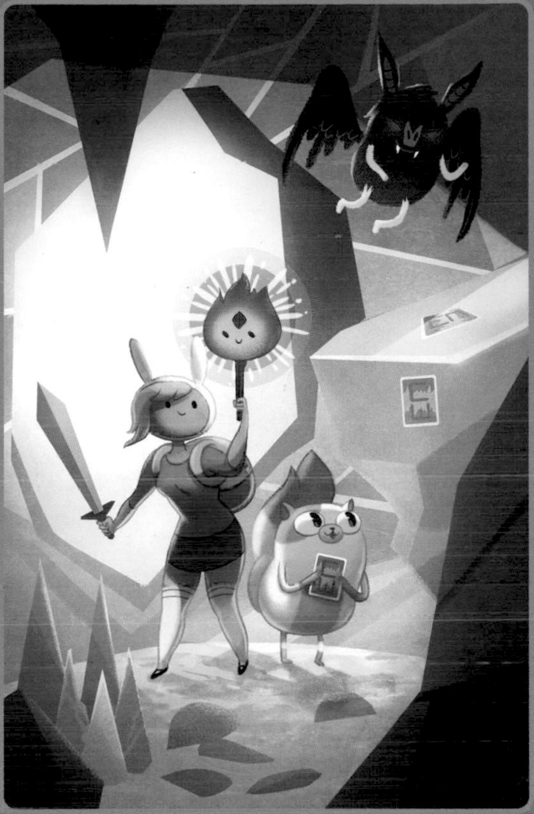

issue three subscription
WENDI CHEN

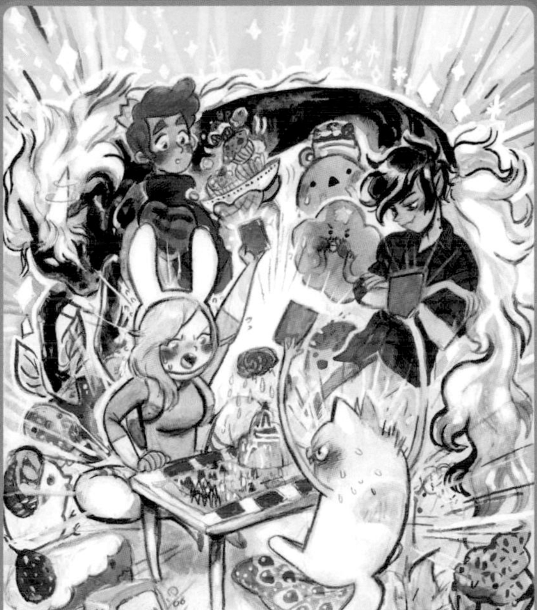

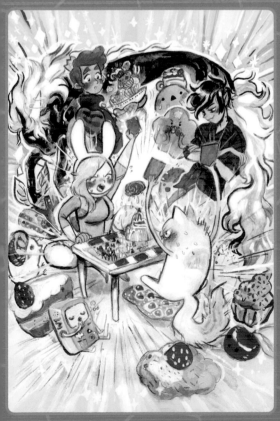

issue three variant
DANIELA VIÇOSO

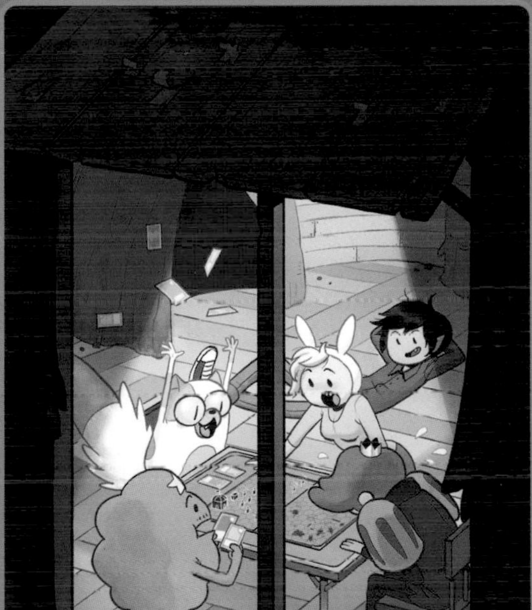

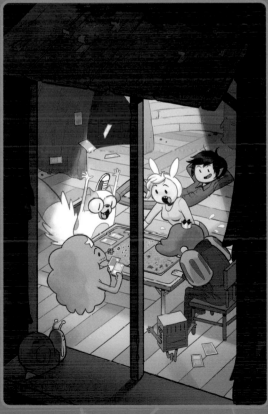

issue four subscription
DANA TERRACE

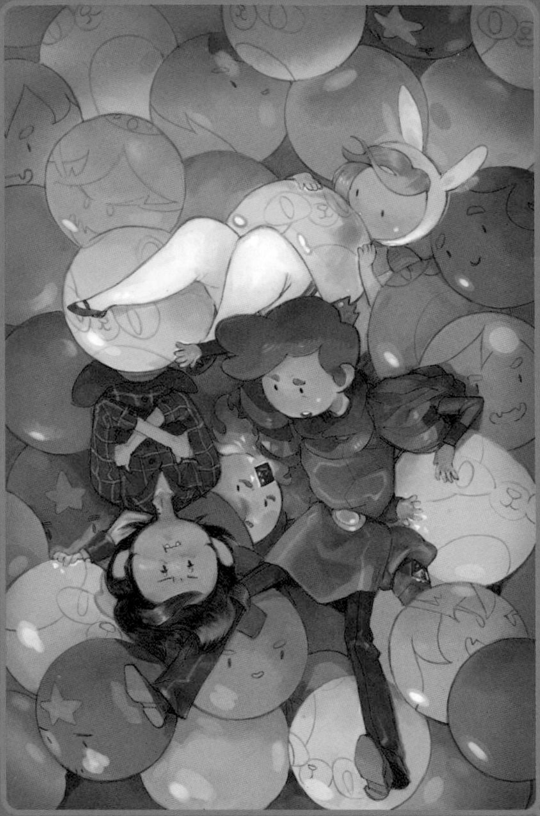

issue four variant
RACHEL SAUNDERS

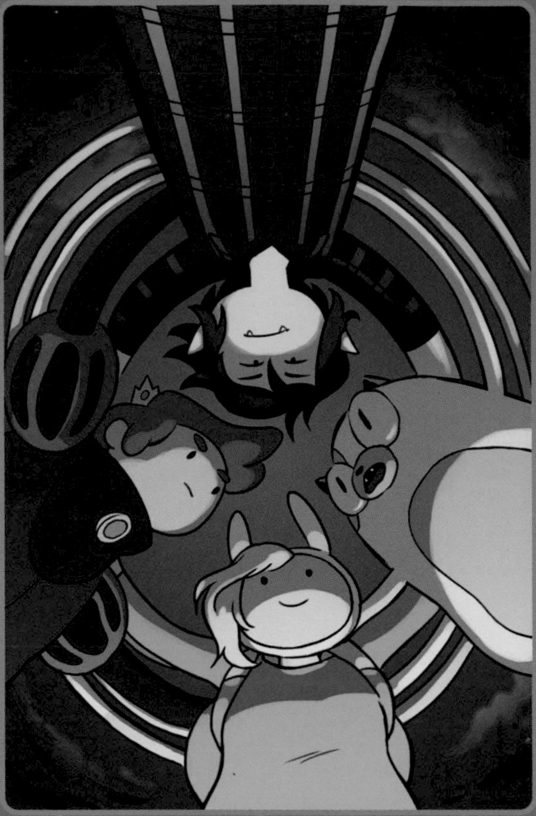

issue five subscription
MYKEN BOMBERGER

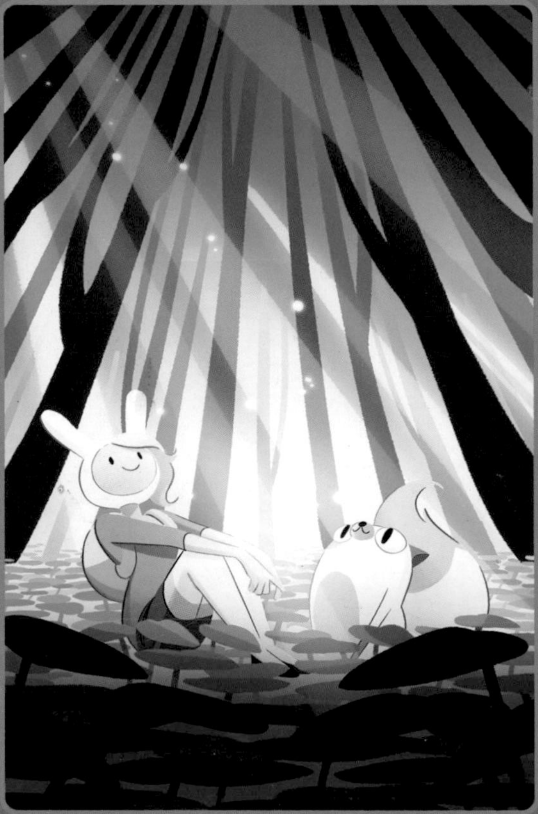

issue five variant
DIANA HUH

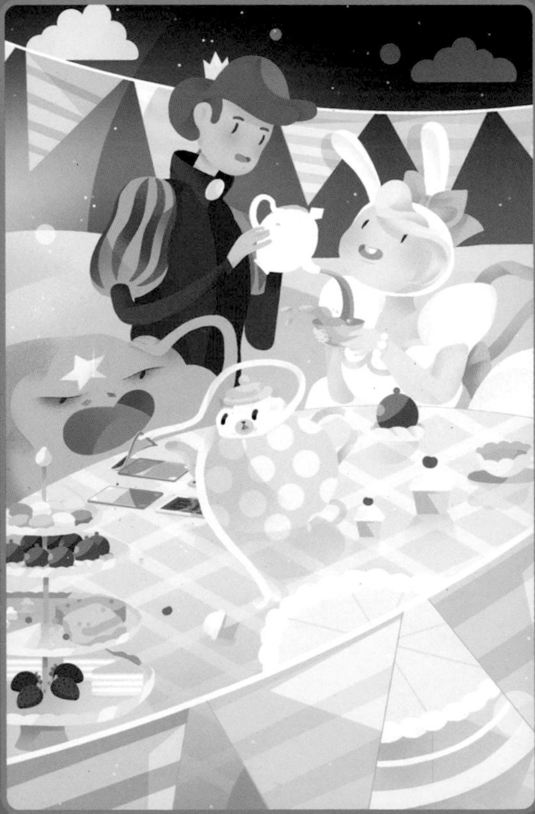

issue six subscription
REBEKKA DUNLAP

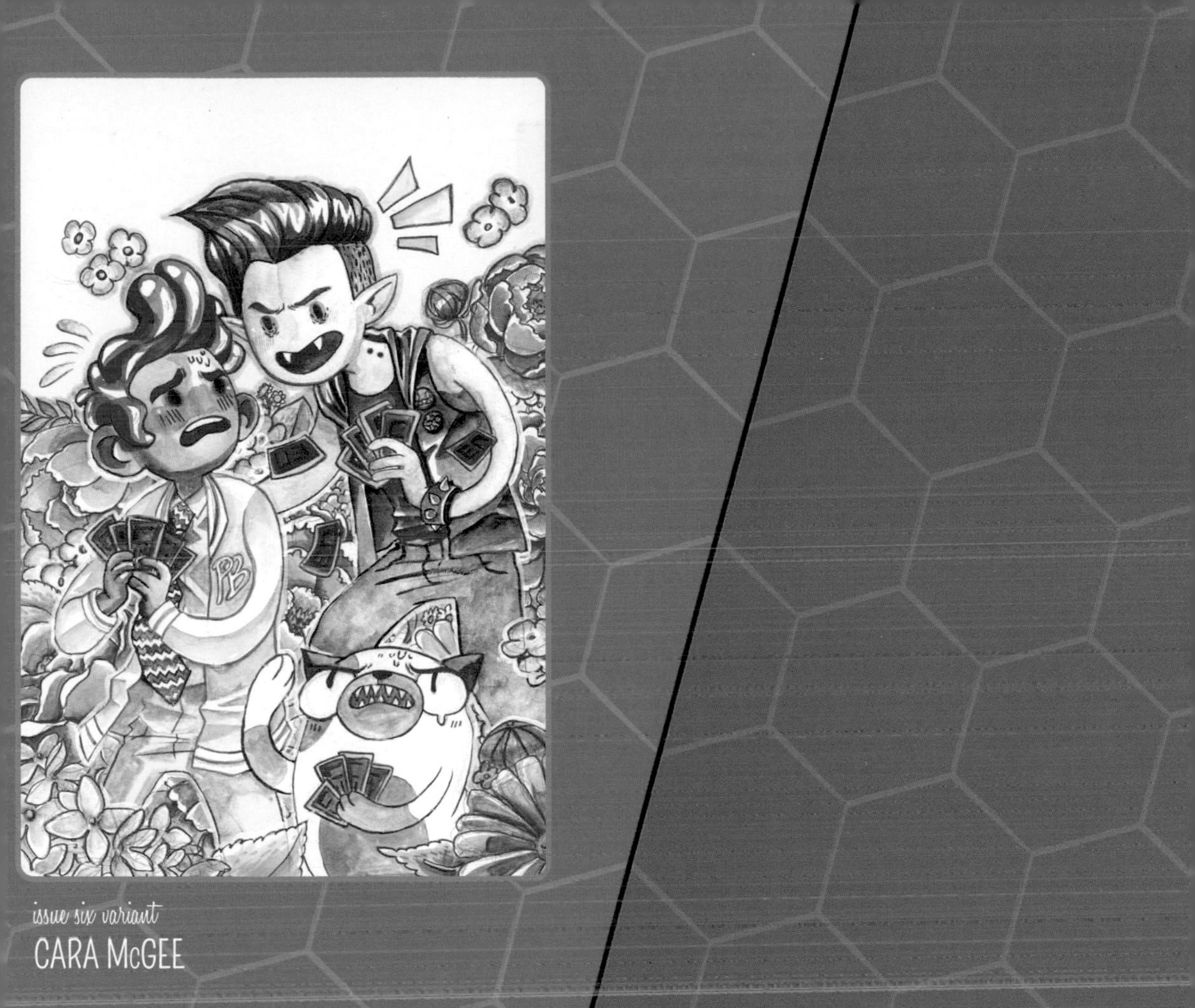

issue six variant

CARA McGEE

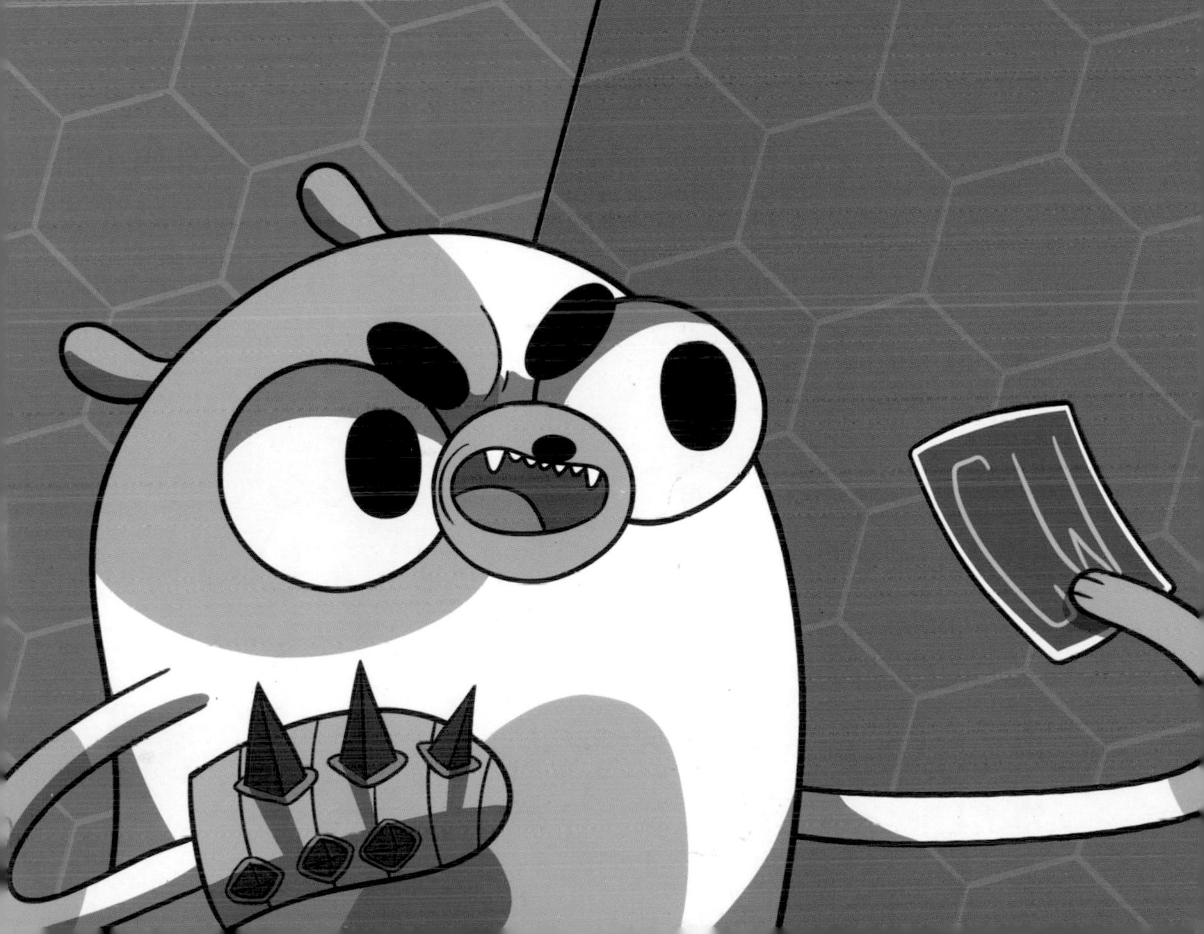